LOOK FOR THESE EXCITING WESTERN SERIES FROM BESTSELLING AUTHORS WILLIAM W. JOHNSTONE AND J.A. JOHNSTONE

The Mountain Man
Luke Jensen: Bounty Hunter
Brannigan's Land
The Jensen Brand
Smoke Jensen: The Early Years
Preacher and MacCallister
Fort Misery
The Fighting O'Neils
Perley Gates
MacCoole and Boone
Guns of the Vigilantes
Shotgun Johnny
The Chuckwagon Trail
The Jackals
The Slash and Pecos Westerns
The Texas Moonshiners
Stoneface Finnegan Westerns
Ben Savage: Saloon Ranger
The Buck Trammel Westerns
The Death and Texas Westerns
The Hunter Buchanon Westerns
Will Tanner: U.S. Deputy Marshal
Old Cowboys Never Die
Go West, Young Man

Published by Kensington Publishing Corp.

EVERYBODY HAS A GUN

WILLIAM W. JOHNSTONE
AND J.A. JOHNSTONE

PINNACLE BOOKS
Kensington Publishing Corp.
kensingtonbooks.com

PINNACLE BOOKS are published by
Kensington Publishing Corp.
900 Third Avenue
New York, NY 10022

Copyright © 2025 by J.A. Johnstone

All rights reserved. No part of this book may be reproduced in any form or by any means without the prior written consent of the Publisher, excepting brief quotes used in reviews.

Without limiting the author's and publisher's exclusive rights, any unauthorized use of this publication to train generative artificial intelligence (AI) technologies is expressly prohibited.

This book is a work of fiction. Names, characters, businesses, organizations, places, events, and incidents either are the product of the author's imagination or are used fictitiously. Any resemblance to actual persons, living or dead, events, or locales is entirely coincidental.

To the extent that the image or images on the cover of this book depict a person or persons, such person or persons are merely models and are not intended to portray any character or characters featured in the book.

PUBLISHER'S NOTE: Following the death of William W. Johnstone, the Johnstone family is working with a carefully selected writer to organize and complete Mr. Johnstone's outlines and many unfinished manuscripts to create additional novels in all of his series, like The Last Gunfighter, Mountain Man, and Eagles, among others. This novel was inspired by Mr. Johnstone's superb storytelling.

If you purchased this book without a cover, you should be aware that this book is stolen property. It was reported as "unsold and destroyed" to the Publisher, and neither the Author nor the Publisher has received any payment for this "stripped book."

All Kensington titles, imprints, and distributed lines are available at special quantity discounts for bulk purchases for sales promotion, premiums, fundraising, and educational or institutional use.

Special book excerpts or customized printings can also be created to fit specific needs. For details, write or phone the office of the Kensington Sales Manager: Kensington Publishing Corp., 900 Third Avenue, New York, NY 10022. Attn. Sales Department. Phone: 1-800-221-2647.

PINNACLE BOOKS, the Pinnacle logo, and the WWJ steer head logo Reg. U.S. Pat. & TM Off.

First Printing: August 2025
ISBN-13: 978-0-7860-5064-2
ISBN-13: 978-0-7860-5065-9 (eBook)

10 9 8 7 6 5 4 3 2 1

Printed in the United States of America

The authorized representative in the EU for product safety and compliance is eucomply OU, Parnu mnt 139b-14, Apt 123
Tallinn, Berlin 11317, hello@eucompliancepartner.com.

Chapter 1

"What . . . else . . . can I fetch for you . . . mister?"

The red-faced shopkeep looked over the lenses of the half-moon spectacles that rode far down his bulbous nose. Beneath that bristled a peppery moustache that looked more suited to being a whisk broom than lip hair. The sides of the man's head sported tufty muttonchops that could not conceal his impressive jug-handle ears. The top of the man's bald head glistened with a sheen of sweat, owing largely to the fact that he kept dashing around the counter and feeding chunks of stump wood into the glowing maw of his potbelly stove.

Then he would scoot back around the counter, seeming to lose his fight with breathing, more and more, with each return trip from the stove.

The customer to whom he spoke struggled to keep a smirk off his mouth. He was a tall, angular fellow holding a low-crown fawn hat in his gloved hands. He regarded the shopkeeper a moment longer through slate-blue eyes the color of high-country river ice in

January. Finally his trim, bearded mouth opened. "I wouldn't mind looking at wool coats, if you have any."

The merchant's bristly eyebrows rose. "Do I have any! Why . . . why . . ." Once more, he bustled around the far end of the counter, his pink hand pivoting on the wood.

The customer noticed that the very spot where the portly man's hand rested and spun had been polished to a honey glow from what he assumed had been years of repeated scurrying to and fro.

Although the day outside had turned out warmer than it had promised to be when the tall man awoke that morning, bedded down in the hay near his horse in the small but homey stable at the east end of town, it was still nippy, a portent of the winter to come.

He followed behind the bustling man toward an annex at the back of the store he'd not seen on his one quick turn through the place long minutes before.

"Here's where my wife keeps the garments that are ready to sell."

"What happens with the ones that aren't?" wondered the stranger aloud.

"Huh?" said the merchant, waddling forward ahead of the man and wiping his sweaty pink hands on his apron.

"Never mind. Just kidding you."

"Oh, okay. Well"—the merchant stopped before a short, built-in wall of shelving. He tapped his pooched lips a moment, his brows pulled together in concentration. "That there line of cubbyholes"—he gestured toward a vertical row of shelves—"is filled with just what you are looking for. Coats for men such as yourself—you know, large size and wide in the shoulder. You could do worse than to walk out of here wearing one."

The man agreed in silence as he eyed the offerings. They were all plaid, of varying shades and hues, mostly with reds and greens and browns, with two showing a distinctive blue-gray color.

"You mind if I go ahead and try one on?"

"No, no, you go ahead. I'll be out front, filling the rest of your order. They're all marked at fourteen dollars, by the way. Oh, and we do have two or three used coats, those are half that price, but I believe you'll find they have less than half the wear on them. They're lower, to the right."

The merchant pointed to other folded coats down lower on the shelves. "You shout if you need help, all right?"

"Appreciate it." The man waited until the shopkeep once more set himself in motion; this time, he burbled on out of the little garment stockroom.

As the man turned his attention back to the stacked shelves, he reached for a new slate-and-black–checked coat. It was folded neatly and he felt bad about lifting it down and shaking it out, but he liked the idea that he might be the first to wear the thing. He set his hat down, tugged off his canvas work coat, and shrugged into the new one—a double-thick mackinaw with an ample collar. The buttons were all ample rounds, cut from the base of antlers, and polished. It seemed like a solid quality coat.

As the tall man looked over the coat, eyeing the seams and the obvious decent workmanship, he heard a noise behind him. It was the merchant again, who looked, if anything, even more red in the face and flustered. But he was smiling.

"Tell you what, you buy the new coat and I'll throw in a pair of wool mittens at . . ." The merchant scratched his chin and looked up at the ceiling, as if the answer to what he was mulling might be nested up there among the hanging baskets, ladies' hats, hanks of rope, and other odds and ends. "At half the marked price."

The tall man nodded and tugged on the top pair of mittens on the stack to his left. They, too, were doubly thick, and he could tell they would be plenty warm, especially inside a larger pair of leather outer mitts, which he already owned. His old pair of mittens were thinner and worn through in the thumbs and a few other spots.

"Sold," he said. "On both counts." He tugged off the mittens and handed them to the man.

"Excellent choice, sir. Now, you don't mind me speculating, but it looks to me like you're making for high country. The mountains hereabouts?"

The tall man waited a moment, then offered a half nod. "I am considering it. Have a mind to do a little trapping."

The merchant nodded. "You'll need snowshoes. The white stuff piles pretty deep in those high valleys. Keep you on top of the pond ice, too. Evens out your weight, you see?" He spread his pudgy fingers wide and walked with his hands in the air in front of him, demonstrating, the tall man assumed, how one might walk in the snowshoes.

"Yes, I had wondered about them. I don't suppose you have any in stock?" Somehow, thought the tall man, he bet he knew the man's response. And he was not disappointed.

"Do I? Do I? Why, only the best sort, made by a man who learned the craft from genuine Indians back East, so he told me. Forgot just where."

As he searched, an old, slow-moving man with a cane and dressed in dapper togs made his way from the door over to the counter, and helped himself to a peppermint stick. He looked at the tall stranger, then down, then up at him once more.

"Ain't you . . ." The old man, who eyed him with a hard sideways glance, narrowed his eyes even more, as if that might help him to make up his mind. "Naw, naw." He shook his head and turned his gray, wrinkle-cheeked face once more to the candy stick.

The stranger stared hard at the old man. Despite the old-timer's demeanor and haggard face, he looked to be well dressed. This meant little to the stranger, but he had learned from life on the drift these many years that, to a person, folks were always far more complicated than he could initially guess. And nothing, absolutely no detail in life, was useless. You never knew when on down the trail, a look or a cough or the custom and cut of a man's clothes might prove useful.

He'd spent enough time on that trail alone, save for his boon companion, Rig, his trusty chestnut gelding, and as solid a companion as man could ask for, for far too long to afford to ignore most anything.

But all that was incidental to him. For the old-timer had done the very thing he didn't want anyone to do—and yet so many folks did. He had recognized the tall man, somehow. And while the old man told himself that he couldn't be right, the tall stranger knew that he was.

And he knew, from long experience, that the old man would dwell on it and circle back to the notion that he was right. He did recognize the man beside him there in the shop. And any moment now, he'd turn back to facing the stranger, with that squint-eyed look of his, his candy stick cradled between his work-hardened fingers.

The tall stranger was Jonathan Gage, also known as Texas Lightning, late of Sourwood Springs, Texas. The Texas Lightning tag was a name that had dogged his back trail for years as he roved the West, doing his level best to outlive and outlast the dark infamy of his gunfighter past.

His success in shedding himself of that grim time was hit or miss, more *miss* than *hit* in the past few years, but when he was recognized, he had vowed long ago he'd not deny it.

Was today one of those days? He never knew, especially when he rode into a town new to him.

The thing that never failed to surprise Gage, even after all this time, was how people could still recognize him. After all, it had been seven years since he'd dropped his six-guns in the street and vowed not to resume the life of a gunfighter.

EVERYBODY HAS A GUN 7

He'd aged since then, grown grayer about the temples and throughout his chin hairs. He'd taken to wearing a full beard and moustache, albeit trimmed and somewhat tidy, for a good many years, too.

He'd also grown a little thicker, if he had to admit it. Mostly, if he'd had a long spell of laying low at a ranch, he'd whittle or darn socks or mend tack with other ranch hands around a potbelly stove in a bunkhouse.

But those times had been few and far between. There were always men, everywhere, it seemed, like the old man here now, who had recognized him. A few of them wanted his head as soon as they found out who he was, for a killing in his past. What he considered a long, distant past, but he knew that was not the case to those who still grieved their dead.

It had never seemed to matter to them that the law found the shootings justified. Truth was, Gage had never been able to figure out how he'd survived all those times he'd been called out to the street.

He'd made certain he never started the fights, but as his father, the long-dead, useless, drunk rancher Jasper Gage, had told him: "If somebody else starts a fight, you make certain to be the one to finish it." And Jonathan had. Too well and for too long.

"You . . ."

Here we go, thought the tall stranger, shifting the new coat and mittens slightly in his arms. He hadn't fully faced the old man yet. He knew what he'd see and he knew it would change everything about his so-far enjoyable, if brief, stop in Higgins, Utah Territory. Based on past experiences, Gage had opted for stopping off at the mercantile first, hoping to avoid this sort of thing in case it might prevent him from laying in his supplies.

At that moment, all he wanted to do was finish this rare bit of shopping, walk outside into the chill October air, check his bags and strapped load, and mount up to ride on out of Higgins, without arousing any further interest in himself.

For Jonathan Gage had no interest in the least in ever discussing his past. A past that, to his mind, was nothing more than a congealing lake of blood stippled with the gore-slick arms of his victims upthrust from the viscous surface, beckoning him, always beckoning him.

No matter how far, or how long, he rode all over the vast West, from mountains to oceans, to deserts and prairies, Gage was never able to outrun the brutal dreams that haunted his scant, restless, fitful sleeping hours. Nor did the dreams pester him solely in the dark.

They lingered on behind him all through his days, as if they, too, were astride horses, ragged mounts more bone than horse. Clopping steadily behind, they always seemed to gain, and never faded behind. Mostly, they were not there when he turned fast in his saddle. He knew they were about, though, for he had come to learn that he did not need to see a thing to believe it existed.

He also knew that someday, when he was caught unaware, he would be called out for his past and its vile misdeeds, and he would be laid low, to bleed out into the dust and grime of some lonely street in some town in which he was forever a stranger. And he knew it must be that way.

"Hey, mister," said a voice, cracking into Gage's reverie.

The tall man looked to his left to see that the same old man had moved closer, and stood staring once more at him. But this time, there was no cloud of doubt on his wrinkled, gray-stubbled features. This time, the old man knew who he was.

Would today be the day? thought Gage. *Would this day be the day when I pay my paltry offering toward the unscalable mountains of debt I owe? Will this be the day that I die?*

"Yes?" said Gage. "Do I know you?" He didn't usually even have to say that, but despite the notion that he'd long abided by—to remain quiet and humble and as unseen as possible—he still found himself annoyed, irritated, by the infrequent, but still occurring, discoveries by people recognizing him.

The old man in the dapper suit of clothes leaned closer, his eyes watery. "You . . . you're him, ain't you?"

Gage didn't quite know what to say for a moment. The man had at least leaned in and kept his voice low, which was appreciated by Gage. But that he knew who Gage was, or had been, tainted this otherwise-promising day. Now he'd have to leave Higgins sooner than he would have liked.

"What I mean to say is," continued the old man, "I

know you are. Him, I mean. I know who you are, and, well, I just want to say. . ."

The old man did something that Gage had not experienced in a good many years. He held out a shaking old hand, more bone than meat to the thing, but from the swollen digits Gage could tell that the old-timer had at one time long since, no doubt, put years' worth of hard effort into his life.

Gage stared at the proffered hand a moment. It had been his long-standing promise to himself that while he would never go out of his way to tell people who he was, and what he had done in the past, neither would he take any extraordinary measures to disguise who he was, and what he had done in the past to earn that reputation.

And what's more, he would always admit it to whoever might be calling him out. He did this because he was no coward, nobody to run away from the truth. He felt he owed it to all those people he had gunned down, and all their families. And to all the family members who would never be, because he had laid those folks low, he owed it to them to tell the truth about who he was.

And so, looking at that old man with the hand held out, he said, "Who is it that you think I am, sir?" in an equally low voice, hoping to not stir any more interest in their conversation from surrounding ears than had already been raked up.

"Why, you're . . ." Then the old man remembered he

was trying to speak low and close to this tall, dark stranger. "You're him!" The man looked about them, although there were no other customers in sight. "You're Texas Lightning."

Hearing that, the final nugget of truth to fall from the man's mouth, Gage could only nod and, since the man still held out his old wrinkled paw, he gave the man's hand a shake, firmly as his father had taught him to do: "Boy, whenever you shake a man's hand, you always look him in the eye as long as the shake lasts, and you grasp his hand firmly. Don't you squash his fingers, for that marks you as a small man with something to prove. Be nothing more than a man, and you'll be fine."

If that had been the end of Jasper's slice of solid wisdom and advice, young Jonathan Gage would have carried it with him with pride for all the long days of his life to come, and without needing to layer on top of it anything else. But Jasper, as a bullying drunkard himself, had continued by yanking the boy close, their nose tips touching, breathing his foul whiskey breath into Jon's face.

And then, in a low growl, he'd said, "And if I ever see or hear of you offering another man a weak shake, or not looking him in the eye, I will beat you as hard and as deep as a child has ever been whupped. You hear me, boy?"

Jonathan had nodded with vigor to his father's

question, and he had never forgotten the moment. Of course, it had always colored how he met other men, and his father's leering, red-veined face was nested there in his mind, riding rough over his thoughts, even all these years after the old man's death following the last in a series of fisticuff brawls that the then-grown Gage and his old, drunken father had engaged in. Gage had punched the old man in the chest and he suspected that's what had finally done the old wreck in.

By then, Jonathan had ridden away from the pathetic ranch they owned, his father too far in his cups to do much more than stagger around the place each morning, issuing orders and cursing at anything that displeased him, which was just about everything.

On that vile day years before, Gage had ridden into town to let his fool of a father rage and howl back at the ranch. It had happened before and Gage knew the only solution was time.

Once in town, that being Sourwood Springs, Texas, Gage knew he would embark on his own excursions into a life of indulging in hard liquor. What else had he going for himself?

And that is when it had happened. A seemingly minor exchange of words with a stranger while sitting at the bar, an exchange Gage took as little more than ribbing, ended up with him being called out into the street. He'd been drunk enough to heed the call, despite the warnings from the barkeep Monty, his old friend, at the Top Palace.

And wonder of wonders, as inexperienced and as

drunk as he was, Jonathan Gage had discovered something about himself: At the moment when he actually faced the man, time had slowed, at least for Gage.

Sound, too, became a muddled blur in his ears, echoing softly in his head, and he had grown oddly keen-sighted and sharper overall, somehow. He could not explain it, but he was thankful it had happened, nonetheless.

And for good or ill, and years later he would decide it was definitely the latter, this slowdown allowed Jonathan Gage to draw, aim, and fire before his opponent had fully raised his own weapon.

Gage's bullet had sought its target, the other man's chest, and had burrowed its way in as if it were a living thing.

It was as if Gage had been born to the task of killing.

It was not until sometime later that Gage, roused from his reverie by the town marshal, learned that man he had killed was none other than famed gunfighter Lee "Lightning" Shiller, late of Arkansas.

Some say Gage's kill had been born of luck, some say rather that he was born into the skill, a divine gift bestowed on him to rid the world of bad men, such as Shiller. As for Gage, he continued the family tradition of climbing down into the bottle, carried ever deeper into that boozy abyss by his backslapping new "friends," who bought him round upon round of drink following that first kill.

They had also bestowed on him the title of Texas

Lightning, an homage of equal parts to the first man he had killed and the place from whence he himself hailed.

When he emerged, groggy and shaking and ill three days later, and stumbled down the saloon staircase from the soiled bed of an equally soiled dove, it had taken the lawman and several others to fully remind the young man of just what it was he had done. And that his father had been found dead, back at the wretched little Gage family ranch, some miles outside of town.

It all came back to him in a sloshing torrent of memory that morning, and from then on, Gage's reputation as an amazing gunfighter grew and grew. It soon outdistanced the facts, until he became, much to his growing unease, a living legend.

For years following his ouster from his own hometown of Sourwood Springs, Texas, after his second kill there on the main street, and not long after laying Shiller low, Gage left a trail of corpses, their blood leaking and leaching into the dry dirt of the West.

At first, he was welcomed into towns and given free rooms, space at every gambling table, offered fine weapons, clothes, food, and more fun, particularly with women, than he could ever have imagined was possible in this world.

It took years, and killings upon killings, before the young man grew not so much older as weary, and began to tire of the adulation of the children chasing him down the streets shouting, "Bang! Bang!" and begging him to show how fast he could draw his gun.

By the end, he had shot north of two dozen men, each

one the result of a round-faced farmhand or a tipsy cowboy calling him out into the street. They had all been for a quick dollar on the growing bounty placed on his head by the frightening number of angry family members of his growing legion of dead.

Despite the raw numbers of his dead, and despite the fact that he did not once beg the fights to take place, nor did he instigate them, his reputation in those early years was such that it trotted on into each town well before he did.

By the time he slid from the saddle and swaggered into the nearest saloon, he was expected, and he heard the murmurings of men and women saying, "He's killed more than fifty," or "No, no, double that and you're still not close! The man can't go a day without laying low another! Stay clear, stay clear!"

Long before he grew tired of the lifestyle he had unwittingly cultivated for himself, Gage longed for an escape from the growing anger of others, the sneers and the frightened looks of women and children, and the unhidden rage of men eager to see him dead. It had not always been this way, he told himself. Surely, surely, it would one day be kind and amiable again.

But no, even then he sensed this was not to be. He was a killer, and the world knew him as such. Somewhere, somehow, the public's view of him had changed. It turned from admiration and awe to fear and loathing. He became someone nobody wanted to associate with. And the bounties on his head grew.

He became convinced he was going to be shot in his

sleep, his head hacked off his shoulders and stuffed in a gunnysack as proof to those posting the increasing dollar amounts that Texas Lightning was well and truly dead.

Gage slept less and less, and worried more and more, and drank more and more, and dreamed more and more. And one day, in a small town in Akin, Colorado, when a slight farmhand called him out into the street, he did not want to go, and yet . . . he did.

And it had happened, as the first had happened, as all his misdeeds had happened, as if time had slowed, as if the clock had been dosed with laudanum. And then it had ended, as they all did—the youth lay dead, while Gage stood dazed and staring at the inevitable.

And yet, that time had been different. That time, as he walked toward the dead or dying young man, pushing his way through the sneering, hate-filled eyes of the gathered locals, as he had looked down, he saw what he expected to see: a dying young fool out to build a reputation, out for money.

And yet, he also saw something he did not expect to see—the tender, unlined, and stunning face of a beautiful young woman, framed with golden hair and with sky-blue eyes.

She had hidden her pretty hair beneath her hat, and the ill-fitting clothes were those of a man, the gun too large for her hand. And too late, far too late, Gage had recalled the voice that had called him out.

It had been a too-high voice, yet the youth had refused to listen to his warnings to back down and walk away. The girl had drawn and fired—and Gage realized she had actually caught him with her own shot, up high on his left side, her bullet digging a furrow in his flesh and bouncing off a rib bone before leaving him.

Yes, the youth had been a pretty young woman, and in a different life, he might well have come to love and to spend his mortal years with her.

But not to shoot dead. And as he had looked down at her, he had seen the last of her precious young life leave her pretty, clear eyes—eyes that far too soon took on the film of death.

"Mister. Say, mister?"

It took another such round of questions to pull Jon Gage from his reverie. "What? Oh, sorry."

"Well," said the red-faced merchant, "you seemed lost in thought, and I believe I'll soon have other folks requiring my assistance."

The amiable shopkeeper nodded toward something beyond Gage's right shoulder. The big former gunman looked to see two men, a woman, and beyond them four or so children—he thought there might be others beyond them back by the door—standing and conversing with each other in low tones.

They didn't pay any attention to Gage or the shopkeeper. But he could hardly blame them, for it looked to him as if they were considering their finances. One of the men held a bulging coin purse in one hand; while the other man, younger and lean, but solid-looking, nodded and whispered something low.

The woman stood with her back half turned to Gage and the merchant. He reckoned this was in part to keep an eye on the brood of mostly behaved youngsters.

Gage turned back to the merchant. "The old man who was in here . . ."

"Oh, old Ronson? Hope he didn't pester you too much. He's old and lonely. Nice fellow, but a real talker. He's gone on home to annoy his wife, I expect."

"Right," said Gage, a small sense of relief washing over him. "I think that about does it for me." His stomach let out a low rumble. He was sure enough hungry, and feeling less rushed than mere minutes before. "Should I wait for the foodstuffs, or would it be easier if I come back later?"

The red-faced shopkeeper smiled even wider. "You wouldn't mind coming back? Say in an hour or so?" He leaned forward and spoke in a lowered tone, nodding toward the other customers. "We got word earlier that a wagon train from Kansas is camped down along the Shaw River, about a half mile east of town. I suspect these folks are the first of what I hope will be many other customers today. Never fails."

Gage nodded, considering the information. "That's fine with me. I'll be back in an hour, then. That will give me time to find a cup of hot coffee and pie. Any recommendations?"

"You bet," said the florid man. "Two doors down, Millie's. Can't miss it. Best pie in town. Also, the only pie in town, unless you are lucky enough to have a wife like mine." He smacked his ample paunch and rocked back on his heels.

Gage laid the cash for the coat and mittens on the counter and scooped them up. "I envy you that. The pie part anyway. The marriage?" He shrugged and nodded, smiling once more, and made for the door.

As he passed the travelers, he nodded and doffed his hat, which he had just plopped back on his head.

As Gage walked out into the street, between wagons, he glanced to the right and saw the sign for Millie's Cafe. He stepped quickly back to the boardwalk in time to avoid getting in trouble with a slow-moving work wagon commandeered by a broad-shouldered, black-hatted man.

The somber fellow wore a thick, square-cut gray beard nested beneath two narrowed eyes that scowled their own grayness at everything they took in. He was a workingman, Gage noted, given the thick, meaty fingers holding the lines well but loose.

The two equally squat, wide workhorses plodded ahead. The man's wagon carried a covered load, but Gage could see the telltale bulging of burlap sacks stuffed full. He was likely ferrying some bagged late crop to a buyer in town.

As Gage strode along, in no hurry, despite the nippy weather, he took in everything else about the street, enjoying seeing whatever his eyes rested on. He could not help but notice a number of men and women, all unsmiling, dressed in black. The men wore beards, trimmed square at the bottom, and black wool coats and black trousers and white shirts, topped with flat-brim black hats. The women walked a step or two behind the men, and wore black dresses over which they wore white aprons. They wore black bonnets on their heads, with little to no brim, and close fitting, as a nightcap might look. It was a dowdy, old look, especially so on some of the younger women.

Not everyone in the town seemed to go in for these fashions, but enough that Gage had noticed. Gage wondered if they belonged to a local church.

That might account for that grim look shared by so many of the men and women in town, folks who had the mannerisms of locals—making for certain stores at a brisk clip; chatting casually with others of their kind, while anchoring what he guessed was a usual spot on the boardwalk.

Gage walked on, musing on the fact that it had been a long spell of being on the trail alone with his horse, Rig. Yet as interesting as this town was proving, he did not mind his own company. In fact, he had always liked it, ever since he was a kid, spending most of his time alone out on the ranch, avoiding his father's drunken gaze and slurred demands.

That comfort and satisfaction of being a loner had never left Gage, and now, all these years later, when he chose to live apart from society, as much as he was able, it suited him fine. The only downside were bouts of loneliness.

As sound and as dependable as Rig was, the horse

didn't much seem interested in learning English, and Gage still hadn't figured out how to form even one word in horse talk. Didn't stop him from trying, though.

He often mused that if someone could hear him trying to converse with Rig while on the trail, and in the horse's native tongue, they'd put an end to Gage right there and then.

No, his life was not bad, but it was the recurrent thoughts that pestered him that he wished he could do without. The deep, demon-filled dreams were the worst of it. They descended when he did manage to slip into sleep after hours of lying awake, staring at the black sky.

Sometimes he'd choose a star and work up a story about how it was a place just like Earth, filled with folks and critters, trees and rocks, mountains and rivers, and he'd send them all on escapades.

But no matter what he thought up, somehow his mind herded those ruminations back to the deaths of all those folks he'd killed. There were plenty of them, although nowhere near the number folks believed and yammered about him having killed. Still, one was too many.

All of their leering death's-head faces stared him down in wakefulness and sleep. Sometimes, in the small hours, it became too much to bear and he would rouse from his blankets and kindle his dormant fire. Then he'd make coffee and sip it until dawn began to show itself.

Despite his proclivity for spending his time alone, when Gage did make it to a town to stock up on supplies, or to seek out work—mercantiles were a decent source for finding out what ranchers in the area might be hiring hands—he always enjoyed the first few hours in a town.

There he would be surrounded with more people than he'd seen in weeks. He particularly liked riding into towns he was unfamiliar with, even at the risk of being recognized. It helped that he had years before taken to wearing a full, trimmed beard. And as the years passed, he often went unrecognized for long stretches of time, which suited him right down to the ground.

He'd vowed to never deny it, should someone name him, nor would he worm his way out of a fight, should someone call him out for a past killing. But he would not follow through with a gunfight in the street. Those days were gone. He did his best to avoid such situations, of course, but sometimes he found himself plunked in the midst of a foolish mess and he had to fight.

He'd done it a few times over the years, and always because some big brute was stomping all over others. That made his blood cold and sparked that old, deep-seated rage in him. He did not like to see people put down by stronger, bullying types. He reckoned it came from being ground beneath his father's bootheels for years.

He'd managed to help a few folks, and in the process make a few more enemies, but he figured a few more wouldn't make any difference.

Gage was almost to the door of Millie's Cafe when he heard a bellowed shout in the street to his left. He paused, as did the dozen or so other folks lining the narrow main street. It did not surprise him to see that the shout had come from the surly-looking man in the work wagon.

"What are you doing here?"

The big, burly man in black stood in his wagon, glaring at a throng of men, women, and children who were huddled, talking on the side of the street opposite Gage. The burly, bearded man was addressing them.

The group of people he spoke to, four men, four women, and six or so children, all looked up at this strange, formidable man, who had stopped his wagon dead in the middle of the street, causing other wagons to do the same behind him and rolling forward from the other end of the street.

"I say again, what are you doing here, curse you!"

One of the men stepped forward, his face red, his jaw outthrust. He wore, as did the other men, a wool mackinaw with a sheepskin-lined collar. He was clean-shaven and tall, with a defined jaw. He nudged his hat brim back, exposing his eyes as he looked over the ten or so feet to the man in the wagon. "You have a problem with us shopping in town, mister?"

A woman beside him wrapped her hands about his coat sleeve and said something to him, looking from his face to the man in the street. Her wide eyes and raised brows showed outright fear.

The tall man beside her patted her own gloved hands with his, and gently removed them. He muttered something and stepped forward once more, this time to the edge of the boardwalk. He was about to repeat himself,

Gage bet, when the man in the wagon plopped down hard in his wagon's seat, shaking his head and speaking in a voice loud enough for all to hear: "Outsiders! Heathens! Up to no good! No good!" He snapped the reins, slapping them hard against the rumps of his team, and the beasts dug in, jerking the freighted wagon forward, gravel popping and grinding beneath the wheels.

Gage regarded the folks across the street. He guessed they were from the wagon train the shopkeep spoke of. It was some moments before the street sounds resumed. Gage regarded the broad, black-jacketed back of the man in the wagon as he rolled onward up the street, still in no hurry.

He reached for the cafe's doorknob, musing on how awful it was that one sour seed could put a whole street full of folks ill at ease and leave them all cringing inside, as if they each had done something wrong somehow.

As he entered, a grinning, red-faced woman, perhaps old enough to be his mother, surprised him just a few feet inside. "That man is a menace," she said, offering Gage a quick nod and smile as she bustled on by.

From her garb, he reckoned she was either Millie or someone who worked for her. She wore a large white apron over a no-nonsense dress, with her sleeves unbuttoned and rolled up to her elbows. Her hands were work-reddened, as was her face, and her hair, more silver than what he guessed from the traces left streaking the grayness, still bore more than a hint of a luxuriant head of chestnut-colored hair.

Her bosom was ample and she was not overly tall, but somehow she gave the impression that she was a giant.

"Take a seat, stranger!" she said, and Gage realized she was talking to him.

There were close to a dozen tables and a long counter fronted with stools at the far side of the room—behind which, from the sights and smells and clanging, clattering sounds emanating from within, was a kitchen.

Gage chose an empty table along the right side of the room, with his back somewhat to the kitchen, and from where he would be able to see the front door. He did not expect to be joined by anyone else, as the room bore few other customers, so he set his new purchases on the seat of the chair opposite his and folded his legs up, sitting down with a slight sigh. It had been a long day so far, and tiring.

As his nose twitched and picked out far too many wonderful, enticing smells on the air, he realized that he was hungry. Perhaps for something more substantial than a mere slice of pie.

"What'll it be?" said the stout woman, appearing beside his table and wiping stray strands of hair from her face with the back of her left hand.

He'd barely had time to consider this, let alone read the board of offerings, but he somehow knew that he could order most anything and she was capable of working it up for him. He also knew what he had a taste for. The smells that had come to him when he entered birthed a gnawing, growling hunger, such as he hadn't felt in many weeks.

He knew it was because his own cooking was so limited, and not because he was impoverished and unable to feed himself. And since he did not like to travel with excessive amounts of goods, he had long since grown familiar with the singular sensations of going without.

"I'd like a cup of coffee. And how about chunked beef swimming in thick gravy and ladled over hot potatoes?" Gage knew it was bold to presume he could have such a thing, but it was what came to mind. Really, given the savory smells in the place, he would have been happy with anything she decided to bring him.

She smiled down at him. "You're in luck. All but the beef anyway. It'll have to be elk. That all right with you?"

"Oh yes, ma'am. That sounds grand."

"Good, it'll be out before long. I'll bring coffee first." She hustled on back to the kitchen and it didn't take her long to fulfill the promise. She set a thick stoneware mug before him and poured out a cup full of steaming dark coffee. It smelled just right and he knew he would have another before the meal was out.

She also set before him a tall glass of water. "A man should drink more than coffee, you know. Particularly when hot food is involved."

"Yes, ma'am." Gage wasn't certain why he felt cowed by the woman, but her rosy cheeks and smile went a long way toward assuring him all would be well if he'd only follow her directives.

"Thank you, ma'am." He accepted the water and nodded his thanks.

Before ten minutes had passed, in which he gazed

about the room, sipping his coffee and enjoying himself, she returned, carrying a platter on which was heaped a more-than-generous portion of steaming meat hunks atop a mound of potato chunks and thick slices of carrots. Atop it all was drizzled brown-black gravy that looked so good and fortifying that Gage felt sure he could have had a mug of that and little else.

She smiled and set it before him, along with cutlery and a folded napkin, and left him to it.

By then, the few other customers in the place had paid and left the establishment, save for a young couple who looked to Gage to be at some stage of courting. He was blond and she was blond and each bore creamy skin, and they gazed at one another the way only youthful lovers might.

Their small, empty plates—they had had pie, he'd seen when he came in—were stacked and placed to the side to give them more room to hold hands and stare at one another.

They were still murmuring to each other when the woman came back to Gage's table. He was halfway through his meal and enjoying each bite as much as the first. "Would you like company?" she said.

He could not reply, as his mouth was full, but he gestured to the other chair at the table and nodded and smiled. She took the hint and set down her own cup of coffee, then pulled out the chair. It held his new coat and mittens.

"Oh, I see you've been shopping at Wenger's." She felt them over approvingly, then set the new items on the seat of another nearby chair. "Well chosen. Should keep you warm." She sat down with a sigh. "So my guess is you're not sticking around, eh?"

"Afraid not, no."

"Ah, well," she said. "Pity. Higgins could use more young, handsome fellows." She winked at him and he liked her even more.

"If I didn't have plans, ma'am, your cooking would be reason enough to keep me here."

She blushed and he resumed his meal, comfortable somehow, eating in her presence. He did not remember his mother, as she died when he was a baby, but he felt certain that this woman represented that ideal of a maternal figure in his mind.

As he finished up, he wondered if he had room enough for a slice of pie, for he felt certain that Millie's pie, no matter the flavor, would be a treat. She beat him to it.

"Do you think you could wedge in a piece of pie? It's pecan today. A real luxury because they're the last of those nuts I expect to see here for some time. It normally costs a fortune to bring them in."

"Normally?" he said.

"Well, I got my last supply of them cheap." She winked. "A family traveling through was selling off some of their goods, trying to lighten their wagon's load. I bought a small chest of drawers and inside one of the drawers was a pretty knitted shawl, green and black, and a package of nuts, all double wrapped, neat as you please. I didn't notice those things until a few days later when I had a chance to rummage. But by then, those folks were long gone. I think of that woman every time I wear the shawl and, of course, when I baked with the pecans."

She sat still, looking at the wall behind Gage, a sad smile on her face.

"As to the pie, I would love some, thank you. And the story will make the eating of it all the more special."

She smiled and stood up. "I was hoping you'd say that. I'll fetch it for you. And more coffee, too."

He finished what coffee he had left in his cup and thumped his belly with his fingertips. Sure, he could make room for pie and coffee. That's what he came in for in the first place! He'd just added a few other items beforehand.

She deposited the pie and coffee and lingered, so he asked her to sit once more. He enjoyed her company and it seemed she was not overly anxious to attend to her kitchen duties. Perhaps she was taking a break after a long, busy morning.

The pie was as tasty as he'd hoped. Even more, and he told her so. She blushed once again.

"Speaking of wagon train folks, do you get lots of them coming through Higgins?" he said between savored bites.

"We do. We're right on the primary route, or one of them, so I'm told, to get through the Chisley Range, which is just thataway." She hiked a thumb beyond him, toward the west end of town.

"There's a pass they all use, just right for wagons to

snake on through there. A couple of hours west of here. Haven't been there myself—me, this is as far as I go. I have a nice little business, a nice little home, and nobody telling me what to do."

"What about those folks I see in black, the men in beards, the women in bonnets. They're a dour-looking bunch," he said.

She leaned toward him. "Hush that talk if you want to get along in town."

"Why's that?" he said in an equally lowered voice.

"Because they're the Brethren. They started coming in here four or so years back, mostly whipped up by one man, a fellow they call Deacon. Well, you've seen him already."

"I have?"

She nodded. "That grouchy, barking fellow in the wagon out front."

"Oh, interesting," he said.

"Yes, when he came in, he brought a handful of the Brethren folks with him. Then others came, and the rest, a growing number of others quite a few now, are local folks he managed to win over to his cause."

"What is this cause anyway?" said Gage.

She shrugged. "I'm not quite sure. It doesn't tempt me, I can tell you. I do my worship in private. Figure anything I need to pray about is between me and my Maker." She looked up. "Me and Him—or Her—we seem to get on just fine."

"And the Brethren?"

Again she offered a shrug. "They didn't start out as

overly friendly, but they weren't mean, not like they've become." She looked about her, as if someone in black was about to pop out from hiding in a corner. She eyed the young couple, but they were dressed in bright colors and looked anything but dour.

"How have they become that way?" said Gage. "These Brethren folks, I mean."

"Well," she continued in her lowered voice, barely above a whisper, "more and more of them moved in. It's because we have decent farming land hereabouts. They don't actually live in Higgins, well, not many of them, but they bought up and settled so much of the land all about us that they might as well own the place. Most of them live beyond that pass I told you about. I heard tell it's a pretty place, good land. They call it the Chosen Valley. Piles of them moved in, once the first ones settled."

She shook her head and offered a rueful, thin smile. "The others must have written to them, told them how good the land was. Before me and the other folks who settled Higgins knew it, we were overrun with them. Now, don't get me wrong, they spend money in town, on things they can't grow or build themselves, but they are less friendly all the time, and they've been crowding us in other ways, too."

"Like how?" Gage was interested, and this information about the Brethren only cemented his resolve to not spend the night in town. He'd thought of lingering, but he now knew he'd be camping once more out on the trail. Which meant he'd have to mosey on, sooner rather than later if he wanted to find a site before the dark and cold settled in on him and Rig.

"They have two folks on the town council now." She nodded and the look on her face was grave, the most serious look he'd seen on her since their short acquaintance began. "And the marshal in town is a convert to their faith."

"I see how that could cause concern, sure." He couldn't help himself and picked up the last bits of the fine pie crust with his fingertips. It would be a shame to let them go to waste. "What flavor is their religion anyway?"

In Gage's experience, nobody overly zealous about anything was ever very much fun to be around. And usually, they were harmful to others, intentionally or not.

"Oh, I don't rightly know. Whatever it is, it sure doesn't look like much fun. They're all so sour all the time. Honestly. Life can be so much fun if you let it be. You know what I mean?" She smiled at him.

Gage did his best to return the smile, but an unbidden stab of memory erupted of the faces of the people he'd laid low. They would never again feel the sun on their faces while picnicking with their families, or see their children grow. He looked past her shoulder to the young couple, still holding hands and chatting, no doubt about a future that looked so bright to them they likely had to squint to see it.

"If you are moving westward yourself," she said in that low voice, "you ought to know there have been folks who've gone missing out by that pass and the valley beyond." She nodded again. "And not heard from again."

This was unexpected. "How so? You think the Brethren had something to do with it?"

"I'm not saying yes, not saying no. But it's odd. That's all."

"There's proof?"

"More than just rumor, let's say that." She pulled back. "I've already said too much, I fear. I'm not even sure why I thought to share such with you." She narrowed her eyes a moment and regarded him.

"Don't worry, Millie. If you're thinking I'm working in secret for the Brethren, rest easy." He smiled. "I'm just here for the pie. But if what you say is true, and I've no reason to doubt you, then that bears some looking into by folks far more official than me."

"Oh, I know it. And the rest of us know it, too. Problem is, this here is our home and our numbers are dwindling, what with the Brethren pulling in folks who used to be my friends. Why, they're taking over the town!" Her voice rose and she caught herself and looked at the table, blushing again.

Gage saw the young man look up from staring at his girl and eye Millie for a moment. *Maybe I'm wrong about him, too,* thought Gage. What a town Higgins was turning out to be. He needed to wrap up his affairs here and make tracks, no matter what was happening. There were enough adults around that he didn't need to poke his nose into their affairs. If there were bad things happening, they needed to tend to that themselves.

Chapter 2

"Pardon me, but do you happen to know the route to a pass that leads to . . . I believe it's locally known as the Chosen Valley?"

For a moment, Gage wasn't certain that the woman had spoken to him. Gage looked at her and noticed a man standing several feet behind her. The fellow didn't quite meet Gage's glance. Gage looked back to the woman.

He had known men such as this, and although he knew it was not his place to judge another, he found it difficult not to think that the fellow, any fellow, who stood back while his wife did the necessary work in a conversation on their behalf, surely was somehow less of a man than he ought to be.

Before he could reply to the woman, the man surprised Gage and stepped forward, nodding and extending his hand. "I . . . I'm Se-Seth G-G-Greenaway. And th-th-this is my w-w-w—"

"I'm his wife, Sarah Greenaway." The woman offered her hand, so Gage went from one hand to the next. He noted that the man flashed a quick look of annoyance at his wife's obviously kindhearted interruption of his painful-sounding greeting.

The man's stammer went a long way in explaining his initial reluctance to ask Gage the question his wife had. It also reminded Gage to avoid judging a man at all, let alone in haste and based on nothing more than an initial impression.

"How do. I'm Gage." He hurried on with his response, lest they decide to dwell on his name. It's not that it was a particularly uncommon name, but he had been surprised many times over the years by the number of folks who associated the name with their hazy, fuzzy memories of stretched truths about a gunfighter from Texas, one Texas Lightning.

"As to the location of this Chosen Valley, I am afraid I'm in the dark about that as well. I'm a stranger here myself, just stocking up on supplies and then passing through. But the fellow yonder," he replied, nodding toward Wenger's Mercantile, "seems a friendly sort." Gage let those words hang for a moment, and gave them each a stern look and nod. "If you take my meaning, and he might be able to answer your question."

"Oh, su-su-sure, thanks. Appr-appreciate it, mi-mi-mister."

"Yes, thank you, sir," she said, not stepping on her husband's words this time.

Gage touched his hat brim and walked on by, back toward the stable and Rig. It was nibbling close to the time he felt he should leave. Somehow, even though he still had the urge to poke around town a bit longer, it being a fine, if nippy, day, he felt he needed to make tracks.

The mood in town had shifted once the wagon train folks arrived and began catching hard looks from some, but not all, of the locals, and certainly not the merchants, who stood to make decent money from the weary travelers looking to stock up on supplies.

He didn't know just what, if any, trouble may be in the offing, but he was in no rush to find out. He wished the travelers luck and speed in getting into town, buying what they needed to continue their journey, and getting on out again.

"Hey!"

The barked word came to Gage from his right. He looked over to see a man seated in a tipped-back chair, balancing on the two rear legs, his right leg crossed over his left knee, his left boot tip gently raising and lowering the balanced chair an inch or so every few seconds.

The man was not particularly memorable in any way—average height, the sad efforts of a young man's beard, drab black wool clothes, a somewhat-white shirt, and, topping it all, a black hat. The black togs reminded Gage of those he'd seen around town on other men and women.

But there was one different and memorable thing about this fellow. He wore a silver badge, a star encircled within a band, up on his left breast pocket.

The man let his chair settle forward to rest square,

EVERYBODY HAS A GUN 37

and he shifted the matchstick he was rolling between his lips, then plucked it free. All the while, he eyed Gage.

"Yeah, I said it, and I am talking to you."

"May I help you?" said Gage, resisting the urge to sneer out the word "lawman." In his long experience, it never paid to start off on the wrong foot with a lawdog, even if this one had the makings of a fool.

The lawman snorted. "Course. Elsewise, why would I call a halt to your walking?"

Gage did not alter his expression, but he wanted to punch the idiot in the face and walk out of there. He waited a long moment and watched the man. Finally Gage said, "Well?"

"Don't rush me now, man. Look, I seen you talking with them strangers. What is it they want?"

Gage regarded the man a long moment. "Why don't you ask them yourself? Unless you're too busy, that is."

"Listen, mister!" The man, still not rising from his seat, pointed a finger at Gage with his left hand. His right slid down to rest on his shiny, well-oiled sidearm.

Gage was not frightened or worried. He was annoyed. This fool of a runt was lazy, full of himself, and had mighty poor manners. Worst of all, if the badge was a true indication, the fool was also marshal of the town.

The urge to point out these things to the fellow washed over Gage like a full rain pail dumped over his head. The sensation was mighty, but it withered as quickly as it came to him.

Long past were the days when he would act on such sensations. The only thing he wanted to do was to get his horse, retrieve his waiting goods at the store, and ride on out of Higgins, Utah Territory, and make straight for the Chisley Range.

He made his intentions plain by walking away, unafraid of the fidgety lawman. That didn't mean he couldn't feel the man's eyes boring holes in the back of his skull and shoulders.

Gage had felt that sensation plenty of times over the years, and it never grew easier, even if he liked the brief sensation of winning a hand every now and again. But risking folks noticing him, particularly law officers, was not something Gage wished to promote.

"I said I am still talking to you, mister!"

The voice sounded a bit keyed up, with a growl to it. Gage laughed to himself and shook his head. *Maybe today will be the day,* he thought. *Maybe today I'll meet my Maker.*

It had been a long time in coming. And although he was in no particular hurry to cash in his chips, he did expect that one of these days more and more people were going to recognize him. It would likely be a family member of one of his victims, and that person would be justified in laying him low, that much Gage knew.

Still, he paused on the sidewalk, but did not turn around. He heard the deep, throaty clicking of a handgun's steel hammer ratcheting back to full cock—the deadliest position of all.

"You best turn yourself around and answer my questions in a civil manner or we're going to have ourselves trouble, you hear me, stranger?"

Gage sighed and raised his arms and turned slowly, his new coat and mittens tucked high under his left arm. His open coat flared enough to show he was unarmed. "What are you harassing me for, Marshal? I am here merely to spend money in your fine town and then leave, which I am fixing to do. Surely, there can be no harm in that?"

Gage knew it was a pinch antagonistic, but he'd said it intentionally, as there were several people walking by who had stopped and were watching the proceedings with raised eyebrows.

Gage searched the younger man's face. He was looking uncertain, his bluster and bravado of moments before having vanished like smoke on a breeze.

But what bothered Gage the most was the fact that the lawman held that revolver on him steady, aimed right at Gage's chest. One twitch of a finger, unplanned or not, and Gage would be dead, gone.

In truth, the thought did not bother him all that much. He'd been on the receiving end of a good many aimed guns, and by now, it did little to rattle him. What did bother him was the fool's attitude and the assumption that because he wore a star, he could do as he pleased.

"It's too bad," said Gage, still holding his hands up equal with his chest.

"What is?" said the uncertain lawman. He'd begun glancing left and right.

Gage knew the idiot was not liking the situation he'd put himself in. And he'd snatch any offered excuse to back out of it, provided it didn't cost him much in the way of saving face before the townsfolk who'd put him in office.

"A shame me and the other folks are having such a tough time in Higgins."

"That's not my fault!"

"Oh," said Gage, squinting at the marshal, "I'd say it is a large bit of your fault, sure."

"How . . . how do you figure that?" The lawman licked his lips, and tried on a sneer. It didn't fit.

"As you are the duly selected representative of peacekeeping in Higgins, I just assumed it was part of your duties to make certain that all these folks, myself included, strangers to your town, were treated at least with the deference and care and concern that the citizens of Higgins receive."

From the look on the young lawman's face, some of those words were tricky for him to comprehend. "Ain't nobody mistreated anybody. Yet!" The lawman tried on his sneer again. It fit for a few seconds, then slid away when he saw that the spotty crowd had grown. Folks were stepping out of shops and staring with interest at what Gage assumed was an unusual sight in their town.

From behind the young lawman, a robust figure familiar to Gage strode up. It was Millie, wiping her work-reddened hands on her ample apron.

"For pity's sake, Rufus! What, in the name of all that is Higgins, are you doing to that poor man?" By the time she finished speaking, she had walked right up beside the lawman and stood not a foot from his left shoulder, her back to the street.

As she spoke and walked, Gage saw the man's eyes widen as he recognized the voice. "Miss Millie. I—"

"I, I, nothing, Rufus Pinkham! I know this man! Just talked with him at the cafe. He's about as harmless to you or this town as a skeeter bite. Besides," she said, sidestepping to partially face the street crowd, "he ain't even armed."

"But—"

"But nothing, Rufus. Put down that fool gun of yours or I'm liable to tell your uncle all about this when he gets back."

That really drained the air from the lawman. If he didn't think he might still be in trouble, Gage would have busted out in a full grin. He kept his face stony and watched the proceedings.

Some members of the gathered street crowd began turning away, while others said, "Aw, leave him be, Pinkham."

Millie nodded. "That goes for the rest of the new folks in town today, too! They have money and I have a business to run. Same as the rest of the folks here. You think we're going to stand by and let you or the other members of the Brethren stamp out our livelihoods?"

A whole lot of small, and not-so-small, towns he'd ridden through over the years had been established by folks traveling together to seek a life where they might not be bothered by other folks not in agreement with their particular religious views.

And he'd found that roughly half of those folks had been kind and welcoming to strangers, likely hoping they might become useful members of their Church, whereas the other half treated newcomers with suspicion and often downright aggression. And judging from what Gage had seen and experienced in Higgins, these Brethren folk were most definitely part of that second group.

What he really wanted to know was how this pup of a lawman was going to save face in front of the town? Gage was getting tired of standing there, holding his hands up and waiting for this fool to make up his mind. And then Gage received another surprise from the town of Higgins.

"Rufus, leave him be! This is not the day for such. The Maker will tell us when."

Gage looked to his right and saw the burly, scowling man from the work wagon. This was the one Millie had said brought the Brethren to Higgins. The one they called Deacon.

The thick, sneering man stood with his big ham fists resting on his waist, the seams of his black coat bulging with the effort. His wide face, florid above the beard, still hosted the two narrowed eyes. They cut over to regard Gage.

"Go," said the grim plug of a man.

Gage wanted to heed the directive, but the surly farmer wasn't the one holding the gun on him. He looked back to the lawdog, and saw he was lowering his revolver. It wasn't until the lawman had it aimed down at the planking beneath his feet that he eased it off cock.

Somebody should tell that fool that's a great way to

drill a hole in his foot. But Gage decided it would not be him. *Let this fool find out for himself.*

"Git gone, and be quick about it!" growled the temporary marshal.

Gage never took his eyes from the young man's face, with its weak attempt to appear menacing. He slowly lowered his hands and, cradling his new coat and mittens, Gage shifted his gaze to the surly farmer, who'd intervened, and offered a slight nod.

Just before turning, Gage saw the man's crabby look turn into a harder sneer, and he wasn't certain, but he thought he heard the man growl.

Gage was not expecting such, but he certainly would find no ally there.

He finished his turn and walked up the street, making for the stable. He'd retrieve Rig, make his way over to the mercantile, and collect his supplies, then bid Higgins a good day, week, month, year, and life. He had no urge to revisit the place. Then he thought of the kindness of the shopkeeper, and of Millie, and of her excellent fare.

Although their pleasant presences, among a number of other folks who looked to be locals who offered smiles and nods, softened the ragged edge of his regard for the town, they did not alter it enough. He'd take his leave as soon as he was able.

It didn't take long for Gage to pay the stableman and lead Rig back onto the street. The big horse walked slowly and jerked his head in a surly manner, irked, no doubt, that he had to leave the convenience and comfort of the warm stable with its hayrick and oats. But Gage smiled as he walked, recalling that on their way in, he'd told the horse that should he find a stable, it would only be for a short while. He'd kept his word.

Gage himself had wanted it to be an overnight visit. "Can't always have the thing we think we most want, eh, old chum?"

If the big brown gelding heard him and comprehended the platitude, he showed no sign of it, choosing instead to plod along with his head down, as if he were being led to a tannery.

"Oh, cheer up, Rig. At least you weren't held at gunpoint by an idiot today."

"Talking to yourself is a sure way for telling others you're not right in the bean!"

Gage looked up to see an old-timer—bushy-bearded, but not wearing black—eyeing him with one eye cocked against the smoke from his long-stem cob pipe.

The man was a good head and a half shorter than Gage and looked to have at least twenty, maybe twenty-five, years on him, but he had the look of someone who'd been around, and not just in Higgins. His full set of well-worn buckskins and tall, fringed leather moccasins told Gage much of the story.

His green slouch felt topper sported a flopping coon tail that trailed down one side and bobbed as the old fellow walked alongside Gage.

"I wasn't talking to myself."

"Oh?" said the man, puffing his pipe and emitting a

fragrant blue cloud of smoke. "Who, then? The head honcho in the sky, like everybody else in this town?"

"Nope, just my horse."

"Oh, well, that's all right, then."

"Thanks."

"Say," said the older gent, "you got something against praying?"

"Nope. But I do it in silence, alone, out there." Gage nodded ahead toward the white-rimmed peaks far in the distance, visible past the end of the main street of Higgins.

The buckskin fellow smiled and ruffled his beard with a gnarled hand. "I hear that, mister. I'm the same." He lowered his voice. "Churches are just fine and dandy for city folks." He looked about him. "But I figure there's all this beauty out there, I might as well take it in when I'm tending to most all my matters of importance."

Gage nodded and stopped before the store.

"Name's Bewley." The codger stuck out a gnarled, thick-knuckled hand.

"Gage." The former gunfighter shook the offered hand.

"Say, where'd you get that new coat of yours?"

Gage glanced at the black-and-slate–checked mackinaw he'd draped over his left shoulder. "Right in there." He nodded at Wenger's Mercantile. "Just stopping back to fetch the rest of my supplies."

"Then you headed out?"

"Yep."

"Me too. I was hoping to find a blanket or some such

to make a coat, but if they have such as that already stitched, why, I might gander on them myself."

The two men moved on up the steps and into the store. Gage pointed the old-timer toward the rear, where he'd found the coat, and made his way to the counter. The genial merchant was chatting with someone by a bin of what looked to be nails.

A stout woman with spectacles with tiny lenses perched on the end of her nose stood behind the counter, tallying figures on a filled sheet of paper. She looked up at Gage, and a smile crinkled her eyes.

She's as friendly as her husband, bet Gage with himself.

"You'll be here for your goods, then," she said, a lilt to her words telling Gage she was Irish.

"Yes, ma'am."

"And you've recovered from your run-in with our welcoming committee, no doubt."

He smiled and nodded. "Somewhat, yes."

She sighed. "Higgins used to be such a quiet place."

"Oh?"

"Yes, then"—she leaned forward—"the Brethren found us." She shook her head. "I tell you, it's not like any Church I've ever known."

Gage wanted no more to do with the town, including knowing anything else about the religious affiliations therein. "Ah," he said, hoping his noncommittal response would stem the woman's inclination to gossip with him.

"Oh, sure, it's a rough lot, I don't mind saying.

EVERYBODY HAS A GUN

T'wouldn't be so bad, but they're running roughshod over folks such as meself and my husband, Mr. Wenger, who helped settle the place. We've a hard enough time making ends meet without the Brethren frightening off customers!"

As she spoke, her voice rose with the color on her cheeks.

"There now, Betty, the fellow doesn't want to hear all about that!" It was Mr. Wenger, her husband, bustling over to her side. He spoke in lowered tones. "Nor do we want the rest of the customers to hear our woes, eh, my love?"

She sighed and returned to her figures.

"Now, then. Ah, yes." The merchant faced Gage. "Let's see, there are your goods, sir." He gestured to a modest mound of packages, bundles, and sacks anchoring the far end of the counter. "And here is the tally." He slid a slip of paper to Gage, who tweezered out the required coins from the money pouch he kept nested within his inner vest pocket.

"One more thing," he said, nodding to a tall, corkstoppered jar containing finger-thick peppermint sticks. "I'd like three of those, please."

"Certainly, sir. That will be nine cents."

Again Gage rummaged in his pouch. "Here's a ten-cent piece."

"Ah, what say we make it four sticks for a dime?" said Wenger, smiling.

"Great," said Gage, sliding the dime to the man and taking the paper-wrapped candies. He slipped them into his breast pocket and nodded. "Thanks for everything. I'm off."

"It is we who thank you, sir. We do hope you will come again. Uh, despite the treatment you've received in Higgins."

"Well, you never know." Gage made for the door, his arms laden. But he was thinking that if he had a thing to say about it, Higgins would soon see the last of him. He had enough to think about without inviting more distress into his mind.

Out in the street, he noticed more folks, many of them not dressed in black, looking up and down the shop fronts as if they were new to the place. He guessed they were part of the wagon train. "Strength in numbers," he muttered as he set his bundles on the edge of the raised boardwalk and scooted Rig closer.

Gage wasted no time in loading up his saddlebags and two small canvas panniers, strapping everything in soundly. He'd repack it all, once he was well out of town. If it rode well enough, he'd wait until he put a good few miles between him and Higgins, then he'd make camp and tend to his new goods.

The last thing he did was to take off his canvas work coat and transfer what he kept in its pockets, checking each thoroughly, to his new wool coat. He strapped the lighter coat down tight behind the cantle and, gripping his new mittens in his teeth, he mounted up. Then he tugged them on, heeled Rig lightly in the barrel, and made for the west end of town.

As he rode, he couldn't help but feel as though his

progress was being watched, and not by kindly eyes. "Soon," he said to Rig, "we'll be able to breathe again."

It took them about four minutes to reach the end of town. He kept their speed restrained and only had to skirt two wagons moving at a plodding pace. Each was commandeered by a dour-faced, black-clothed man, with the second carrying a similarly clothed woman and four children in the back, sitting on hard wooden benches. Their unsmiling faces matched that of the man up front.

CHAPTER 3

Gage rode for much of an hour, marking the sun's slow descent toward the far mountain peaks. He'd hoped to make it farther from Higgins, but it was nippy and he was full from the fine meal at Mattie's, so he'd not kept a brisk pace once he left the environs of the town.

Since the day was a bright one, but on the cold side, he knew from experience that the evening would freeze his canteen and shiver his bones.

That meant riding off trail soon and making camp, preferably hunkered at the base of a cliff, in the lee of the wind, which had picked up since leaving Higgins. It blew from the northeast, nudging his right shoulder aslant on his ride west, which was better than having it buffet him full-on.

That was never any fun and was most often something he would avoid at all costs, choosing instead to lay low in a wind-free spot, if possible, until the bluster blew itself out.

His new wool coat, he was pleased to note, did a fair job in keeping out the cold. He knew, though, that if he chose to spend the winter in high country, he would need another layer atop, something of hide, preferably with hair on. Maybe buffalo or elk.

If that were the case, it was a good thing he bought heavy waxed thread and a new set of needles. The awl he had—but what he didn't have were the hides. Yet.

It had always pained him to take another creature's life, particularly given his past, but for survival, he was up to the task. An elk or two would not go to waste, nor would a bear. Once he established a solid, long-term camp, he would hunt up what he could, skin them out, render the meat, perhaps smoke it, and do his best to store what he could for the harder months.

He'd learned the rudiments of the fine skill of smoking meats from a German ranch cook named Johann, who had grown up in Bavaria, but had decided to seek his fortune in the wilds of America's frontier.

As a young man, he had heard the gold-laden stories two men had related in a tavern one evening while passing through his small town on their way north, and home. Based on their fantastic, riveting stories, he determined that it should take him no longer than two years to reap a lifetime's wealth and then return to marry his young love, who would be waiting.

When Gage had met Johann, the cook's time in the American West had just passed the thirty-one-year mark. In that time, he had made and lost two solid fortunes, certainly enough to return to Bavaria and be considered a success. Somehow he kept wondering about the next seam, the next dig pit, the next sluice full, and on and on.

After three years, he had received a letter from his love informing him that she would wait no longer. She would marry her second cousin, a shopkeeper two valleys eastward. And since the letter did not reach him, due to his perpetual case of itchy feet, for eleven months after she had mailed it, Johann raised a bitter glass to the couple, and spent the evening working through the rest of the bottle of rye whiskey.

Then he resumed his makeshift career as a miner. He also discovered, once he'd grown weary of breaking his back rooting in gravel for more gravel with little or no color, that he was naturally inclined to enjoy cooking—and what's more, he was quite good at it. Good enough, in fact, that he was hired on at a ranch. He'd agreed because it seemed like a decent enough place to ride out the raw cold of the winter months.

By the time spring rolled around, the ranch owner had become smitten by the man's culinary concoctions. Most of them were second-rate versions of his talented mother's hearty Bavarian dishes, among them many recipes that required deeply smoked meats. He built a smokehouse, but was also not afraid to use tarpaulins, hollowed logs, pits in the ground, and such.

Gage recalled Johann's story with a smile as he rode, eyeing the terrain for a suitable camping spot. As Rig walked on, it occurred to him that he needed to ride to a patch of high ground and scout the terrain. It would wait until morning, if he could find a campsite soon.

And as if he had ordered it tailor-made, he spied a narrow game trail to the left. It appeared to angle down toward an overhang that faced west. He slid from the saddle and led Rig, taking the lead and proceeding down the varied switchbacks until they reached the bottom, roughly twenty feet, no less, from the cobby trail they'd been following.

Light from the late-afternoon sun angled through the leafless trees—he saw aspen and a couple of others he could not name at the moment. It was far easier to find the spot in the daylight. He was grateful for his trail experience.

"Looks decent, Rig."

And then he received a surprise. At the bottom, tucked to within a few feet, no more than six, from the bottom of the inward-sloping overhang of granite, he spied the scorched rocks of a well-used fire ring.

Instinct and habit tensed him. Gage ground-tied Rig and moved forward slowly, his coat already unbuttoned halfway from the bottom, and his left hand feeling for the antler handle of his big wide-blade knife.

He saw no one about, no tracks on the sandy spot, and, squatting, held a palm above the rocks and the midst of the ring, where the half-sandy charcoal bits sat. No heat, as he knew he'd find.

He turned to take in the view from beneath the overhang and saw that the tree-stippled land sloped gently away, ending some twenty yards down at a small stream. He saw it in the sun glint like a traveling snake.

He glanced back up at the close-in overhang and

noted scorching above where the fire ring sat. It would not surprise him to find ancient artistic renderings on the rock, at man height, depicting huts, animals stalked and slain, of horses and of people, too.

He'd seen such before and was always fascinated by the thought that perhaps there had been people other than those such as himself, whites, but people who had lived here perhaps thousands of years before. How long ago, he did not know. Only their ghosts would know for certain.

Indians, he guessed they would be, perhaps of Mexican stock, perhaps from deeper and more southerly places. He knew not. But was it possible this was an unused camp for all this time? How tempting it would be to stay here and explore the region. Were it not for thoughts of the still-too-close-for-his-blood town of Higgins and its zealots, he might well let that notion unspool awhile.

"Time enough for that later, Rig. Right now, we need to make camp. Maybe indulge a little and make a full pot of coffee and another feed, what say you?"

The horse, as usual, did not reply much. He snorted and eyed the sparse, brittle brown grasses not far away on the gentle slope.

"All right, man, I'll get you picketed out there, but let me unload the gear. Unless you prefer to lug it all night long? Hmm?"

It took Gage a while to unburden the horse and stack his gear where he could tend to it once he had fetched water and had kindled a blaze. Neither chore, it seemed, would be too onerous or difficult, given the proximity of trees, plenty dry and down, as well as water. He suspected that since the stream looked to be flowing all right, it would be safe to drink from.

It was always a risk and he had experienced the gastric turmoil that a poorly chosen water source could bring a man. But usually, his choices were good ones.

He picketed the horse, then fetched wood, dragging back the biggest lengths first. Much of it was well-dried pine, its bark long gone and its body like gray lined bone. He'd snap what he could, stomping with a well-aimed bootheel, then take his camp axe to the rest.

Once he'd laid in a supply he doubted he could burn through in a single night, he unpacked his canvas water bag, which traveled collapsed, as well as his canteen.

He lugged the water up to camp, and on his return trip, he carried his battered gray enamel coffeepot with him, and led Rig down to the stream, too, knowing he should have done so first, before he'd picketed the lad.

"Live and learn, eh, boy?" he said, filling the kettle upstream from the big horse, who had slurped for a spell and then stood looking about him.

The breeze from the northeast had abated, but still offered enough to ruffle Rig's mane and forelock. Gage saw gray and white hairs there, where he swore they had not been a week earlier. He squatted once more in the streamside sand and looked into the water.

It was too difficult to tell how much grayer and whiter he'd become, but perhaps it was just as well. He'd never liked looking at his own reflection, and knowing what he did about himself and what he'd done with his life, he wasn't so certain he needed to see the ragged, haunted look in those eyes staring back at him.

"Hey there!"

The voice spun Gage fast; he rose from his squat to a crouch, his left hand, out of instinct, snatching for the gun that hadn't ridden on that hip for years now. Instead, it closed around the handle of his big knife. He looked upslope through the sparse trees, while angling to his left and grabbing Rig's dragging reins. He walked behind the horse, transferring the reins to his right hand and once more resting his hand on his knife.

The man who'd called to him was visible now, wearing brown clothes a bit darker than sand, darker hat, beard . . .

"Hey! Mister!"

The stranger waved an arm in greeting. It didn't appear to Gage as if he held any weapons. The man was, however, close by Gage's camp and all his gear.

Gage took a route different going up than he had walking down. He carried his full coffeepot in his right hand, along with the reins, and kept his left on the knife handle, though he had not yet pulled it free. No need to show aggression. At least not yet.

As he emerged from the trees, he saw the man standing to the right side of the overhang, twenty feet or so from Gage's gear, but respectfully, with arms and hands visible, beside his own horse.

That set Gage's mind at ease. And then he recognized

him. It was Bewley, the old-timer from Higgins, who'd asked him about his new wool coat.

He didn't know the man at all, but somehow he'd trusted him, found him to be friendly, and to see him here, despite the fact that he liked to camp alone, the man's presence took some of the funky edge off the oddness of the day. As if good things could emerge from Higgins, too.

"Hello to you," said Gage, facing the man as he retied Rig. He walked upslope to stand before his gear.

"You been busy, I see," said the bearded old-timer.

Despite the fact that he looked to Gage to be a good twenty years older—or even more so—than him, he seemed tight and sprightly somehow.

"Was about to make myself some coffee," said Gage, hefting the pot. "You're welcome to join me."

"Hoo-boy, now you're talking. I'll help you with the wood, if'n you like. I can't stay long, got to get back to the trail, but imagine my surprise when I recognized the game trail down to this old site."

"You know it?" said Gage.

Bewley nodded. "I do. Been a whole lot of years since I camped here, though. One of the best spots I ever did find. Long before that silly little town was around. Hey, you see the art on the rocks yet?"

Gage shook his head. "No, not yet. But I wondered if there might be some."

"Sure is. I'll leave you to find it. Imagine the stories them old-time hunters could tell us, were they hereabouts now."

Gage liked the man even more on hearing that.

They worked to build the fire, then conversed while the coffee got to work in the pot.

"Well, I expect you're curious, so I'll tell you. I ain't here to bother you. Just scouting for the wagon train. You likely saw all them hopeful, shiny faces in that odd town, huh?"

"I did."

"Well, I was heading back out West myself anyway, a month and a half back, so I figured that since I know the terrain—for the most part anyway, though it has been a few years since I come through thisaway—I figured I might as well get paid to make the same trip."

"And how's the trip so far?"

The buckskin-clad man shrugged and ruffled his beard with his fingertips. "Oh"—he eyed the steaming coffeepot—"you know, good and bad. Thankfully, the good bits still stack up higher than the bad."

Gage nodded. "I hope that continues for you."

"Thanks. Say, you mind if I poke the fire a little, sort of hurry it along? I would downright welcome that coffee you offered, but I got to be getting back before nightfall."

"Sure, be my guest," said Gage.

"Ha! I guess I sort of am at that." Bewley smacked the thigh of his buckskins and a small cloud of dust rose. "Dusty country, even in the cold months. You'd think it would leave off choking a man, once he's good and cold. I tell you, for every pretty mountain range we got ourselves out here, there's a whole lot of ornery country that aims to do its level best to kill you every time you draw a breath."

He prodded the coals a bit, bent and blew on them, and stuffed in a few more twigs. The effect was slight but impressive, even to Gage, who had been tending his own campfires for years. It told him that no matter how long he had been at a task, no matter how much experience he had, say, in building fires, there was always someone out there who might be able to teach him a thing or three.

"Been at this awhile, eh?" said Gage.

"Huh?" The codger looked at him. "Oh, making smoke and cinders and ashes out of trees? Ya! You bet. Oh, I'd say I been at it a good half a century, at least. Been alive longer than that, but I didn't get serious about it for a spell. When I was a young man, I was too busy doing things young men do, if you take my meaning." He winked.

Gage nodded, wondering, as he had now and again, on how he had missed out on a youth shared in love with a woman. That thought led him right into thoughts of his grim past and he shook his head in an effort to bring himself back into the present moment he was spending with this interesting fellow named Bewley.

"Say, you all right?"

Gage looked at the man, his beard fluffed and his kindly eyes, which were surrounded with crow's feet, gazing at him as if he knew Gage's travails and sympathized.

"Sure, I'm fine. Been a long day."

"I hear that," said the man, snatching up Gage's hand-size leather scrap he used to haul his skillet and coffeepot off the hot fire. He held the pot up and nodded at Gage, who held out his battered tin cup. The man poured hot steaming coffee into it, then did the same into his own such cup.

"If coffee cups could talk, eh?" said Gage, gingerly testing the scalding brew.

"Oh, if that was the case, I'm not so sure I would want mine to tell all my campsite secrets."

They sat in amiable silence for a few moments, enjoying the brew. Finally Gage said, "So you're scouting for the wagon train. Is it a big one?"

"Oh, big enough. Near three dozen wagons, plus a few other conveyances, not to mention a sizable herd of cattle, a remuda, also passably sized, and other bits and bobs—chickens and pigs and such. One fellow even brought a cage full of baby turkeys! Can you imagine? No wonder the coyotes skulk around at night, nibbling the edges of the firelight."

"You're a poet," said Gage.

If he expected the man to chuckle and shake his head, he was mistaken.

Bewley looked up at him. "You like poetry, do you?"

"No less or more than any other man, I'm afraid," said Gage. "Why, do you?"

"Why, sure I do! Ain't nothing better I like than to rummage in the words of Tennyson or Chaucer. You ever read *The Canterbury Tales* or 'The Charge of the Light Brigade'?"

Gage sipped. "I've heard of each, but I can't say I have read them, no."

"Oh, son, you are missing out. You could do worse than to find yourself a book or two of poetry. No better companion, or nearly so"—he winked—"on a cold night than a fine pipe full of tobacco and a book of poetry."

Gage nodded. "You know, I might just do that. The pipe, I have. Something I break out now and again, most often in cooler weather. The poetry, no, not yet, that is. Next town I come to, I'll see what I can scare up."

"You do that, son, and I guarantee you won't ever regret the purchase." Bewley stood up, his knees popping audibly, though he neither winced nor showed sign of stiffness. "Now I have to get back to the train. This was a little detour for selfish reasons. But it's over and I have commitments. I am glad to have met you, Gage."

Gage had risen, too, and offered his hand. "It was a pleasure to meet you as well, Bewley. Maybe our paths will cross again one of these fine days."

"Could be, could be. But they have once, and with coffee, no less! And that's as good as a meal." He smiled. "Now, I reckon, I'll unpack that dandy new wool coat you talked me into buying back in Higgins and be on my way."

He walked over to his horse and stuffed his cup back into his saddlebag, then unlashed a green-and-black-and-white–patterned coat with a tall collar.

Gage remembered seeing that one. He'd liked the pattern, but had been afraid the white wool might take on soot and dirt quickly. But seeing this wiry fellow wearing it, he was glad he'd passed on it. It looked just right on the man.

"Handsome togs, Bewley. It looks like it will serve you well."

"It ought to, cost me the price of a couple of books. But a man can only travel with so many of them in his saddlebags anyway. My mule, back with the train, she's showing signs of revolt. Every time I walk on over to her carrying new books, she sidesteps and brays as if I'm about to cut open her throat with a dull spoon! The antics, I swear." He shook his head and mounted up.

"Until we meet again, then," said Bewley from atop his horse.

He saluted Gage, who replied in kind. "And may it not be in Higgins!"

The older man chuckled, turned the horse, and they picked their way back up the slight switchbacks toward the trail top.

Gage walked back to his site, and stared at it for a few moments, hands on his hips. It was not a little depressing, now that the lively fellow had gone his way, to see that he was once more alone. He'd enjoyed the company and the conversation, and, under other circumstances, he would have enjoyed an entire evening of banter with the man.

But he chose this life, and that was all there was to it. Gage sighed and laid more wood on the fire, then set about sorting his new purchases.

First he stretched out a six-foot-square canvas tarpaulin he carried for all manner of reasons. It made a decent little tent, or a ground cloth, or something to huddle beneath in the wind, rain, or snowstorm, either while riding or in camp.

It also made a clean, smooth surface to lay out his gear and repack, something he did with regularity. Gage kept a list in his mind of everything he owned and often was able to winnow it down by an item or two.

He discarded worn-out goods, usually socks that had been mended beyond all good sense, and even then he tried to devise new ways he might use them. Once laundered, they made all right hand warmers, albeit with holes.

He'd been taught to knit and darn by an old-timer at a ranch over in New Mexico way some years back, and since then, he'd saved his choicest worn wool socks, picking apart the weave and winding them back into a ball.

The saved yarn made all right materials for repairs, and sometimes for new socks and mittens. But his skills were such that when he was able to find decent, well-made socks and mittens, and if he needed them at the time, or knew he soon would, he gladly made the purchase.

Gage kept his clothing collection in check as well, owning two shirts, two trousers, one set of long-handles, and two full undershirts. He also carried a double-thick stocking cap of knitted wool for use in low temperatures.

It had saved his ears more than once, from frostbite when working out on open ranch land. It wasn't the temperature as much as the wind shoving all that cold at a man that would lace him with those telltale gray patches on his face, neck, and anywhere he had skin exposed.

That was another lesson an old-timer had taught him. The man's name was Rollie and he had wrangled cattle from Mexico clear on up to Canada's vast plains. And he knew the value of staying warm in winter weather.

"Don't be a fool and think you can outwit Mother Nature, boy! Tug on a hat, wrap a muffler about your face, wear elk-hide mittens, fur in, and double up on your socks. And for pity's sake, don't get wet. Got it? Good! Now get back to work!"

Gage smiled at the memory of the surly old fellow ambling in three layers of clothes up and down the center aisle of the bunkhouse, shouting at the younger men. They all listened to him, but mocked him behind his back. Gage respected Rollie and vowed to keep the man's advice in use. And he had, and it had proven invaluable.

Next he sorted his foodstuffs, beginning with what remained of the older goods in the bottom of his pannier. "Not much," he muttered, feeling with a thumb and forefinger the last scraps of cornmeal in a light cotton sack.

His coffee bean supply had dwindled down to dust and aromas the day before he'd reached the town of Higgins. Coffee was an indulgence he was willing to spend a little extra money on.

After all, he thought, what else did he spend money

on in life? He lived like a traveling monk, replacing only necessities when he had to. Surely, enjoying the occasional pipe of tobacco or cup of coffee was all right.

He had long since given up on thinking that he should live as bare bones a life as possible in order to somehow do penance for the murders of his past. Living a thin life would not bring back those he killed. Nothing would.

Perhaps his penance was the nightly hauntings, awake and asleep, and the regular replaying in his mind throughout his days of the deaths he had caused. Over and over again, as if time had slowed, he saw the bullets travel from his gun straight into the flesh and blood and bone of others.

Gage poured himself another cup of coffee and sighed and repacked his bags, preparing for an easy and quick departure from the campsite, something he always did, just in case a fire or a flood or an attack by trail bandits forced him to get up and go with all haste.

He fried up a couple of strips of lean bacon, made four simple biscuits, and cooked it all in his small skillet. While he ate, he did his best to not dwell on anything other than the pretty view from his fine little campsite.

Rig required moving twice, as he had cropped even the brown brittle grasses down to paltry nubs.

Soon darkness moved in. Gage brough the horse closer, built up the fire, laid out his blankets for sleep, visited a thicket of rabbit brush to relieve himself, then called it a day. He would see what the new day might bring. And, he thought, perhaps he could finally get far enough from Higgins that he might forget about it for a spell.

He had plenty to think about, as it was, nurturing the notion of spending the cold months in high country, perhaps establishing a trapline. Time would tell.

CHAPTER 4

In the morning, Gage, with much reluctance, departed from the campsite. It had been, in so many respects and for so many reasons, one of the best two or three sites he'd had the privilege of staying in, in all the years of his roving.

He paused at the cut of the first switchback and gazed downward, wondering if he'd ever return to the site. He also mused on the fact that he felt wistful about it at all.

Still, he thought as he and Rig picked their way back up to the roadway above, it had been an instructive spot. There had indeed been paintings on the vast angled rock that served as a ceiling of sorts for the night.

He'd seen the tracings of hands large and small, with the smaller, curiously, at the same height, roughly six feet up on the smooth stone, as the larger. He thought on this and came to the conclusion that whoever the warrior was who had made the adult-size handprints, he must have then hoisted a child up high to also contribute to what seemed, to Gage's untrained eye, as a story scene.

There were other depictions—beasts that looked like deer, but with much larger racks than any he'd seen roving the wild. And there were renderings of what looked to be campfires, birds, and one curious creature that looked manlike, but stood taller and wider than the other obvious depictions of warriors. This one also looked to be covered all over with hair.

Perhaps it was a bit of humor, wondered Gage. Or perhaps it was a rendering of some beast little known and, he hoped, long since passed from this world. He had enough trouble spending much time with most of his fellow humans, let alone running up against a freakish creature such as that.

Having once again gained the trail he'd departed the day before, Gage guided Rig westward along it, relieved to once more have Higgins receding behind him. Although he could not see the town from where he was, it felt good, nonetheless, to be shed of humanity for a while. For how long, he knew not. But for the time being, it felt right.

Ahead, the trail rose, slightly southwestward, leading him along a ridgeline and into higher country, two of his favored terrains. It's one of the few times he was able, even for a brief spell, to forget the mess he'd made of what he told himself was his former life as a gunman, to dispel, however briefly, the wince-inducing memories of the lives of his victims and their families.

They rode on like this, enjoying the blue-sky day. He

stopped once for a couple of minutes, to take off his new wool coat, needed when he awoke because it had been nippy. But now, the sun was warming the land and, in turn, the air rising from it.

The land to his left, southward, opened up. Far below, he spied a rolling expanse of lush land, what looked to be a wide river bottom stretch, the green not yet given over fully to the dry and brittle ways of autumn, with its palette of tans and browns, the moisture having gone from the grasses for the season, pulling back into the earth below.

Cutting through this river bottom stretch, close to its northern edge, he saw the telltale twin tracks of a roadway frequented by wagons. And although it was quite far below and away from him, to his south, Gage could swear he saw movement along it, but not of wagons. They were smaller, and singular in their progress. Riders, had to be.

Ahead of them, to the west end of the lush patch, Gage saw a double-shouldered pass flanking a narrow declivity, or so it seemed from his vantage point high above. That pass, to where the roadway led, must be where the distant riders were headed.

He reasoned it could well be the very pass Millie had mentioned. And if so, beyond it sat the Brethren's own Chosen Valley.

The roadway leading to the pass roughly paralleled his own direction, and for a moment, Gage's guts tightened as his thoughts turned to the inevitable—would the two roadways, his and the one far below and southward, meet up?

"Foolishness," he muttered, chiding himself. Of course, they would not. For ahead, he saw that his own track began to angle northward, deeper, and higher into the mountains. That trail to his south was likely a wagon train trail, making for a practical and easier route through the massive Chisley Range looming ahead.

Due to the ragged array of jutting landscape and sprawling reach of trees along its edge far below, Gage saw there was more, much more, of the lush stretch he hadn't seen, between the few stray riders and the narrowing that he assumed was that pass into and through the mountains.

And in that newly revealed section, Gage saw wagons, and what looked to be cattle and other beasts, small dots, light and dark, from this distance, and they were all making for that pass.

Indeed, it looked as if when they all reached it, they would clog the entrance. Of course, they would not let that happen.

Part of him was envious of the thrills they were encountering along their journey. He knew they were in a hurry to escape this side of the mountains and make it farther west, toward warmer climes before the snows trapped them in these foothills.

And he bet they would make it, because they needed to. With men such as the rangy, old, bearded, buckskin-clad Bewley helping to scout, he felt certain they were going to make it through in fine shape.

"Godspeed, you travelers," he said.

Rig snorted.

And then Gage began to hear odd, far-off clicking sounds. *No,* he thought, *it's not clicking. Snapping, popping sounds.* He halted the horse and squinted at the field once more and noted that the wagons at the front were beginning to slow.

Gage also noticed that there were riders emerging from out of the mouth of the pass. And small puffs of smoke rose up all over the scene, mostly from the pass and the dark dots. He looked back, eastward, and saw that the riders he'd seen earlier were many now and sending up smoke as well. And he knew just what the smoke clouds were—the exhalations of gunfire.

And so the odd popping noises were also explained. He groaned and slid from his saddle, then rummaged in a saddlebag and pulled out an eight-inch leather tube and unbuckled the end. Out slid his battered brass telescope. He'd found it, already well used, in a shop in Fanta, New Mexico, a few years earlier. He thought it might come in useful in spotting game, and he'd been correct.

Now, though, he was using it to spot men. And those he saw chilled his guts. Yes, it was an attack, and the wagon train was the victim. And the attackers were all men, and all were clad in black, save for their white shirts.

All of them wore beards of varied colors—from short and black, brown, and ginger, to long and streaked with gray, to flowing and nearly white, and all cut straight across at the bottoms. Each of what looked to be dozens of bearded, black-clad men rode as if chased by wolves.

But their mission was not to escape from an enemy, saw Gage, but rather they were riding hard at a perceived enemy. At least that was Gage's guess, because the other things the black riders each had in common were the many guns they wielded.

He saw them much closer now, their rifles and revolvers and shotguns barking and snapping and blasting away. Their horses, most of them black and brown, ran white-eyed and foaming, terrorized by ferocious howls of rage shouted by their riders and by the frightening, thunderous sounds of the guns just behind their heads.

"Oh no," he whispered. "Oh no, no, no, no, no . . ."

He shifted the scope to his left and saw the wagons up close for the first time. He could not be certain, but one of the men in the lead sure looked like his pleasant visitor from the evening before. The scout was delivering rifle shots toward the black riders and looked also to be barking directives over his left shoulder toward other wagon train men, all wheeling on their horses and looking confused.

Since they were too far to clog through the pass, the wagons cut southwestward toward a jut of trees, which looked to Gage to perhaps be the downslope of a cut in the land that rose up behind the trees. He bet they were going to secure themselves against that and use it to fight from. That's what he'd do.

He scoped farther left and saw more wagons cutting in that direction, word no doubt having reached the drivers, along with the gunfire from fore and aft the train.

Gage looked eastward behind them and saw riders, not dressed in black, hurrying a mass of bawling, stiff-legged cattle—red and white, some horned and some not, and none of them used to running great distances. These riders were doomed if they kept themselves behind that slow mass of beasts.

"Leave them!" growled Gage. "Save yourselves—those zealots won't kill the cows, they'll just steal them!"

He knew, of course, that his snapped words were a waste of breath. There was no way anyone twenty feet from him could have heard them, let alone however far below the frenzied men were.

And then he saw one of them, a fellow in a tan work coat and brown cap, suddenly whip his arms skyward. His handgun pinwheeled out of his grasp, and though his horse kept moving forward, the man himself slammed backward, his back, high up between the shoulders, bounced once off the horse's rump, and he slopped to the brown-and-green–speckled earth.

"Oh no."

Gage looked behind the man and saw that the black riders, many more of them than he'd suspected earlier—dozens, perhaps—were gaining on the herd and on the men, who still doggedly tended the bawling, wild-eyed cattle.

Gage saw enough to know this was not going to end the way he hoped. He let loose a long pent-up breath, and as it leaked out of him, he lowered the spyglass and collapsed it. He looked at the dented brass thing in his lap and groaned as he slid it back into its sheath.

"Oh, Rig," he said, securing the saddlebag, and then checking his game rifle. He hoisted it from its scabbard and had to rummage for his bullets—it had been so long since he'd used the thing. More than two weeks since he'd had to kill to eat. He hated to, though it was vital to maintaining his body, his very life. But he'd had his fill of such things.

And yet . . . "Here we go, chum, back into the midst of madness, I expect." As he said this, he turned the horse on the ridgeline trail and searched for a route down. They walked back a few yards the way they'd come, keeping his eyes down to his right, at the long, sloping shoulder of land that led to the valley floor below.

He seemed to recall seeing a game trail branching off this main trail. The distance to the valley was great, but although steep at times, he knew, too, that such distances might prove deceitful, and hopefully easier to traverse.

But that all depended on the ability the game had of navigating the sloped landscape. "Switchbacks," said Gage, easing Rig down onto the trail. "We're looking for switchbacks, chum. They are a sure sign that if a deer made it down, there might, just might, be a chance for us to do the same."

Of course, thought Gage, he had no idea if the beasts that had used the trail ever actually made it all the way down or if they found it impossible and turned back, making for the top once more.

He spied a long stretch of the trail below that became hidden from sight beneath a branching veil of rabbit brush and stunty ridge pine. He wasn't certain just what sort of tree they were, something piney, but it didn't matter, for he suspected he had to dismount and scout the terrain ahead.

There was no way on this stretch of trail for Gage to see more than a dozen feet ahead, and sometimes not even that far.

"Rig, if I didn't know in the deepest rattly part of my bones that the folks in that wagon train were being attacked by the black-wearing brutes in that Church, I'd never try this, my friend." He let the thought hang there, because he decided he had to slide on down out of the saddle and inspect the coming trail on foot.

He lashed the reins to a sizable gnarled tree, a juniper, he thought. "Stay put. I'll be right back—with any luck."

Gage probed ahead a few feet with cautious steps, then returned to the horse and slid his rifle out of the scabbard. He didn't want to tote it, but he had no idea of what he faced up ahead. Or rather, he thought with a grim smile, down ahead.

He returned to inching along the trail, parting the brush and overhanging branches, at times up to his chest, with care. In this manner, he managed to keep both a sharp eye on the distant down trail, as well as probing forward, foot by foot.

After several minutes, the shrubbery thinned and relinquished its grip on his legs. He was also able to see that the trail broadened and did indeed lead to a switchback to his left.

From there, the trail bent downslope and to the right, westward, and although he could not be certain, he thought he saw, some hundreds of yards away, that it ended, only to appear once more, angling eastward and farther downslope.

Seeing this gave him the confidence to risk the route with Rig. He turned and began making his way back to the horse, not but a few minutes' walk back upslope. The steepest part of the trail that he could make out was at the start. While he searched and then made his way back to Rig, he heard the slow, random popping and snapping sounds from far below.

All told, he mused as he drew closer to Rig, he'd only spent less than ten minutes at this venture so far, but it had been well worth it if the trail would get him down there quicker. To what, though? he asked himself as he slid the rifle back in its sheath.

There were ample armed men on the wagon train, had to be. Even if the attackers had played on the element of surprise, he doubted there were enough of the black-clothed brutes to take the upper hand. The wagon train folks could circle, or at least crescent their wagons, keep the women and children and old folks and animals tucked from harm within, and close with their backs to that far slope he'd seen them making for, off to the southwest, across that patch of valley bottom land.

What was the plan of the Church members? Why not let the wagon train pass, unmolested?

He gathered the reins and led Rig along, planning to guide him through the clawing, raking low branches. If he were ahead, the horse might tolerate the annoying closeness of that stretch of trail.

He walked the horse slowly along the decline, speaking in a calm voice to him. "By the time we get down there, Rig, it may well be time for all those fools to take a noonday break for tea, hmm?"

The horse snorted and shied, jerking his head back, but Gage growled, "Hey now!" and jerked the reins once to let Rig know he was going nowhere but where Gage told him to.

Of course, Gage thought, if the big brown gelding decided to bolt, there would be little Gage could do about it. But where would he go? Thunder off the side slope, either east or west? Spin and scrabble his way back to the top? Or shove Gage aside and mince on down the trail, just where they were headed anyway?

He tugged the horse ahead, and each time he heard a *pop* or *snap* from far below, he winced inside. They were still at it down there, trading shots; one party defending, the other attacking.

Another ten minutes, he reckoned, and they'd be well below timberline. He doubted anyone had seen him from that far away, especially given that their concentration would be on their jobs at hand; but just the same, he'd be pleased to have descended into thicker tree cover, instead of the whippy, shrubby growth they were slowly emerging from.

He also reasoned that once they were down into the

trees, it would still be another half hour before they made it to the valley floor. He didn't know what he'd find at that point.

"Once we get shed of these steep, tight switchbacks, we'll move faster, okay, Rig?"

If Gage expected a response from the big horse, he was destined for disappointment.

Perhaps, thought Gage, it was all the same to Rig. Being shot at, shooting, climbing down the mountainside or climbing up, it seemed to matter little to the horse. And he was thankful for it. The last thing he needed to put up with was a horse balking at everything and then deciding to run.

He said no more, but kept up with a steady tugging on the reins. The big horse had resigned himself to the task of following Gage, and they made it down into the trees, the last stretch beforehand, however, was a rough one.

Ahead, the trail, which he was traveling from west to east, cutting slowly downward, had narrowed due to a landslide roughly a dozen feet across, then another perhaps six to eight feet across.

The right side, which was also the downhill side, had sloughed away in places, forcing them to dig harder into the uphill side of the trail. He noted that other beasts, for he saw no horse or man prints, had done the same, cutting into the thin layer of topsoil, the edges of which were ragged and the roots of the scant cover already brittle and dead in the unforgiving sun of the place.

"Nothing for it, Rig," Gage murmured as he chose a cautious foothold.

He was not concerned for himself, but for the horse, who had four hooves and a whole lot more girth to manage on such a dicey run.

Ahead he saw where the trail resumed its wider, more promising shape. But not yet. This treacherous stretch was a reminder that he might expect anything ahead, as they were but two-thirds of the way down the slope, at best.

He still marveled at how much steady gunfire he was hearing, from the popping and snapping to brasher blasts that told him someone, likely threatened emigrants, were using shotguns. And that told him that if someone was using a shotgun, it was likely for close-in fighting.

He tugged harder on the reins, increasing their pace as much as he dared, given the sliding, tender slope. The last thing he needed was another landslide while he was in the midst of walking it.

As they strode hard forward, the sounds from the fight below, not visible to them now, grew slowly but steadily louder. And with the increase, Gage's concern rose. But it didn't make the final click in his mind until he heard the shouts of men's voices. And then a scream. And he would have sworn it was the scream of a woman.

"Oh no! No, no, no . . ." Gage spied another turn in the trail ahead, westward, a sharp one that would lead him, he felt sure, to yet another and another. He bolted for it, not yet daring to mount up on Rig, for fear of encountering some new flaw in the terrain that they might be unprepared for. A fresh landslide that had collapsed the trail was his primary concern.

But soon enough, once they rounded that sharp turn and barreled downward and eastward all at once, the landscape below him, to his right, showed signs of promise. It sloped gentler; and though they were still some distance above the valley floor, he saw that it was now reachable by their own trail—even if it was a haphazard game trail made for nimble mule deer and elk, more so than a man and a horse.

He realized he had, once again, decided on a course of action based solely on emotion than on thought. But the sounds drove him onward: the woman's scream and the increasing shouts of men, of horses neighing; the clatter of weapons smacking other weapons; the bellows of agitated cattle; the babble, albeit far off, of youngsters, perhaps.

All these noises reached him, and he knew he must do something, no matter the consequences to himself.

Hadn't he, after all, agreed to forfeit his life in the pursuit of just causes those long years ago, following the killing of the pretty young woman in the street?

When, after wandering with no guns and sober, but blinded with grief and emotional wreckage, he had roused from that period of madness, he had found he bore a new, and strange to him, way of existing.

It was one that came with plain but obvious structures: He would never deny who he was if someone accused him of being Texas Lightning, the gunfighter, also known as Jonathan Gage.

He would not own a six-gun. For a long time after that, he did not own any gun at all. But he found, in order to live the roving life of a trail hound, he needed to make meat now and again. And so he had acquired the old but serviceable rifle solely for that purpose.

Most important of all his new discoveries about himself—he would only interfere in the lives of others if he thought he might be able to help them in some way. And he would only take the life of another man if that other man was causing grievous harm to innocent folks.

This, to his dismay, had happened to him more than he would have, could have, expected. But of the many scrapes and grim situations he'd found himself in since then, he regretted none.

For he believed he had brought some level of relief, perhaps comfort, to downtrodden folks, among them widows, farmers, small ranchers, a blacksmith, a woman on a train, and on and on.

He took little satisfaction in this, but he considered it a sliver of the penance he knew he must undergo before he would one day be laid low by a bullet delivered into him by someone avenging the death of a loved one. And he would deserve that bullet, and there would be an end to it.

That it had not yet happened mystified him, but neither did it make him reckless. For, despite his shame and grief at what he was and what he had done to others, he found that he did not want to die. At least not while there were still people to whom he might be of some small, simple use.

CHAPTER 5

As Gage neared the trees, he slowed Rig and peered through the tree line into the open, rolling swath of land beyond. Up close, he saw that it was not as he had seen from high above on the ridgeline. It curved and rolled such that he could not see more than fifty feet into the field, for that's still what it looked like to him.

He paused a moment, cocking an ear, and looked east, then west. He heard nothing from the east, Higgins way, and then he heard the *crack* and the *pow* of gunfire to his right, westward.

He muttered to Rig, "Here goes," and gently heeled the horse out into more open terrain, emerging from the trees into the shade thrown by those same trees.

He glanced right first, as that's where the sounds of guns had come from last. He cast a quick look to his left, then urged Rig up the slope ahead, angling slightly westward.

They topped the slight rise and he was able to see most of what he assumed there was to see, most of what had attracted him to make the long journey down here. And it was not pretty.

Between him and the far southwestern corner of the field, which he could only partially see due to the undulations of the landscape, he spied at least four large, downed beasts, whether horses or cattle, he could not tell. He cut south, cresting the next slight rise. He knew he would be seen there, but he had to get a sense of what was happening.

Now he took it all in, noting that there were dozens of riders in black, from hats to coats to trousers, riding an array of horses. Most of the men bore long guns or revolvers held high, and they cut left and right, spreading out in a wide curve. It appeared as if they were loosely holding their line for the time being, but that at any moment, they might resume their advancement.

Beyond them, Gage saw clearly, though they were all still a good quarter mile away, the wagons, save one, clustered as if huddling hard against the rocky slope of the southwest edge of the open land.

He also saw, far to his right, that the spot he assumed was a pass, which he could barely see from on high, was indeed a pass that looked to cut through the sloping shoulders of the foothills directly westward.

There were more men in black arrayed in and out of the pass, most on horseback, or so it seemed from that distance. Closer in toward him, southwestward, making toward the wagons, sat a wagon that had apparently been cut off from the rest. Surrounding it were milling riders in black.

It was a small Conestoga-type wagon and it sat as if parked. The team looked to be a four-horse setup, and were angled enough that Gage could see the long sides of the horses to the right of the wagon they pulled.

At that moment, he heard shouts from one of the men in black, a swarthy, blocky-shaped fellow, also to the right of the wagon. Then that bulky man raised his right arm, pointed; then smoke, and a *crack, crack, crack,* three shots, came from that pointing arm.

He'd delivered bullets to someone at the front of the wagon. Gage assumed it was someone in the driver's seat.

Then between and beyond several black riders ahead, Gage saw a white-shirted fellow with braces and a fawn hat running away from the wagon to the left side. He made it from the wagon a good fifty, seventy-five feet; then his arms whipped upward just as Gage heard another *crack,* and the running man flailed and jerked, ceasing to run. Another *crack* whipped him upright stiffer; then he fell backward.

"Oh no!" growled Gage. He was too far away for anyone to hear him, and, he noticed, a moderate but persistent breeze swept the little valley from west to east, bringing the sounds he didn't want to hear—gunfire and shouts and screams—with clarity, while sending his own few noises away downwind.

Gage didn't quite know what to do, but he knew he had to do something. Anything that might help save someone, he reasoned, was better than standing here feeling shocked.

As bad as he felt about what was happening, he knew that if he rushed on in there, he would accomplish nothing, save getting himself killed. "Time enough for that," he muttered, and retreated, keeping an eye westward to ensure nobody saw him.

Soon he was hidden once more by the rolling terrain of the field, a span he now noticed was likely tended for rough haymaking. It was a large, open space, and one he suspected was flooded in the springtime by the river that flowed roughly east to west at the far edge, south of where he and Rig stood.

He was inclined to give the black-clothed brutes very little in the way of consideration, and even less now, considering the blatant murder he'd just witnessed, but it was obvious they were workers, given the size of the tended field.

In the time it took for him to make it back to the tree line, he heard five more shots, two screams, both sounding as if they came from men, and then the jarring sound of cheers. As if the fiends were pleased with their efforts.

Gage cut Rig well back into the trees, perhaps thirty feet in, and made westward. There was no other option, other than riding back to Higgins for help, which he doubted he would be able to rouse, considering what Millie told him and what he experienced on his own. The Brethren all but owned the town, and thus the residents—even those that Deacon fellow had yet to seduce or coerce into becoming followers.

No, his best chance in helping the folks in the wagon

train lay in somehow cutting wide around the Brethren and reaching the train. It would take some time, but that was all he had, whereas the folks being bombarded did not even have that luxury. They were confused and in a strange place and not wholly aware of what it was they had done to provoke such ire.

What can I do? thought Gage as he rode. *Other than travel toward them as fast as the sparse tree cover will allow.* He had to hope he didn't come upon any Church folks patrolling this edge of what apparently was their river bottom domain.

Gage heeled Rig harder and bent low, keeping a tight but reluctant grip on the rifle laid across his thighs.

CHAPTER 6

As Gage hustled Rig through the trees westward as fast as he was able, given the fact that no trail existed there, he kept an eye to his left at the snatches of sward visible through the sparse tangle of tree growth, stunty shrubs, and bracken.

The base of the foothill to the west that formed the northern flank of the pass, which the emigrants had been making for, loomed ahead of Gage. He rode as hard as he could, but only until he drew as close as he dared—about one hundred yards—and then he halted quickly and slid down from the saddle. He hadn't yet seen any black-garbed men about, but that didn't mean they weren't salted in among the trees to keep watch on the perimeter.

He walked on, reins in one hand and his rifle cradled across his midsection, ready to drop rein and swing. He made it to within twenty or so yards of the pass, which, as he suspected, was wider than it had looked from above; he halted then.

He smelled something . . . smoke, campfire smoke,

coffee, maybe bacon frying. He sniffed, arching his head back a bit. No, the breeze wasn't coming from the southwest, so he doubted it was from a fire made by the likely still-petrified and confused travelers.

It was coming from ahead, by the mouth of the pass. He saw no one, but the smells, faint as they were, were there. And that's where the breeze had been coming from for some time—west to east, roughly.

The coffee tickled his nostrils and suddenly made him want a cup. He tamped down thoughts of the tasty brew and concentrated on the task at hand. There, ahead, he could just make out a fold in the landscape, a smaller rise before the north-side shoulder of the pass opening. And yes, now and again, he saw what might well be smoke rising up.

Had to be a camp base of sorts for the zealots. Somebody was tending camp, while the rest of them attacked and savaged the wagon train. A campsite had to require planning. More and more, he began to think these weren't the actions born of quick-triggered rage. These zealots, these Brethren, planned this. Had to have. It was too bold and too well orchestrated.

Gage slowed his pace and moved more silently forward. He had to somehow get up and past the mouth of the pass so that he might melt back into the tree line along the west edge of the field. From there, he could make it to the emigrants' campsite.

He paused. Was that the best course of action? Could he do more good staying outside the fray, doling out some semblance of balance from the periphery? He did not want to shoot men at all, and certainly not by sniping at them. But they were terrorizing and killing seemingly innocent folks.

Rig walked behind Gage, content or at least resigned to put up with being led through a mire of raking branches. Then the big horse stepped on a sizable dropped branch. The brittle, hard snap of the wood sounded to Gage as if someone pinched the trigger of a rifle from afar. It was loud enough that Gage jerked to a halt and looked about him.

Yes, indeed, there were human voices ahead and they rose and fell as if in regular conversation. It sounded to him like a conversation between two or perhaps three men, one louder than the others.

Undecided as to what his course of action should be, Gage held still, his right ear cocked toward the voices. Although the wind played in his favor, he could not make out individual words yet. He trudged on, walking with more care, and hoping Rig didn't step on any more branches. He made it another dozen feet before *crack,* another branch snapped under one of the horse's hooves.

He held still once more, and held his breath, too, half expecting a black-clad brute to come crashing through the trees and confront him. But as he listened once more, he detected no lull in the chatter ahead. But he knew he had to make another decision, so he turned Rig, and shaking his head at his foolishness, he made to head back the way they came, eastward.

From the far end, he would cut southward, then westward once more, along the far side of the valley floor.

From here, it looked as if there would be ample tree cover to shroud him from roving eyes.

The journey would take a fair bit longer, but he suspected it would be a whole lot safer than risking prancing right on through the Brethren camp.

Just then, he heard hooves drumming and horses snorting from the pass. He halted once more and held, listening. More voices. This time, they were raised, but not in argument, or at least he didn't think so. He felt certain he needed to hear what they were saying, so he lashed Rig's reins around a tree trunk, tied them off for safety, and, with his rifle, ventured closer.

Gage peered through the trees, hunkering out of instinct. There were about a dozen black-clothed riders ahead, to his right. It looked as if they'd come from the pass, and then he saw others coming from the south, from where the wagons were holed up.

Gage low-walked closer, until he figured he didn't dare risk either making a sound that might give him away or by being seen. Still in the tree line, and thus in shadow, was a slight advantage, but not one he could rely on for long.

Then he heard a voice from one of the men who'd ridden up from the scuffle. He recognized it as the man from the street, the blunt-shaped, gruff, squinting, sneering Deacon. And judging by the direction from which he rode, Gage suspected he was also the man who'd shot the poor fool who had tried to flee from the wagon down in the field.

"Gentlemen, good of you to come! I know the day is

a busy one, what with winter preparations and all, but it is of the utmost importance that these interloping heathens be made an example of!"

A round of barked voices affirmed they were all in agreement with him.

The plug of a man continued: "This will show the world that the Brethren will no longer tolerate uninvited travelers through our lands!"

Again the thick voices of men braying in agreement came to Gage and turned his guts to stone. He had a feeling the man wasn't through yet. And he was right.

"We have grown weary of these heathens traversing our lands!" The plug of a man smacked one hamlike fist into the palm of the other as the gaggle of black-clothed men bellowed their agreement.

"And so we say *no more*! No more! We have shown these heathens our true intentions and we shall not stop until they are fully dealt with!"

Again the assemblage, all his peers and all in obvious agreement with him, nodded their heads. It was a small sea of dozens of flat-brim black hats, wagging in unison, with revolvers and rifles raised.

It was obvious by now to Gage that had these zealots wanted the wagon train out of their lands, they would have, could have, done little more than lob insults at them and stampede them on their way as quickly as possible.

But no, it came to Gage what their real motivation was. It was not merely that these zealots wanted the travelers gone from their land, they wanted them to pay a toll. The highest toll imaginable. And they intended to justify this by telling each other they were doing the bidding of whatever deity the Brethren bowed to—which, at present, seemed to be Deacon.

As he listened, Gage learned that these religious fiends had grown weary of travelers, a seemingly never-ending river of them. They did not want them rolling through their established lands and lives, inadvertently trampling their hard work beneath the grinding wheels and stamping hooves of their wagons and beasts. They would not tolerate the shooting of game that the zealots regarded as their own.

The Brethren represented the worst of humanity to Gage, for they had determined that they alone were worthy of procuring and maintaining whatever they would—and they would maintain their grasp on it at any cost.

All this was bad enough to hear, but the blatant hypocrisy espoused by Deacon as he continued his red-faced tirade told Gage more than he needed to know. If anyone listening had maintained any doubt about it, Deacon's fever-pitch proclamations left none.

"There will be no quarter given by the Brethren!" He flung an arm behind him toward the distant flanks of the canvas-topped wagons still high-tailing it to the base of a cliff in the far southeast corner of the field. "These people . . . these heathens making their way westward . . . carry with them everything they need from their old lives. And I can tell you for a fact that most of them have no intention of moving back East ever again! These heathens sold up all their goods and turned into cash money whatever they did not, or could not, carry with them, nor readily buy or make once they reach their westward destinations!"

This declaration of the obvious—for had they not all done the same not long ago in search of a brighter life on the frontier?

His rant brought a ragged cheer from Deacon's audience, but it sounded to Gage as if his people were confused. If Deacon detected this, it did not slow him.

"There is a whole lot of cash money passing by us! It is being carted away by the very heathens carving a road through the Chosen Valley, and thus through the lives of the Brethren! I hope I need not mention the animals and wagons as well! Consider all the horseflesh suited for hard work and for hunting and riding; all the cattle, the chickens, and the goats; the wagons; the household goods that their own helpmates, the women in their lives—mothers, daughters, wives—all wished they might have in their own humble cabins.

"Then there are the clothes, the tools, the harnesses, the foodstuffs, and the spices. Why, there is enough to keep each and every Brethren family in comfort for years! And it is all rolling on through our lands, trampling our efforts in the process."

Deacon let this ragged rage echo for but a moment, the faces of his people beginning to shine anew with possibility. He had them.

"And you just know, being the foul heathens that they are, that none of what they possess was gained through hard work and honesty! Such virtues are unknown to the heathen. Nay, they must be stripped clean of these ill-gotten gains. And it is the Brethren who must perform this task, on behalf of the Maker!"

The swarthy man did not let up. "My fellow Brethren, what we have here is the opportunity to honor the Maker! And how do we do this? By accepting this gift from the Maker! If, that is, we are not too dull, not too inept, not too swayed by the wicked spell of the heathens, to grasp it!"

CHAPTER 7

Gage felt as if he just awakened from a three-day drunken spree, with the sour gut and pounding skull to match. What he'd heard was madness, and they weren't done, not by a long shot. He knew he had to keep listening, but it made him angrier than anything had in a long ol' while.

They were laughing now, talking of the bonus of it all. From stray words, Gage understood that the Brethren were now looking on the travelers as an evil to be eradicated. They were deducing these were no poor farmers to have such large, slow-moving wagons, likely filled with fine home goods, and trailing such fine stock and herds. And such fine horse and mule and ox teams . . .

Gage gritted his teeth so hard they were about to powder, but he kept still, kept silent. He was not certain he could take much more, but something told him it would all be worth it. Soon he knew he had to make it either to the law or to the wagons to help them, somehow, to break free of this madness.

"And then there are the children, my friends!" It was

Deacon again. "And boys grow up, and do you know what they grow up into?"

There were murmurs among some of the men, lobbing out half-hearted guesses, all sounding eager to please the brute. The word "heathen" was lobbed by more than a few.

"Ha!" said Deacon. "True, but they grow up into workers. The best farm laborers we could ask for. Keep them lean and hungry and wanting and they will do our bidding. Don't you see?"

"What about the girls?" shouted one high-pitched voice.

"Leave it to you, Snider, to ask that!"

The plug of a man chuckled and smacked his big, thick hands together. "Why, the little girls will grow up to become breeding stock for more laborers. I tell you, men, this is only the beginning. Now all we have to do is figure out a way to not let any of these folks escape. One of them does that and makes it to the law—"

"Not the law in Higgins!" shouted one man.

"True, true. But beyond that, it is a big world. We can make all this work if we just keep our heads. Make certain from here on out that you all wear the burlap sacking masks that Pomfrey will be handing out."

"Why? Ain't it a little late for that?"

The plug of a man nodded. "I admit we should have gone into this wearing them, but now listen, we never got all that close most of the time. And the ones we did get close to, why, they have been dealt with, haven't they?"

"Yes, they have, but why the masks, Deacon?"

Gage saw, even from a distance, that being pushed on this point annoyed the thick man.

"I was getting to that. Now don't interrupt me. See, here's what's going to happen. We are going to make like we are willing to negotiate with them. They'll think they can buy their way out of this so we'll let them pass. As if filthy money is the only reason we're doing this."

"Ha!" shouted the high-pitched voice again. "It's also for the girls!"

"That is enough of that, Snider! You risk being called out as a blasphemer! You are new to the fold and we shall overlook that last outburst. But no more!"

"I . . . I'm sorry, Deacon."

"Now, where was I? Oh yes, the masks. We'll need them to shield our faces as we negotiate. At least the emissaries. We'll tell them it's for their own good. That if they don't know who we are, and can't identify us as individuals, we will be less likely to keep them here indefinitely. But once we make personal contact with them, up close, we will be able to gain some of their trust, and that will be far easier than having them hole up and shooting at us every time we draw near."

"I think that's a fair estimation of how this could play out," said a voice Gage had not yet heard. "But I think the mask idea is not necessary." Gage could not see the speaker.

"Oh, you do, do you?" growled Deacon.

"No need to get riled, Deacon," said the new voice.

This man, thought Gage, *might be one to be aware*

of, and one to be wary of. He was a voice of calmness and one the others would be inclined to follow more so than the ranting Deacon. But how long a voice of calm and seeming reason would be tolerated by the self-proclaimed leader remained to be seen.

CHAPTER 8

It took another hour before the last of the Brethren members rode away from where they'd been gathered. Gage was relieved, as he had had limited ability to shift and stretch his tall frame. He was certain Rig was also annoyed and fidgety, because he heard every now and again a crunching and stepping from in the trees, back where he had tied the sizable horse.

The breeze had remained consistent and helped to keep him and the horse from being heard. For that, he was grateful. But that was all he could be happy about. He was cramped and caught betwixt the age-old proverbial rock and a hard place.

Gage didn't doubt that he could depart the scene, but that wouldn't help his conscience, and it darn sure wouldn't help the travelers.

Once the last of the Brethren cleared out, he eyed the terrain with extra scrutiny, then made his way back to Rig. No, he decided, untying the head-wagging horse, there was no way he could leave and save his own skin, even if it meant his own hide. But since he'd already written himself off as expendable in life, he knew he had to try.

"Come on, boy," he said, once more leading the horse along the trees. This time, he ventured eastward.

For the fifteen minutes it took him to reach the far northeast corner of the cleared valley floor, he kept a sharp eye, but saw no black-clothed brutes. In fact, he saw no other humans. He did see three mule deer that melted out of the woodsy shadows and were now nibbling grass along the edges of the greensward.

"Bold choice," he muttered, knowing that anything interfering with the livelihood of the Brethren was apparently fair game for killing.

He reached that corner and eyed the track ahead that led from the east and Higgins straight to the field.

If the Brethren posted any sentries, this would be a likely spot.

And a moment later, he heard the telltale sound of a man spitting. He followed with his eyes where he thought the sound came from. It took him a few more moments to locate the man, but there he was, perched on a boulder just into the trees on the far side of the track. He was plainly hiding, and he was armed, most certainly.

The man was also chewing tobacco, and this offered Gage an idea. With little more thought than that—he knew from experience that if he overthought a thing, he was likely to dither and change his mind, and often later regretted that change.

Gage stepped into the open and made no effort to

hide his or Rig's footfalls. It only took a few seconds for the man on the boulder to react. He spun to face their direction and brought his rifle to bear on them soon after.

"Hey! Ah, halt there!" he said.

This told Gage the man was likely a farmer or some such and not engaged in gun work as his first choice in occupation. "Hey there, yourself." Gage walked three more strides so that he and Rig were not standing in the middle of the lane.

"Halt, I say!"

"And I say you had best keep that rifle aimed anywhere but at me, you understand?"

"Who are you?"

"I am sent by Deacon to do two things. First, to check on you, and the second, to infiltrate the enemy camp." While the man thought this over, Gage sized him up. He looked to be about twenty-five years old, perhaps older, and a hard worker, judging by the thickness of his hands and the calluses on them. He also had that slope-shouldered look of a tired man ready to drop into a nap at any moment.

The man licked his lips, and though he had lowered the rifle when Gage ordered him to do so, he still held it at waist height and aimed in Gage's general direction.

"Deacon, he wanted you to check on me? But I don't know you. Never seen you before, in fact!" That notion gave the man some renewal in confidence and he raised that rifle once more.

Gage had already gotten the measure of the man and he doubted very much that the fool would shoot him.

Gage closed the distance of three yards between them in three quick strides.

"Now, the reason you don't know me is because I am new here. Brethren headquarters sent me, on request, for this special operation. Do you understand me, boy? You had best keep it down *now*. Voices carry on the wind and I don't know who else is around here." Gage narrowed his eyes and squinted left, then right, as if eyeing the terrain for spies.

"'Brethren headquarters'? I never heard of such a thing." Although the man said it in a defiant tone, his demeanor had wilted. He looked two steps from dejected. "How come nobody told me about you coming?"

"Look here, the more folks know about us special operators from headquarters, the more chance there will be for mistakes to be made. Folks such as yourself might let slip with important information."

The fellow thought this over, but was already lowering his rifle. Now would be the time, thought Gage, to rush him and club him quick on the side of the head. But he'd risk the fool cranking off a gunshot, which, he guessed, would bring black-clothed brutes descending on them from every point of the compass.

"How long have you been with the Brethren, son?" said Gage in a lowered voice and in a tone he hoped came across as not unsympathetic.

The man shrugged. "About a year, year and a half. Mostly, my wife's doing." He looked at Gage then, and his eyes widened. "But I like it, too. Oh, it's been a good thing for us, to be sure."

Gage smiled. "I was practically born into it. What did you say your name was?"

"Tate," said the man. "Georgie Tate."

"Well, Georgie Tate. As I say, I'm a lifer in the Brethren, and one thing I know that is valued by the higher-up members, and I think you know who I mean." Gage waited for this to sink in and for the man to nod.

It worried Gage not a little that all these lies came to him with such ease. This trait, one he'd always had, reminded him of how much like his father, Jasper Gage, he was.

"Sure I know who you mean." Tate nodded, although his eyes told Gage the man was uncertain.

"All right, then. And that means you know how the Brethren feel about the use of tobacco."

The man's brows drew close. "No, I guess I didn't hear about that. No, sir."

But he'd stopped working his chaw. The bulge sat inside his mouth, puffing out his cheek like a hard-earned lump in a battle of fisticuffs.

Gage leaned in once more. "I will refrain from saying anything about your chaw habit, if you resume your post and forget that you saw me."

"But Deacon already knows you're here, right?" asked Tate, shifting his quid in his mouth and setting loose another quick stream of brown spittle to the side.

"Yes," said Gage with a sigh, as if Tate was too thick in the head to catch on to what he was saying. "But not many others. I am not at liberty to say who does and who does not know I have been called in to work this situation. Do you understand, Georgie? Now, I've wasted enough time with all this talk. I have an enemy camp to infiltrate."

Gage stepped back and eyed Georgie Tate up and down. He pitied the poor fool, especially as he was just another duped man roving the world, taken in by ill-intentioned folks more powerful than he.

"Long live the Brethren," said Gage, touching his right palm to his heart. He had no idea if that was even close to something these zealots might get up to.

In dicey situations in which he found himself knitting up lie after lie out of whole cloth, Gage found that false but seemingly well-intentioned solemnity rarely went amiss in gaining him an emotional edge, no matter how slight.

Georgie Tate's eyebrows rose and he watched this, then nodded. "Oh yes, yes." He clapped his own right hand to his breast. "Me too. Long live the Brethren."

"Good man," said Gage. Then, without another word, he led Rig past the slack-jawed Georgie Tate and into the forest beyond. He didn't dare turn around to see if the man was watching him, but he felt certain he was.

Gage somehow knew that his stream of lies had done just what he needed them to do. But only because Georgie Tate was a rube, and a new and ignorant member of this mad Church.

The terrain Gage cut through was, if anything, thicker with tree and bracken growth, likely because they weren't all that far from the river. He did his best to keep well inside the tree line so he would not be visible from anywhere in the field.

Ahead, southward, flowed the east-west river. He then recalled the name of the flowage, the Shaw River, but the fact meant little to him. After all, the river didn't know or care that humans named it one thing or another.

This line of thinking was something he often mused on as he rode along. Did a tree know it was a ponderosa or an aspen? Did it care? Did it even know it was a tree? No, he had long ago decided, was the answer to all those questions, and more.

He decided, barring any other sentries, that they would rest at the river. If the bank was forgiving enough, he would lead Rig down for a cool drink, something the big horse had long needed.

Gage gazed upward through the branches to the clear blue sky and guessed, from the way his gut rumbled and by the sun's glow, that it was near to midafternoon. He only had another few hours before the cold and dark set in. He had to make the emigrants' camp by then.

And what sort of welcome might he receive there? Skeptical, no doubt. He hoped they would at least listen to him and not shoot him on sight.

As they neared the river, Gage's thoughts turned to the wiry old scout, Bewley, who had shared a pot of coffee with him the evening before. *Was that only yesterday?* thought Gage. *My word, it seems a lifetime and a half ago.*

The riverbank turned out to be a low and easy one to navigate. He poked his head through and looked upstream and down, but saw no one. "We have to make this quick, Rig," he told the horse. "No dawdling."

A low, chesty rumble was the big beast's response. He slurped and slurped up enough water to fill a whiskey barrel, or so it seemed. Gage also took a decent drink, and he topped up his waterskin and canteen, a practice he always got up to whenever he found a good-running flow of clean water.

"Okay, horse," he said in a low voice. "Time to leg it west along the river. Tricky," he said, "because we have to stay between the open land to our north and the water to our south."

The tree line was plenty wide, for the most part, to accomplish this. But he noted that in places ahead, it narrowed right down to low scrubby brush.

As he cut ever closer to the emigrants' forced encampment, he heard more noises, shouts of men, weeping of a woman—more of a wailing—and at least two children crying, as only children can. The sounds tore at him inside and hardened his resolve to help these folks somehow.

Then, as he and Rig threaded their way through the increasingly thinner scrabble of trees between the river and the open land, he wondered why these folks didn't try their luck by cutting southward and crossing the river. Unless the Brethren had somehow made it an impossibility. Perhaps they set up some sort of bulwark preventing this.

"We'll find out soon enough," he said to Rig. And

within five minutes, he was within sight of the camp, such as it was. He paused and watched for a moment.

What he saw looked like little more than a hastily arranged cluster of wagons, a few tied head of bawling cattle, three loose horses that two young boys were trying to catch, and people with wide eyes trying to look everywhere at once.

If he walked blindly into the camp, he might well be shot, given what they'd been through and how jumpy they seemed. But Gage knew of no other way to go about it. He let out a deep breath, said, "Here we go, Rig," and with his hands raised, the reins held high in his right, he walked forward. Within twenty feet, he broke through the ragged line of scrub growth and halted.

For a comical long moment, nobody noticed him. He was about to clear his throat when a woman holding a baby on her hip saw him and offered up a quick scream.

A handful of men all turned their weapons on him, and Gage faced more drawn guns than he'd ever seen all at once.

"Who are you!"

It was no question, but a barked command, by a tall young man with the makings of a dragoon moustache on his face. He looked hard at Gage, his evident rage simmering through narrowed eyes, and his jaws flexed with hard-gritted teeth.

"I'm just traveling west alone, up on that ridge to the north." He nodded beyond them. "And I heard shots, thought I'd come to investigate."

"Liar!" growled the man. "You're a spy—a spy from those crazy, religious farmers!"

Three men advanced and snatched Rig's reins from Gage's right hand. He didn't resist, and the other two grabbed him by the wrists and held him, arms bent back to the sides.

"Look," said Gage. "If I'm a spy, why would I walk in here, hands up? I tell you, I'm just a fellow traveling through and I happened to hear shooting. If being nosy is a crime, fine. But it doesn't mean I'm a spy."

The group's spokesman shook his head, his jaw muscles flexing and jouncing more than ever, his eyes narrowed into slits that never left Gage's face. "You are not telling us anything of worth, mister. Time's up." He ratcheted back the hammer on his gun and raised it to Gage's chest height.

"You fool," said Gage. "I didn't have to come down here. I was doing fine, on my way west on that ridge right up there, riding from Higgins."

"Yeah? Well, where were you last night? If you know so much, why didn't you ride on down and tell us what was to come, should we try this pass? Huh?"

The man clicked the hammer back to the deadly position.

"I camped on up there a few miles back." Gage nodded northeastward, toward where the ridgeline snaked from Higgins and points east. "And I didn't know any more than you did about this cursed pass!"

"Likely story, mister." The man advanced on Gage,

but the former gunfighter didn't move. He planted his feet and stood firm and tall.

The tall young man shook his head. "I don't trust a thing you say, mister." He raised his rifle to his shoulder. "You got something more to say, spy, you had best get to it. And consider it your last words, because we hang spies hereabouts."

"Oh, 'hereabouts'?" said Gage, more angry than afraid. He saw the worried looks on the faces of the man's fellow travelers when he had uttered the word "hang."

"Look, I'm not even armed! I didn't have to come down here. But I did. Why? I'm beginning to wonder that myself!"

"You done?" said the man, not flinching one bit.

Gage jerked his chin to the left. "I see trees over there behind your wagons, but none of them are good enough for hanging a man! Not until you drag me out into the open yonder." He pointed northward along the tree line that led to the pass. He let that hang while he and the tall man exchanged flinty looks. "If you are dead set on killing me, then you best get to it," he said, echoing and mocking the younger man's phrase. "Otherwise, let me speak."

"Let him speak, Chase," his accomplices urged.

The younger, angry man barked his pent-up anger. "Fine. Make it quick."

Gage noted that he and the young man, Chase, were equally matched, heightwise, though the younger man looked leaner and hungrier, an almost wolfish demeanor hung about him like a raw pelt on the shoulders of a mountain man.

"Just go ask your scout, Bewley."

The mention of the man's name rattled Chase and he pulled his head back a smidgen. "How do you know him?"

"I met him in town. In Higgins, yesterday. Then later, we shared a pot of coffee at my campfire. He was scouting late in the day yesterday, came upon my camp, and explored, as any scout worth his salt would do, inspecting the land ahead for his train."

Behind Chase, folks mumbled and murmured and parted as someone shoved his way through them. "He's telling you the truth, Chase."

Bewley emerged from behind the tall young man. "And for heaven's sake, put that gun away."

"How do I know you ain't in this with him?"

The old scout let his arms hang by his sides, his shoulders sagged, and he looked up at the young man's face. "You have to be kidding me, boy. What makes you say that?" He held up his left arm and shook it before Chase. "You think I'd risk taking a bullet if I knew what all this mess was about? Huh?"

Gage saw that Bewley's arm had been grazed, the buckskin tunic he wore now sporting a ragged, long furrow dug in it. The edges of the tear were blackened, and beneath it, Gage caught a quick glimpse of a raw red wound that had congealed enough to staunch the blood's flow.

Chase hadn't much to offer, so Bewley said, "Now put that away, Chase. And you, Rice, and you, Dawlish, let go of his arms. The man's as innocent as we are in this mess. And what's more, he ain't lying! He could have as easily ridden on and left us to deal with the Brethren nuts on our own, but he didn't, did he?"

Bewley looked at the faces around him. It was obvious to Gage that the old scout had earned a few notches of respect from them all in their journey so far.

"You string him up, you might as well do the same with me. Because I rode on out here yesterday, well, up thataway first, as he said, and I didn't see anything that would have told me we ought to shy clear of this cursed valley. Though I wish I had. Truth is, there ain't no other way through this stretch of the Chisley foothills, leastwise not for days' worth of journeying, north or south!"

"As far as this pass goes, I'm not certain it would have mattered," said Gage.

"What do you mean?"

The two men holding Gage's wrists behind him released their grips and he pulled his arms forward, slowly, then rubbed his wrists as he spoke. "If I was a betting man, and I am not, I'd wager that they made up their mind to do this to you long before you ever got to Higgins."

That caught Chase's attention. "You think they've been following us?"

"No," said Gage. "That's not what I mean. I think they decided recently, or at least the man in charge of the Brethren, that they were going to do this to the next substantial wagon train that came on through their lands. And I think this is legitimately their land. Trouble is, the roadway was here before they even got here. But now, they want to control the traffic through it. And instead of being civilized like the Sioux, and demanding a payment in order to cross their lands, they decided they want everything you have. All of it."

"What?" said Bewley. "What are you saying, Gage?"

Gage saw all eyes on him, and all the fearful faces looked as if they knew what he was going to say before he said it.

"I know it, because that's what I heard them saying earlier. You folks just happened to be in the unfortunate position of being the next ones along to suit their needs."

"But how do you know all this?" said Chase, his hand still resting on his gun.

Gage also saw that the man licked his lips and flicked his eyes down to Gage's waist, as if he might see a hidden revolver pop out of nowhere.

"If you hadn't interrupted me before and threatened to hang me, I'd have told you what I heard. I was trying to, in fact."

"What do you mean 'they want everything you have'?" asked Bewley.

Gage nodded. "That's what they said. They want the wagons, the animals, the household goods, your money . . ." He listened to the gasps and growls from men and women alike. "And they made a point of saying they want your children, too."

"Wh-wh-what?"

This burst came from a man Gage hadn't paid much attention to. He'd stood off to Gage's left, back a couple of folks, and partially hidden. The man stepped forward, eyeing Gage, his face bright red, and his teeth gritted hard.

Gage recognized him from town: Seth Greenaway, the man with the stammer.

"Hello there, Mr. Greenaway," said Gage, offering a rueful smile. "Nice to see you again."

"You know him?" said Chase.

Greenaway ignored him. "Wh-what . . ."

"We met in Higgins," said Gage to Chase. He turned back to Greenaway and the others. "What I meant was what I said. Those brutes"—he thrust a finger toward the pass where he'd last seen the Brethren—"said they want your children for laborers. Mostly, the boys." He glanced at the faces closing in around him, the raw anger and fear there was pitiable and a little frightening, too.

"And . . . th-th-the g-g-g-girls?" Greenaway questioned in a hoarse whisper.

Gage chose his words with care and pressed on. "They said they wanted to grow them up for . . . other purposes."

The gasps and stifled, choking sounds of anger being bitten off forced him to redden and look down at his boots. He didn't know how else to state it. This was a rum business and he didn't like it one bit. But who would?

Then they had no more time for talk because a boy from far in the camp shouted, "Pa! Pa! Hurr—"

His last word was clipped off, as if he'd had a hand clamped over his mouth.

As they all broke and ran for the wagons at the rear, where most of the women and children were secured, Gage heard someone say, "Where are the sentries? Who's standing guard?"

Gage made for Rig, who'd been taken from him when he'd first entered the camp. Whoever had held his reins had just dropped them and bolted. He couldn't blame them, but he didn't fancy the idea of Rig running out into the middle of the field where some fool might shoot him.

He snatched up the reins and ran to his left along the river, then cut in by the cliff face, making for the wagons arrayed at its base. As he reached the corner, he looked once more to the river, wondering why they hadn't simply crossed and done their level best to hustle the train on out of the Brethren land.

Then he saw why—the cliffs had continued in that direction as well, and the embankment was steep, steeper than even a work wagon might roll down without fear of tipping over.

Still, he thought, they might stand a chance, especially early on like this, if they backtrailed east along the river's edge and crossed at the first spot that would allow for it.

Perhaps if they set up a line of defending fire to cover the wagons. He suspected it was an idea one of them at least had already come up with, but now was not the time.

CHAPTER 9

Gage lashed Rig's reins to a stout pine and slid his rifle from its boot. He walked closer to the crowd, in time to hear a man shouting.

"I said, why'd you leave her alone like that? I told you to mind her!"

The man bellowed in the face of a young boy—perhaps eight or ten years old, thought Gage. The kid, who was already shaking and red-faced, covered his eyes with his hands and Gage saw the lad's shoulders working up and down with heavy, hard breaths.

The irate man tried to comfort a weeping woman nearby, but she shouted and shrugged him away. He stormed off, following the others, who had moved on, spreading out northward along the rocky west edge, armed and afoot.

"What's happened?" said Gage to the few who remained near him. Nobody paid him any attention. He low-walked closer to the far edge of the poorly arrayed wagons and hunkered below one, partially hidden by a crate.

Soon he was joined by Bewley, the wiry scout. "They're riled because someone made off with a baby," he said.

Gage nodded. "I gathered that."

They watched the irate men stream out along the tree line that led to the pass. "This is what the Brethren want, to get them out in the open, separated from the feeble safety of hiding behind these wagons." Bewley waved a hand at the ragged cluster of wagons about them.

Shots cracked, and one of the men in the lead of the pack of travelers, a shortish fellow with long hair and wearing a derby hat, screamed and snatched at his right shoulder. He spun and dropped to his knees.

This was all they needed, thought Gage. "What would you like me to do?"

"No idea just yet," said Bewley. "But once we convince these fools to get back here and hunker in, somebody has to go after the Henning baby."

Gage looked around the crate. The shots from the Brethren had sizzled in from throughout the field. Gage had not seen any men out there and he wondered when they had established themselves. The grass was not that tall, and more brittle and brown than green, but it looked to be high enough to cover a prone man sniping from a distance.

The group of travelers hustled back to the wagons, the mother of the missing child holding her other child, the weeping boy who'd been blamed by the shouting man. Gage learned, as he'd guessed, that the man was the boy's father, and father to the stolen child.

Of the thief, no one saw a thing.

"Is this the way it's going to go?" said a woman's voice beside him. Gage looked down to see Sarah Greenaway, the wife of the man with the stammer.

"How do you mean, ma'am?" Gage suspected he knew what she meant.

"Are they going to chip away at us, one person at a time, until they have achieved whatever it is they hope to gain?"

For a long moment, Gage was tempted to skirt the truth, but the woman's narrowed eyes never looked away from him, and she showed no sign of being hysterical about the situation.

"Yes, ma'am," he said, deciding to tell the baldest truth he knew. "If I had to guess, I'd say that is the most likely outcome."

She nodded. "Okay, then, Mr. Gage. As long as you speak the truth. After all, that's the only acceptable response we require. So, what now?"

"Now we make a plan."

"We?" shouted Chase, striding toward him. "Who's this 'we'? You are a spy, and we ain't yet proved otherwise!"

"Oh, Chase," said Bewley. "Leave off that, will you?"

"Why? That child was snatched right from our own camp while everybody was distracted with him!" He waved a dismissive hand at Gage.

"That's enough of that, I said!" The rooster of a scout

jammed himself in between the two men and Gage backed up a step, then turned and walked toward where he'd tied Rig.

Chase shouted, "Where you going? I ain't through with you!"

Gage sighed and turned around. He saw Bewley storm off at a trot, making for the wagons to the far western corner of the rough encampment.

Gage walked back to the small group. "I am going to get that child back. And if I do, maybe you, Chase, and the rest of you all won't think I'm a spy."

"Won't prove nothing."

"Fine, then you won't care if I try."

"We let you go, you might tell them all about us!"

"Tell them what? That you're a frightened bunch of folks who can't seem to think straight, nor can you work together to do the things you should be doing?" Gage looked at the rest of them.

He guessed about a third of them were here, with the rest manning guard posts and tending stock. The faces all around him already showed signs of the heavy weight this unexpected attack was having on them.

Women, with dark circles beneath their eyes, each held one baby, and several had two babies on their hips.

He noted, too, not for the first time, that the zealots he'd overheard had been quite correct in their assessments of them. They were not a down-at-the-heels bunch, but from the looks of them and their gear and goods, they were all fairly well-to-do, or at least had been before they embarked on this journey.

He imagined a good many conversations were taking place, or would tonight, between husbands and wives about the prudence of their choice to venture out this way. These people needed a victory—and they needed it soon. But before that, they needed to tighten up, use their heads, and work together.

"We're only hours into this, folks!" Gage addressed them all, looking at faces in turn. "And already you're turning on each other. You had best pull together and come up with a plan, because it's likely that you'll be here for some time!"

He spun once more and departed. This time, nobody said a thing to him. He wondered what Bewley was up to, but decided he was running around the camp, trying to appease all the flustered travelers and make certain the outer lines of defense held.

Dark would be coming soon and he needed to make his move quickly. There was no way those zealots would keep a baby in camp any longer than necessary. In fact, he bet they had someone carry it on through the pass to one of their homesteads tucked in the hills or lining the roadway.

He didn't think they would harm the child, given what he heard them say about wanting the wagon train children, but then again, the Brethren seemed to be fairly demonic in their judgments.

"Hey, Gage!"

Gage spun. It was Bewley. Gage finished pulling on his new wool coat as he approached. "You serious about trying to go after the child?"

"I am. That's what I am headed to do right now."

Bewley nodded. "I have to tell you, I think that child's long gone."

"I figure that, too, but maybe I can learn something. Will you watch my horse for me?"

"Sure, yeah. You know you don't have to do this. These folks, they don't trust you, and they don't seem to have trouble showing it, neither."

"I can't say as I blame them. They don't know me at all. I just show up in the midst of all this? It's fishy, I understand, but I couldn't live with myself if I didn't try to help. Believe me, it would have been far easier to keep on riding west, but I have to live with me."

"I hear you on that, Gage. But it's risky, man," said Bewley. "You don't need to stick your neck out like this. I'm the scout. I can do it myself or send someone else."

"I know, but I don't have anything of value to lose. If I can help someone, then so be it."

"Nothing to lose? How about your life? That's a mighty valuable thing to a man, no?"

Gage finished checking his game rifle and bullets, then tugged on his leather gloves. "Like I said, I have nothing of worth to lose."

Bewley had nothing to say to this, but Gage saw the man's raised eyebrows. He'd seen the same look many times before when folks realized they were dealing with a man who had little personal regard. *If you only knew,* thought Gage, *you'd wish me dead.*

"Besides," he said, "maybe I can find out more useful

information. Or . . ." He shrugged. "I don't know yet. We'll see."

"Don't you at least want a handgun? That relic of a rifle ain't much to look at, if you'll excuse the insult."

Gage smiled. "It's not an insult if it's the truth. But this gun"—he raised it a bit—"has served me well, and kept me in food for a few years now."

Bewley nodded. "Good luck then, Gage."

Gage rubbed Rig's long nose, then strode away. The horse watched him go, ears perked, and Bewley murmured, "Gage . . . Gage . . . Where do I know that name?"

Then his eyebrows rose once more and he whistled low. "If he's the Gage I think he might be . . . well, that's something else, that is."

He turned to the horse and gathered up the reins. "Too bad you don't speak the human tongue. You could confirm my guess for me. Well, no matter, no difference. We have bigger fish to fry up, son. And I best get to it."

Gage skirted the rear of the camp, drawing narrow-eyed looks and a couple of snorts, but little else. These folks were beginning to annoy him, he didn't mind admitting it. But then again, he thought, he wasn't here to make friends with them. He was here to help.

And the first thing he needed to do was find that baby.

Barring that, he might be able to cause some sort of headache for the Brethren. And the best place to start that, he thought as he took once more to the trees, would be at their own camp.

CHAPTER 10

By the time Gage reached the far northwest corner of the wagon train's makeshift encampment, the daylight had dwindled, leaving in its wake dark, shadowed spots he might hide in as he made his way to the pass.

He knew he needed to wait a bit longer before stepping out from behind the end wagon, a high-topped Conestoga affair with a surprising amount of cargo, both inside and strapped to the outside.

Compared with the other wagons, it had sunk several inches into the earth of the field. It was not a particularly damp spot, so that told Gage this family had not heeded the prudent advice found in all the emigrant guidebooks telling potential travelers to pack light. He reckoned it was difficult to convince folks that new goods would eventually be available at the far end of their journey.

One of the rear flaps of the wagon was tied back, and light from the waning sun to the west, above the ridge behind them, cast its dim rays into the wagon. Within,

Gage thought he saw a pianoforte, and beyond it, also trussed with rope, a small cast-iron cookstove.

The rest of the interior was largely hidden in shadow, but it looked filled, nonetheless. Just where did the family members sleep?

The outside of the wagon was just as filled: There were buckets and crates and hinged boxes and ricks of hay. Lashed to the sides of the wagon, there were small wooden pens filled with what looked to be ducks and chickens and some other, smaller birds. Perhaps pigeons, he couldn't be certain.

There also seemed to be a full assortment of new-looking hand tools, from shovels and axes to picks and brooms. Perhaps the man was a vendor?

As if reading his thoughts, a fellow moved around the side of the wagon and saw Gage, hunkered a dozen feet away, trying not to look like a nosy stranger, and failing.

Gage recognized the fellow as the long-haired man in the bowler who'd taken a bullet in the shoulder but a short while before.

"Can I help you?" said the man, holding a hand just below the freshly bandaged wound. It still wept blood and the white cloth binding it bore a stark red splotch.

"I'm waiting for the sun to leave us," said Gage. "Then I'm going to try my luck at their camp."

"What's that mean?"

"Means I have to try to find the stolen child. If not, I

don't know. There must be something I can do. I have to try."

"But why?" The man shifted and leaned against his wagon. Even in the low light, Gage could see the man's face was drained of color. "You're not one of us."

"No, no, I'm not. But I am a man who doesn't like to see other folks ground down for no reason."

"Oh."

Gage looked away to check the day's waning light and realized he could barely see his own hand. Soon, soon.

"Are you a merchant?" Gage asked the man.

"No, what makes you say that?"

"Oh, it's just that your wagon seems a tad—"

"Overloaded?" said the man with a weak chuckle.

"Well, yes."

"You're not the first to tell me that. I figured I'd make it as far as I could before I begin discarding possessions. Truth is, I don't much care one way or another."

"Oh?" said Gage.

"Nah." The man walked a few steps toward him. "I was going to set up a home out in California. Maybe near the ocean, even. She . . . she was going to join me when I had it all perfect for her. But . . ." He looked away and didn't speak for a few moments.

Gage didn't interrupt. He sensed the man wasn't through speaking. Sure enough, he resumed, but his voice was thicker, lower. He was stifling back some hard emotions.

"My intended, she . . . I got word a few weeks back that she had . . . passed."

"I am sorry to hear that. Truly," said Gage. That would also explain why the man had run willy-nilly right out into the open, on hearing of the child's abduction. The danger there had been that others had thoughtlessly followed him.

Gage hoped the shoulder would be enough to keep them all at a simmer. At least until he was able to wreak some havoc of his own at the Brethren camp.

They stood that way, eight feet apart in the growing twilight, not speaking for long moments; then the man cleared his throat and in a near whisper said, "You're him, ain't you?"

A cold, fist-size stone dropped from the top of Gage's throat right down his gullet to land hard in his gut, chilling him from the inside out. It always seemed to happen this way.

Gage would be in the midst of a quiet moment of the deepest emotions possible and someone would, almost apologetically, though sometimes in a braying manner, cut in and hack the tender moment apart with news of their discovery of who he was. It was never about who he had been, which is how he tried to think of himself and his life.

"Who do you have in mind?" said Gage. He might have promised himself to never lie about his identity, but he wasn't that much of a fool—he'd not admit it without them saying his name.

"The gunman, what was that silly name? Texas Something-or-other." The wounded man dragged a shirt cuff across his teared eyes. "Lightning," he said, nodding as if to himself. "Texas Lightning. That's you, isn't it?"

Gage let out a quick sigh. "I am Jon Gage."

A sound from the shadows, nearby the half-empty work wagon to his right, caused both men to look.

The tall, youthful firebrand, Chase, stepped from the shadows, one hand resting on the butt of his revolver. "I knew there was something about you that warranted watching. And now I know what."

"Oh?" said Gage, his cold gut now hardening into stone itself. "And what's that?"

Here he was, in the middle of absolutely nowhere on a map of the world, and he was caught playing the foolish game of riddles with an idiot. He regretted, not for the first or last time that day, not riding on out, sticking to the ridge, and getting good and gone.

He'd be miles and miles and hours and hours west of here, trekking into the high country he'd come to love over the years. It was his most favorite place, and he'd be encamped out there right now, were it not for his blasted conscience.

Simmer down, Gage, he told himself. *Nobody to blame for this situation but yourself.*

He looked at Chase, then back to the wounded man

and touched his hat brim, then turned his back on the two of them.

"That's right," said Chase, far too loud. "Walk on out of here. I'm surprised you don't shoot us before you do."

Gage stopped, knowing he shouldn't act on how he felt, but not able to help himself. "The night's young," he said, then kept going.

He walked a couple of paces and heard the man he'd mistaken for a merchant say, "I'm sorry about this, Gage."

Gage held up one hand as a gesture of kindness and then stepped out beyond the protection of the far edge of the wagon and low-walked to the tree line a couple of paces to his left.

He wormed his way in, he hoped, with less noise than he suspected he was making, and rued the fact that he was not really qualified to go on such an adventure. He was armed with a decent hip knife and an old rifle that, while reliable, was a far cry from a brace of pistols that most folks in his situation would pack.

So be it, he thought, and cut with caution to the north. He figured that at the snail's pace of progress he was making, he'd reach the outer edge of the Brethren camp, across the roadway cutting through the pass, in fifteen or perhaps twenty minutes.

Between now and then, he told himself, you have to come up with a fair notion of what to do once you get there. First thing was to determine somehow if the stolen child was still there. The next step all depended on the answer to the first point. And if the camp was swarming with men, he would have to back away and retreat once more to the scant safety of rocks and trees.

CHAPTER 11

Twenty long, cautious minutes later, Gage found himself crouched in shadowy tree cover, once more eavesdropping on the coldhearted brutes known as the Brethren.

"Why can't we just burn them out? You know, shoot lit arrows into the canvas of them wagons."

"You idiot!" growled a voice Gage remembered he'd heard earlier. It was Deacon. "If we set fire to those wagons, we'll lose most of what we are doing this for. Honestly, how did you make it out of childhood without something happening to you?"

"What do you mean by that?"

Gage heard a sigh; then Deacon said, "You see what I mean?"

"All right, all right," said a third voice. "What we need to decide just now is how we are going to smoke them out."

"Yes, yes," said Deacon, sounding surly. "That's what I was about to suggest. No need to set fire to the wagons, *which we need.*" He said this last part loudly, no doubt emphasizing it for the lout's benefit. "We can drive them from their camp, coughing and gasping, and then we can choose who lives and who dies as they stagger on out of there."

The third man asked, "How on earth could we do that?"

"I haven't decided that yet," said Deacon. He stood, groaning and yawning. "But it's dark and we all had a big day. We have enough sentries on duty now that I'm not worried about keeping those heathens pinned down for the night. Let's all get rest and we will see what the morning brings. We'll get an early start on it. I want everyone here and assembled before dawn."

"What about services?" queried the third voice.

"What about them? Curse it, man, we are engaged in a tricky situation here! Services can wait."

"What? You ... you can't mean that," said the lout's voice.

"I most certainly can, and I do. Are you questioning me, Fletcher?"

"Well, no, sir. No, Deacon."

"Fool. And by the way, just who is Deacon here?"

The younger man said, "You are, sir."

"That's right. You forget it again and I will see to it that you are expelled from the Brethren and branded a heathen!"

"But—"

"No, I say! You keep your mouth shut and go to your bedroll before you can't!"

Judging from the sudden silence of the various noises

Gage heard leading up to that—breathings, sighs, cups being set down, boots sliding on gravel—Gage figured that there were no more than the three men sitting around the fire and participating in the conversation, and at Deacon's outburst, they all grew quiet.

Then he heard one set of boots crunching gravel and depart. The third voice said, "Deacon, don't you think you were a little hard on him?"

"Hard on him?"

Deacon, still worked up, blew out a long breath. "Look," he said in a lowered voice. "Men like Fletcher are all right for one thing—they are expendable. They're too dumb to grasp what it is we stand to gain from all this. And he thinks we're doing this for the glory of the Maker."

"Well, isn't that a large part of this?"

There was another pause. "Well, yes, sure, but look, Schenk, we can't play this game anymore. The longer it drags out, the more danger we'll be in."

"How do you figure that?"

"Because this might not be the last wagon train westward this season."

"Oh, it's so late, Deacon. Surely folks aren't stupid enough to keep trying their luck."

"Those folks did," he said, and Gage could picture him pointing toward the barely visible white shapes of the wagon tops hovering above the darkness of the field.

"What's our next step, then?"

"I've been thinking on this," said Deacon. "And I am

convinced we can draw them out, and quick. First thing we need to do is use that baby as leverage."

"How?"

"We tell them if they don't do as we say, the baby, well, you know."

"No, I say. No! I don't care if you are Deacon! That's unacceptable. You can't even think that about a child."

Deacon didn't respond right away. Then he sighed as if he were on a stage.

Gage hunkered even lower, and through the scrubby brush, he gained a better sight line and saw much of the man now, silhouetted against the fire's low glow.

Deacon walked around the fire, toward the other man, and rested a hand on his shoulder. "You're right, Schenk, you're right. It's late and I'm not thinking clear. I told you we needed a rest." He looked about him as if to make certain no one could hear them. Gage saw no other folks around.

"Look, Schenk, I have something important to tell you, couldn't do it when Fletcher was here. Walk with me. I can't risk others hearing this. You're the only one I trust, you know that, right?"

"Sure, sure, Deacon. What is it?"

Gage froze. They were walking his way! He narrowed his eyes and held still.

When they were within a foot or so from the cleared edge of the trees, Deacon looked about himself again, casting a glance back toward the camp. "It's not that we don't have good men, but, well, they don't understand the real importance of what we are doing here."

"Um, right, Deacon."

"Yes, we are up to the work of the Maker, the ultimate founder of our Church. You see that, don't you, Schenk?"

"Yes, yes, I do, Deacon."

"Good, I knew you did. What I need you to do now is have that pretty wife of yours bring that baby into camp first thing in the morning, before light."

"But—"

"No, no, now, Schenk, hear me out. We'll just use the baby for negotiations, that's all. Like playing poker, you see?"

"But that's blasphemous behavior!"

"Oh." Deacon moved closer to the man. He lifted the hand that was resting on the man's right shoulder and draped it around Schenk's shoulders, then pulled him close. "Never mind, Schenk."

Gage heard the man gasp, and a coughing, gagging sound, low and wet, rose up from his mouth.

Deacon hugged him close. "Shh, shh, hush now, hush now. Don't worry about that baby. I'll fetch it myself. That is, after I go and comfort that pretty little wife of yours tonight. She'll hear what brutes those heathens are and how they sneaked in and killed her poor husband, and I'll be there to make sure her night is comfortable and soothing."

The gagging sounds rose in pitch, and then Gage saw Deacon's right arm, barely outlined by the distant low firelight, rise outward and slam inward, then upward.

Just before it had plunged into the man again, in

midstrike, Gage had seen the shining wetness that he knew now to be a blood-slick blade. Deacon had gutted his own friend and was going to blame the killing on the travelers, once Schenk's body was found.

Deacon supported the man as a long, last, gasping wheeze rose up and out of him, then guided him gently to the earth. "There now," said Deacon, laying the stabbed man down with barely a thump.

Gage had seen and heard enough deaths to know that the gutted man had shoved out his last breath in this world. It was fast, and he guessed that the stabber, Deacon, had pierced the man's heart with that final upward stroke.

"There now, old friend," the Church leader whispered low and harsh as he crouched over the dead man. "You and I both know what we know. And what we know won't help any of these fool farmers one whit. It's best I continue to lead them as I see fit.

"The Church of the Brethren, such as it is, will thrive now that you are not here to question me at every turn. I, for one, welcome this, and I know that in short order, everyone else will, too.

"Know, my friend, that your death will do many things. One, it will make it easier, far easier, for me to keep the sheep in line, or at least keep the flock from straying. Especially the thickheaded ones, such as young Fletcher."

Gage heard the man's voice tighten, as if with a momentary flare of anger, when he spoke of the younger man, who, not many long minutes before, had endured a harsh scolding and then had departed for the evening.

"Another thing your demise will do is help me to convince the skeptics that we are indeed doing the correct thing in taking these traveling heathens to task. And I, as Deacon, will naturally have the pick of the spoils, and that includes women and children.

"As you know, I have discovered that the Lord of All Brethren wishes us to take as many wives as we may safely support so that we can raise up the first generation of unwavering non-doubters within the Church. We will need many if we are to help the Church to grow far beyond our fertile valley.

"Ah," he said, sinking back on his heels. "It will be glorious to have a mansion on the hill behind where my cabin now sits. It will, of course, be the pulsing heart of the Church of the Brethren."

Gage hadn't dared stir for the long minutes all this had taken place. Now he felt a knot forming in his lower right thigh, just behind his bent knee. It felt as if someone were sticking a handful of hot needles into his seized muscle. He clenched his teeth tight and waited for the foolish killer to leave—for surely, he would soon. If not, he risked becoming discovered. It was, after all, a likely spot for a man to wander on by to relieve himself, Gage guessed.

As if he had heard Gage's thoughts, Deacon shook his head, as if rousing himself from a daydream, and patted the dead man on the shoulder. "Okay, then, Schenk. Hey, you remember that name I gave you?

Old Reliable? Well, you came through for me one more time. I can use this, your final sacrifice, for the betterment of the Brethren. Which really means the betterment of me. But that's between us, eh, old chum, my second-in-charge? Old Reliable! Ha! Okay, my work here is done, but I daresay yours has only begun. You will be discovered at some point, and I will, of course, be surprised that you have been taken from us far too soon.

"But rest assured, your wife and son, and that new baby, will not be left to fend for themselves. I will step into the vacant spot you have just made, my friend. And your killers, those heathen travelers seeking to take our fertile valley from us, will not get away with such demonic brutalities!"

Deacon had raised his eyes skyward as he uttered this last; then with a grunt, and using his dead friend to shove off from, he stood, stretching and his knees popping. "I am getting too old to go through all this again. But nobody knows me out this way. Perfect, perfect . . ." The killer walked off westward into the night.

Gage saw beyond him that the two campfires he'd seen earlier had now dwindled to a paltry glow. Now and again, he heard the quick, stray sounds that he presumed were made by men on sentry duty.

He would have to be extra cautious in getting back to the emigrants' camp. He did not accomplish what he'd hoped, the success of which he had doubted even before he'd set out. The baby, by Deacon's account, had been taken into the family of the dead man, and brought farther west, to what Gage assumed was this fertile valley that he had heard of, the home of the Brethren families.

When he was certain that Deacon was well and gone, Gage rose to standing height, letting the blood seep back into his lower legs. He massaged roughly the knotted, pinpricked spot behind his right knee.

It had been painful enough to make him wish he could howl in pain, but he'd refrained. Now he had to retrace his steps, with no source of light, back to the travelers' wagons. And all this without getting discovered and shot by a panicked Brethren farmer more used to snoring than standing guard duty.

The first hundred feet or so went well, with Gage barely making any sound. Then he toed a fist-size stone and it rattled into what sounded like a dead, hollowed log. He recalled from his cautious venture out here earlier, there had been a log he'd stepped over.

The sound wasn't particularly loud, but it did catch his breath in his throat. He held in place, but heard no sounds of approach or gun hammers ratcheting.

He knew that his approach to the wagon camp was going to be equally dicey, especially if that pigheaded Chase fellow had his way. He stood an all right chance of getting back into the camp with the wounded man, who had talked with him before Chase had intruded.

And then there was Bewley. He was busy keeping a lid on the simmering pot of anger and confusion that was the wagon train encampment.

They were pushed into an unexpected spot, without much warning, and already Gage could sense that their civility was on the wane. Certain of them, mostly the men, would soon do away with any thoughts of civility and attack at will. Anything, Gage suspected, to get them out of their predicament. Even if that meant a slaughter of their attackers.

He hoped it wouldn't come to that, but time, and not much of it, would tell.

He knew, by lamp or fire glow, that he was approaching the camp, and so he was not surprised to hear a harsh whisper call out, "Who's that? Show yourself! We are armed to the teeth and in no mood to put up with you rascals!"

The whispering voice was perhaps twenty feet in front of him, just at the point where he'd taken to the trees earlier, tight to the granite slope behind the rough assemblage of wagons.

Gage knew the voice, or thought he did. "Bewley? That you? It's Gage."

A moment passed, then Bewley said, "Come ahead then," still in a growly whisper.

Gage assumed the man was mostly certain who he was, but not entirely so. He swallowed once, and still keeping his rifle held before him and ready to fire, he advanced.

Bewley didn't lower his own gun, a revolver, until Gage was right in front of him. "You alone?" said the older fellow in a low voice.

"Yep." Gage didn't blame him. It was the very question he would ask, and verify for himself, which is what Bewley was doing by looking past him and not lowering the gun just yet. Gage knew why—it was entirely possible that the Brethren could have used him as a decoy to get into the camp.

Finally Bewley said, "Good to see you, Gage. Any luck?"

"Well, not with bringing the child back."

"Did you see her? Is she—"

"No, no, I didn't see her. But I heard one man tell another that they'd taken the child farther in, down the pass, which is where their farms lie, to somebody's home. A woman has her, and it sounded as if she would be well cared for."

He sensed that last bit was a stretch of the truth as he knew it, but overall it had seemed hopeful, so why not further that thought?

Gage eased his rifle down and Bewley did the same with his pistol.

"Any other news?"

"Yes, there's a fellow called Deacon. I remember him from Higgins. A mean piece of work. He seems to have them all cowed. It's as I said earlier, they only want one thing—and that's everything. I don't think there will be any quarter given."

Bewley groaned. "Any chance we can fight our way through?"

Gage thought a moment. "On the whole, I'd have to say no. Not given what I have seen and heard. There are lots of them. I counted as near as I was able earlier, guessing at how many outliers there are on sentry duty, and I came up with about three dozen, likely more. And that's just the men. There are more of them on through the pass. As I said, that seems to be where their homes lie. Deacon kept referring to it as the Chosen Valley."

"So making for the pass was a bad idea from the start." Bewley sighed. "Why on earth didn't the folks in Higgins warn us? We were there long enough for me to learn they weren't all members of this so-called church."

"I don't think they knew how ruthless the Brethren have become. Or maybe how angry they'd become with wagon trains driving through what they consider their land."

"Even if it is the main route out of Higgins westward."

"Even so. But there's something else, Bewley."

"Oh?"

As they spoke, they had retreated twenty feet or so with another man, from a nod by Bewley, quietly slipping in to fill his post on guard duty. Then he and Gage continued to a small campfire, where a number of haggard-looking men perched, tense and tired all at once, around the fire.

A large coffeepot sat quietly steaming on a flat rock to the side of the fire.

Without a word, Bewley poured a few swallows into two tin cups and handed one to Gage. They stood to one side, sipping and conversing.

Gage could not help but notice that the men all flicked hard looks his way. When he caught their eyes, they looked back to the fire quickly. A couple of them were whispering low and looking over at him.

"What's the other thing?" said Bewley over the rim of his cup. He kept his voice low.

Gage did the same with his reply. "That one I mentioned, the self-proclaimed Deacon, is most definitely the leader of the Brethren. I was hiding in the brush, not twenty feet from him and another man, a fellow named Schenk. He guided the fellow over, until they were no more than five, six feet from me. I kept still as a stone. Deacon kept referring to the fellow as his friend, that sort of thing. Then he knifed him in the gut twice."

"What?" said Bewley, his cup halfway to his mouth.

Gage nodded. "The second plunge was a heart blow, for the man stiffened with nary a sound and slipped to the ground and bled out. But he was dead when he hit."

"Oh, my word!" said Bewley in his low voice.

"Yeah, and this Deacon fellow said he was going to go comfort the man's wife tonight, the very woman with the baby from here. He also as much as said that the Church was a sham, that it was something he'd done in other places. But now that he has quite a following, it seems he intends to use the goods and money from this train to set himself up in a big house, to be built behind his own cabin in the valley."

"You got all this from your foray just now?"

Gage shrugged. "It helped that Deacon is a chatty fellow. Even when there's no one around. But the worst part is that he plans on the Brethren finding his so-called friend's body and blaming the killing on someone from here."

Bewley let out a low whistle through his teeth. He

tapped the cup's rim against the same teeth. "That ain't good."

For a few moments, neither man spoke. Then Bewley sighed. "Well, time for shut-eye. Sentry duty will come quick."

"I want in on that."

"Figured you would. I'll wake you in a couple of hours so we can spell some of the boys. Got your horse tied yonder, along the river end of camp."

CHAPTER 12

"When will you be back, Deacon?"

The man who asked was an eager man, a good farmer, anxious to please and to be useful to others, and willing to take on tasks that might otherwise be onerous.

Deacon released a theatrical sigh. "I will share with you, Samuels, that something among the Brethren is not right. Somebody has been . . . harmed, I believe, in some way. The Maker hasn't yet shared with me just what it means. But I must speak with Schenk."

He looked at Samuels, who stared back with wide eyes and nodded.

"I assume Schenk has ridden home," continued Deacon. "Likely to see how his wife is coping with the farm and being saddled with that heathen baby from the wagon train. I need to talk with him on . . . on urgent business. If I am incorrect and he shows up here, would you tell him that I have gone after him, and to come find me at his place? If he's not there, I shall wait for him. But not all night, I daresay. We have things to do!"

Samuels nodded. "But if you both happen to be

gone from here . . ." He shrugged his shoulders and his outstretched hands, palms up, took in the entirety of the largely quiet camp. Only the glow of two small fires cut through the night's darkness.

"Ah, what you are asking, Samuels, is, who is in charge of the men, at least until one of us returns. Is that correct?"

Samuels nodded and looked down at his boots.

Deacon pursed his lips and gazed skyward. "I have given this matter much thought in the past few days, Samuels, and it should come as no surprise to you that I would like to think I can rely on you to be our third in command. Not just for this mess"—Deacon wagged a hand southward—"of an interruption with the foolish heathens and all, but going forward."

He leaned closer to the man and lowered his voice. "I need folks I can rely on close to me. There are forces"—he cast his eyes to each side as if expecting untold enemies to lurch out of the dark at him—"who feel I am, shall we say, making decisions that require a broader agreement among Brethren members."

"But that's not how the Church is set up," said Samuels.

"That is exactly what I told them," said Deacon, nodding. "They don't seem to grasp the notion that the captain, say, is required to make the ship move forward. But you let the sailors of that same ship make all the decisions, and nothing—and I mean nothing—will get done, except the sails will slacken, the craft will drift, and never get anywhere at all. Eventually the crew will starve to death, and what will have been gained? This is especially sad, knowing that the Maker has provided us with all the fruits of reward we could dream of, if only we get to the land of goodness and light he has offered."

Samuel's eyebrows rose. It was obvious to Deacon that the man might be confused, which was what he intended. *If I keep the sap perplexed, he'll work himself to death on my behalf,* thought Deacon.

"So I take it from the solemn look on your face that I may rely on you, Samuels?"

"You bet, Deacon. I . . . I won't let you down."

"Good man. The Maker will be pleased knowing solid men are willing to steer the ship in the temporary absence of the captain."

As Deacon mounted up and looked down at the man, he said, "Pray, Brother Samuels, that all will be well among the Brethren."

"I will! I will, Deacon! I promise."

"Good." With that, Deacon turned the horse and, suppressing a smile, rode west along the pass road toward the valley of the Brethren. He smiled wide. He had done the right thing and he knew it. Right for whom?

"Why, for me," he chuckled as the horse trotted toward Schenk's homestead, and the man's unwitting widow. "And, of course, for the Maker." He shook his head. "Careful, Deacon. Otherwise, you just might begin to believe this nonsense yourself!"

His dry chuckle drifted into the otherwise-silent night as he rode on, grinning and thinking of the task ahead.

Chapter 13

The next morning, Gage and Bewley were touring the camp, lending a hand with tasks where they could.

"Is there any good news today, Bewley?" asked Gage.

"Well, one thing," said the old scout.

"What's that?"

"Folks found a freshwater spring smack-dab behind where we've snugged the camp, up close to the cliff yonder."

"That's good. There's also the river, for fish. For the time being anyway."

"Heck, everything here is for the time being, son." The scout winked and walked on.

"How many men are there in camp?" Gage questioned.

"Well, we started with near two dozen. We're down by two men, one's wounded, you met him, but he's game. Fights like he has nothing to lose."

"Maybe he feels he doesn't."

Bewley nodded. "I know what you're referring to, and that may well be. At least in his mind." He shrugged and set flame to the tobacco in his pipe. "Then we lost a good man. Fellow named Hastings. Those animals shot him in the back. He'd sent his wife and child ahead when the attack first come on, insisted on taking up the rear with his own wagon so the rest could get to safety. And it worked, too. He was able to slow down some of the attackers." Bewley shook his head. "But then those brutes got around him and he got bogged in the field. His wagon's still out there. They've near picked it clean. Shot him in the back when he tried to run for it."

"I saw that. It was awful."

"Doubly so for his wife and child."

As Gage walked briskly beside the old scout as they threaded their way through the tight damp, he was impressed with the efficiency of the setup. They'd parted the wagons that had earlier been jerked in close to the cliff wall, affording some space for them to set up a make-do kitchen.

There was even a growing pile of firewood tended by what looked to be two young boys, perhaps twelve years old. They went at the dragged-down trees with their axes, just like they were seasoned men working a woodlot. He was impressed.

There was a central fire, kept low and a little smokey, but it served the purpose that all fires do—be they in a stove or a fireplace in a house, or a campfire out of doors. They provided a central point, as with the heart in a body, from which all other vital tasks were made possible.

Gage saw that there were eight or so sentries posted

along the front edge of the camp, partially protected by wagons and stacked barrels and trunks and crates, and propped tailgates. And one of them appeared to be looking everywhere but toward the field.

Chase and an older farmer named Billings walked toward them. Chase was his usual narrow-eyed self, his hand resting on the butt of his revolver. He was just aching for Gage to give him the opportunity. How on earth did a fellow like him come to be on a wagon train of folks who seemed so darned normal?

"Morning, men," said Bewley. "Me and Gage here are going to check the possibility of getting across the river."

"Never mind that," said Chase. "Look here, Gage. I have let it be known among the train just who you are, and ain't a one of us who feels comfortable having you around."

There it is, thought Gage. He noted that Billings looked a bit red in the face and not inclined to look either him or Bewley in the eye.

"What's all this about?" said the scout, looking at Gage, then Billings, and clearly not at Chase.

Billings didn't say anything. Gage was going to, but Chase beat him to it.

"That there man!" He pointed at Gage with a long finger.

Gage thought that if Chase's hand had been six inches closer, he'd snatch that finger and snap it backward.

"He's a famous killer. Shot him, oh, about how many?"

Chase looked at Gage, a slight smile on his face. It was apparent he was enjoying himself. "Thirty? Forty men?"

"Chase, you're an idiot." Gage couldn't help himself. And it was not unpleasant to see the tall, thin man tense, his jaw muscles working, and the fingers on his right hand crabbing around his gun's butt.

"Oh," said Bewley, "that gunfighter business? You know how long ago that was, boy?"

"That makes no difference. A man is what he is and he don't change."

"Then that's unfortunate for you," said Bewley. He winked at Billings, then glanced at Gage.

The former gunfighter had to hand it to the scout—he was full of surprises, such as knowing and dismissing Gage's past identity. He was impressed that the old fellow was doing his best to keep the members of the wagon train at ease. Or as much as was possible, given they were being attacked and outnumbered.

Billings cleared his throat. "Aw, that can wait, Chase."

"But—"

"No, now what we need to do next is to try to talk to these folks. I'm certain if they just hear what we have to say, they'd be willing to let us pass on through their lands. Nobody's out to harm them or take anything of theirs, or even stay around! Ain't none of us want that."

"I'm afraid that's not how they see you, Billings," said Gage. "And it's not how they will treat you."

"I hear you on that, but somebody has to take the first step. A peaceful compromise is the only way to go about this."

Gage liked what the man had to say, but he knew more about the Brethren than Billings or any of them, and the Brethren weren't about to make a deal with anyone. Especially not after they discover the body of Schenk.

"Look, Billings, I don't disagree with you, but these Brethren folks are not about to bargain with you. I spied on them last night. They are ruthless and only want your goods."

"And then some!" said Bewley.

"That doesn't matter," said Billings, shaking his head. "The Good Lord says to turn the other cheek, and so we have to try."

Gage and Bewley exchanged glances, and the scout said, "Look, men, Gage isn't kidding."

"You expect any of us to take the word of a killer?" Chase was still seething, his fingers flexing as if he could not wait to draw on Gage.

Bewley sighed. "Billings, what is it you have in mind?" He said this as if he'd given up.

"We are going to send an emissary with a white flag, unarmed and obviously not harmful to them."

"Billings, look—"

"Shut it, killer!" Chase poked that finger at Gage again. Quick as lightning, Gage's right hand whipped outward and snatched that man's long, thin hand and encircled it with his thick, large hand. He squeezed, forcing the man's pointer finger skyward and Chase's knees dropping down in the opposite direction.

While he was slowly being rendered incapacitated,

Billings shocked Gage by gently reaching over and lifting free Chase's revolver and transferring it to his other hand. He held it out away from himself, between two work-thick fingers, obviously not intending to use it.

"Boy," said Gage, leaning in and down to Chase's gritted mouth, "you poke that finger in my sniffer once more and we're going to have to do something more than play slap and tickle about it. You understand me?

"Now I said I'm here to help, and I meant it. Nothing more, nothing less. I have no interest in killing anyone any more than Mr. Billings here does. I just want to see that you all aren't treated any worse than you already have been by those Brethren clowns. Got it?"

Chase said nothing, but tried to rise up to a standing position again. Gage worked the pressure on the man's digit a little harder.

Chase made pitiful, whimpering sounds. "Got it, got it. Let go!"

Gage did—after he gave the finger one last quick jerk. Chase pulled his hand free and held it down to his midsection. The encounter hadn't endeared Gage to the man, but then again, he didn't care what the fool thought of him.

"Now, Billings—" said Gage, but he was interrupted by Chase, saying, "Give me back my gun, Billings."

"Not just yet, son," said the mature farmer.

That appeared to put a damper on Chase's enthusiasm. He stood still, holding his sprained hand and scowling.

"Billings," continued Gage. "Those men mean business. They aren't going to let you all go, I just know it."

"We have to try," said Billings. "Or we are not Christians."

Gage let go a pent-up breath. "All right, then, so be it. What can I do?"

"Nothing," said Billings. "I will depart shortly."

"You?" said Bewley. "But you're a senior member of this here drive!"

"He's the one who arranged the whole thing!" said Chase, nodding as if it were his own accomplishment.

"Chase," said Billings. "Leave us for now."

"But . . . my gun."

"I will give it to you later."

The tall, childish fellow stomped off. Billings watched him a moment, then said, "He wants to marry my Evelyn. But that will not happen as long as I'm alive. He's too short-sighted."

That is a mild way of putting it, thought Gage.

"No way I can talk you out of this?" said Bewley.

"What?" said Billings with a smirk. "You mean I should reconsider him as a son-in-law?"

"No, I— Oh, man, you are a stitch. Look, Gage here doesn't lie. These Brethren folks are out for blood."

"I understand that, but a man ought not to stray from his convictions in life, you see?"

"What if those convictions get you killed?"

Billings offered a slight smile. "I have to try, men."

Neither Gage nor Bewley could argue. Billings turned and walked from them, still holding the revolver away from himself as if it were a writhing snake.

Several minutes later, out from the wagons stepped

Billings. He wore no coat, nothing clothingwise that might be construed as concealing a weapon. He wore no hat so that his face was plainly visible. Both arms were raised, and in his right hand, he held the end of a stick roughly three feet long from which was draped a bright white length of what looked to be cotton bedding.

It hung as a flag might, and a light breeze fluttered it. Billings waved it left, then right, slowly, and repeated this. He walked steadily, but with slow, measured steps, out into the middle of the open space. He made it about two hundred feet from the emigrant camp when a voice from the Brethren camp shouted, "Hold it right there, heathen!"

Billings halted, still holding the flag aloft.

"What do you want?" shouted the voice, and Gage guessed that the voice was Deacon's. It sounded thick and full of itself.

"We wish to negotiate with you! In good faith!"

"Ha! You are heathens and have no idea what 'faith' means!"

Even from his distance from the man, somewhat off to the east end of the scene, just enough to see the side of Billings's face, Gage saw the humble farmer flinch. He was, Gage had come to see, a true quiet and peaceful man of God—the truest he'd come across in some long time in all his travels. For he dared to risk his most precious thing, his own life, for the promise of peace, on the notion that there was goodness in everyone.

Gage did not like the odds Billings faced, but he hoped he would be surprised.

It was not to be.

A puff of smoke rose up from the Brethren camp, and on its heels a sharp sound parted the air. Billings was hit and spun around. He staggered and began to lean to his right, but held the flag aloft.

Gage saw a spot of blood spreading on the man's blue cotton shirt. Then another bullet jerked him the other way.

Screams and shouts of shock, then rage burst from the travelers' camp, but were stifled by return fire from one, then two, then nearly all of the sentries of the camp.

"Cover me!" shouted Chase, and before anyone could stop him, the tall young hothead, with his revolver barking and snapping, ran out, straight for his sweetheart's father.

The wagon train folks, with Gage and Bewley helping, lobbed enough lead at the Brethren that the air was filled with smoke.

Beyond all probability, Chase was able to bring Billings back without getting shot himself. But it was too late for the older farmer. He was near death, and drew his final breaths within moments of his wife and daughter bending low over him.

Gunfire from both camps dwindled and pinched out, and for a long time, the wagon train encampment was silent, save for the sobbing of Billings's womenfolk.

His death did not result in something that might please the pacifistic farmer. Instead, it incited the wagon train folks to create stronger bulwarks, bolstering their perimeter defenses with everything they could lay their hands on, including chests and trunks filled with clothing and personal goods.

All of this activity gave Gage a grim relief in knowing that the emigrants finally understood it was unlikely the zealots would ever negotiate with them.

They cut down more trees, careful to save every bit they could for cooking and warming fires, and they took stock of every bit of ammunition and weaponry, including items such as axes, hoes, and sickles that would be useful in close-in, hand-to-hand fighting, should it come to that.

And Gage saw no reason to think it wouldn't.

CHAPTER 14

"You doing this for any reason, son?" said Bewley.

"What do you mean?" Gage paused in loading his pockets with shells and regarded the man.

"I mean, well . . ."

"You mean, am I trying to gain favor with these folks? Trying to win them over?"

"Now, I didn't—"

Gage offered a half grin. "It's a fair question, Bewley. But no, I have no urge to win any friends. I don't have many, and I don't need many, and I prefer it that way. Keeps life less complicated."

"Sounds lonely to me," said the old scout.

Gage said nothing, but shrugged and checked his pockets.

"So, why are you doing this? I know all that business you said before about not liking to see folks getting stomped on by big, rank, ill-intentioned folks, but . . ." Bewley let that thought trail off, mostly because he didn't know quite how to round off his point.

"Isn't that enough of a reason? Or have we all

become too suspicious of one another that we always assume there has to be more of a motive behind everything we do?" Gage paused and looked at the old-timer hard. "You think I'm in this for some gain? Maybe on the side of the Brethren, after all?"

If he had reached out and backhanded the old scout across the mouth, Gage could not have received a more surprised expression staring back at him. A cold look followed the surprise, and Bewley lowered his voice. "If you think that, Gage, then you and me, we ain't got much more to discuss."

"No, I don't really think that, Bewley. Just wanted to give you a taste of someone doubting you."

"Oh, I get it. All right, all right. I deserve that shot."

"It's how I live my life these days, cat-footing through them, not looking for trouble, but somehow finding it anyway. I figured a long time ago that if this was how it was going to be, I might as well give in to it and do whatever good I can along the way. Until . . ."

"Until?" said Bewley.

"Until it all catches up with me. Bound to one of these days. I only hope when it does land in my lap that I won't fold like a poor hand of cards, and whine and beg and grovel. The folks I killed don't deserve that."

Bewley said no more, but slid his revolver out of its holster and handed it to Gage, butt first.

Gage didn't take it, but looked down at the walnut-handled tool. "What's this?"

The old scout rolled his eyes. "They call it a pistol. I thought you might know that by now."

"Ha ha. I mean," said Gage, still not taking it from his hand, "why are you offering it to me?"

"Because you don't seem to carry one, and where you're going, you'll need more than some old-relic rifle and a hip knife."

"Hey, I'll have you know this rifle has kept me from starving on the trail, thanks very much. And as for the knife, it was a lucky find some time back in a mercantile. Originally belonged to a 'mountainy man,' as the fellow who sold it to me said. One of his kind found him killed and buried him, then gathered up the man's goods and sold them. I hope the money went to the man's family back East somewhere, but who knows? It's been one heck of a knife. Slices meat, chops kindling, and makes a decent defensive weapon, should the need arise."

"And has it?" said Bewley, still holding out his pistol.

"A few times, yes. Once against a timber rattler."

"Judging by the fact that you're still here, I'd say the rattler came out shorter than he woke up that day."

"That's about it, yes. Hated to do it, but as an old English cowhand I know once said, 'Needs must.'"

"So, how about it? You going to take the pistol or not?"

"I thank you, Bewley, but no. I'll stick with my trusty pieces for now. I'm balanced out and I will need that if I'm going to get in there and cause a ruckus."

"What do you have in mind?" said the scout, sliding his gun back into its holster.

"That remains to be seen. I just don't know until I

get in there, but if I can knock a few heads before they know I'm there, I might be able to . . . well, I just don't know. I don't usually plan these things too far in advance. My experience with planning is that there's someone somewhere in charge and he's just waiting on us to make plans so he can toss troubles at our feet and then watch us stumble around."

"I hear that. In fact, that's why I have decided I can't do any more good here. At least for the time being." Bewley held his hands on his waist and surveyed the camp, all the bustling folks, the sentries, the lot of them.

"You mean you're leaving them?"

"Sure I am," he said. "I signed on to be a scout, and that part's done for now."

"Oh," said Gage, not certain of what he was hearing.

Then Bewley grinned. "Had you wondering, didn't I? Naw, I only mean that I'm going with you, that's all."

"Oh no! No, Bewley. Look, I appreciate it, but I do better working on my own. That much I know about myself."

"That's too bad, because I'm going with you. Already decided it, and when I decide a thing, I don't backtrack. Got no interest in seeing where I been, only where I'm headed." He turned and made for the riverbank. "You coming?"

Gage growled and grumbled as he strode after the light-footed, buckskin-clad old fellow; then he realized, as he always did, seemingly too late, that grumbling and growling and grousing never made a bit of difference to the task at hand. It still needed doing, no matter how much whining he got up to. So he shut up and walked astride of the scout.

"What about the others?"

"Oh," said Bewley, waving a hand. "I already sorted it out. Everybody knows, and they're on top alert, especially after those beasts murdered Billings."

Gage nodded. "You already know I don't have a plan beyond getting up and over that massive granite knob behind the camp, right?"

"Yep. Good thing you got me along." Bewley tapped his temple. "'Cause I got me one whopper of a plan."

They reached the riverbank, eyeing with care up and down, before they broke cover from the trees. "Going to let me in on this plan of yours?" said Gage.

"Nope. Not all at once."

"You don't have any more of a plan than I do, do you?" said Gage in a whisper.

Bewley looked at him and Gage grinned.

"Was it that plain? I am usually a world-class fibber. Must be out of practice."

"You don't play poker, do you, Bewley? I'd recommend against it."

The scout stepped into the water, the icy flow reaching up to his knees tight against the bank. A shiver rippled up his spine. "Never could understand folks who gamble. What a waste of hard-to-come-by earnings." He shook his head and kept wading, his own rifle held in his right hand. As with Gage's, it was ready to swing into a firing position.

Gage stepped into the river just after Bewley did and

kept an eye upstream, eastward, and across the way. Fortunately, the far bank hadn't much in the way of trees, and what shrub and brush there was would not conceal a man, as the foliage was mostly long gone. The tangles of gray pricking branches hid little, save for the small black entrance holes of rabbits and other riverside critters.

They walked westward with the flow, and when they were about even with the far-off wagon train camp to their right, with the mass of raw gray rock against which it was wedged tight, they slowed.

Gage looked behind and then to the far shore once more, then edged up beside Bewley. He wanted to see around the bend that cut to the right.

It wasn't a sharp curve, but enough to conceal men with guns. Gage stepped forward and took the lead. If it offended the older man, he didn't make it known. Gage did so with intention, as he had wanted to do this on his own anyway. Bewley seemed competent enough that Gage didn't think he had to worry about the man.

"Anything?" said his companion in a whisper.

The loudest sound was the flow around a fallen tree ahead that created a bobbing wash of low, irregular splashes and gurgles.

"Nothing yet." Gage continued on, the rifle butt tucked just under his left armpit. If someone drew on them or jumped at them, he wanted to be ready.

It went on like this for another forty feet or so; then they came to a rocky promontory that looked to have been boulders that tumbled down from the cliffs to their right. Gage glanced up to see juts of rough-edged rock high above, several crags of which looked as if they wanted to drop away from the mother rock at any moment.

If they did, they'd hit the mass of shale and boulder-strewn slope to their right, and then continue on, crashing likely right into, onto, and over Bewley and Gage. He pulled in a deep breath and continued on.

Wading the river was the only way, or so they had suspected, of getting around the rocky mess, and they were relieved to note that they had chosen the best of the paltry options available to them.

They climbed up and out of the river, clambering over the rubble pile, their steps awkward and dangerous. A wrong-placed boot could mean a snapped ankle and an end to whatever meager progress they'd made.

They paused to catch their breath and glanced up and down the river, across the flow, and back to their right, into the tree cover beyond which sat the camp.

"Still don't know if we'll be able to get up and over that hard menace up there!" Bewley was breathing hard, but his color was good and he looked as fit as Gage felt, which meant they were each ready to move on. Gage decided that if he made it to whatever age the old scout was, he hoped he was in as good a shape.

"I think the land tapers down a bit up there a ways, beyond the back of the cliffs."

Bewley nodded. "Let's get to it. We'll find out soon enough, if we don't run into any Brethren first."

They stepped once more into the flow, hugging the

riverbank. They'd gone a dozen feet when Gage stepped into water that rose well above his knees. He held up a hand. "Deep here. Have to cut wide toward midstream."

"That's dicey. Might be exposed, but there's nothing for it." They both moved to their left, following the shallower edge of that dark pool. Gage knew enough about sizable rivers to know it could well be eight or a dozen feet down to the bottom. And neither man thought much of the notion of swimming the fifteen or so feet across it.

They'd made it back to water below knee high. An unspoken agreement led Bewley to keep an eye behind them and Gage ahead.

Just as Gage shifted his gaze from the riverbanks before them, cutting his sight line to his left and up, a shot echoed and something drove like a demonic bee down at them, punching into the water between them.

Both men spun to their left, rifles shouldered. With no more thought than it takes to pull in half a breath, Gage sighted and, as if he was back ten years and standing in a dusty Texas street, time slowed and he touched the trigger of his old meat-maker rifle.

The shot was true, and a tall, thin man in black, but wearing a white shirt, yipped a tight, quick, coyote-like sound, and then folded forward. He dropped his rifle and it spun, end for end, clattering off sharp rocks as it traveled downward.

The man's heavy body did the same, a pinch of a moment later. His hat was the next thing he lost. It pinwheeled and sailed away into the treetops far below him, yet up to their left, behind the wagon camp.

The man's arms flailed as if he were trying, despite a lack of wings, to gain mastery of the air. It didn't work and he dropped hard and fast.

That's when time regained itself and sound washed back into Gage's ringing ears just as the man smacked with his upper back off a horse-size wedge of rock before continuing on downward and outward.

That hit lessened his arm waving, but it wasn't until he smacked headfirst—an explosion of red spray plumed outward—against another outcrop that Bewley and Gage knew the fellow was well and truly dead.

His body slammed to a stop right below that, with one leg and an arm hanging off the edge, all that was visible to them.

Both men held their positions, with Gage glancing quickly upstream, and Bewley doing the same behind them. So far, there were no others lurking that they might be able to see.

Finally Bewley whistled low. "That man won't pester us anymore. I know you might not want to hear this, but I will tell you, I never saw a shot like that in all my days."

"You're right," said Gage. "I don't want to know." He bent and puked in the river, dragged a cuff across his mouth, and said, "Let's get back to the riverbank before his chums show up and finish what he started."

"You bet."

They'd slogged a good twenty more feet downstream,

doing their best to hurry it along, when they heard shouts from on high.

The cliff top was above them by at least seventy feet, but it was not a distance a bullet would think twice about traveling.

"To the base, quick!" growled Gage. He slogged ahead and gained the rocky embankment as the first of a volley of shots sizzled down at them. Their only cover would be an overhang of sorts jutting along the river farther downstream, perhaps fifty feet away. Gage glanced back to the scout, who was himself just emerging from the water. "Hurry up, Bewley!"

"Keep your hair on, boy!"

Gage continued to be impressed with the man. He was at least old enough to be Gage's father, yet he moved nearly as quick as Gage, and he kept cool in a tight situation.

Bewley made it to him and they hotfooted right to the craggy, uneven wall above, confident that the shooters—Gage thought there were at least two, no more than three—had lost sight of them.

As they scooted along, the shots from above kept on plinking and zipping down, now closer in, but they weren't able to reach them, which told Gage they weren't seen from above. And that suited him just fine. Twenty more feet and they would be able to duck under the overhang for certain cover.

He arrived to it first and found that it sported what looked to be a charred ceiling, similar to the campsite he'd spent an agreeable time in, not long before. If he had the time, he assumed he'd also find more of that mysterious artwork painted on and chipped into the sloped ceiling.

"Well," said Bewley, crouching beside him, "that wasn't unexpected. Shot one of theirs, they'll do the same."

"Yeah," said Gage. "But it's a shame. Now they know we're out and about, and what's more, unless they're idiots, and I know they're not, they'll have a pretty good guess as to what we plan on doing by traveling downstream like this. Especially only two of us."

"Yep," said Bewley, "but there are enough holes in that notion that we might find one big enough to climb through."

"What do you mean?"

"They might be smarter than we want them to be, but they're greedy and they might not think we're worth the effort of a big push. With any luck, they'll keep most of their men back around the wagon site. That'll leave us to deal with a handful of those brutes. Might be, we can spoil their days for them." He winked.

"But it won't happen if we stay here," said Gage, making for the far end of the overhang.

"Right." Bewley scrambled close behind. "Good thing I ain't as tall as you, or I'd forever be whacking my head against the rocks hereabouts."

Not ten seconds after Bewley said this, Gage came to the end of the overhang and poked out a bit, intending to scout. But he stood too soon and clunked the back of his head against the rock. *"Gah!"* he growled. "See what you made me do?"

Bewley chuckled. "Been blamed for a whole lot of things in my life, most of them I earned, but not another fellow smacking his bean, that's for certain. See anything?"

"The brush is too thick, but it looks to me as if the rocky knob pinches out not far ahead. And there might even be a game trail."

"Good. I about had enough of this skulking around like we're the ones who've done wrong in this setup!"

They made for the spot and it was indeed a game trail. And judging from the hoofprints close to the river, where the rocky debris from the mass of rock now behind them turned to hoofprint-stippled sand and muck, it was still in regular use.

"Well," whispered Bewley, "if all else fails, we know we can make meat!" He chuckled at his own wit and they proceeded to climb, with Gage in the lead. They half expected to see a black-clothed shadow up ahead, or to one side, but they saw none.

"So far, so good," muttered Gage.

They followed the game trail, even though it brought them on a long stretch paralleling the river. It climbed upward, though westward. They both recognized this would not be a bad thing, as it was taking them away from the rocky knob, which formed the southern side of the pass, and so, of the Brethren camp.

Just when Gage thought they'd have to depart from the game trail and carve their own way back toward the northern rim of the slope, the trail began its own meandering cut in that direction. He grunted his approval and kept on, watching ahead and to the sides, trusting that Bewley was doing the same to their back trail.

The terrain leveled and provided them cover from above in the form of a jut of boulder, so Gage paused and was not surprised to see Bewley not six feet behind, and not winded much from the climb up the incline.

"Good place to take stock, see if either of us has any more idea of what we'll get up to, once we draw closer to the camp."

"Yep," said the scout, leaning beside Gage against the rock. They both faced downslope.

The massive granite chunk was taller than they were by a foot or so, and wide enough to shield half-a-dozen men. Gage wondered if it had cleaved off the rocky knob to their left, visible aplenty looming beyond and above the rabbit brush and sparse tree growth. It was an arid place, suited more to heat-loving ponderosas that favored thin, sandy soil.

"If I were a tree," said Gage, letting his thoughts come out in words, "I wouldn't mind rooting hereabouts."

"Oh, I would. This close to them Brethren fools? Bah, as soon as they moved into the region, I'd have tugged up my roots and skedaddled elsewhere."

"Where to?" said Gage, wishing he'd brought a canteen.

"Anywhere but here."

They were silent a moment; then Gage said, "I hadn't expected to have anyone along with me, so my plan was to scout the perimeter of their camp, as much as I can anyway, and get a sense of how they're set up. Might be able to see a weakness or a flaw of some sort. If I have the time, I thought I'd take a look at their so-called Chosen Valley, but I don't know how far west it lies."

"Yeah, that's about as far as my paltry planning got, too."

Gage glanced at him. Bewley was smiling.

"So?" said Gage. "Anything more specific to add?"

The scout thought a moment. "We don't have enough man power or bullets to do much more than kill a few before they'd descend on us like starved coyotes."

Gage nodded, and said nothing.

"But, we could set fire to a few things. Items they might find of use. Wagons or such. Maybe they stash their ammunition in a central spot."

"The fire idea gave me a thought," said Gage.

"I'm listening."

"Seems like most of the men are here, bent on dealing with your wagon train. But to hear them speak, and from what evidence we've seen, they are farmers. I grew up on a ranch, which is a whole lot like a farm, and one thing I know is that ranches require a pile of daily work. Chores don't wait because a man has a wild hair about stealing from another man."

"I think I'm getting you," said Bewley, a slow grin spreading on the mouth hidden halfway by his beard.

Gage nodded. "We make for the settlement—it can't be that far if they're riding back and forth, spelling each other. We can get a sense of what it looks like, and maybe cause a little havoc there. A fire or something. I don't know yet. I think we'll need to see it before we can decide exactly what to do. That might draw some of them back from tormenting the wagon train."

"I like how you think, Gage."

"Only trouble is, there will be the families—wives, children, old-timers."

"Yah," said Bewley. "There's that. Well, as you say, we'll play it as it comes up. Might be, we can scare some of them off. But if we can set enough distracting fires, or some such, that'd be certain to bring back most, if not all, of them. At least I'd think so."

Both men leaned there, guns at the ready, yet each mired in thought. Then Gage spoke: "Maybe we save fire as a last option. I'd hate to turn families out to face the coming winter with no place to go, nothing to keep them warm."

"You don't mind me saying so, Gage. But for a fellow with as ruthless a reputation as you are supposed to have, you sure are a softy."

"I'll take that as a compliment."

They'd been talking low, and each eyeing the downslope and their respective sides of the boulder and trail. In that last pause, Gage looked up, then glanced at Bewley.

The old scout narrowed his eyes and held his tongue and his pose, the first trick a seasoned hunter knew to do. It was what game did when it was being pursued. It held, be it prairie chicken or mule deer or rabbit or snake.

Then they each heard it—a soft, light scuffing sound.

Each man looked at the other. Gage angled his head to the left, nodded at Bewley, and then to the right. The old man nodded once. Gage sighed and said, "Aw, I don't know. Maybe those Brethren folks are just too smart for us. This whole thing has come as quite a shock, really."

As he spoke, he moved, catlike, to his left, shifting his rifle around to bear on whoever or whatever might be there. Something was there, making that scuffing sound.

As he let his last words taper, he glanced at Bewley, who was in position as well. Each man nodded, then Gage leapt away, free of the cover the rock provided. Bewley did the same.

Neither man said a thing, but each saw at the same moment what it was they'd heard, and they both kept their rifles trained on it. For they each knew that there could be nothing deadlier than a twelve-year-old boy.

This one was armed with a gun, too, a service revolver far too large for his thin arms, but he held it fairly steady, right on Gage. The kid glanced jackrabbit fast to his right and saw Bewley, but cut his gaze back to Gage.

They also saw that the kid was likely a Brethren offspring, given his attire—black trousers, leather braces, and a white shirt. Atop his head sat a black hat, looking to be a handed-down affair, given that it sat low and bent the lad's ear tops forward as if they were hinged.

His eyes were wide, but his mouth was set tight and his lips pursed.

"Two on one, boy," said Gage. He did his best to keep from trembling. It had been a problem for him since giving up the life of the gun years before. Never more so than when he was facing down someone who ought not be carrying a weapon for any purpose other than for hunting. And anyone carrying a revolver in the woods, creeping too quiet, had to be up to no good. But that didn't matter.

Here I am, thought Gage. *Holding a rifle on a boy. One bad slip and that'd be it for either of us.*

"Set that thing down, son," said Bewley, stepping boldly upslope, feeling the incline, the leaves and twigs and stones and roots with one moccasin-clad foot leading the way.

"Won't," said the kid. "Won't do it."

"Why?" said Gage, drawing his brows together. Maybe he could keep the kid chatting, give Bewley some sort of advantage. It was a tricky situation. He didn't doubt for a moment, given how calm the boy seemed, that the gun was loaded.

"Because I heard you two chatting. Going to burn down our farms, our homes, leave us all to die in the snow and cold. No, sir!" The kid raised the revolver a few inches, narrowing one eye and taking careful aim on Gage.

This is it, thought Gage, for he knew as sure as the sun rose and set each day that he could not pull a trigger on a mere boy. He had a hard enough nowadays doing so on rascals and rogues, men who had caused others dire harm or were about to, let alone a boy.

"You didn't let us finish the conversation, son," said Gage, adopting Bewley's word of choice for any male, it seemed, younger than him, which was just about everyone.

"Heard enough."

"What makes you think you know the entire story, then?"

"Know enough."

"What do you know?" Gage played it out because he'd seen the whisker of a flinch touch the corner of the kid's mouth.

"Killed my father, you all did."

"I assure you neither of us killed anyone." Gage wondered briefly if the man they'd shot off the cliff had been the boy's father. It was unlikely, because it hadn't happened that long before.

"You all. The heathens in the wagon train."

"How'd he die, son?" said Bewley.

The kid flinched then, unnerved by the voice to his other side, from a man he was not doing a very good job of keeping in sight.

Despite this promising development, Gage did not move, save for angling his rifle barrel a pinch to the right, just enough to graze the boy's upper left arm. If Gage could shoot while dodging to his own right, he might be able to avoid the killing shot the boy seemed intent on delivering.

"You know. You know how he died!"

This was the first time the kid showed that much fire, startling Gage.

"No, no, we don't. Nothing we did, I can tell you that, son."

"Don't call me 'son.' I ain't *your son*! I am his. Was his! And you killed him! Stabbed him and left him for dead!"

That's when Gage felt certain he knew who the kid was. And who the kid's father was. Schenk. The one that Deacon gutted right in front of him. Gage loathed himself at that moment. *Yep, it was just a flare-up of rage, but why hadn't I done something to prevent it?* Gage thought.

As quickly as the fire flared in him, it subsided, because he knew there had been nothing he could have done. A thought came to him that he might not have been able to save the father, but he might yet be able to save the son.

And then another thought followed on the heels of that one—Deacon had said he was going to make sure he took care of the dead man's wife, was going to comfort her. But there was something off about this. And then Gage knew—it was the timing. If he could convince the kid . . .

"Boy, when did Deacon go to your house and tell your mother about your father's death, hmm?" Gage made sure to avoid the word "son."

That rattled the kid and he thought for a moment that he'd blown his slim chance by blurting too much, too soon.

"What are you saying?" the kid asked.

"I'm saying," said Gage, careful to choose his words

with caution, "that I saw Deacon stab your father, twice, and he told him that he was going to go to your house and comfort your mother. Am I right, kid? Did Deacon show up at your house last night?"

"No! That's a lie, mister!"

"No, son, it ain't," said Bewley. "And I'm right sorry to say it, because no man should lose his pappy like that. But shooting us won't end this thing any sooner. And it has to end, you know."

"It will end when all the heathens are driven out of our land like the scourge they are!"

"You been listening to that Deacon fella, haven't you?" said the scout.

"Course! He's our leader. And he's . . . Deacon was a good friend of my father! You are heathen liars, just like Deacon said. Now get over there with him!" The kid glanced toward Bewley once more, risking averting his eyes from Gage for a brief moment.

Gage made his move, knowing it would not end well for him. But he was running low on choices with each moment that passed.

He ducked low to his right and barreled for the kid. At the same time, as the kid was glancing at Bewley, who he was trying to get to comply with his intentions, the old man had not wasted his own scant opportunities.

Before the kid shifted his attention to him, the scout had covered the ground between them, a distance he had been nibbling down with each moment the kid looked away. He was a nimble old fellow in his moccasins, and as silent as a Lakota Sioux brave on the warpath.

He didn't shoot the kid, but he did slam into the kid's right side with force and intention. He hit him so as to spin the boy. If the blow didn't knock the revolver free of his hands, Bewley felt certain his slamming blow would at least spin the youth toward him.

As it happened, both possibilities came to pass, and Bewley landed atop the boy in a spraddle-legged sprawl, his own revolver held on high in his left hand. The kid's dropped revolver slipped from his grasp and spun away in the air.

Gage had been making his own move toward the kid and saw the gun drop. He also knew that a fully cocked revolver dropped like that would, more often than not, fire. And in this instance, it was anyone's guess as to where it would deliver its deadly messenger.

The boom of the big handgun rattled the sloped glade this scene played out in, and was followed immediately with the distinctive spanging, whining *zing* of a bullet that had just ricocheted off rock.

Instinct drove both men to jerk low, though Gage knew that since the bullet bounced off the rock, it could have gone anywhere, and most likely at any height.

Nobody grunted, screamed, or moaned, and Gage knew he'd not been hit, or at least he didn't think so. He'd check himself later for blood. But right now, he was busy.

But not busier than Bewley, who had managed to subdue the wriggling youth to some degree.

Since Bewley still held his own gun high in his hand and away from the boy, Gage knew that it was only a matter of moments before the boisterous kid landed a solid blow to the old man. And as Gage scurried to them, now on his knees, he kicked the kid's revolver farther away with his left boot, then laid his right hand on the kid's thrashing left arm. He'd already flailed a couple of solid knocks to the side of the scout's head.

"Easy, boy! Easy!" Gage shoved his rifle behind him and laid his left hand over the kid's chest. The boy tried to arch up and bite at him, but was too far to render him any harm.

Not so with his right boot, however, as it whipped upward and drove squarely between Bewley's buckskin-clad legs. High up enough that the old gent wheezed and groaned and crab-walked his way to the side and off the kid, leaving Gage to deal with the feisty varmint himself.

Not a problem, he thought, and proceeded to crush the kid from the side, keeping those kicking boots of his away from his own crotch.

"Get off! Get off me!"

"Not so fast, boy," said Gage, trying to flip the kid over. He suspected he'd have a whole lot more control of the situation if the kid were chewing gravel instead of bellowing in his face.

He was close to dosing the kid with a quick backhand across his biting, lippy mouth, just to startle him, but he couldn't spare the hand just yet.

The thought of doing that brought to mind his own father, and the regular lashings and backhands and punches young Jonathan himself had received at the hands of the old brute.

So instead of striking the boy, knowing that would only make relations with him worse than they were, Gage wasted no more time on growling at the kid. He gritted his teeth, and with a heave, he flipped the wiry youth over, first onto his right side, where he clawed and kicked, and then Gage slammed him face down on the rubble-strewn slope.

That seemed to knock the wind out of the kid for a moment, and Gage knew enough to not let off his pressure on the boy. He caught his own breath and felt the kid, still tense and breathing hard and fast as his wind came back, tensing and ready for more struggle.

Gage had to hand it to the boy, he was a fighter. Gage glanced to his left and saw Bewley's normal color rising back into the cheeks above his voluminous whiskers. There was also a flinty look in his eyes.

"You all right, Bewley?"

"Been better," said the old-timer, after a few more puffs of his cheeks. "But I reckon I'll live." He knee-walked on over, and helped Gage subdue the kid, having already slid his own revolver back into his holster.

He took pains to make certain he kept the gun's side to his right, away from the boy's grasping, flailing left arm. Then he grabbed that arm by the wrist and helped fold it around, behind the kid's back.

"Got a rope?" said Gage, huffing as he worked to kneel on the backs of the kid's legs as he held the boy's right arm behind his back.

"Nope," said Bewley, "but I have a strip of rawhide that'll do."

As he said it, the scout freed a hand and rummaged in an inner pouch pocket of his buckskin tunic. Both men had left their new wool coats behind, back at the camp, each wondering if they'd ever see them again.

Next to a horse, which each man had also bid a worried farewell to, Gage reckoned that a new, practical, and, as a bonus, handsome article of clothing, such as a coat, was a tool every bit as useful as a gun, a knife, or boots.

But they had to travel light and generate their own warmth. The day had turned out decent so far, not too cold, though he knew that would change later.

He got himself adjusted, pinning the kid's flailing legs with his knees, and reached up to help Bewley, who was struggling, trying to ready the rawhide while keeping a grip on the kid's left hand.

"Thanks," said the old scout. He made quick work of it, and Gage guessed the man had experience, somewhere in his long past, of roping and tying off calves' feet for branding.

All this time, the kid had been making growling, angry noises, and he finally got his head turned to the left. After he finished spitting out gravel and bits of leaves and twigs from the slope, he commenced to shouting.

Gage wasn't too worried, because the kid's position was such that he wasn't able to pull in a big lungful of air, and half his face was mashed into the dirt.

"Gonna have to gag him, Gage," said Bewley, giving voice to the thought Gage had himself just come to.

"Yep," he said, tugging out his own oversize kerchief, which he kept folded and tucked inside his vest's inner pocket. It was a much-used blue-and-white affair of thick yet soft cotton, large enough that he often tied it around his face in a snowstorm or windstorm or when riding drag on a trail drive, which he'd had to do more than he liked over the years.

To date, he'd not had to use it to hush up an unruly adversary. *But then again,* he mused as he worked to inch it beneath the kid's neck, *that's what life is all about, new experiences.*

He grinned, thinking that he'd much rather see a fine new vista than deal with this enraged youngster.

"Glad you find this amusing!" said Bewley.

"Oh, just thinking of all the fun I'm missing out on."

"Oh, you and me both, man," said Bewley. "Cursed Brethren fools, went and ruined a perfectly good journey for us all!" He leaned close to the snarling kid. "Yes, and that means you, too, unruly child that you are!"

"Feel better?" said Gage, tying off the bandanna as best he could.

"No, but the day ain't over yet. Now let's get this whelp upright and see what we need to do next, okay?"

Gage nodded and, shifting his weight off the kid's pinned legs, kept a firm grip on the lad's arms. He jerked him upright, spinning him around to a seated position on the slope before them, and out of kicking range of them.

"Hoo-boy," said Bewley. "If eyes could fire bullets, we'd be goners now. Look, kid, I don't think we can convince you of a thing. Fact, I *know* we can't. But we have ourselves a problem now—and it's you."

Bewley looked at the kid, who was breathing hard through his nose, with dirt and sandy bits stuck to the right side of his face. The scout reached toward him to brush it off and the kid shied and shouted around the gag, but he wasn't able to make much of a sound. His nostrils worked and Gage felt awful.

He no longer saw much of the raw rage on the kid's face. It was replaced with a fear that danced in those dark eyes. "We truly don't want to hurt you, kid," Gage said. "Look, if we wanted to, we would have already. All we want to do is try to figure out how to get you Brethren from killing us."

"What say we trade promises, all right?" Bewley let the question hang there.

Gage was interested, too, in what Bewley had in mind.

"I know that you think we're heathens, and all that foolishness," the old man continued, "but what say we promise not to cause you any harm, right? And in return, you promise us not to scream and shout or try to run off, at least not until we all come to some sort of agreement. Okay?"

The kid just stared at him. His breathing had begun to slow. Eventually, after long moments, perhaps half a minute, he nodded once—a curt, quick nod—but there it was.

"All right, then," said Gage. "I'll untie the gag and we can all talk like civilized men."

He reached slowly so the kid wouldn't flinch, and with one hand, he untied the knot he'd made behind the kid's neck. He tugged the bandanna free and let the kid stretch his jaw and move his head back and forth.

Then the kid looked at Gage and then at Bewley and pulled in a deep breath.

Gage never saw the old man's move, but all of a sudden, there was his revolver, in his hand as if conjured. Bewley's half-cocked gun was leveled right at the kid's chest.

"We had us a deal, son." Bewley's voice was low and even. "You don't see the heathens among us laying into you with knives or guns, do you?"

"You almost just did," said the kid, eyes narrowed. The fear on his face, Gage noted, had once more been shoved aside. But it was there, and Gage was glad of it, for it might just keep the kid alive. *Everybody needs a little fear in their hearts,* he thought. *Otherwise, they'll end up as a grizzly's dinner, or dangling from a rope.*

"I pulled that gun on you to show you how quick retribution can be if you cheat a man," said Bewley. "Now, me and him, we're real sorry about your pap. That's a rum deal. Now, I know you have no reason to trust a thing we're saying, but I'm telling you straight out, when he said Deacon did for your father, he meant it."

The kid looked at Gage. "Then why didn't you stop him?"

Gage nodded. "I would have, but he was too quick. He put his arm around your father and . . ." Then Gage remembered something, something that might help the kid believe them.

What was it? Deacon said something. He called the kid's father something.

"And what?" said the kid, his eyes flaming and his bottom jaw outthrust.

"And I'm just remembering. Deacon called your father Schenk, so I assume that's your surname. But he also called him his second-in-charge, something like that, and . . . what was that? Oh yes, he called him Old Reliable. Does that mean anything to you? He said something such as 'Schenk, remember that name I gave you, Old Reliable?'"

Gage knew he'd hit a hard nerve in the kid's memory, for his rage-twisted face froze and his eyes glistened with angry tears. "Deacon, he always says, said, that my father is . . . was his right-hand man. He called my father that name all the time—Old Reliable. I think Papa liked it. I bet it made him feel like he was doing good. Deacon, he has names for folks he likes. He says the names are part of the studies from the Old Book. Only his special chosen helpers get those names. But he only ever says them to that person when they're discussing something important."

"Then how do you know that's the name he gave your father?"

The kid looked at his lap and didn't look up. After a few moments, Gage saw that the kid's cheeks and ears had turned red. He thought the kid might be fighting back tears. When he spoke, his voice was hoarse and little more than a whisper. "I heard Deacon call him it."

He kept looking at his lap, but he seemed to have sagged into himself, and looked older than he had moments before. "Only time Papa ever beat me was when he found out I'd been hiding when Deacon and him were talking. I did it a couple of times. 'Nobody else was supposed to hear those things!' he shouted at me. Then he gave me a smack across the face. He didn't talk to me for a day, that's how important the Church is, was, to him." He looked up at Gage.

"Then you know he ain't lying to you," said Bewley.

"No," said the kid, in a calm, level voice, but looking right at Gage. "He could have heard that and then killed my papa."

Gage nodded. "That's true. I could have. But I didn't. And that's all I can say on the matter."

Again, for a short while, they were silent. Bewley and Gage waited on the boy to decide what might happen next. Then the kid spoke.

"Suppose I believe you. Why would Deacon want to do that? Papa is, or was, his second-in-charge of the Church. You heard it yourself! He called Papa his right-hand man, and Old Reliable. He—" The kid stopped there.

Something, thought Gage, *must be forcing doubt into the boy's mind.*

EVERYBODY HAS A GUN

The two men watched the possibility occur to the boy for the first time that perhaps Deacon was not a truthful man. Maybe even a murderous one.

He shook his head. "No, no, I just can't believe it."

"Fine," said Gage. "But I think we should pay a visit to your mother and that new baby she has."

"How'd you know that baby went home to my mama?"

"Because I heard Deacon talking about that, too."

"You know, son," said Bewley, "that baby has a mama already. And a papa, and even a big brother. And none of them are bad folks. They're grieving just as hard as you are, because right now, they think you Brethren folks stole that baby and killed her."

"What?" The kid sat up straight. "No! That's not true. We don't kill folks for no reason—especially not babies!"

"Then help us prove that," said Gage. "Let's go see your mother and we'll explain all this to her as well. Okay?" Gage didn't wait for a response. He grabbed the back of the kid's trousers and hoisted him to a standing position.

"Now let's go. On up the hill. And at the first sign of you playing us false, we promise we'll set fire to the first Brethren building we come to."

Bewley spoke to Gage in a low voice: "Do you think the kid's mother will listen to us?"

"No idea," said Gage. "But we have to try." He turned back to the kid. "And don't worry, I'll bring this revolver of yours along."

"It was my papa's."

"Fine. You'll get it back. If you do as we say."

They had nothing else to gather up, so they all turned and trudged on up the steep slope, the bulk of the big rocky knob sitting cold and gray through the trees far to their right.

Gage surmised that once they crested the ridge above, they would be granted a view of whatever it was the Brethren held so dear they felt compelled to murder and steal to keep folks from traveling through it.

He had no idea what he was about to see.

CHAPTER 15

"They got us pinned down here," said Chase, risking a look toward the northeast, where he thought the nearest Brethren sniper lay in wait. It was the fourth time in as many minutes he'd done so.

"If you don't simmer down, you'll get yourself killed," said a short, pudgy man everybody called Gramps, despite the fact that he was traveling alone and had never mentioned having a family of his own, let alone children and grandchildren.

"Well, what do you suggest we do?" Chase plunked down on the nail keg and crossed his arms. "They got us pinned down here, and our food's going to give out long before they get sick of keeping us—"

"Pinned down?" Gramps asked with a grin.

"You funnin' me, old man?" said Chase, his rangy jaw outthrust.

"Aw, no, son. Look, just what is it you want to do? You keep acting all agitated and you're going to upset the women and children even more than they already are."

"Well, they should be upset, man!" Chase sprang up again. "We got to do something."

"Can't you at least wait until Bewley and that new fellow, Gage, get back? They asked us to give them the day, maybe less, for them to return with news."

"News? *News!* My word, man, we ain't got time for news. Besides, that Gage fellow is a killer. Admitted it to us all. He kills for fun. Shoots people dead and all."

"Then leave him be. Maybe he'll lay waste to some of these Brethren fools and we can be on our way."

Chase shook his head. "No, no way. They ain't trustworthy. Besides, they're long gone from here."

"'Long gone'?" said Gramps. "They left their horses and gear here. They went on foot."

"Yeah, you heard those shots not long after they left, making their way upriver. They got themselves killed is what they did. And we're supposed to sit and wait for no word from them? Sit and wait for the Brethren characters to finish us off? All they have to do is wait us out."

"If you go up there and start shooting at them, they're going to shoot back. You ever think about that?"

"Good," said Chase. "Then we'll know where they are and we can get a sight on them, lay them low."

"You have a mighty high estimation of your shooting abilities, Chase."

"What's that supposed to mean?"

"Means I've seen you shoot."

"I'm a good shot."

Gramps shrugged and turned away, finding conversation with Chase to be a frustrating, annoying, confusing task.

"Tell me this," said Gramps. "Why do you think, if they want us gone so bad, did they stop us? All they had to do was haze us on through their so-called fancy valley and take shots at anyone who ventured out of line."

Chase shrugged.

"Well, I'll tell you why." Gramps looked around at the faces of his fellow travelers—young and old, men and women, even a few children who were horsing around together in the small area in the midst of the camp, where they were allowed to play. "It's because they want the wagons. All our things, our goods, our cattle, the works."

Chase snorted. "You're just saying what Gage said."

"That's because it's the truth. And I'll tell you it all over again, if need be! Now, why are they willing to kill us off, but not send, say, flaming arrows into our wagons?"

The haggard faces of his fellow wagon train members told him they likely already knew the answer, but Gramps plowed on ahead anyway. All of it bore repeating, if only to sink the notion into their heads that when the time came, they would need to fight like demons to keep themselves and their children alive. "Because they don't want us alive, they want us all dead. Save for the children. Maybe even the teenaged young. For reasons of work . . . and such."

"So, what do we do?" a tired woman named Mrs. McGraw asked, shifting the sleeping bairn cradled in her arms.

"I say, we keep doing what we have been doing," said Gramps. "Keeping sentries looking in every direction, and spelling them so they don't doze off and miss something. And if the Brethren folks shoot, then we shoot back."

Gramps looked at their faces. A few of them nodded. "See, they don't need to do a cursed thing, save for waiting us out. And if it takes a month or two for our food to run out, why, they'll still get most of what it is they want. Which is our goods and gear."

"What about our cattle?" said Mrs. McGraw. "We can eat them."

"Sure we can, but considering they already took most of them, we're looking at what's left, a dozen head, including oxen? How long do you think they'll keep?"

Mrs. McGraw shrugged. "Long enough, I expect."

"For what?"

"For us to do something. Get someone to ride on out of here and fetch help, that's what."

Gramps nodded. "Yep, it's a good idea, I'll grant you that. But by then, it'll probably be too late."

"Then let's send someone now!" said Mrs. McGraw.

"I think it's worth waiting to hear from Bewley and Gage. If we don't by, say, tomorrow at this time—"

"Gramps is playing too cautious. Tonight is the latest I'm waiting," said Chase. He looked around. "Anyone else with me?"

Gramps watched as one, two, three, five, eight, and then more and more hands went up; folks were nodding.

"All right, so then what?" said Gramps, sitting down, with a groan, on a nail keg.

"Then we kill every blasted one of them."

It wasn't Chase, but a lean man with a full beard, sharp gray eyes, and a quiet, keen way about him, as if nothing escaped his attention. He went by the name Silks, and was father to a boy and a girl, both as lean as he was. His wife was less lean, but no less intense and quiet. All four of them were quiet, but generous in helping with chores.

"Might mean we need to bust on out of here, a couple of us, and scout the perimeter. I got up to such in the war. Good way of dispensing with any enemy you might come across."

"Gunshots will be heard and responded to, day or night," said Gramps.

"I ain't talking about guns," said Silks. He spat a rope of brown tobacco juice and laid a bony hand on the hilt of the huge hip knife that hung at his side.

"Who else has such experience?" said Gramps, warming to the idea. "I'd go, but I'm too old and fat and noisy."

A few folks chuckled, but nobody else raised a hand.

Silks spoke again. "My boy knows such. Taught him

all he knows. Ain't that right, Mother?" The man looked briefly at his wife. She nodded her stern face once.

The man's son stepped forward. A mirror image of his father—save for being shorter by a few inches, a pinch leaner, and with a wisp of a beard on his face—stepped forward to stand beside his pa. He also laid a hand on the hilt of the huge knife he wore about his own waist.

"You would try this for us?" said Gramps.

The man spat again. "Nope," he said. "Trying don't keep us all alive. It's doing that will."

After more discussion, the small group broke up. Gramps was surprised when the lean woodsman walked over, leaned close, and spoke in his ear. "I'd be obliged if you'd keep that idiot, Chase, away from me and mine. Better, even, if he didn't keep spouting off and riling up folks. We do this my way, and we might come through. Leastwise until Bewley and Gage get back. If they do."

He backed away, and he and Gramps exchanged looks. The older man nodded. "Agreed. I'll do what I can."

"Good." The woodsman walked away, joined his family, and they all made their way back to their wagon.

It's a thin plan, but decent enough, thought Gramps.

The first they'd had since the start of this bizarre situation. But it relied on the stealth of two men. Actually, one man and a boy.

Somehow, thought Gramps, *that is not going to be enough.*

He looked up toward the great rocky knob high above. It was quite high, but maybe possible for the

Brethren to get up there and shoot down at them. So far, they had not seen any snipers perched up there. But it could happen at any moment, he knew. And then, where would they be, with death raining down on them from on high?

"Come on, Bewley and Gage," muttered Gramps. "Do something back there. Anything."

CHAPTER 16

Somewhere on the journey trudging up the hill with the kid in the lead, prodded forward by the notion that there were two "heathens" nipping at his heels with guns, Gage decided that there was no way he could set fire to anyone's property just to provide a distraction. Not that he didn't have just cause, but the faces of women and children and old folks, all vague but very much alive, floated in his mind and he put himself in their places, wondering how he'd feel if someone did that to him.

He suspected Bewley felt the same way, but he didn't really know the man all that well yet. Up to this point, the old buck had surprised him repeatedly. He could well turn out to be ruthless if pushed, but somehow Gage didn't think so.

All these concerns nibbled at him, but the primary thought that shadowed each step he took upward was what to do with the kid. Finding him and then getting the better of him were not events that he'd expected.

Gage was seasoned enough in dealing with dire situations to know that too-tight planning was a doomed effort from the start, and it was wise to always keep a loose notion of what should and shouldn't happen. With that in mind, the kid's appearance in their trek was just something to work with—indeed, they had no choice.

But a decision about the kid would have to be made soon. Sooner than they expected, because though Gage knew they were approaching the top of the ridge, it came up quick. The kid and Bewley reached it two strides ahead of him, and the old scout whistled as he stepped up between b

oulders that looked to have been cleaved just wide enough to accommodate the narrow walking path they'd been on.

To either side, brush and scraggly pines he now saw were largely responsible for his inability to see the dawning vista of the valley below.

Bewley glanced back at him as he strode up. "You have to see this."

Gage edged through the narrowed declivity between the boulders and said, "Wow." For below, as if the scene had been rendered by an artist in paints, sat an idyllic valley with a patchwork of fields and paddocks, set apart by log fencing and stone work.

The road that cut through the pass wound in a nearly straight line from right to left and onward, westward, as far as the rolling landscape allowed him to see.

Far below, to either side of the roadway, scattered far enough apart for elbow room aplenty, sat tidy homesteads built of log and stone, mostly cabins, modest in size, and each attended by a similarly constructed barn and other various outbuildings. He saw cattle and sheep in pastures, laid in and around the valley, horses in paddocks close by the barns, and wagons near most of the places, each parked at tidy angles nearby the barns.

A robust mountain stream flowed down toward the center of the valley from on high across the way, from somewhere high above on the northside ridge. At the base of the slope, the water had been allowed to gather in a sizable pool, perfectly oval enough in dimension that it had the look of being hand dug. At its outlet, he saw what looked to be a long dam; then a bridge sat perpendicular to this to allow traffic to flow along the east-west roadway.

Gage wondered if he would have seen the valley, had he kept traveling even just another hour farther westward a couple of days before. But perhaps not, he thought, since he'd intended to cut northwest, departing from the narrow trail he'd been following out of Higgins.

None of that mattered now, as they were obviously gazing down upon the Chosen Valley. It seemed to Gage to be perhaps longer than a mile, perhaps a mile and a half from the east end; the men could just about see the roadway emerging from the massive cut in the pass to their right.

Far to the left, the rolling landscape and increasing foothills impeded his view of the settled, farmed valley, but it was obvious that the settlement continued. Here and there, as the treed slopes were cleared for logs for building, for firewood, and for pastureland, there were signs that yet more farmsteads were being cobbled together wherever the slope lessened into a usable shelf of land.

"Ain't it something?" said the boy. He, too, Gage saw, was impressed, and he was a resident of the place. It was nice to see the troubled, grieving young lad's face relax into a softer look, an almost smile and eyes wide.

"You're a lucky fellow to live in such a pretty place," said Bewley.

Gage knew the man meant it sincerely, but the kid's eyes narrowed and the cloud descended over his face once again.

"And you want to take it all from us, you and all those heathens."

"Not true, son," said Bewley, sighing.

"Then why else did you all come this way so late in the season?"

"Fair question." The scout nodded. "We got a late start, that's true, but it's a gamble you take in life when there's something that you want to do bad enough. And the folks in that wagon train want nothing more than to make it out to California and build their own homes, like you have here. Not a one of them had the idea of staying on here at all. You understand me?"

"I understand you're lying, you and all the heathens." The kid glanced over his shoulder at Gage. "Him too."

At that, Gage had to chuckle. "Kid, the last thing I wanted or expected was to be saddled with a fight such as what the Brethren brought to the wagon train. But then again, I seem to have a habit of sticking my nose where I shouldn't. It's gotten me in a passel of trouble over the years, and I suspect if I make it through this mess that I'll find more trouble before too long. But I just can't help myself. I see bad things happening to folks, and I have to try to help."

To this, the kid said nothing. Gage looked at Bewley, asking in silence the question they both were considering. Finally Bewley, half looking at Gage, said, "What say we head on down there to your mama's house, eh, son?"

The kid was confused and didn't respond right away. He just stared at the old man.

So did Gage.

Bewley continued: "While we do that, I think my pard here will take a look around, just to be sure there aren't any surprises awaiting us. Besides, as an honorary heathen, he might just be in the market for a fine homestead of his own, eh, pard?"

Gage snorted, getting a grip on the edge of what Bewley was saying. He was freeing up Gage, giving Gage what he had wanted from the start, which was to pack light and move fast, scout the scene and figure out next moves. But what of Bewley? Gage wasn't certain what the man was doing himself.

The kid was wondering the same, for he said, "You're letting me go?"

"Well," said the older man, "not just yet. And we won't be moseying down there straight out in the open. What I need from you is to show me the way to your family's place. Then we'll see what we'll see. I have to talk with your mama, and try to explain a few things."

"Big risk," said Gage. "She will not be amenable to meeting a stranger, having just lost . . . well, you know."

The kid heard this and his face tightened. His mama lost a husband and he lost a father. And Gage wanted to find that Deacon fellow worse than ever and make him pay for his vicious ways.

"Well aware of it, pard, but somebody has to make the first move of civility, don't you agree?"

"I do. Good luck." He handed Bewley the kid's revolver, which he'd lugged in his waistband. The feel of the killing tool had chilled him the whole while and he was glad to be shed of it.

"You'll need it," said Bewley, holding up a hand of refusal.

"Nope. Don't want it."

"It's mine!" said the kid.

"Yep," said Gage, "and it's up to him to give it back or not. Now mind him and you'll be all right. Fail to, and you'll answer to me." At that, Gage leaned closer and, in as menacing a voice as he was able to muster, said, "You understand me . . . boy?"

To his surprise, the kid gulped and nodded as if genuinely frightened, even if just for a moment or two.

Gage muttered, "Good luck, Bewley," and instead of switchbacking down into the valley himself, he cut eastward back along the top of the ridge, making for the rocky knob that far below would lead to the wagon encampment eventually.

But it wasn't a return he was looking for just yet. He had a notion that there might be men there doing what he and Bewley had done, namely to come into the enemy camp from a wide-ranging loop. And that ridge, nearly down the same slope he and Bewley had come up, in part with the boy, might already be crawling with Brethren.

At the very least, there might be a man or two looking to find the man who'd shot at them. He knew there was at least one other, for he fired down at them from on high. He'd been surprised that nobody from the knob had tried to ambush them on their way up, but that only meant they hadn't yet been seen. The man was likely a scout sent out on a solo mission.

The journey took Gage about twenty minutes, longer than he wanted, because there was no direct route to the end of the ridge. But there were a whole lot of boulders in his path. Gage held his rifle at the ready and kept his big hip knife unthonged and ready to pull. He hoped he wouldn't find any of the Brethren ahead. But hope, as he had found over the years, was a notion he'd never felt comfortable with.

The east-west ridgeline, which he traveled atop, bisected neatly with the rocky knob, which somewhat abruptly marked the end of that ridgeline. To either side, sturdy, scrubby pines and thick brush provided a deceiving cover.

Here and there, slides of gravel had carried away the vegetation, leaving raw, sun-baked washouts. He kept to the ridgetop and stayed low, partially disguised amid the brush and gnarled trees as he looked hard to his left, toward the slope that led to the pass, and then to his right, the end of which was too far to be visible. It was the spot from where the felled Brethren member had fired down at them. And the spot that Gage had dropped him from.

It wasn't too far, just enough that he knew he had to investigate. He might get lucky and discover a little encampment of the enemy.

As he hunkered low and walked along the narrow rocky way, he wondered if it really would be lucky to find such a thing.

And then he didn't have to wonder any longer. The phrase "Be wary of finding that which you seek" popped into his mind as he saw, not thirty feet ahead, three black-clothed men seated on rocks about a small fire.

Gage sniffed woodsmoke, and cutting through that acrid scent, the smell of coffee on the boil. It made his gut rumble loud enough, he was certain, that the men would all swing their black-hatted heads his way. But no, they remained talking low with one another.

"Speak plain, man!" said one, smacking the man beside him gently on the near shoulder.

The man who received the touch looked not with amusement at the man to his left, but with narrowed eyes. "You wouldn't say that if you weren't trying to lure me into some sort of trap—now, would you?"

The first man pulled his head back. "And if you hadn't said that with narrowed eyes, I might think you were funning me. But I see somehow that you are not."

The third man, who rose and stretched his back, leaning a rifle against the sizable rock he'd been seated on, looked down at his two companions.

He was facing Gage, who remained motionless and hunkered low. He didn't think they could see him unless they looked directly at and through the dense gray mass of twiggy branches that made up the rabbit brush at this time of year. Still, movement would give all away, and he did not want that. Not yet.

"Boys," said the fellow, rubbing his lower back with both hands.

He looked to Gage to be in his fifties or so, judging by the bit of a belly and the sizable gray beard adorning both his chin and chest.

"Boys, boys, this bickering will not do."

Gage noted that both the seated chatting men were younger, their beards darker and their forms leaner.

"But, Father, he's—"

"No! I won't have it!" The standing man held up a hand, palm outward, to cease the man from talking. It worked.

The other two men looked at the older man, and Gage assumed the obvious—he was likely their father. He looked bone tired and was most certainly weary of their bickering. Gage could sympathize. They reminded him of the growing problem of increasing tensions due, no doubt, to fear and a feeling of helplessness, found in the wagon camp and now here.

He weighed his options and found that he had few. Stand up and bark orders at them to drop their weapons . . . and what? Tie each other up? He didn't even have rope on his person, which he realized was a serious bit of poor planning. What else could he do?

And then the decision, he realized, was about to be made for him. The father said, "Raymond, you run back home and start chores. Your brother will be along in a bit. I need to have a talk with him first."

"Aw, Father—"

"Shut your mouth and do as you are told!"

One of the men, seated mostly with his back to him, stood with a heavy, quick sigh, as if it were the most painful endeavor he had to undergo in his young years.

The other fellow, still seated, smiled up at him. "Have fun, brother."

"You shut it, too!" The father bellowed this and stroked one big, thick plank of a hand against another, as if he could not wait to lash out and strike them each.

The first one, Raymond, stood fully and, bending, snatched up a rifle. He gave his seated brother a long, withering glance, and then stomped up the path, right toward Gage.

All this happened in mere moments, and even if it hadn't, Gage knew he had nowhere else to go. He'd be discovered running off back down the patch. He'd also be discovered if he stayed hunkered, because there was nowhere for him to hide off the trail.

And the idea of crouching, as a petrified rabbit might, stank to him like flyblown meat in the August sun.

He was about to stand—the young man was still a decent twenty feet away—when a voice from down trail, the direction Gage had traveled, sounded: "Hello there!"

The young man halted, his rifle jerked up halfway to his shoulder. Behind him, his brother stood and did the same with his own rifle, as did the father beyond.

"It's Per Schneider, Father," said Raymond, half looking back at his father.

"Good," said the older man in a lowered tone. "That idiot is early. I am pleased, as I don't want to waste any more time up here for no reason."

The man called Schneider was still some ways off, but he shouted, "Hello, men! May I approach? I am come to spell you!"

"Yes, yes!" shouted the father. "Come ahead. Then my boys and I can go home to do chores!"

Gage thought fast. This situation was not at all what he had expected.

He glanced to his left to verify that he had a couple of feet of rocky but level earth before tumbling backward and downslope.

His first option was to try to bluff his way out of this, as he did with the fellow a few days before, but somehow he thought that this time his yammering about being sent there by the Church hierarchy would not convince any of them, especially the older father.

Gage's second option, the one he least liked, but felt he was stuck with, was to trust in his old deadeye ways and wait for the Schneider fellow, who appeared to be alone, to advance close enough that he might wing him. He did not want to kill unless he was forced to.

Schneider advanced, and Gage could see that the man held no long gun, but would likely have a revolver about his waist. That was helpful. His hands were occupied, cradling several snapped lengths of wood, which he obviously intended to use for the little campfire.

One end jutted out several feet to his left and clunked, snagging in a branch. He wrestled with it and kept talking. "Any problems up here? No sign of heathens?" He laughed and shook his head as he freed the branch.

Raymond turned and walked back to the campfire, to which the father had just added small lengths of dry tinder.

The man Schneider was almost to Gage when his firewood knocked, once again, against the trees. Once more, he continued to talk, not waiting for a reply. One of the young men interrupted, though. "Brother Mueller was up here before us. We were just arriving to spell him when he began shooting from over there."

"No!" Schneider blundered ahead, and walked right past the tensed, gun-ready Gage.

"Yes, I tell you the truth."

The father took over the story from there. "We ran up the trail to see what was happening, but then we heard a quick shout from him, but when we got up here, he was gone!"

"Gone?" said Schneider, dumping his armload of wood on the earth beside the fire ring.

"Yah, so we looked over the edge, just there." The

older man pointed to the edge of the cliff top, a dozen feet to his left. "And we saw he had fallen."

"We think he had been shot from below. But he might have lost his footing."

"What?"

The father and his two sons all nodded, pulling solemn faces.

"What did you do then?"

"We shot down, and Raymond thought he saw someone down there, but—" The young man shrugged.

"I did see at least one man, maybe two."

"Did you go down to investigate to see if Mueller was all right?"

"All right?" bellowed the father. "You are joking, no? He fell all the way down, and hit rocks on the journey. He will never wake again. Besides, he was probably shot, too."

All four men fell silent again.

Gage had grown weary of this conversation, though it did provide him with some information; however useful it might be to him, he had no idea. Nor at that moment did he care. He wanted to get out of there, but he calculated they would see him, should he depart. But he could not risk staying put any longer.

When the father and his sons left the spot, they would walk right in front of him; and this time, he would not have the luck that an armload of firewood and a distracted, chatty man brings.

Since I'm in for a penny, he thought, and rose fast to his feet.

"Raise your hands," he shouted, standing and leveling on them.

"What!" said Schneider.

"And drop the guns! Now!"

All four men stared, wide-eyed, at him; none had a gun raised. But none made a motion to drop them, either.

Gage knew that very soon that might change. These next few moments were the quick ones that would determine everything else for him and for them. He eyed each man in turn.

He expected that the first to try something foolish would be one of the younger men, the father's sons.

He wasn't wrong.

The one whose name he did not know, and who looked to be the younger of the two, showed the telltale signs first. His left eye began to narrow, his mouth corners spread, the beginnings of a sneer pulling at his face beneath the dark, wispy, little moustache and beard he was no doubt proud of cultivating.

He would be first, thought Gage. And although he hated having goaded them into violence, he tried to keep in mind that it was they who had shot down at him and Bewley. And they were part of the Brethren, the very men intent on thieving and killing innocents, and all for personal gain. He had to keep that in mind.

Their previous words implicated them in the heinous crimes they were perpetrating in the name of their so-called Church.

Despite all this, Gage promised himself he would try to deal with them without killing them. Somehow.

The man Schneider had his hands raised above his head. Gage could see that he wore a gun belt, with a revolver hanging limply at his right side. He looked confused. He would not be a worry. Yet.

Raymond narrowed his eyes and, with a snarl, threw his rifle to the ground.

The youngest kid, in one quick motion—but only quick by inexperienced farm boy standards—began to inch his rifle up.

"Don't do it, kid!" growled Gage.

"Jason! No!" shouted the father, who still stood on the far side of the fire.

But Gage noted that the older man had also not released his rifle. And he was inching his upward.

One more warning, thought Gage, *is all I have time for.* "Drop them now!"

Gage saw the conviction in the eyes of the kid Jason as he jerked his rifle up to his shoulder and prepared to shoot.

That's your first mistake, thought Gage, *and maybe your last. Never take the time, especially this close in, to aim. Just point, that's all you do.* Even as he thought it, he heeded his own long-buried, dreaded advice.

It was a freakish skill he had somehow acquired to lay men low in the streets, the dusty streets of his foolish youth. And it all came back to him now. And as it always did, sound pinched out and time seemed to slow.

He often thought back on such moments and pictured

the face of a large clock and the hands barely nudged forward. And when they did, they made a huge, cavernous sound that reverberated within him. And yet he heard none of this, none of the other sounds around him.

He only saw the bullet leave his rifle barrel.

The bullet caught the foolish farm boy, Jason, in the left shoulder, smacking hard into the meat, jerking the kid's black-clothed frame as if he'd been yanked by an unseen rope. His rifle whipped to his right and fired as it flew from his hand to clatter on the rocks of the fire ring.

Gage kept his rifle up, aimed at the man behind Jason. But Jason's bullet had not whistled harmlessly into the cold, clouding sky. It had found a home in the midsection of Schneider, the lummox among them, and he screamed and staggered backward.

Gage wanted to shout a warning, but the man was screaming and looking at his bloodied hands clutching at his bloody, pumping gut, the white of his shirt now red-black with gore. He staggered backward over rock and shrubs, and then he had nothing else to step upon, and he dropped away, off the edge.

He wouldn't go far, Gage suspected, because the slope was treed.

But Gage ignored all this, because his attention was pinned on the father of the boys, whose face was a drawn mask of raw, hate-filled rage. His mouth was wide beneath his white beard and he jerked his rifle chest high, then fired.

That was also the moment young Raymond lurched to his left to help his fallen brother.

And that was the moment when their father's bullet—meant for Gage's chest—drilled hot, fast, and hard right into Raymond's chest, entering under the youth's raised left arm and nesting somewhere in there. It did its job, even as the young man was dropping down to help his younger brother, Jason, who lay on his back, howling and clutching his shoulder.

Both boys lay at the feet of their father.

"What? What?" The older man seemed suddenly, with finger-snap speed, so much older to Gage.

Gage kept his rifle raised as the old man stood staring down at the bodies at his feet. The one on top of the other was dead, blood leaking out in a thick, dwindling run.

The younger brother, beneath his dead older brother, whimpered; and, half-conscious, he moaned, making sounds that were more animal-like than words.

"Oh, what have I done?" muttered the old man, a sob leaking from his trembling mouth as he dropped to his knees. He let go of his rifle and knelt, his hands raised as if in supplication to a deity. Then he collapsed on top of them, sobbing and moaning.

Gage kept his rifle trained on the old man, but backed away one, then two steps, trying not to make a sound. All he could think of was that he had to get out of there. None of this had happened as he could have imagined. Instead of finding answers and leaving, at worst, tied-up prisoners, anything to slow them down. He had once more caused death.

Gage's left bootheel clunked against a stone and the

boys' father raised his tear-smeared face and red eyes and seemed to see Gage, but also not see him. Then he shook his head and his face hardened, his eyes narrowed, and a low animalistic growl rose up from his throat.

"You!" he barked "You!"

Then the storm subsided and his face sagged once more as he looked down at his sons. The younger boy was still alive, but Gage saw that he had passed out and lay unmoving beneath his dead brother's slumped form.

Gage looked again at the father and saw that the man had slid a revolver out from beneath his parted black coat. The man had it cocked in his left hand, but was not aiming it at Gage.

He seemed once again to be in a trance. "First their mother last winter, and now this? Now this?"

As if the sound of his father's voice roused him, the younger boy made mewling, moaning sounds. "Papa? Papa, what happened? It hurts! Oh, it hurts so much, Papa."

The father's face drew tight and he rested his right hand on the boy's matted black hair, stroking it. Then he did the same to the dead boy's hair. Then he rested his forearm across their close faces.

Before Gage knew what the man was doing, the boys' father held the barrel to the living boy's skull and pulled the trigger.

"No!" shouted Gage, already on the move toward them. "He was alive!"

In the time it took Gage to reach the man and his

sons, the father had raised the revolver to his own left temple and had pulled the trigger.

The right side of his skull bloomed outward and burst in a sopping mess, spraying blood and bone and gray gore as he slopped forward and collapsed atop his dead sons.

"No! No, no, no . . ." Gage stood before them, looking down at what he had wrought. He trembled with the terror and madness of the moment, but nobody moved, nothing happened.

After some long minutes, he remembered the other man, Schneider, and wondered if there was still a chance he might be alive, somehow.

Gage crossed the few feet to where the man had slipped from sight over the edge and into the thickly treed slope. He peered over and didn't have to put any more effort into it than that. He saw Schneider not ten feet below, staring straight up at him, with eyes wide in agony . . . and death.

The man had landed atop a stout, stunty pine. The rugged tree had not bowed and bent, but it instead had snapped off when the man slammed into it. The trunk's ragged, freshly broken end had punched through the man's back, and his falling weight had driven him down hard onto the now blood-wet stick.

It was no bigger around than a shotgun barrel, but it had been stout enough to shove on through the man's coat, shirt, flesh, meat, bone, lungs—and outward again. A jagged, glistening length of it protruded out of the man's chest by nine inches.

Gage did not know what to do with this situation. It had not worked out at all as he had expected, that thought kept ricocheting in his own skull, like a never-tiring bullet trying to find its way out.

He turned away from the edge and looked at the father and his two dead sons. How easy it would be, he thought, to end it all as that man had done. And would the world miss him? Would anyone in the world?

As if in response to his unspoken question, he heard, from far below to the east, far below and beyond the garish, gruesome mess that had been Schneider, the sudden sounds of gunfire. He could not be certain, but he bet it was from the Brethren, lobbing lead once more at the wagon train folks. Then he heard muffled shots—return fire?—and knew he was too far away to do anything more than continue on with his initial intention.

He looked down at the heaped dead at his feet and thought for a moment of snatching up the youngest man's revolver. But as soon as the thought came to him, another snapped at its heels.

The face of the last person he had shot in a gunfight, in a so-called defense of his life, the pretty young blond woman not but a few years his junior at the time.

He'd thought of her, now and again, in the small hours when he could not prevent such thoughts from seeking ingress to his mind. Had she lived, had she never come to town that day, had he never killed her father in a similar gunfight some time before then, he might have somehow gotten to know her.

Had he been inclined to roam earlier, with no killings

behind him, trailing him like slavering dogs, he might somehow have found that family's small hardscrabble farm or ranch.

He might have offered to help them in return for keep, and perhaps he would have met her. Perhaps she, too, might have found him of interest, and perhaps they might have courted.

They would have children by now, he'd thought. And a place of their own.

The far-off stutter of gunfire from below roused him from his reverie. Gage growled and shook his head.

Gage abandoned the notion of taking the youth's revolver with him and, with a last look at the dead, said, "I am sorry. For what it's worth, this is not what I had intended. I'm so sorry."

He turned and, in a crouch, loped back along the trail, confident of little, except that when the dead were found, for the bodies would be found by one or more of their fellow Brethren, the wagon train folks would be blamed. And while that was somewhat true, it was not the entire truth.

And did it really matter? he thought as he ran. All in all, none of it would change the fact that those men were dead and needn't have been.

Gage shook off thoughts of them and of the bizarre incident and hurried along the ridge. Far below to his right, he heard intermittent snaps of gunfire.

How long could the wagon folks hold out? Their ammunition had to run low at some point. They had water and they had food for a while. The Brethren had succeeded in peeling off much of the herded beasts the travelers had brought with them, but still, there were chickens, pigs, geese, and horses. He hoped it wouldn't come to that.

He made it back to the east-west ridge and paused. Another twenty feet brought him to an easterly overlook of the settled Brethren valley, so serene and idyllic in setup and appearance. Directly below him, the trees thickened and seemed to converge on the roadway that led from the pass.

What to do? If he scrambled down the slope, and stayed well tucked into the trees, he might make it to the Brethren camp without being detected. But it was still a couple of hours until dusk and he needed to act soon. Lives depended on it.

His initial thoughts of setting fire to something in the valley still had merit—the kid and their promise to him, notwithstanding. But the idea of killing innocent animals, and perhaps even people, was too awful to consider. Still, there might be some other way.

And then he knew. Gage nodded at his new notion. Yes, that might do it.

He tried not to think of what Bewley was getting up to with the kid and the kid's mother, but he suspected it was all well intentioned. Gage could read folks pretty well after spending so many years as a drifter, watching and working alongside them, mostly men, listening more than he spoke.

He'd learned somehow to get a good sense of people and their intentions. And he had a good feeling about the innate goodness of Bewley, despite still being baffled by how the old fellow was as spry as a man half his age.

The thought of him brought a quick smile to Gage's face as he picked his way down the slope, angling westward toward the settlement. He slid across an open stretch of scree and raised more dust than he intended as he trekked downward toward the nearest copse of pines.

Lingering in the open was a certain way to attract the attention of someone familiar with the terrain hereabouts, although a darting dark shape on high was apt to attract the eye more than a still figure. Any stalked animal knew that. But standing still was a surefire way of getting nowhere.

He used the high vantage point to his benefit while he could, fixing in his mind the course downslope that would afford him the most cover. Past that scree slope, and on down the lower slopes, the pitch eased and vegetation thickened.

Soon enough, he came to the rocky cairn that marked, he suspected, the corners of what he saw was a tended pasture with its perimeter being set by the farmers, as time allowed. Or, more likely, their sons and daughters.

The more ambitious the farmer or rancher, the bigger the spread and the more children the farmer had. And the more haggard his wife invariably looked. That was Gage's experience, and he doubted it proved differently here.

As settlements went, this place was in its early days, but if they made a go of it—and by all signs, they were certainly doing that—this settled valley would only become more of a nexus of prosperity.

"Or it would have, if they had been kinder," he muttered as he took a last look downslope before him toward the nearest farm, some eighth of a mile below. "They can't get away with this. At least not any longer. And not without a fight."

It would take a few days of hard riding before the law could be alerted. And by then, who knows how many more deaths and thefts would have taken place?

He realized as he crouched and ran, his rifle held in his upslope hands, that the shadows were lengthening. He might avoid being seen if he stayed on the east side of the nearest structure—what looked to be a sizable, open-faced pole barn, with its back and roof to him, and so to the slope.

As if he had willed it, Gage's next step forward was with his right boot, and instead of landing on the firm, grassy slope, it kept going for another six inches or so. A hole reared up and tripped him. As he slammed forward, hard to his knees, he knew it was either a divot from a dislodged rock or the entrance of a critter's den. Didn't much matter. But what mattered, he knew, stifling a groan, was the hot pain from his right kneecap. It had slammed against a jag of rock.

He felt with his ungloved hand and there was a slice in his trouser leg and a wetness beneath. He sat on his backside for a moment and massaged the slammed kneecap, waiting for the pain to subside. Waiting and hoping that he had not broken the cursed thing.

It took a couple of long minutes before Gage felt able to stand and put weight on the thing. Hot lances of pain flowered within his knee, but he gritted his teeth and forced himself to walk on, slower and with more caution, covering the remaining fifty feet to the back of the pole barn at a baby's pace. But he made it.

As he leaned against the rough, vertical planking, he was heartened by the fact that nothing in his knee felt broken. He was just badly annoyed with himself. He had to pay more attention. Particularly now that darkness was coming on.

He had a good idea of what the settlement looked like, and he cast his thoughts back on the view he'd had of the valley from on high. This pole barn, which he now knew to be a shed for hay storage, at least partially, was the nearest structure on his trek.

Gage felt the half-round boards with his fingertips. What bark was left on had puckered and curled and was doing its best to take its leave from the wood beneath.

He turned to his right and edged to the rear east corner, his cheek tight to the wood as he peered around the end. The wood still smelled mildly of the pitchy tree it had once been. Through a gap between the planking, he had felt dry, brittle grasses through.

He also smelled a distinctive odor of mustiness overriding an underlying sweetness, the last, lingering scent of the hot summer's grasses. These hay stores would be crucial to keeping the Brethren's livestock, particularly the cattle and horses, alive throughout the winter. He knew that what was in the barn represented a whole lot of work.

But then again, so did everything the wagon train folks owned, and everything they had put into their journey so far. None of it deserved to be stolen. But if he could distract the Brethren, at least some of them, from the massacre they intended, he might be able to give the wagon folks a leg up.

He needed to set the Brethren men on the back foot, and taking away their feed stores and whatever else he might be able to, without harming lives directly, was what Gage knew he had to do.

He saw no one eastward of him. The next nearest structure was a low, tight log structure, which he knew was a barn, given the manure pile off to the east side.

That barn, he reasoned, would be filled with critters, especially considering how few animals he'd seen dotting the grassed pasture slopes flanking the pass roadway.

He'd worry about them when he got to them, but first things first. He edged low around the east side of the hay barn, hugging the wall and keeping an eye toward the barn. Now that he'd made it nearly to the front corner of the pole barn, he saw a corner of another structure beyond the edge.

Had to be the cabin. It had looked to be such from above. He bent low and looked to his left. This glance verified what he'd suspected—this was an open-faced hay storage barn, with a boarded bay within, containing what looked to be neatly stacked wood—logs, stumps, extra planking.

From the chopping block with the axe embedded in it, Gage knew it was extra firewood. The farmer who'd attended to this was a man with foresight. The winters here, he bet, would be cold and long and packed with snow.

Too bad he wasn't going to be able to enjoy the warmth from it that Gage was about to create.

He knew this action he was about to take—setting fire to the barn and its contents—was also going to harm the innocents in this mess. That is, if the Brethren wives and grandparents and children could be considered innocent in any of this.

He thought of the terrified looks on the faces of most of the wagon folk and he firmed his resolve to carry through with this questionable plan.

Gage bent low and wormed to his right and into the barn. It was tall in the front, perhaps a dozen feet at the peak, and the roof tapered toward the rear to about eight feet. From front to back, he guessed the space within to be twenty feet or so.

What breeze that had kicked up was blocked by the rear of the barn, and he knew the farmer had chosen the spot with care, keeping the front open for simple access to the hay and wood, while shunning the persistent downward buffeting from the wind.

The stored hay took up at least two-thirds of the space, leaving little room for more. The wood stored at the far end, with the chopping block in front, sat dry and waiting.

Gage leaned his rifle against the wall's log crosspiece, tugged off his gloves, stuffed them into a coat pocket, and fished out his matches. He had taken all he had stored in his saddlebags. He used them occasionally in place of his char cloth and flint and steel setup, because they made his life so much simpler on the trail.

But when he had time, he forced himself to use the steel striker and flint to shower sparks into a nest of fine tinder. There was something far more satisfying in conjuring flame that way, and he did not want to lose the slight skill it took.

But matches were just right for the job at hand.

He flicked the head of the match off his thumbnail once, twice, and on the third time, it flared to life. He cupped it and the warmth in the darkening stillness of the open barn made him long for a quiet, warm camp all to himself far from here.

He let that thought go and knelt, cursing himself for not twisting up a few brands of dry hay before lighting the match. *Too late,* he thought, and held the dwindling match to a hastily twisted handful near the base of the stack.

It singed, glowed, crept; then just when he thought it was going to dissipate and go out, right when his thumb and forefinger were heating up from the dying match, flames—tiny, but growing, and hungry—licked up the front of the dry haystack.

He hastily snatched up hay and twisted and knotted several handfuls, then lit them one at a time from the growing flame and, leaving his rifle for the moment, dashed along the front of the stack.

It would not take much to put out these flames at this point, he thought, provided there was a water trough and bucket within an easy run. But that's not why he was there.

The wood might take longer to burn than he thought, so he made another two twisted brands and wedged them here and there, then added two more. He was gratified to see fire begin to taste wood and like it.

The flames were climbing the face of the haystack now and would subsume the lot within minutes. *Time to go,* he thought, and dashed back to where he'd begun. He snatched up the rifle, then beelined for the far corner of the nearby log barn.

Gage glanced back once and was alarmed at how easy it had been to destroy one family's entire planned winter. Then he hardened his mind, narrowed his eyes, and worked his jaw muscles and planned his next move.

Across the valley floor to the other side, where another farm sat waiting. He would zigzag his way along the valley and get as far as he was able before cutting up the south slope. Then, hopefully, he would find Bewley and make once more for the ridgeline, then up and over it, and down once again to the river, and so on back to the settlement.

Or maybe not. Other thoughts bubbled in Gage's

mind as he bolted, aware he might still be seen in the coming dusk, not yet dark, dashing fast across a cleared pasture. But there was no other way across.

I've got to get there, he told himself, *and then worry about next steps. Just get there, Gage,* he told himself.

Chapter 17

Gage made it away from that first farm and down to the roadway that cut along the valley floor. Here he found more cover, as the farmers had left a handful of trees, and there were boulders aplenty.

Despite these possibilities for cover, he decided to cut west toward the bridge and the widened mountain stream the settlers had controlled for their purposes. He could not blame them, as it was ample and had the look of a fine flow—perhaps even in summer when the rains were at their least.

It also provided him with decent cover, enough so that he could cut upslope along it, provided he did not mind getting his feet wet. Well, he did mind, he thought, but not enough to stop him.

Gage's knee throbbed like a too-tight hat, but he'd worry about that later. He knew if he slowed for any length of time, it might well swell up and prove even more of a hindrance to him.

He reached the stream just south of the bridge, ducking beneath it and noting it was shy north of his six-foot height. Before he emerged from the other side, he paused and listened, then looked up to the east first, then west. He expected he looked a little like a prairie dog.

Seeing no one, he continued on up the streambed, hugging the east bank. If he crouched, which he had intended to do anyway, he might well avoid being seen by anyone out and about.

He was a little surprised that he'd not heard shouts from alarmed folks about the fire. He would soon, he just knew it. Bad deeds rarely went unnoticed.

When he'd worked his way upslope, equidistant to the nearest farm to his right, the east, he kept going in order to emerge and hopefully avoid any eyes. One more prairie dog impersonation, then he popped up and onto the grassed field.

It was stubbly and somewhat smooth, obviously worked to be free of anything that might hinder horse-drawn implements, and he knew the effort put into that task had been mighty and every member of the family, and community likely, had participated.

It would provide for them next year, but not this. This year's crop lay ahead in another pole barn; and although the day's light was waning, he suspected it was also filled with hay.

He covered the last fifty yards at a low lope, eyeing the downslope the entire way. This farm, he saw as he ran, had an oil lamp burning in one window that faced west. Somebody was home.

And he still had to cross a span of open ground that would take him within sight of eyes that might happen to be peering outward. But he had to make time while he could, before the first fire was discovered.

He bolted for it, keeping low and wincing each time he planted that gamey right leg. He shoved on through the mounting pain, gritting his teeth, and reached the near sidewall of the log barn. With little variation, it was a near duplicate of the one across the valley, behind which he'd set the fire.

He clunked into the wall harder than he intended, so fast had he been loping, but held still, not liking the fact that he was on the west side of the structure, and not in shadow. He didn't linger, but kept the rifle at the ready in his left hand. He low-walked along the wall, looked beyond the rear corner, and saw no sign of people or of any windows or open doors.

He had expected to bump into somebody, likely a woman or old-timer or growing child tending to the afternoon barn chores. Surely, each barn held chickens and at least a milk cow, perhaps goats.

He bet it was warm in the barn, too. And for a flicker of a moment, he considered slipping inside through a side door just to smell the earthy scents of a stable in cold weather: the sting of urine, and the warm, oddly familiar smells of manure mingling with hay and animal musk. Horses had their own smells, as different from those of cattle as cats from dogs, he reckoned.

But as tempting as the warmth and the nostalgic aspects of dipping into a stable might be, he had to keep going.

He wished he had thought to take along his new knitted wool mittens, but they sat back in his saddlebags, unused and waiting. Fat lot of good they were doing him there. He hoped Rig was faring better than he was.

He hadn't liked the idea of leaving his horse and spartan gear back at an encampment full of people who knew of his past—and who, it seemed, had wanted his help before they'd found out about him. That number had dropped like a stone once they found out he used to be known as Texas Lightning.

The second hay barn, another open-fronted structure, sat about one hundred feet from the rear of the log barn. He pulled in a quick deep breath and dashed for it.

Again the right knee caused him to grit his teeth and wince, but he didn't let up until he'd reached the short side facing him. The open front of this barn faced eastward, in an effort to keep the wind from driving snow into the stored feed.

His operation was a near repeat of the first hay barn, but this time he remembered to first twist handfuls of dry hay into knotted hanks that could be stuffed in, here and there. And as they were now denser, they would burn slower, giving him time to vamoose and make for the next farm before the smoke and flame caught anyone's attention. At least that was his plan.

He was halfway through setting fire to this hay barn, and having decent success at it, too, when he heard shouts, far off, but human voices raised in alarm, nonetheless.

One fire and they might assume it was some sort of accident. But a second fire? All bets were off then. And arson would be the immediate assumption. It's what he would think and how he would react.

This barn held no stored wood, just hay, so setting the fire was a quicker matter. He hobbled along the length of the open face of the barn, lighting one twisted hank off the next; and within a couple of minutes, he had the entire mess alight.

He wasn't kidding himself in thinking they might lose all their feed for the season, because the hay barns were deep and densely packed, but his attempts would certainly do the thing he wanted—draw the attention of some of the Brethren men fighting up at the pass east of the valley.

With any luck, a goodly amount of them would come quickly. That was also the downside of his plan.

Gage heard more and more shouts, from farther off, deeper down the valley. Along the roadway, he saw someone riding hard from west to east. "Keep going, go fetch your pappy up at the pass," muttered Gage.

Me, he thought, rounding the hidden far end of the smoking hay barn, preparing to bolt to the streambed once more, *I'm off to make more distractions.*

He felt as he ran that he needed at least one more fire, preferably two more, burning on down the valley, enough to keep the Brethren members hopping and spread out.

So far, he had only heard high-pitched voices, and he assumed they were women and children doing the shouting. Good. They'd have their hands full. He hoped they weren't foolish enough to get themselves hurt by the flames or smoke, but of that he had no control.

He made it to the streambed and slid down into it. His feet felt as though they had solidified into blocks of frozen wood, but there was nothing for it, he had to keep going. There would be time for thawing and healing later.

Down in the waterway, Gage decided to alter his plans and stick with this, the north slope side of the road. To try to cross, this close to the two fires, would be a mistake. And he needed to bolt for the third place without pause, because the second fire would surely be seen any moment.

He made it halfway to the next small farmstead, wishing he had more to duck down behind, but thankful that the dark was descending quickly in the valley, somewhat shrouded as it was by the heights of the cupping range in which it sat, blocking the dropping sun's rays from the west.

At that halfway point, he left the cover of a boulder half the size of a bull, but large enough to catch his breath behind. He resumed his low, bent-over lope. He knew he wasn't making as much progress as quickly as he wanted. His banged-up knee had by then begun to dictate the pace at which he would travel. It also had begun to throb and made his every movement a painful endeavor. He tamped down the pain as best he could and kept on hobbling.

Then he heard another voice, young-sounding and

higher pitched than a man's. Was it a woman? Did it matter? He glanced downslope toward the roadway he was roughly paralleling and saw a dot of light swaying there. Someone with a lantern.

"Hey there! Hey, you! Who is it?"

The voice was shouting at him. Apparently, it wasn't as dark as he hoped, for this person likely could tell he was a human and not a creature of the night—a deer or wolf or fox or coyote, loping for cover.

He crouched even lower and kept on toward the safety of the nearest island of rock and scrubby brush, likely the result of cleared rocks being piled there.

He was grateful for it—he needed to catch his breath once more before continuing on. The black bulk of the next building seemed so far off. He glanced down the road once more and saw that the lantern was still slightly swaying, but the person had ceased shouting and looked to be turning and making eastward.

Perhaps the woman, for it had sounded like a female's voice, had decided it was a critter, after all. He hoped so. Anything to slow down folks who wanted to track him.

That would happen soon enough. But by then, he hoped to be gone, or at least on his way, with Bewley, back upslope.

The third hay barn was similar to the others, but it sat much closer to the nearest house and stable than had the others. That gave Gage pause. Would they lose their home because he was about to set their gathered crop alight too close by?

Then, as if in answer, a door in the side of the barn facing him squawked open. It was an unnerving sound, and confusing until he figured out that it might provide him with a bit of cover. He might be unseen if he could get there without whoever was emerging from within the stable not looking his way.

Any luck Gage had had up to that point had been depleted by the frenzy of the past long minutes. The door shoved open even wider and a gimpy older man stepped out. It was as if he had been looking in Gage's direction the entire time.

He stood like that, the door ajar, and a quicky volley of calf bleats escaped from within.

The man stared at him, then bent low and visored his eyes. Gage had paused in his run and kept low. The fingertips of his upslope hand, the right, balanced him while he held his position. He supposed he should be grateful that darkness was near enough that his silhouette might appear to be a critter.

Still, the old-timer looked at him, backlit from within the byre by low lamplight. The man shuffled farther out into the night and stood, hands on hips, the calves continuing to bleat behind him.

He turned his head and looked eastward, down the valley toward the pass, and shouted, "Oh!" Then he turned and entered the barn once more, this time leaving the door open.

Gage figured he had seen the fires, which a quick glance behind showed Gage to be glowing and smoking and engulfing the barns enough that the glow was visible at that distance.

The old man in the barn emerged again, this time holding the lantern, and muttered something.

When the man ducked back inside, Gage had decided to stay put and lowered himself as much as he could without lying down on the cold, grassy ground. He'd wait out the man, who was now more concerned with the fires than with what he had or had not seen on the slope nearby his barn.

The man ambled away, looking as though he was hurrying, but too old to move any faster. Gage watched his dim lantern's glow swinging at the old-timer's awkward gait and pace down toward another building. He presumed it was the man's log home. Even before the man reached it, he was shouting, "Mother! Mother! Fires! Come! Come!"

Gage wasted no time in reaching the barn, from which he could still hear the hungry calves through the log walls. He legged it around the upslope end and looked ahead, but saw no hay barn. He'd seen from above that some of the places were smaller and only had a small barn behind the house. This was one of them, and he told himself it was likely the home of an old couple with fewer needs and no children to feed. He kept on running, knowing he could not set fire to that barn now.

The next place was a fair piece on down the valley,

but it was a sizable spread and he vaguely recalled it from his earlier vantage point above, looking down at the peaceful vale.

If it was the place he recalled, it looked to have several storage barns. He presumed it was the home of a large family, one that might be able to muddle through the cold months with less feed.

That's where he would make for next. And he did, taking care to dart as much as his knee would allow from copse to stunty bush to boulder, each one a massive rock that had tumbled down from the high ridge to the north lording over the site.

By the time he drew within one hundred or so feet of the nearest building, he heard more frequent shouts, with dots of orange lantern light glowing here and there along the roadway, some of them hustling toward the fires, and at least three looked to be making their way westward, perhaps looking for him, or whatever culprit they suspected had emerged in their midst.

Did they not think retaliation would occur? Gage saved the heady exploration of motives for himself and the Brethren, and nearly made it to the building, when he heard a dog barking ahead.

It had to happen at some point, he thought. Dusk had descended in full and whatever the dog may have seen of him would soon be overruled by how fast the dog could make it to him and what its keen nose smelled of him.

He'd not had to kill a dog in all his years on the trail, and he didn't want to begin tonight, but neither was he going to risk capture or lose his life—because of a dog, a cow, a goat, or a person. Not if he could outthink it somehow.

Shapes of buildings were still visible, although barely, and other low structures also appeared within yards of him, as if they had emerged from the ground like mushrooms. A low building, no bigger than a wagon and perhaps half as tall, jutted close by a snag of trees growing hard by a neat pile of rocks. As he drew closer to it, he paused and sniffed. There was a smell to it and he knew it, but for the life of him, he could not recall what it was.

It had been some time since he'd been around a farmyard, so the smells took time in triggering memories. But then, in moments, he had identified that odd smell as that of pigs. It was not a pleasant odor, and as the slight breeze had been carrying itself from the southwest, he was in the path of whatever it carried with it. In this case, it was the stink of hog muck.

No wonder the family kept the beasts well away from the house. He cut higher upslope, and as he passed the pigpen, he saw that the west side of the structure opened into a sizable fenced yard for them. His guess as to its inhabitants was soon rewarded by a grunting and a quick burst of squeal as one pig harassed another.

Gage's boot scuffed a rock and the squealing pinched off in favor of a chorus of eager grunts. They must be used to being fed about this time, he thought, and are on high alert, watching and listening for sign of their feed.

He hurried on, the dog's barks the only constant sound as he progressed.

He could see downslope toward where he knew the home to be and spied no lantern lights from within. Another few strides brought him closer to a larger building, which he guessed was the primary barn.

As with the pigs, the beasts within the new building offered random bellows and snorts. Gage recognized among them the sounds every overhungry cow he'd ever heard made. This time, he heard two—a deep, chesty rumble, which he took to be a bull, and the lighter, younger sound of perhaps a heifer or bullock.

He thought he also heard the drawn-out croaking and cackling of chickens. He passed by that building, and it took a while, as it was sizable. Once he gained the far west side of the barn, he paused, listening for the dog. It was almost worse not hearing it now, for he wondered if perhaps someone had set the beast free so it might hunt him.

There had been, according to what he recalled, at least two other buildings out this way that had the look of storehouses, likely hay, and perhaps wood. He made it to the near corner of one and and saw nothing, save for creeping darkness and the lighter color of mounds of loose hay piled high inside, to his right.

Now he had no time to waste, for a quick glance back to the road far below showed him that there were more swinging lanterns making their way slowly up the road in his general direction.

Once he set fire to this barn, he would be all but shouting to them to find him. He must make this quick. He repeated his efforts, twisting hanks of hay, and when he had four, he struck a match . . . and broke it. He cursed and snatched at another, his hands trembling; this time, the match caught flame.

He lit the first twisted hank, a soured smell of summer rising up in the first curls of light smoke from the fired hay, tickling his nostrils.

He kept on, and soon had four somewhat spaced spots of flame doing their work. The breeze from the southwest nibbled at and wagged the new flames. They danced, but none went out.

He retreated to the corner of the building he'd come from, intending to make his way up around the top edge and move as quickly as he was able, westward, before dropping down and across the valley.

He'd reached the corner and glanced back, and the light thrown by the new, low flames glinted off something at the far end. Or rather two somethings. Eyes.

The dog had rounded the far corner, then jerked to an abrupt stop alongside the front of the flaming hay. A low, chesty growl burbled up from the beast, and it did not seem to care that just a half-dozen feet to its left flank, hungry orange flames licked at the hay.

The dog had ceased its barking, perhaps a half minute before, and Gage knew in that moment as he saw the black shape barreling at him that he should have been more suspicious of the renewed silence.

He pulled back around the corner, guessing the dog would have to slow up to get at him. Not much, but he'd take any leverage he might gain.

It had been a large shape, but he knew it was a dog

because of the knee height and the chesty growl. He waited, his rifle spun around and held in both hands as one might an axe, ready to come down hard on the brute's skull once it showed itself.

But it didn't. In fact, it had ceased its growling, and though he had not had a lifetime of dealing with dogs, he knew that, for every kind and goofy or diligent and hardworking cattle dog he'd met, as with people, some canines were clever and some were devious. And some were killers. And if you combined all three of those traits, you had the makings of a bad situation.

Gage leaned to his right, the rifle still held aloft, club-like, and peered around the log post that formed the corner of the open-fronted building that held an ample supply of mounds of loose hay.

He saw no dark shape awaiting him. He pulled back. Had he imagined it? And then, from behind him, he heard a swishing, rushing sound, and quick, light breaths. He spun, the notion of what it was already coming to mind, but too late to be of use to him. For the thing drove into him as a battering ram might a bolted door.

Gage's wounded knee gave way and he collapsed with the pummeling force of a large and frenzied beast that had found its quarry and was not about to surrender it.

Despite his intention to remain silent, Gage yelped as the beast drove him backward. His rifle flew from his grasp and he was rolled halfway to one side with his left arm pinned beneath him.

He had no time to right himself, for the sleek-coated,

thick-muscled brute, growling loud now, was on him fully and seemed to be using every bit of its rock-solid body against him.

Gage managed to jerk his left arm free, while holding his right up, to protect his face, which the lunging hound seemed intent on destroying. It slashed and slavered at him, sinking fangs into the meat of his forearm, even through the thick canvas of his work coat, shirt, and undershirt sleeves.

He drove a gloved left fist hard at the dog's head, but it did nothing, save bounce off. He snatched at it and felt a short, tight fold of an ear as he grabbed it, twisting hard, but it also did nothing. Aware that he was in a bad spot, Gage was also aware that he was making growling, grunting, yelping noises—and he could not help it.

He jammed his left thumb into what he hoped was the dog's left eye, but that effort also yielded no results. The beast lunged and bit and the face jerked away, then slammed harder at his face.

Its breath stank of rancid meat and rankness that clouded his senses. Spittle flecked in great gobs all over his face and in his open mouth and eyes. He gritted his teeth and shoved hard upward with his knees, trying to roll the beast from him. It worked, but for barely an instant; then the clawing resumed and the thing was atop him once more.

He regretted wearing his hip knife on his right side, for that arm was the one most occupied in fending off the growling, frenzied brute's attack. But he managed to shove his left arm in its place, feeling the beginnings of pain on that forearm as well, while he jerked his savaged right arm down to his side, flexing the fingers and finding them still able to work, although they were numb and slick with gore.

They scrabbled, shaking with the dog's attack, and with what surely must have been damaged muscles and nerves in the arm. But he managed to feel the rawhide laced thong that secured the handle of the knife within the sheath. He had to untie it, he knew, but his fingertips were benumbed and sopping with blood, *his* blood.

The grimness of the situation washed over him, as did a sudden boil of nausea. With the awareness of everything that seemed to be happening at that moment, Gage threw up—a quick, hot geyser of vomit that coated his own face and chest and somehow stunned the dog, at least for a sliver of time, for it ceased its growling, mad savaging, and pulled back.

Gage managed to jerk the knife handle hard and somehow it came free, either snapping the rawhide or perhaps it had stretched enough to allow the knife to be pulled free.

He did not care how, but the knife—the big bladed knife that he used for so many chores, and kept honed to a keen edge—slid free of the sheath as fast as he could make it do so. As the dog renewed its lunging attack, Gage slammed the thing at the dog's massive rib cage inches above his own.

It yelped and then kept on, perhaps even angrier. The knife was still in Gage's hand and he was beginning to lose his senses, for sound and smell and what little light was left in the sky high above began to blur and fade and pinch.

The smells of the cold and the dog and hot blood and vomit mingled and the sharpness of each softened, replaced with the sound of a dull buzzing in his ears. And still the dog bit and lunged and then he felt its fangs on his face. He was weakening.

Gage knew this was it—that he had to make some effort, a last effort, to defend himself; and the weight of the hefty knife, which was awkward in his numb, slick right hand, was reassuring.

He forced himself to close his fist tight around the handle, and with what felt like the last of his strength, he raised the knife and swung it hard. It was almost at himself, but just high enough, he hoped, to reach the dog.

He felt the knife's thick, curved tip pop skin and drive on deep into the beast's innards. He gritted his teeth harder, sure they would turn to powder at any moment, and not caring a whit.

The wide, keen blade opened a three-inch gash in the side of the dog's belly, behind the ribs, and angled in and upward.

As with his past gunfights, time seemed to slow, and sights and sounds and smells grew strange, stranger than before; and the blade drove deep, deeper in and upward, high in the dog's chest, and still his hand shoved with all the force Gage could muster.

The blade led the way and his fingers, slicked with his own blood, now were washed in a drenching of hot blood from the dog's spasming, sagging body.

It had yelped, he was sure of that, but still it was atop him and he could not understand why. With a last effort, he rolled it off him, using his right hand, still gripping the knife's handle, though much of it was now inside the dead beast.

He shoved, and the body flopped to his left and it lodged there, chest to the sky and legs akimbo, wedged between Gage's spent body and the log wall of the hay barn.

CHAPTER 18

"Now look, ma'am," said Bewley, standing where he'd stationed himself inside the doorway of the cabin. He was finding it difficult to explain to this woman just what it was he was doing there, who he was, and why he had escorted her son home at gunpoint.

Plus, she had hold of a squalling bairn, and the boy, once they got near the house, bolted for the cabin and wouldn't comply with Bewley's growled threats. The kid knew full well that the old scout wasn't about to put a bullet in him, despite the fact that the kid had laid a solid kick to the old gent's eggs earlier, back up on the ridge.

"You tell me what you want here!" shouted the woman, her left hand creeping along the top of the worktable, while her right cradled the fussy baby.

Bewley couldn't be certain, as it was a dimly lit cabin, but he thought the fingers on that left hand of hers were crabbing toward a big ol' knife, the sort of honed wedge of steel a man didn't want to find wagging out of his innards.

"I told you, and I will tell you again, that your son there bushwhacked us—"

"Us?" she growled, bouncing the weepy baby on her hip as she continued her reach.

"Yes, ma'am. I appreciate you have your hands full, ma'am, with the bairn, but I don't want to see that left hand of yours moving any closer to that big ol' knife there on the table, okay?"

She stopped the hand from moving, but didn't retract it. She was a tough one, and wily, he thought. Full of vim and spirit. Normally, he liked that in a woman, but he was tired and cold and sore now, and feeling as though maybe he'd run his last race.

Turned out that these Brethren folks sure seemed to have a powerful way about them—more so, anyway, than his wagon train folks.

"Yes, ma'am, me and my pard. You see—"

"He's telling the truth, Ma," said the kid. "I . . . I didn't tell you when I left because I figured you wouldn't let me go."

"You're right there, little mister!" She managed to crook a work-reddened finger at her blushing son.

The boy pulled himself up to full height, which was taller than her, but not by much. "I set out to track down Papa's killer. I reckon that any one of those heathens will do, as they are all guilty of so much in the eyes of the Maker."

"That's enough of that talk," she said, narrowing her eyes at him.

"But that's what Papa said!"

"I know." She looked to Bewley as if she was exhausted and about to cry. "But he's not here now."

The kid recoiled as if he had just been slapped in the face, but he said nothing.

The woman glanced at Bewley, who still stood just inside their closed door, his back to the log wall. His revolver, not aimed at anyone, hung by his side.

Not only was he more tired than he could recall being in a long ol' time, he wasn't being helped in the least by the room itself. The low light and the heat of the cabin and the smells of food cooking—he thought that big black pot hanging on a hook by the fire was bubbling with toothsome-smelling and thick stew—were enough to lull a body right down to sleep, even while standing up.

"Look, ma'am, I didn't come here to argue or to hear you squabble amongst yourselves. I came here because your boy tried to kill us and we turned the tables on him. Now"—Bewley held up a hand to stifle the words he knew were going to come flying at him from the woman, or the boy, or both—"look, ma'am, I am right sorry to hear about your husband. Really, I am. But that boy of yours seems to think that one of us heathens from the wagon train took his life. But it's simply not so."

"Then *who* did?" She was shaking and her face was red, but her eyes were fixed steadily on him.

The boy said, "Ma—"

"Son, shut your mouth. Now!" And to Bewley, she

said, "You had better explain why I should believe anything you say, mister."

The scout swallowed and nodded. "I intend to, ma'am. And for what it's worth, we explained all this to your boy. See, my pard, he heard your Deacon fellow whispering to your husband, telling him all sorts of things, and then he . . . well, my friend saw that Deacon fellow of yours—"

"It ain't true, Ma!"

Instead of shouting the boy down yet again, the woman, her jaw clenched, kept her dead-on stare at Bewley and said, "Continue, mister. And make it count."

"But Deacon ain't here to defend himself, Ma!"

"Deacon," she said, surprising Bewley, "would certainly be able to do that, wouldn't he?" She said this to the boy, but Bewley sensed something else behind it.

"It was Deacon, ma'am, who stabbed your husband. My friend saw it, but it happened so quick, he had no time to prevent it."

"Convenient that your friend was there and yet did nothing. And where is he now? I am inclined to think you are as silver-tongued as Deacon."

Then Bewley remembered what Gage had said. "When did you find out about your husband's death, ma'am?"

Her face turned stony once more. "Why?"

"When?" he asked again.

"Late last night. Why?"

"And who told you?"

Her eyes narrowed. "Deacon." Her voice was lower, colder.

Bewley nodded. "Yep, and Deacon was betting that nobody would find him, at least not until the morning, not until sunup this morning."

"So?" she said, but he saw the doubt widen her eyes. "Deacon, he . . . he found my husband, he said so. And then he came here. He said—"

"He said it was to comfort you, am I right?"

"Yes, but . . . but that's something people say all the time when someone dies."

"That's true, ma'am. But it don't add up, ma'am."

"No, no." She shook her head. "This doesn't make any sense! My husband and Deacon, they were friends. Deacon called him his second-in-charge of the Brethren. He called him his Old Reliable."

"That's right he did," said Bewley. "But see, that Deacon fella, he doesn't want anyone else in charge of his Brethren."

"That's preposterous," she said, taking her eyes from him for the first time in long, long minutes.

"Is it, ma'am? How long you know this Deacon fella? How long has he been around these parts?"

"Three years or so."

"You all happy before he came?"

She looked at him then with what appeared to be exhaustion on her face, her head leaned to one side. "Yes. Yes, we were. We all were."

"You all happy now?"

"Not really, no. But Deacon says we should all endure hardship here on earth so we might gain the keys to paradise afterward."

"So you all work harder than ever, but you're not as happy as you were. Funny thing, that is," said Bewley. "Look, ma'am, I don't have all the answers. But I do know that those Brethren men are attacking and killing innocent folks, stealing our cattle and other livestock, and Deacon was heard telling the Brethren men that your so-called Maker wanted them to take everything from the heathens and send them packing. Am I right?"

"Yes, but only because the heathens carry the taint about them. He said they would infect our people and lay us all low and keep us from entering paradise."

"The taint. Heh. I'm sure he did say that," said the scout. "But all I can tell you is it ain't right what they're doing to my friends. We didn't pick any fight. We just wanted to roll on through on the road and keep on going. This is your home, not ours. Half those folks on the wagon train have land and family already waiting on them out in California way! Why would they want yours, too? Can't take it with them."

"I think . . . this is all so confusing."

Bewley shook his head. "No, no, it ain't."

"Don't listen to him, Ma. They lied to me all day getting here. And they said they were going to set fire to our homes and kill us in our sleep!"

"Now, boy, that is the biggest lie I've heard all week, and I've heard some doozies of late. Ma'am," said Bewley, looking back to her pinched face, "don't take my word for it, but wait to hear when someone tells you of your husband's death. Someone other than that Deacon fella."

"I already heard."

"You did?" said Bewley.

"Who?" said the boy.

"Doesn't matter, but it was a friend. Not Deacon."

"Then you know what I said is true."

"I only know that he could have found my husband's body and come here right away last night."

"Could have, yes. But I'd wager he would have set up a hue and cry and everyone would have known in the Brethren camp within minutes, no?"

She sighed and shifted the now-sleeping baby to her other arm. "I don't know, mister. I will not pretend to know what goes on in the mind of Deacon. All I know is that you are a stranger. You are one of the people we have been told are our enemy and will cause us harm. And you are in my home holding me and my boy at gunpoint."

"Because I want that baby back, ma'am. Plain and simple. I know she's not yours. She was taken from the wagon train. Her mama is a wreck, I tell you, without knowing what's happened to her baby. Her *stolen* baby."

"No . . . Deacon said she was abandoned by you all! Another reason you are heathens, he said, for who else but a heathen would throw a baby away as if it were an old, worn-out boot?"

"Ma'am, Amy Henning, she's a mother. And you're a mother, too. Would you honestly think anybody who feels as you do about your son there would behave that way? You see any marks on that baby that show she's been hurt in any way?"

She slowly shook her head.

"Why in heaven's name would I lie to you? Why would I risk my neck to be here?" The questions hung in the air between them like heavy smoke.

"Now," he continued, "no offense intended to you or anyone here in your pretty little valley, ma'am, but I got me other things I plan on doing with my life, and so does each and every one of the folks back in that little wagon train your men folk have savaged, and I suspect it's all because of that Deacon fellow. If I'm wrong, then so be it. But answer me this, was everything dandy before he came into your midst?"

She didn't answer him, nor did he expect much of an answer. But after a few moments, she looked down at the now-sleeping baby and said, "Mister, you may leave if you care to."

"But, Ma—"

"Hush now, son!"

To Bewley, she said, "I appreciate you bringing my son home to me, and I am sorry for any misunderstanding he may have caused. He is . . . was fond of his father."

"As any boy should be of his pa, yes, ma'am. I'll take my leave of you, but I can't yet, ma'am. And you're holding the reason."

"But it's just a baby and you're—"

"I know, I'm a rough-and-raw sort of character, but I promised that baby's mother I'd bring her home."

"But—"

He held up a hand. "As a show of good faith"—he tugged free the boy's revolver from his waistband—"I believe this was your husband's. And so it belongs to you. Or the boy. At any rate, it's yours and not mine. Never let it be said that I stole a thing in this life."

He set it on the near corner of the family's dining table. "As to the bullets"—he pulled them out of his coat pocket—"I'll leave them over here on the windowsill." He smiled. "Okay?"

At that moment, the kid looked to one side, beyond Bewley's left shoulder toward the half-shuttered window. "What's that?"

He stepped forward, pointing toward the window. Bewley looked to his side and saw something, too. A light, maybe, but far off.

"It's a lantern," said the boy. "Someone's coming!"

Bewley sidestepped to the left of the doorframe and unlatched the door, then peered outside quick, not forgetting the boy and his mother were but a few steps to his right in the room.

Within seconds of looking out, down the length of the dusky near-dark valley, he saw no one approaching, lugging a lantern. What he did see, however, caused him to mutter, "Oh no! He didn't . . ."

Whatever thoughts he might have had of rescuing the baby, of finding Gage, and getting on out of there with no harm caused to them or to the dwellers of the valley evaporated as his eyes fell on the fires he saw in the distance.

There were two far down the valley, eastward toward the pass, one to either side of the road. And then something to his left caused him to glance that way, too. Upslope, yet still east of them, he saw yet another fire, higher up the hillside.

From behind, he heard boot steps, and the kid reached toward Bewley and yanked the door wide. It swung inward and the youth stood close behind him, the revolver in his hand, his mother shouting behind him.

But as the scout swung around to look at the kid, the kid saw what Bewley had seen and stared past him, slack-jawed. His mother, with the baby whimpering in her arms, also saw what they both had seen.

"Oh, my," she said.

"What have you done?" shouted the kid. "That man, that friend of yours . . . what did he do?"

"I . . ." Bewley looked once more out the door, not certain what to think. And then, from behind, he heard the woman shout, "No!"

Bewley swung around in time to see a dark shape pass before him, then a hard, sharp pain flowered up the side of his head. He spun, facing the small, warm room, and the room somehow was moving, too.

The woman was there before him, her eyes wide, her mouth shouting, saying something. But all Bewley heard was a pulsing, pounding sound, as if he had been slammed hard by a pummeling, foaming current at the bottom of a waterfall and he couldn't get up out of it.

The room kept on moving and soon he was looking upward at beams and planking and what looked to be dried herbs and smoked meats hanging above. The sounds grew louder and the hot pain flowed right over his head and down his body; and try as he might, he could not keep his eyes open. And then darkness closed in on everything he was seeing, crowding out the glow of the lantern light in the room. And then he saw nothing but blackness and felt nothing but pain.

CHAPTER 19

"I told you, Fletcher, you'll want to stay on the Maker's good side. And as the leader of the Brethren, you must do as I say!"

"But, Deacon, it . . . it ain't right." The tall, thin young man shook his head. "I'm sorry, but it ain't right."

Instead of shouting him down, as Deacon had been prone to do to everyone lately, the swarthy plug of a man pulled his big sausage finger back and rasped his hand over his whiskered face.

"All right, Fletcher. Tell you what." He set his big ham hands on his waist. "This is not good—surely, you see that? Here I am, trying to do what's best and right for the Brethren, and you're doubting me. You're talking as if I am doing this all for my personal gain." Deacon walked in a wide circle, his hands raised to the sky, his gaze looking upward.

"Why, everything I do, awake or asleep, everything I am, everything I have, it's all for the benefit of the Brethren, for the good of the Brethren. Do you realize how very precious and sacred and delicate—yes, that's the very word, 'delicate'—the Brethren's existence is right now?" He turned his steel-eyed gaze on the young man. "Hmm?"

"No . . . no, sir, I guess I don't."

"I didn't think so. Well, I'll tell you."

Deacon looked at the other men standing there, ringing the now-cold fire. "And I will tell you by way of a story. It's one I have not shared with you all yet. The only person I have shared this with is now no longer among us. Yes, Brother Schenk, who was taken from us without mercy by heathen hand last night under our very noses."

He waited, eyeing the dozen men one at a time. They all looked suitably saddened at being reminded of the gruesome thing that had, indeed, happened in their midst to one of the top members of the Brethren.

"When I was a younger man, not much older than you, Brother Fletcher"—he nodded to the lanky young man—"I had a home, a wife, and a child. Yes, it's true! And what's more, it was a son. And his name was Noel."

Deacon closed his eyes and bit his lip, then nodded and continued. He let his gaze rove their faces once again as he slowly walked in a circle around the low, crackling fire.

"We lived in a place far from here, on land that we had wrested from the wilderness. We worked hard to clear it, felling trees and pulling stumps and moving rocks. I built a cabin, small, but it kept us dry and warm.

"And after a year of hard seasons, with more rain than we wished for, more snow than I could shift, and then more drought parching our hard-won field, we managed somehow to grow enough root crops to keep body and soul together, but that was all. My wife, she came down with the croup, and soon my boy had it as well.

"I had to leave them, had to ride our one and only beast of burden, our mule, more suited to a plow than to carrying the weight of a man on his back. But I worked him without mercy, hoping to reach the nearest settlement for the tonics I thought might help my wife and son.

"And I did make it, and with the rest of my savings, I was able to purchase the last bottle available of the tincture. I also secured a promise from the one person in that tiny place who might be able to help me. She was a midwife, and her husband promised to drive her in their wagon right away. I did not wait for them, but left for home.

"The mule gave out when I was still an hour from our cabin. I ran the rest of the way, and try as I might, I could not keep on running the entire route. I staggered the last mile or so. It was almost dark, and as I neared the cabin, I saw a brightness in the sky above our humble clearing. I remember being confused by this for a moment, and then I smelled smoke and, cocking an ear, I heard a rushing sound, as if there was a windstorm up ahead.

"Of course, I knew by then what all this meant. I

screamed and ran once more, though I had no strength left in my poor, battered body. Still, I ran; and the closer I drew to the cabin, the more dread I felt. I broke through the tree line, already knowing my home was ablaze, having seen it with more clarity with each passing step.

"I screamed for my wife and son, shouted myself hoarse, and tried to rush at the fire, but by then, it was already too powerful and had engulfed the entire cabin. Indeed, timbers were falling. I ran up, as close as I dared, screaming and bolting!

"Nothing but the crackle of flames and thick, choking smoke responded to my pleas. I shouted and ran around the entire cabin—and that's when I saw that our small barn, too, had succumbed to flames. And I remember thinking, however fleetingly at the time, that this should not be. Was the barn not some hundred feet away from the house? How could this have burned, too?

"It did not yet occur to me that the devil, in one of his many guises, had caused this nightmare. But it would occur to me soon after that. Very soon. For as I ran back around the house, I saw a blackened, smoking shape sprawled on the earth some yards from the cabin . . ." Here, Deacon paused, his voice trembling, and he held a hand to his mouth, then bent his head and covered his eyes.

None of the men in the circle spoke. Some of them looked ready to sob, others looked at Deacon as if for the first time. They had, of course, seen him preach an untold number of times in the past few years since he came into their midst, but this was a much more intimate affair, not the somber situation they found themselves in, in one of their barns each Sabbath eve. No, this was . . . different.

Deacon pulled in a deep breath and opened his hard-rubbed, reddened eyes, and walked his slow circle about the campfire stones, glancing at the men. He bent and laid with care two lengths of snapped branches over the sputtering fire, then prodded the coals with a charred poker stick. "Fire," he muttered. "The life giver, the life taker." He stood upright and faced them once more.

"I did not know at first what this thing on the ground could be, but as it was not of the house and not something I recognized, I ran to it, and before I reached it, I knew that it was my wife. My dear wife. I dropped to my knees, hope pounding in my breast that she had somehow escaped the killing flames.

"And she had escaped the fire, it seemed, though her clothes were charred; and beneath her, my son, shielded by her body, had also, it seemed, escaped the blaze."

Deacon looked at each man in turn, his face a mask of horror, his head shaking no, no, no, so that each man he looked at also wore the somber mask and also shook his head no, no, no.

"But alas, she was dead. And so was my son, my Noel." A jagged sound erupted from his mouth, a sob ripped from him by force, it seemed to the assembled Brethren.

Deacon held up a finger skyward and his red eyes

glanced at each man as he spun in place slowly. "But it was not the fire that killed her!"

As he expected, several of the men, the more simple-minded, in his estimation, gasped, and most of them wore knitted brows, confusion crawling over their faces.

"Yes," he said, nodding. "It's true. While the fire did not do my wife and son any good, I discovered as I knelt by their side and grasped my wife's shoulder, then turned her over to face me, that . . ."

He gasped again, and once more, he held a trembling hand to his face. Between his fingers, he spoke loud enough for them all to hear him. It helped that they had leaned forward. ". . . that their throats had been sliced open!"

Deacon ran a shaking fingertip across his own throat as he glared at the men as if they had somehow been responsible for the heinous act.

"Who?" said Fletcher.

Deacon spun, fixing the rangy young man with his wild-eyed gaze.

"That is the question, the very question I asked myself, Brother Fletcher!" Deacon nodded, and he could tell by the slightest flicker of relief across the young man's face that Deacon's response had somehow made the fool feel as if he had been somewhat forgiven for his earlier insubordination.

Not so, thought Deacon. *For I do not forget or forgive the questioning of my ways or policies.*

Sensing he might be losing his audience's patience, he plowed ahead with his story. "It did not take me long to determine the identity of the culprit, no, for even in my grief, even through the river of tears bursting forth from my very own eyes, the eyes I wished to pluck from my head for seeing this terrible sight . . .

"Even with the blistering flames and raging power of the towering inferno that was at that very moment devouring all that we had worked so hard for, worked so hard to wrestle from the wilderness, to build with our own hands . . . these very hands!"

He held up both hands before him. They were clawed and shaking, and he could tell by the looks on the faces of the gathered Brethren as he peered at them from between his fingers that they felt as if they were right there with him, watching as if their very own homesteads had been driven asunder by flames, foul flames, their loved ones cruelly killed.

"Even as all this torment swirled about me, I spied, across the clearing, through the trees, one, then two, then three, and more leering faces, not just smiling, but laughing, howling mad with glee, and pointing at me!"

"What?"

"Yes! Yes, I tell you a thousand times! Yes, they were not phantoms, but men!"

"What sort of man would do this to another?" said one Brethren, a grizzled older man, pious and steady as a tight-wound clock with his attendance of services. Quint was his name, and he was one of the Brethren that Deacon could count on to help sway the others, for he was a forthright and respected man among his farming peers.

"That is what I asked myself, Brother Quint!" Deacon pointed a thick finger at the man and nodded. "And I found my answer soon enough. For as I bolted toward them, they held their ground. I did not care what was going to happen to me, but the closer I drew to the trees behind which they hid, poking out their foul, grinning faces, I saw who it was and I was chilled to my very core. It was then, my friends, that I knew without doubt that which I had all but ignored all my living years up to that point."

They all leaned toward him and he knew he'd not lost them yet. "I learned that the world is populated with two types of folks." He held up a finger "The righteous!" He nodded. "And the heathens!"

Most of the men nodded, a couple held their hands to their chests, and several muttered. "Yes, yes!"

"I don't think I have to tell you that the beasts I saw leering at me from the trees were not righteous folks! No, no, they were heathen folks!" He let that sink in a moment or two, then resumed. "They were the roughest sort of heathen, for they were the red savage Indians!"

The gasps and nods that greeted this news told him that at least some of them were not surprised by the revelation.

"I see by the faces on the younger among you that you do not at first understand the fact that they do not deserve our pity, but rather our dedication to eradicating them from the earth! For that is the only way to combat this creeping sickness. The only way!"

"Yes, yes!" shouted Quint.

Deacon replied with a solid head nod. "Indeed! And that is what I did! It did not happen immediately, but I was able to chase them deep into the forest. I was not worried about getting lost. No! I was not worried about myself in the least, for I felt that I had lost all hope.

"With the murder of my wife and son and the burning of our home and barn and possessions, I hoped I might somehow avenge them. And it was, if I must admit it, my fervent hope that I, too, would lose my life in the effort." He bowed his head and nodded slowly, hearing the slight gasps of the assembled men. He had them in his palm. Now it was time to squeeze.

"The next thing I knew, I was in the forest, chasing the heathens, who, when not faced with a woman or a child, it seemed, were little more than frightened forest creatures. I did not heed a thing, for I had no conscience about me. I had pure, raw animal rage. In that respect, I was no different than, and no better than, the heathens I was chasing."

"Then what happened, Deacon?" asked Fletcher, his curiosity overcoming his fear of the man. The change was apparent to Deacon as he looked at the younger man's face.

"What happened next, my friend, is that I soon became lost. I ran and ran, confident for a long time that I was tracking the killers. Soon enough, however, I realized I had seen neither sign nor signal from them, since after I had plunged into the gloom of the dense forest.

"Rage, such as I had never known, filled me. I wished only to find them and kill them with my bare hands. For I had no weapon on me, save for a folding knife in my trouser pocket."

He shrugged and let his shoulders hang, along with his head. He hoped he looked mighty dejected.

"I wandered then, for one day, two, then three, who knows? The true count I have never been able to discern. Eventually I was able to realize, as I crawled out of the thick fog of shock and grief, that I was still alive and still very much lost. And I did not care. I lay down under a pine with low-sweeping branches and wished for death to take me. Lo, I will admit to you all now that at that time, I was not a praying man!"

The gasps rising from the Brethren who ringed about him sounded more like steam released from valves than men in shock.

Deacon nodded. "But somehow, as I lay gasping beneath that pine on its thick matte of needles and duff, close to death, for I had neither water nor food since well before the fire, many days before, I prayed, if you could call it that. I begged is what I really did. I begged the Maker for death, for release from this hard, cold world."

Deacon looked at them. "He let me down. He let me down because I remained alive. How long? I don't know. A week? I don't know. Long enough to find I was indeed still alive, that my fondest desire, death, had not happened. But my journey was not yet over. No, no, dear Brethren."

He slowly circled the smoking fire again, his hands behind his back. He sensed some of the men were growing tired or impatient. "It was then, when I was at my weakest, that the most frightening thing happened to me after I had entered the thick, bleak woods. I could scarcely move, save for opening my eyes.

"In addition to the fact that I was weakened from no water and no food and had never felt so utterly close to death, the thing that eluded me, it was then that I heard the sound of branches snapping. I had forgotten that I had crawled beneath the pine and lay in a state of stupor and grief.

"But I soon became aware that the sounds of branches snapping drew closer. And closer, and closer still. Yet I could not move, and part of me was beyond rage, for I felt certain it was the savages come to attack me. But another part of me thought, 'Yes, yes, let it happen, for then I will be with my beloved and all this sadness and suffering shall be behind me.'

"But it was not to be, for I heard the sound of deep, heavy breaths. I did my best then to raise my head. And do you know what I saw, my brothers?"

He looked at them, and each man shook his head, eyes wide.

"I saw the face of a great grizzly bear, staring at me. It had poked its way beneath the branches, its massive head parting them as a hand might open closed curtains to see who is outside.

"And that bear huffed and chuffed and blew its rank, rotten-meat stench at me. Its great mouth hung open, its lips sagging, its mighty teeth parted as if it were about to open its jaws wide and rip great chunks from my feeble body!

"But it did not. No, it stared at me for the longest time. It moved closer and stared down at my face, its breath clouding me. I gagged and my eyes teared and still it stared, sniffing me and gazing at me in the gloom with its massive pig-like eyes! They stared straight into mine, deeper than any creature had ever looked at me. And with a great huffing gust of breath, it growled—a low, thunderous sound as of a storm far off, but moving closer with each second. And then it swung that mighty head down and I thought, 'Here it is at last, the killing moment.' I closed my eyes and awaited it.

"But it did not come. Instead, the great beast turned and walked away. Soon afterward, a cleansing rain gushed down. It rained all that day, all that night, and well into the next day. Then the sun emerged and soaked into me, and somehow I found the strength to drag myself out from beneath the pine.

"I found that a small, clear stream had grown overnight not far away. I drank my fill and then some; and heartened, I stood. Once more, on wobbly legs and without any effort at thought, I walked in a direction—the choice I had not made, so much as felt, and soon came upon familiar ground.

"I emerged into a clearing just as several people, the midwife and her husband among them, were gathered around a grave. It was the clearing that had once been my home, and the grave is what they had dug and were laying my swaddled wife and son to rest deep within.

"They were, naturally, shocked at the sight of me. And it came to me just then that they might all think I had done this foul thing, for some odd reason. And I did not care. But no, one of the men told me how they had found many sets of moccasin tracks about the clearing and had seen my own trail leading off into the forest and they had assumed I had given chase. But they could not find me, though they tried, calling and shouting my name for days.

"They had given me up for dead. But as you can see, I did not die. At least not in the way one might think. For I have come to believe, my fellow Brethren, that I died deep in those woods and was reborn as the man you see now.

"For as I gazed at the fresh grave entombing my wife and my son, it came to me that I was spared by the Maker for a purpose. And in the coming weeks and months and years, as I wandered, alone and footsore and without possessions, that I was spared for one reason, and one reason only."

He looked at them all and they waited for him to speak.

"To spread the word of the Brethren so that we might rend asunder all heathens from the land. Those we cannot turn to see the power and rightness and grace of the Brethren must be vanquished. And that, my friends, is what I have devoted myself, my life, to doing."

Deacon turned once more to face Fletcher, the lanky youth whose questioning of his authority had set Deacon off on this path of what he chose to call explanation.

"Brother Fletcher, that is why my authority on this matter of how we deal with the encampment of heathens—and any matter to come—must be supported wholeheartedly by all Brethren. Or else."

"Or else what?"

Deacon swung his gaze around and his eyes fixed on the speaker, Quint, the oldest of the Brethren. "You, too, dare question me, the embodied representative of the Maker?"

The old gent cleared his throat, fluffed his beard, and said, "I only asked what the comeuppance will be if somebody rubs your fur the wrong way, as the saying goes."

Deacon regarded the man a long time through narrowed eyes. Long enough, in fact, that other of the gathered Brethren men began to fidget and look away—anywhere, it seemed, but at this awkward exchange between two men they trusted, admired, and followed.

Deacon knew that as an elder among them, Quint was revered and looked up to. If Deacon had any reason to be nervous about Quint's position—and his own, too—it would arise because of the fact that Quint was one of the original settlers of the vale. Whereas Deacon, by comparison, was a newcomer.

This was a fact he was well aware of and not something he liked to remind any of the Brethren of, nor to be reminded of himself. He considered this and thought that it would be best to once more amble down the path of humility, a trail well-trodden by him.

"You are correct, of course, Brother Quint. It is the

part of me that is but a man, a base creature constantly at war with his heathen self. But that, my friends, is what I wish to help you all to conquer! And if my efforts on your behalf result in a lack of humility and a directness, instead, then know that it is because I alone realize the importance, the urgency, the necessity, to dispense with the heathens before their taint spreads among us like a wildfire! Lest the heathens burn us out and murder our wives and children!"

Any further questions, or objections that might have been raised by the old man or the young, lanky Fletcher, were quashed by the fervent cheers and gestures of supplication that the rest of the Brethren feverishly engaged in.

Hands rose to the sky, eyes closed, heads were bowed, and loud murmurings of beseeching prayer to help them do better rippled through the group. Soon even Quint and Fletcher had no choice but to join in. They also felt Deacon's gaze, steel-like, settle on them with a cold, hard, unforgiving weight.

Just then, a lad rode up fast on a horse, jerking to a stop right in their midst. He held a lantern, but it had blown out on the journey up to the pass from the farms beyond.

Deacon turned his angry gaze on the youth. It was one of the Schnee boys, but his face was writ large with alarm and he was breathing almost as hard as the horse.

"What's wrong, boy?" said one man, stepping forward to gentle the stamping steed. It was Brother Schnee.

"Pa!" The lad looked at his father, then over at

Deacon, then back to his father. "It's the hay barn. Ours and two more! They're on fire!"

"What?" shouted the man. At the same time, the others barked oaths of shock and bolted for their own mounts.

During the next few minutes, Deacon barked orders and the men paid attention to him, although he could tell it took effort to do so.

He told four men to stay behind at the Brethren camp and to await the return of the other men still in the field. He knew, as did those he spoke to, that those men were likely dead. He didn't care about them, but he did care that the Brethren remaining continue to bow to his will.

Deacon entertained dark thoughts about the spineless fools he'd saddled himself with. And that cursed boy who rode up to tell them that hay barns were on fire. *Hay barns! Just when I had them lapping anew from my palm after that silly story I made up about having a wife and son, and finding them dead. Ha! The saps.*

But still, perhaps the burning hay barns would play to his benefit. Perhaps he could use them to prove his point that only heathen savages, such as those in his fanciful tale, resorted to fire. Thus proving him correct—the only beings worthy of life were Brethren. All others were heathens and should die.

Yes, these fires could prove to be just the thing. Perhaps there should be other fires as well.

Deacon grinned in the dark as he rode back into the valley, the Chosen Valley, with his fellow Brethren. Fools, though they were. He looked about him at their dim outlines. If they only knew that the Brethren was his very own fabrication. An invention he'd been testing in various small ways all the way westward.

These fools were the first large group he'd been able to convince so well and for so long. But perhaps they were beginning to become suspicious. Perhaps he needed to bundle the collected tithings and ride into the night. It was worth a thought.

But not just yet, Deacon, he cautioned himself. *Not when there is so much to gain, and so soon. So very soon.*

CHAPTER 20

Something cold and wet slapped down over Gage with the suddenness of a backhand across the face. He groaned and tried to figure out just what was happening.

He was in darkness and coldness and something else, something that eclipsed those two sensations. He felt a throbbing jaggedness all over his body, his right arm felt as if it were on fire, as did his face, his left hand, spots on his neck and chest. What was happening?

As painful as were the agonies pulsing all over his body, they also had the effect of reviving him. And the darkness, he came to realize, was because he still had his eyes closed.

He worked to open them, and felt as if he had been slammed first through the ice of a frozen-over river, then shoved into a massive forge fire at a smithy's shop.

What was happening? He kept working to open his eyes and tried to speak, to get a word in around the other noises someone else was making. They were groaning and moaning and he wished whoever it was would shut up.

It took another few moments of effort before he could pop open one eye, his left, and then the right followed suit. He smelled the tang of woodsmoke and the coldness of a bitter autumn night.

"Good," said a cracked, hoarse voice. "You are awake now."

Gage thought maybe it was the voice of an old woman. Was she the one moaning?

Then a sudden cold, wet blast hit him in the face and chest. And he knew what it was—water. Cold well water dumped on him, as from a bucket.

It had also come to him that the groaning and moaning was no one other than himself.

"Wake up, you!" the old woman's voice shouted, close by his face this time. "And stop that bothersome noise or I'll give you something to cry about!"

That last phrase helped Gage to force open his eyes again and looked upward. He saw darkness, yes, but set with stars. And closer in, the dull glow of a low-lit lantern. Closer still, he saw a face.

That phrase: "Something to cry about." That was a favored saying of his old man, Jasper Gage, who used to tell him that whenever he'd pull a sad face or begin to sob as a child.

Young Jonathan had learned early on to always do what Jasper said and to never indulge in anything like crying. It earned him a backhand or a striking boot, most often both.

For some reason, hearing it now, and from the mouth of what sounded like an old woman, made him chuckle.

"I am glad you see humor in this. I cannot," said the voice.

He watched as the face that spoke moved closer toward his. The wrinkled thing was surrounded with a black bonnet and its squinted eyes stared at him.

"Why?" she said.

"Why?" His word unintentionally echoed hers, but his voice, he realized, was strained and barely above a whisper. It had come out as a wheeze. He swallowed and tried again. "Where am I?"

"Ha!" she said, and kicked him in the right shoulder. "You don't remember, huh?"

He closed his eyes once more, and that was the very thing that began the trickle of memory.

"Why set fire to our barns? You have doomed our livestock to starvation. And the Brethren, too!" The woman slapped his face again.

The slap didn't hurt, but the pain caused by his jerking away felt like hot needles and coals. He groaned once more.

"You ought to moan, you . . . you killer!"

"Ma'am," he said, then dragged his tongue over his sore lips. "Ma'am, please, a drink of water."

Of all the reactions he might have deserved—denial, rage, another slap—it was laughter that he did not expect. But that's what the old crone was doing, she was wheezing through a smile on her face. Her shawled shoulders worked up and down as if she were being goosed from behind.

"Ain't going to answer my question yet, eh?" she

said after a few moments. "Well, maybe if I leave you out here, the cold will loosen your tongue."

"No! Wait, wait . . ."

She laughed again and stood, revealing that she'd been seated on a stump of wood that looked to be a chopping block, and hoisted her lantern. "I will not wait. Nor will you. Not long, that is, for the others are coming. And they are a whole lot less kindly than I am."

"But—"

"No, sir, no sugar talk. Time for that is over, you dirty heathen!"

She shuffled away. Gage turned his head and saw that they had been but a dozen feet from the door of a cabin. She stopped with the cabin door just nudged open, her hand on the latch.

She turned and looked at him. "You just wait until Deacon gets ahold of you. The man cannot abide a heathen, and that's a fact. Why, him and the menfolk are dealing with a nest of them right now!"

She held the lantern up near her face; for the first time he could see her features clearly, and he saw that she was indeed an old wrinkled thing. There was no mirth there, no mercy on that scowling, withered apple of a face.

"I don't doubt that nest is exactly where you crawled out from! Heathen!" She spat at him, a paltry, dry effort, but a hard gesture, nonetheless. Then she shook her head and turned away.

Now that he recalled what had happened to himself, and what he had done to the three hay barns—had it been three? Were there any others? That memory was fuzzed, but the waves of pain and welling nausea kept him awake and alert.

He'd been attacked by a dog—a big, vicious death dealer. He remembered the most menacing thing about the beast was that it barely made a sound as it attacked him. Growls, to be sure, but they were low and menacing.

Gage knew it was the signature of a successful stalker and killer. The thing had savaged him and he knew he was likely in pretty rough shape. How bad, he had no idea, for right then, the coldness from the water the old crone had dumped on him began to stiffen his clothes.

The night's temperature was dropping. He'd known it was going to be a nippy one, as the breeze earlier and indeed all afternoon had carried with it the particular and peculiar scent that precedes bitter cold, and often snowstorms.

None of that much mattered to him at that moment, for his body spasmed, wracked with cold; and hot lances of pain shot through him from so many wounds. Every time he moved a limb, another jag of pain sliced into him.

He could not blame the old woman, for he had indeed caused them grievous harm. But it was nothing, and he still felt confident of this, compared with the horrors that awaited the wagon train families, should that Deacon brute get his way.

And from what he'd seen, there were precious few Brethren who were about to go against the man. He seemed to have them all bound up tight with his powers of persuasion.

Chapter 21

The long, nippy afternoon had been made longer for the pensive wagon train members. The gunfighting stranger, Gage, who they knew now as the cold-blooded killer of legend, Texas Lightning, and their very own scout, the grizzled but friendly Bewley, had gone off together.

They said they were going to rescue the Henning baby and maybe cause a distraction in the so-called Chosen Valley of the Brethren. But were they? The fact that the men left behind their goods and mounts went a ways in keeping folks calmer than they might have been. But in the circumstances, that wasn't saying much.

It hadn't taken long for what tender trepidations they had to begin to crumble like old sandstone in a flood. Not more than an hour after the two men had departed camp, the wagon train members heard shots from the west, upriver and low, then from above. And then nothing—no sounds for what felt like days.

Despite the situation, it was the waiting, the feeling

of being trapped and helpless, that wormed its way into their minds. It mattered little to them that they knew they could be in far worse shape—after all, they had a source of fresh water, albeit the flow was modest. But it was pure water, come down from on high, from somewhere within the bowels of the cliff behind them.

Still, the lot of them felt uneasy. The only sounds were the occasional cackle of a flustered chicken, the lowing of one of the few cows they had managed to keep from being herded off by their attackers, and the occasional cries of one of the babies on the trip.

"Hollow promise," Chase had said to the handful of men sharing his shift as they stood about the smoldering, smokey central fire ring. "Not Gage or Bewley is going to bring that Henning baby back. You mark my words."

"Shut it, Chase," muttered Silks, the rangy backwoods loner. He'd become more talkative, which is to say uttering four or five words once a day, instead of his usual none.

Chase cut his eyes to the man, but kept his mouth closed. The rest of the men were more apt to stand behind this no-nonsense, quiet man than they were Chase, and Chase knew it.

Didn't mean he had to like it. He was tempted to say that Silks would go too far one day, but he figured he'd let it be for now. But not forever.

The rest of the men were at their scouting posts, dotted about the ragged, tight perimeter of their camp.

Then Silks surprised them by speaking once more

"Should be obvious to us all by now that the Gage fellow was talking the truth."

"Oh, which lie do you believe?" Chase challenged. He could not help himself. Both Silks and Gage rubbed his fur the wrong way.

Silks glanced at Chase, then let it slide. "These Brethren folks are only half serious."

"Half? How do you figure?" This was the somber, pudgy fellow who'd been winged in an early attack. Folks found him curious because he wasn't overly chatty, yet he traveled with enough gear to set up shop as a hardware merchant. He'd never said it wasn't his plan.

"They ain't killed but a couple of our beasts, ain't attacked us with flaming arrows. About the only thing they don't seem to care about, or want around, is us. Mostly, the full-grown members of us. This tells me these Brethren folks want our goods, our gear, our money, our beasts, and apparently our children."

"But why?"

Chase cut in then, with a snort. "Because they're greedy, as well as being stony cold killers."

Silks drizzled brown chaw juice in a demure stream down between his feet, then glanced, as was his habit, to make sure no womenfolk had seen him. If they had, he would have blushed, not at all in keeping with the whip-lean, no-nonsense image he showed the world.

"Much as I hate to do it, I will agree with Chase here. Them Brethren are the worst of the worst. Where I come from, when someone does their worst to you, they have given you permission to do the same, and then some, to them."

"That's an eye for an eye," said the pudgy, somber man, nudging a blackened fire ring stone with the toe of his scuffed brown brogan.

"You bet it is. That's why I ain't waiting for those two men to come back and tell us what they got up to."

"What are you going to do?"

"Me and the boy are going to do more of what we said we'd do yesterday. Only this time, we're heading out and we're not coming back until we have a few scalps, so to speak."

The man they called Gramps stared wide-eyed at Silks, and he stiffened, standing straighter. "But . . . but you don't mean you're going to literally—"

"What? Separate them from their hair? Might be, might be. Been a while since my blade tasted the hairline of another man." Then Silks did something none of them had seen him do in the weeks and weeks since he and his family joined the train—he grinned, his tobacco-stained teeth showing briefly nested beneath his moustache and beard. He patted the broad leather sheath at his waist, in which sat a keen, wide blade, only the slab walnut handle and solid brass hilt showing.

Just then a low whistle sounded from the north edge of camp, closest to the infernal pass none of them wanted to travel through any longer. They'd all lost their taste for travel, for the jolly adventure their journey from Kansas had been, until they reached Higgins, that is.

All the men about the smokey little campfire ring looked toward the fellow who'd whistled. It was Rice, and he stood inside the Nowlan wagon, which, along with two others flanking it, sat broadside facing the brunt, thus far, of the Brethren attacks.

The three wagons had been emptied of precious goods and had been filled with crates and such that might slow, if not stop, bullets.

Rice stood inside, behind crates, almost like a podium, protecting him, save for his shoulders and head. He was hidden from the attackers, as were some of the other sentries, by the wagon's arched canvas cover. A hole for eyeing the terrain of the field and the pass beyond had been sliced in the canvas, and below it, another for the rifle's snout.

Behind him, another hole had been cut, larger, and he had stepped the width of the wagon to poke his head out of that hole. "They're on the move, spreading out and making for us, circling wide! Get set, boys!"

The men about the campfire scattered, hustling to their meager camps for more arms and ammunition, and spreading the word throughout the small camp, although everybody already knew.

The many children and the few feeble, which amounted to three old women and one doddering, softheaded old man, were herded into the center of the camp, within which they had built up a bulwark of planking and crates. Ringing this from within were five women, mothers and wives, who would see to it that the innocents among them were defended.

Of the womenfolk, Silks had said days before when helping to build that central structure, that in a grim fight, he trusted them above and beyond any man. "My mammy was born with a gun in each fist and a knife in her mouth, and she died ninety years later about the same way. Wouldn't have had nothing if she hadn't laid low a passel of savages each year of my youth. And my wife is the same way. Good woman, but don't get on her mean side."

"Which side is that?" said Dawlish, with a half grin.

"All of 'em," said Silks, not grinning back.

Now that a renewed attack was imminent, most of the wagon train members felt an odd sense of relief. What they had feared was coming true, and as they could do little about beginning it, they could, sure as the sun rose and set each day, do something about how it ended.

Stations were taken up and the surprisingly well-barricaded camp was laced with men and women bearing guns. Near to hand were laid shotguns, revolvers, pistols, pitchforks, axes, mattocks, hoe handles—anything that might prove useful in a close-in fight. For surely, it would to come to that at some point.

Silks, for one, was tired of the Brethren playing games with them. He was also a little disappointed because he and his son had wanted to take the fight to the enemy, and had only stifled their urge for a day because the others wanted to wait.

"Wait for what?" he had asked, but none of them wanted to risk letting the guerilla tactics, should they backfire, bring the wrath of their attackers any sooner than they had to.

Time for that foolishness was over, thought Silks. Once the tide had turned, he and the boy were going to use the smoke and the noise of the fight to enact their plan.

It was a simple one—scout the perimeter of the field, preferably under cover of dusk and then darkness, and slice throats.

But that, Silks realized, would have to wait, because the first bullets were whistling in. If the attack was anything like the Brethren's previous efforts, they would arrange themselves in a crescent about the camp, hunker low in the field, and commence to firing, taking their time and sighting in well. That made it important that the wagon train folks all stay hidden, but not at the risk of getting a decent sight line on any attackers.

Silks aimed and waited for one of the black-clothed men to show himself from behind one of the slight rises in the landscape of the field. What did the Brethren hope to gain? Kill a few folks at a time to help speed the plow, all the while waiting for the rest of them to starve to death, or get so desperate from the thought of starvation that they might give up?

He'd adjusted what he felt was the right distance for windage, for there was a stiff, if slight, breeze laying in from the northeast, just dragging its fingers over the field. Had been for a few hours now. Enough so that at the distance between him and the killer he'd chosen to concentrate his bullets on first, there would be no mistake.

He had to make each shot a successful one. And that meant . . . "Blood," he muttered, and squeezed the trusty, smooth-worn trigger of his rifle.

It whistled in, parting air and dried grasses, and bored dead center into the prone, peeking Brethren man's forehead, just below his pepper-and-salt hairline. His head jerked upward hard and fast, as if he'd been punched from below on the jaw. Then he smacked forward and that was it.

Silks heard one of the Brethren men, close by his victim—for there were enough of them that they were not but fifteen feet or so apart—shout his rage at them. Silks was too far to hear what name the man shouted, but it did not matter. That he'd riled them was enough for the lanky woodsman.

And then the man, as Silks had hoped, jerked back around, shouting oaths of anger, and peeled off a shot, which plunked into a wooden chest to Silks's right.

"Eye for an eye," muttered Silks, and delivered unto the riled Brethren fellow's forehead a hole that matched that of his now-dead friend. "Make that a third eye."

In a nearly identical move, the head of the newly shot man snapped up, revealing for the slimmest nibble of a second, his eyes wide with shock. His head dropped and, once more, cries of rage rose up here and there from his fellow believers.

Silks allowed himself a thin grin, then waited on another one.

"How'd you do that?" shouted Rice from behind stacked crates and kegs to his left.

Without moving, Silks kept his eyes on the field for any telltale movements. "Take your time, wait them out, then let them have a lead sweetie. Because rest assured they are doing the same to you and yours."

"You make killing a man sound easy."

"It is. Don't let sentiment sugar it up. Just decide if you want to die knowing you could have, should have, done more to protect your wife or daughter from the foul hands of those praying grubs."

"That's a hard view."

"Hard life." Silks decided he'd said enough for a week. Now it was time to kill.

Word spread around the camp of the woodsman's two successful shots and the men quietly cheered. The women in the central barricade whooped loudly, which brought a quick grin to Silks's face. He did love to hear a woman shout when he'd done something well, and the other men, he guessed, felt the same. It was natural for a man to feel such.

Soon a crack was heard from their lines, along the southern edge, then another.

"Need a hand over here—pile of them are trying the river to get around us!"

"Then shoot 'em!" growled Silks, shaking his head and readjusting the gaze through his sighting eye.

"Ain't that easy!" shouted one of the men just before he yipped.

Silks looked his way, taking care to keep his own head down, and knowing what he'd see before he turned. Yep, it was Rice, the young man with a pretty young wife and a little boy, and another bairn on the way, was flopping around on his back in the dirt.

He'd just toppled backward from his height of seven or eight feet up on a water barrel, and when he'd shouted back to Silks, he had lost charge of his thinking for a finger-snap length of time. That was all it took for one of those Brethren beasts to tickle his trigger.

But the shot wasn't a dead-on one, and it looked as though, despite the obvious pain the young man was in, he might pull through if he could staunch that bleeding.

"Get a woman on over there! Now! Where's his wife?"

As it turned out, she was shouting for her wounded man, struggling to get out of the central barricade, but having a heck of a time with it because of her ample belly.

"You ain't in no condition to help your man! Get back. I'll go!" It was Silks's wife. She shoved the pregnant woman back down into the arms of the others, and made to scramble over the barricade herself. As she did so, her eye caught her husband's and he gave her a quick nod. She returned it and made for the writhing, squealing wounded man.

The shot fellow was holding the left side of his face and offering up strained shouts forced through tight-set teeth.

"Hush yourself now!" she said. To anyone in hearing range, her tone didn't sound the least bit comforting.

EVERYBODY HAS A GUN

"You think he'll be all right?" said Dawlish to Silks's right.

"Oh yes, Mother will tend to him, don't you fret. She's been doctoring shot folks since she was four." The lanky man squeezed off a shot. "Got a late start, she did, but she's made up for it since."

His bullet had found man flesh, but he did not think it was a fatal blow. Still, it would slow the fellow. Shoulder wounds were not a trifling thing. He reckoned the pickings were slim along this northern edge because of what the young man had shouted before he got himself shot in the face. It seemed the Brethren were working up a side attack, by way of the river.

Silks wanted to make for the southern edge of the camp and pop a few of the Brethren making their way along the riverbank. "You get yourself set, stay calm, and choose your shots. I got to get over there. We're a man down by the river."

With that, Silks slid his buckskin-clad frame down out of his station amid the barrels and crates. With instinct keeping him bent low, he made for the southern edge of the outer barricade, over to where the young man had been stationed.

On the way, he snatched up the fellow's own rifle from where it had fallen to the earth when the man dropped.

From his quick glance, Silks reckoned it looked all right. He'd try to use it in a moment or two. Had to get himself up there to see if what the man said was true.

Judging from the shots of the other wagon train men aiming riverwise, there were more Brethren making their way along the river than before.

"New tactics," he muttered. Keeping his head low, he sighted down the long barrel of his rifle.

It would be like popping squirrels back home in the hills as they scampered way up high, blocked part of the year by leaves on the oaks. Experience had taught him what he considered one of the most precious things a woodsman could know about making meat—if you waited long enough, every critter you stalked would tire first and pop up to see if the way was clear. That's when a hunter's patience would pay off.

He did that now, silently cursing the other two men along this stretch for not taking their time. "Bullets will run out." He said it loud enough in a pause for them both to hear.

One of them slowed his squeezing, and the other one, Silks saw it was Chase, offered up a snort loud enough for the entire camp to hear. Then the fool doubled his efforts at pulling on his rifle's trigger.

Silks ignored him and waited. Soon he would have his patience rewarded. Had to.

Behind, down below on the ground, he heard his wife's hard tone begin to quiet the writhing young man. He knew her ways weren't to everyone's liking, but they suited her and they suited him, and that's all that mattered. She was a good helpmate and was as tough as a mule.

There, between the rattly stalks of bankside alders

and thickets of rabbit brush, Silks spied movement, and it was not a mere shadow. No sun to make them just now. He waited, giving whoever it was time to think he was clever and had outfoxed the defenders.

It worked. The man by the river—one of how many?—dared to move forward, eager to gain ground.

The woodsman let him have a lead snack. It caught the man low, though. At least the shot was lower than Silks had planned on. It cored a hole a man could stick a pinky finger into in the right-hand side of the fellow's neck.

He'd intended for the bullet to nest itself at the temple. *Must be my sights are off,* he thought. He was pleased, nonetheless, with the fact that he'd lobbed four bullets that day and all four tasted blood.

Two of them caused death where they lay. One of the victims, his third, was savvy enough to keep from moving about any more than Silks expected of a shot man. The man, shot in the shoulder, lay there, silently grim and waiting out the onslaught. It was a credit to him, thought Silks, that he hadn't shifted much.

Not so with the man at the river. Silks's shot punched into his neck and likely would kill the man. It was not a way he wanted to die, choking up blood and unable to scream. He held still and thought he could detect a gurgling, gasping sound. He knew it was wrong to take pleasure in the pain of another, but these Brethren thieves had brought it on themselves.

Long minutes passed without shots from either side. "Chase," said Silks, "I'm going to get my boy and make for the riverbank. Can't do much more from in here, but out there we can."

"That's foolish!" growled Chase. "You'll get killed and . . . and we need you and your son here!"

"Thanks for the left-handed compliment, but we can do a whole lot more out there than we can in here. You and your men here can hold down the situation without us." Silks knew that he was stroking the man's feathers, but if there ever was a fellow who needed that sort of thing on a regular basis, it was that blasted Chase.

"All right, then," said Chase, sounding bolder. "You go ahead, but don't be long! And don't get yourself killed!"

The woodsman was already on the move, not needing anything from Chase that resembled permission. "Yes, Mother." Silks knew it would ruffle the very feathers on Chase that he'd just smoothed, but he could not help himself.

He slid back down, laying the young man's rifle beside him. His wife had the man's head in her lap and was wrapping muslin around the groaning fellow's wound.

"He hurt bad, Mother?"

She didn't look up at him, but kept working. "He'll live. Gonna have hisself an awful scar, lose some teeth, likely have to wear a beard, and his wife will have to get used to him talking funny, but yeah, he'll live."

All the while she spoke, the wounded man's eyes grew wider.

Silks shook his head. *Leave it to Mother to yank off*

any tenderness and let the fresh air of bald truth in.
"Okay, then. The boy still in the far corner, yonder by the river and the rocks?"

"I expect so. He'd stay where you told him to. He's a good boy."

"Yep. I'll fetch him then, take to the bottoms along the river. See what sort of ruckus we can muster."

She looked up at him. "Okay, then." Once again, they nodded to each other and that was that. Silks was off, padding fast and low on his moccasin-clad feet toward the camp's southwest corner to retrieve his son.

It took him but two minutes to find the lad, who was sighting down the barrel of his rifle, aimed toward the riverside bank brush. He glanced at his father and they greeted each other with a nod. The boy snugged his rifle tighter to his shoulder, let out a breath, and touched the trigger. The rifle, a brute of a piece, kicked slightly, but the lad held it firm.

"Get him?"

The boy squinted a bit more toward the river, then nodded. "Yep."

"Good. Ready?"

"Yep."

They set off, as if they shared one mind, toward the tumbled-down stone that helped form a natural bulwark at the corner of camp. Before they clambered over, each checked his shells and his sheath knife again. They each also had a hide-out knife tucked in a pouched pocket low on their buckskin leggings.

Beyond that, they were armed with no more than the

wisdom gained from lives lived in the mountain country of North Carolina. And as far as Silks was concerned, this was not an insignificant trait. It had served them well in tracking and bringing down game enough for their family and others on the long journey westward.

As he and the boy crept through the bracken, Silks mused on the oddness of life that had brought them out here.

He never once questioned his decision, but a man's mind, he thought, could not help toying on the notion of "what if". No matter, he and Mother had discussed one time why they were making the move away from kinfolk off into a land none of their relations had ever ventured.

"Getting crowded hereabouts," Silks had one day said to his wife.

She looked up at him from making lye soap and he knew that she saw in his eyes a man who had decided on a thing. She also knew that her time in her beloved hills, not but one hollow removed from her sister and ma, was drawing to a close. That part had given him pause, but not enough to stall his thinking.

She had nodded then, because she was devoted to her man, as was he to her. They had been inseparable since they each were children, growing up on neighboring farms. And now here they were, thought Silks, smack-dab in a feud.

Thought we left all this foolishness behind, he mused. And then he realized that would be impossible, as long as men were roaming the earth. Even if there were only two left, they would get to feuding and fighting and eventually killing, sooner or later.

He paused, crouched, and held up a hand. His son stopped beside him, ears keen. It didn't take much effort for them to hear the heavy breathing and snapping brush of a man unaccustomed to woods walking.

Silks glanced at the boy, pointed at himself, then ahead, which meant that Silks would take on the coming fellow. He then pointed at his son and wiggled a hand to indicate the sign they both knew was meant to mimic a fish's movement. That meant the boy would take to the river, while the father stuck to their bankside path. The boy slipped off to the right and his pa barely heard when the kid entered the flow.

It was not a matter of keeping the boy safe, but it was a matter of not being held up or worse by a less sure-footed fellow in the river. The water would chill and thus slow a fellow, but the boy could overcome that, being lighter and quicker.

Silks was thinking that some of the Brethren would cut wide along the river. It's what he'd do, were he trying to sneak up along the southern edge of the battleground.

After another twenty feet, he remained still once more, keeping low, his rifle held somewhat at the ready, but his knife was unsheathed and keen to taste skin, flesh, and bone.

The noisy fellow was visible now, so Silks let him advance. The man was not as fat as he had pictured him. Given the lumbering sounds the other man had been making, Silks had figured he'd see a big brute with thick hands and ears and equally outsize feet. But no, this fellow, not large in stature, surely had to be a stranger to the forest.

He was also obviously one of those Brethren, as Silks had expected. The fool's odd clothes gave him away—black boiled wool trousers and coat, a black wool hat, a beard that ignored the merits of growing ample hair up and over the top lip, and that white shirt that in the thin autumn woods was as good as whistling and begging an enemy to shoot him.

Silks held, knowing that movement would be the first thing to give him away. The next would be if the man chanced to see him before he was close enough for Silks to strike.

Luck, or rather long experience paying off, was with him. For the man blundered on, his eyes rarely roving down to where he set his boots, and so he was nearly alongside Silks before something caused him to slow and glance about himself.

But it was far too late for casual glances.

Silks remained poised like a panther waiting to strike, his body tense, every buckskin-clad muscle tight and ready.

The Brethren stopped, his rifle held uselessly across his chest, not even at half cock, and he glanced toward the cleared land to his right. Had he glanced to his left, the river's side, he would have glimpsed Silks springing upward, his own rifle laid neatly down out of the way, his big, gleaming sheath knife held in his right hand, blade pointed downward.

The black-clothed man spun his head to his left, but the last thing he saw in this world, without searing, lightning-bolt pain zagging down his body, was a blur of brown as the buckskin-clad woodsman leapt up, gaining height for the blade to do its bidden work.

Silks used his body's dropping momentum to give his right arm extra weight in driving downward. He aimed the gleaming blade's curved tip right at that spot, close in, where the man's left shoulder joined his neck.

The tip entered, popping through wool, linen, cotton, skin, and flesh, and wormed right down into the man's chest, tickling whatever was in there before it sought its intended destination in the man's thumping heart.

If the Brethren man had had the inclination to scream, it was a wish unfulfilled, because Silks's big, callused left hand closed over the man's nose and mouth. His eye took it all in, though, and a man's brows never rose so high, thought Silks as he glared straight back into them while riding his failing victim down to the earth.

The blade did its work well, for the man, although still barely alive when he hit the ground, was unable to do more than blink once. Tears oozed from his open eyes as the woodsman laid him out on his back and gave the knife, which had sunk to its brass hilt in the man's neck, a quick turn before dragging it free.

With the twist, the Brethren had stiffened and spasmed once, then sagged against the earth and his body relaxed as if he'd slipped into a deep sleep. But from this one, he would not awaken.

"Maybe you'll wake up in the arms of the Maker you believe in enough to kill innocent folks for," whispered Silks, shaking his head and wiping his blade on the man's coat sleeve.

He looked at the man's waist, but saw no gun belt. Ah, well, he did not wish to lug another rifle with him, but he reached into one coat flap pocket and felt the familiar shape and heft of brass bullets. He snatched them out and, with the man's rifle, laid them to the side, hidden by duff.

He figured it likely that the wagon train encampment would soon grow hard up for guns and ammunition. He or the boy could sneak back along this way and retrieve whatever they would each stash today.

To his right, he heard a quick splash and a muffled grunt He held his knife halfway slid in its sheath, his own rifle grasped once more in his left hand. The grunting sound was not the boy's voice. He nodded once, knowing his son had also taken a life.

"Good boy," he whispered, and, bending low, continued on. Silks felt neither bad nor good about killing. But the feeling the act of the hunt instilled in him was something that could not be matched or denied. The solid feeling was not surpassed yet in his life, and he suspected his wife felt the same, for she was a rare woman who also enjoyed the trail and the seeking of meat for the pot.

He continued on, wondering how many of the Brethren

had chosen to take this somewhat-hidden route. It would be in an effort to circle wide around the camp in hopes, no doubt, of coming in on it from the extreme southwest corner, tight to the base of the cliff the wagon camp was snugged to.

A sliding, then quick-muffled snap of branch told him he did not have long to wait to find out. He considered repeating the same procedure as he'd just gone through, but rarely in life did anything work well successively. Or at least that's what he chose to believe.

Instead, Silks glanced to where he was about to set his left moccasin and, seeing it safe and clear enough of anything that might produce the slightest offending noise, stepped to his left, off the scant game trail he'd been following. He continued onward, the sound ahead having given him enough information to proceed.

It was another Brethren, of that he felt certain, and the man was more cautious than the first. That also meant he was likely more afraid. And a fearful man in the woods meant someone who didn't have the abilities to get along well, a man whose discomfort overrode his sense of logic.

None of that mattered at the moment, for Silks bent low and risked another stride forward. And that's when his right foot scuffed a half-buried rock, hidden beneath the low brush through which he was wading.

It smarted, sure, but the sound his moccasin made—a sliding, scraping noise, although slight—was enough to pull him once more into a low crouch and jerk him to a halt. He gritted his teeth together hard and raised his rifle. He would have to wait out the man. The fact that he heard no other sounds from ahead told him the man was also holding his ground.

It irked Silks to have to wait, because the boy would be moving ahead. Just his luck, he had to come up against a nervous man. He held his position, his rifle at the ready, and let his breath drift in and out of his nose.

Within two minutes, a sound beyond the nearest man, and closing in toward them both, could be heard. It was yet another of them, and this new one, as with the man Silks had already dealt with, was a lumbering fool.

Good, he thought. *That will set them both up for me.*

Although he preferred fighting up close, he would, if he had to, deliver bullets into the devils. That was far from his ideal notion, not only because it would alert every critter within earshot, but it would defeat the purpose of a stealthy hunt.

But he wasn't about to act the fool and bring a knife to a gun battle—without also toting a gun.

The sounds ahead continued, not as if the man was intending to lay waste to every twig he came across, but neither was he taking precautions to keep quiet.

Then he heard another voice offer a quick shushing sound. It did the trick because the second fellow also held his ground. Silks would wait them both out, for he had no option, and he hoped they did not feel the same.

He was granted that hope after three or four minutes, for the newest of them grew weary, as Silks suspected he might, and the fool even began whispering to the still-as-stone man.

Evidently, he was not getting any response that he cared for, because he set forth, once more toward Silks, at a brisker pace. The bumbler bypassed the silent Brethren fellow, and it wasn't but twenty seconds later that Silks saw the man, shoving his way through the rabbit brush.

He reached ahead of him and snapped branches that hung where he wished to move through with his body.

It was the brazen act of a person more comfortable with the field and farm life, not of forest and stream. It annoyed Silks that folks could be so careless as to snap branches and crush the very things that, had they bent to notice, would bring them knowledge and satisfaction, perhaps pleasure in discovering something new about the world of which they were part.

The man was closing in. He was thickset, wearing no coat, but he wore a white shirt with the usual black trousers and hat, braces holding up the trousers, and a beard, more brown than gray, and also with no moustache.

He carried a revolver in his right hand, and with his left, he continued to grab and snap branches.

Silks also noted that the man wore a sheath knife swinging at his left side.

That might come in useful.

A plan came to the woodsman. He would wait for the oaf to come abreast of him; then he would take him with his knife. Then, as it now sounded as if the other man was making his way forward once more, Silks figured he would try to keep from firing his rifle.

He waited.

Within short moments, passed in patient silence by the woodsman, the man emerged in the trail before Silks, who wasted no time in driving his blade up and into the man's chest, stifling the heart in midbeat.

At the same time, he spied, over the shocked man's left shoulder, the second man in the trail. They exchanged glances, but Silks had already snatched the first man's own hip knife out of its sheath and had whipped his arm back.

The man in the trail raised his rifle, and that's when his comrade's knife sailed straight and true for his chest.

He had no time to squeeze the trigger, for the thick sheath knife drove itself into his chest, flying perfectly between the man's raised arms, half the blade buried there.

Silks eased the first man to lie flat on his back on the soft earth of the trail even as the second man began to crumple, first dropping the rifle, then collapsing to his knees, and finally falling face-first, driving the blade even deeper into his dead chest.

Knife throwing was a skill Silks had always been proud of, often sinking throwing axes and knives, from little mumblety-peg pocket stickers to big belt knives, quivering smack in the center of a log round. He'd also brought down many critters for the stewpot when he had gone out either with a sling or knife or both, leaving the booming long guns at home.

Using the skill to kill two-legged predators was something he'd done a bit of in the past, in the war, and it was not a thing he enjoyed, but it was, after all, a thing that needed doing. He would be content to leave it at that, and for the most part, he knew that he could.

But, as he slid his knife free of the man's heart and wiped the broad blade on the man's white shirt, Silks knew, too, that sometimes life's grimmest tasks would never fully leave a man alone. They would come back to him in the small hours.

"At this rate," he whispered as he walked on, "I may never sleep again."

CHAPTER 22

"You think he's coming back?" said Bewley after a few nervous moments. "He took his father's pistol again. Didn't think I saw him. But I did."

She regarded the man for a moment, then shook her head. "If I know him, and I do, better than anyone alive, I expect, now that . . . now that his father's gone, I'd say he's off to find Deacon, or someone to come back here and deal with you."

"Well"—Bewley scratched at his beard with his free hand—"I'm not just a 'you,' ma'am. Name's Bewley. And I'm not leaving here without that baby."

Her gaze fixed on him once more, sharp and direct; even in the low light of the cozy cabin, he felt it. She said nothing, but her arms seemed to cling tighter to the child.

"Ma'am, you will always look on that baby as the stolen child and you will know in the deepest part of your heart that keeping that baby from her rightful

EVERYBODY HAS A GUN

mama and papa isn't right. It just ain't right." Bewley did not let up there, but bore his gaze straight into hers.

She looked away, then down to the once-more-sleeping babe in her arms. He saw on her face that her impressive resolve and fortitude, which he had seen plenty of in recent long minutes, was slipping away.

He decided to keep his mouth shut and not push his luck. This was something he had always had a hard time doing, ever since he was a boy. That, and eating. Man alive, but he liked a good meal. It was always a wonder to him how he stayed so trim.

But as with having a thick beard when other men didn't seem to have steam enough to grow anything more than a wispy, patchy thing on their faces, so Bewley accepted as a gift from above the fact that he was blessed with the ability to eat like two horses and stay lean and feisty.

If he had to describe himself to a stranger, it would be that he liked a good chin-wag only after he'd had a good meal. And a cup of hot coffee. And a nice, slow smoke on his pipe.

His mama, sainted and bless her, always told him if he had wings she'd have sworn he was one of those mouthy little birds always sitting there with his mouth open, waiting for her to shove in more food. She also told him once that she'd been feeding him worms, just like a baby bird would get, for months and he'd never noticed.

He had pulled quite a face when she'd said that, though. And then she'd winked.

Bewley glanced once more at the woman and he saw she was weighing a decision in her mind. He bet she was a good mama to the boy. Surprised they didn't have more than the one child.

As if in answer to his thought, she looked at him with tearful eyes. "My husband, he suggested to Deacon that the babe be brought to me. We lost a little girl, you see, some years back. It was hard, so hard."

She pulled in a breath, straightened, and looked at him. Speaking in a bolder voice, she said, "That's why I know just what this wee one's mother is going through. And please tell her I am right sorry to have been part of all this." She walked to him and handed him the baby. "Right sorry."

Now that Bewley had the baby in his arms, he wasn't at all certain he could do what had before been a conviction in his mind—that he could bring back the child to the wagon train. It had been a conviction, yes, but one with no clear notion attached of how to actually get the child back safely, through enemy lines, without being seen.

This must have shown on his face, because her eyes widened. "How are you planning on getting this child home?"

"I, uh, well . . ." He wanted to fluff his beard, a thing he did when he got flustered and had to resort to thinking a thing through. But the baby required both arms. This would surely be a problem.

"I see," she said, and took the baby from him. It stirred and wiggled a little and made a scrunched-up face as if it might awaken and cry, but she held it close and it snuggled in deeper and dozed again. "I think that under the circumstances, and given the fact, as much as I hate to admit that my son has . . . I think—and it's quite obvious to you—become a handful of a young man. And now that his father is gone . . . well, he'll be better off for a spell while I accompany you."

"Oh no, ma'am, I can't let you do that. It's not right. It's—"

"You don't have a choice. Either you leave the child with me and we take our chances, or you bring her back to her mother now. Tonight. With me."

He fluffed his beard and scratched at his hidden rangy chin and said, "What would you do?"

"Ordinarily, I'd say she would be safer with me. But I am also in danger, if what you say about Deacon is true. For I cannot hold my tongue any longer around that toad of a man. I cannot do it." Her eyes glistened.

"My husband is the reason we fell in with Deacon. If it had been up to me, I would have sent the man packing before he could unload his so-called Holy Book. I was raised with the proper Holy Book. I can quote at length from its wonders. And I can tell you now, with no hesitation of thought, that this man's book is something no honest, God-fearing person would have within reach. He's a thief, plain and simple."

"You think you're in danger then, ma'am?"

"I know I am. I didn't want to say it in front of my son, but the more I heard what you were saying, and the more I thought about it, the clearer it became. I was correct then, several years ago when Deacon came into our midst, our pretty little valley, and I'm even more correct now.

"The man is foul. Foul enough to kill my husband out of fear, because while he was weak enough to fall in line with what the man had to say, my husband was also a good man, honest and true, and he would not abide what Deacon is up to. In fact, he had been increasingly worried about the direction the Brethren had been taking for some time now.

"Deacon came here, as you said, just after he killed my husband, with my husband's blood still fresh on his hands and in his mind, and he had the nerve to tell me that I should consider moving into his home with him. For my protection."

"What?"

"Yes," she said, the anger unconcealed on her face. "He said that as one who has the look of wanting to stray from his flock, he felt I needed close guidance and observation."

"Oh, he's a rich one," said Bewley. "But look now, ma'am. If you're serious about going with me, then we got to head on out. It's only a matter of time before one of them comes a-knocking."

She nodded, said no more, and handed the baby back to him. He held it as gentle as he would a lit stick of dynamite, while she bustled about the place, snatching up several short, squat tallow candles, a sturdy little outdoor lantern, and a knitted hat and mittens for herself.

She topped that with a shawl and draped a slouch bag over her shoulder. Then she stuffed matches, bread, two glass bottles of milk, stoppered tight and bound with oilcloth and waxed string, into the sack. Then she wrapped the child in woolens, leaving only the babe's soft, puffy pink face exposed.

Bewley checked his weapons, and then opened the door and peered out. Nobody shot at him.

The night was dark, but he could still see one low spot of coals glowing far down the valley, and still smelled smoke on the air, washing over in waves as the wind carried it toward them.

"Okay, then?" he said. "I think it best to keep the lantern quiet until we need it—if you have a sense of the land hereabouts."

"I do," she said.

"Good. Now I was thinking we should make for the ridge to the south, same way we come down."

"We could," she said, "or we could walk straight up the road, eastward, to the pass."

"But—"

She held up a hand. "Hear me out. We make it to the camp of the Brethren men—"

"Oh, really? And then what?" he said, sounding a pinch snippy. "Sorry, sorry."

"Then with you as my prisoner, we tell them that I am going to march you straight to the wagon train camp and give them the child, but we'll demand something in return."

"Like what?"

She shrugged. "I don't know yet. I never said it was a good plan, but I think it's better than trying to climb that rise and then descend it without tumbling off the steep bits into the river. If the fall didn't kill us, the cold water might. Oh, and all that without using a lantern."

"Okay, then," he said. "I'm desperate enough to give it a go. But I have to think of something better than being your prisoner. I don't think those men will let me pass through them at all. Not with how worked up they are. And will be when they learn their hay has been all burned up by heathens."

"Right," she said. "We had better go."

"What about your boy?" he asked. "You going to leave him a note? They're liable to think I took you as prisoner."

"Will it really matter?" she answered, poking her head outside, looking about, then stepping out into the night.

Bewley watched her a moment, thinking what a rare woman she was. Then he shrugged and followed her, closing the door behind him.

Chapter 23

"Well, now."

Gage had felt himself slip into a sort of half-conscious state some time before he heard the voice. It served to rouse him, more so than the shivers wracking his body, from the cold. He also figured he was well into some sort of state of shock from the savaging he'd received by the dog.

He bit the inside of his cheek in an effort to stay awake and stay with the situation. He felt the cold stinging his face, the exposed parts of his body, his arms, through the tears in his trouser legs where the dog's claws had ripped and dug at him. That was good, he thought, that he felt the cold stinging him, as moments before he felt himself benumbed by it, a certain sign that he was slipping into a slow death by cold.

The fight with the dog had begun the slow wheel of pain spinning, and then the old woman's dumping of cold water over him had set it to whirring faster and faster until he'd begun to lose the fight. But no! This was not how he imagined dying, not in such a foolish, passive way. He had expected—needed, he guessed—to be punched with lead delivered by a gun handled by the loved one of a person he had long since sent to the grave.

By a vengeance-seeking relation of the girl with the golden hair . . .

"Hey! Hey, you!"

Whoever said that had also delivered a kick to his left-side rib cage, a fitting reminder of the girl, for it was she, in her last act alive, who had shot him there, barely. Her bullet had plowed a furrow of blood and meat high up on the left side of his chest.

It still twinged more than he liked, but it had become a daily reminder that he was nothing more than a killer drifting on luck through the land of the living.

"I said, hey there! Wake up! I know you're still with us because the Maker deems it! A Brethren knows, am I correct, Brothers and Sisters?"

Gage heard this voice clearly, and it was followed with a ragged chorus of others who sounded weary, annoyed, exhausted. He slitted his eyes and moved his head to his left.

Lantern light dazzled him and caused him to squint tighter. He fought it and the lantern light receded. Someone had held it close to his face, for he had also felt its heat for a moment on his cheek and ear. He wanted to tell the holder of the lantern to bring it near once more so he might hug it.

"There now, see? I told you that what the Maker wants, the Maker receives. And what he wants is for this rogue heathen to reveal his plans." The voice bent low, and as it spoke again, Gage knew now who it was—Deacon. And the burly killer continued to speak loud enough so that they all might hear.

"There is nothing you can do, heathen, to hamper the will of the Brethren! Oh yes, you might set fire to the stored feed for our beasts of burden. You might mutilate for your freakish, foul pleasure the lesser beasts, such as dogs. But you cannot alter the fact that you are a heathen and are, as we speak, already tasting the licking flames of a nightmare eternity in damnation!"

More murmurs of half-hearted agreement arose from the vague shapes ringing the night behind Deacon. Gage saw that this annoyed Deacon, for he turned slightly toward them, but said nothing.

Gage felt as if he were a child once more, forced to sit at a desk in school and listen to the schoolmarm drone on in her withered voice, scolding the children and pacing the front of the room, for that is what Deacon was now doing close by.

After two tries, Gage forced himself to rise up on his left elbow. His right was too numb, either from injury or cold, perhaps both, to function as he wished. "Deacon, you . . . are a—"

The man looked down at him as Gage forced the words out, but a voice from someone in the night, running toward them and shouting, interrupted the budding exchange.

"Deacon! Deacon!"

Everyone turned to see a running young man emerge into their midst carrying a swinging lantern. He was red-faced, and as he said "Deacon" a third time, he looked down at Gage and his words stoppered as his eyes widened. *"You!"*

Deacon grabbed the youth by the arm and spun him. "Where were you, boy? You were needed fighting the fires!"

"But, Deacon, that's what I'm trying to—"

"Foolish boy!" growled Deacon, and turned back to Gage.

"But, Deacon, I couldn't. We were being held by—"

"What?" said one of the voices of the crowd. A man stepped forward. "What's that you say, son?"

The kid nodded, still trying to catch his breath and clearly confused by Deacon's reaction to seeing him. "I was going to, but one of them"—he pointed at Gage—"heathens, I mean, they, oh, it's a long story. But I was their prisoner and then they split up and one came to our house."

"And the other one?" said Deacon, turning back to the boy.

"Well, he's . . . he's right there!" He pointed at Gage. "What happened to him?"

"Shut that mouth of yours, boy!" snapped Deacon.

"Yours is not to judge!" Then he turned back to Gage, sneering. "Prisoner, eh? That gives me an idea."

"But, Deacon," said the kid, backing up, his fear of the burly leader apparent, "the other one, he's—"

"Yes, out with it!"

"He's at our cabin. Ma's got a gun on him."

"What?" Deacon turned hot eyes on the boy. "Why didn't you say so, you oaf!" He turned to the crowd. "Tate and Foster, you come with me to Widow Schenk's house. The rest of you go on home, save for the men. You all get on back to the pass. But you, Marstow, you keep a watchful eye on this one. I don't want him out of your sight, do you understand me, boy?"

Deacon had leaned close to the face of the man he addressed as Marstow. "I shall see to it that the Maker looks with disfavor on anyone who dares to disobey me or fail me in any way. Is that understood?"

The crowd dispersed, per Deacon's instructions, although Gage noted none of them moved too quickly. They were soot smeared and smelled of smoke and were weary. He felt terrible guilt, for they appeared to him no more capable of murdering innocent strangers than he might. And yet, was that not what he had done as a way of life some years ago?

Humans, it seemed, were capable of justifying anything, particularly if they were led by the nose by a persuasive leader playing on their fears. That said, none of them had seemed terribly impressed with Deacon's ranting.

The man left to tend him, Marstow, was a medium-build, bearded fellow about Gage's size, but shorter and less wide at the shoulder. He'd been left behind to guard Gage, but he looked little better than Gage felt.

"For what it's worth, I wish I had not been forced to set those fires," Gage said.

"'Forced'?" The man shifted the rifle in his uncovered hands. They looked red, chapped, and cold, as did the man's face, which was even redder, a result no doubt of being too close to flame while battling fires. "Nobody is ever *forced* to do such a thing."

"Just like nobody is ever forced to shoot innocent travelers, steal their children and goods and beasts, lay siege on them, and enact plans to starve them to death?"

The man looked down at him, and it seemed to Gage that his words tickled something in the man's mind, made his eyes widen a moment.

Then he tamped down that emotion and shook his head. "Deacon said you lot would try to work your will against us with your honeyed tongues. I see now he was right."

"Only now?" said Gage. "Did you think before that maybe you weren't so certain about him?"

Again the man shook his head. "You had best stop talking, mister. I . . . I am liable to pull this trigger."

"I don't think so," said Gage, sitting up and patting his aching head with his left hand, the less savaged of the two. "Look, I am not so naive to think you'll let me go, but I sure could use some help standing up."

"You stay right where you are, mister!"

Gage shook his head. "No, sir, I can't do it. I am in flaming agony and I need to stand up!" It was no lie, but he had more ambitious motives. Gage didn't wait for approval, but went right ahead and worked on bending his legs to get them beneath him.

He felt better than he expected just stretching himself. The shivering had abated somewhat, but he still was wracked by shudders, which he hoped would not turn into pneumonia. It would be a foul little victory for Deacon.

The guard backed up a step and wagged the rifle at him with a stiff motion. "You keep still, mister! I'm warning you! Deacon will not like this one bit!"

"Do you really think"—Gage moved with slowness and caution, afraid to stir up the many bleeding wounds the dog had given him. They had dried a bit of their flow of blood, but it would not take much for them to resume—"I care what your precious Deacon thinks?"

He was not usually so bitter, but then again, it had been a while since he'd been savaged by a wolfish dog and then had cold water dumped on him by a crazy old woman.

"You're not going to shoot me and you know it, Marstow."

"How do you know my name?"

"Calm down, man," said Gage. "The dog didn't eat my ears."

The man looked at him with brows drawn.

Gage sighed. "I heard what he called you. Now let me stand. I'm in no danger of running away," said Gage. "Only because the dog did claw my legs."

"Oh."

Gage slowly got his feet under himself, and using first one knee, then the other, he managed to stand. He rested there with his hands on his knees and glanced to his left. The man's boot toes were about four feet from him. He wanted to lunge, but didn't trust that he'd be quick enough, given his current condition.

"Keep the gun on me, but, man, offer me one hand, will you, just grasp mine and help me stand straight up. Then let go. Keep the gun on me, okay? I can't straighten up and I am in bad pain, mister."

"No way nothing like that is going to happen . . . you . . . you heathen!"

Gage sighed, still bent over. "Look. Deacon said for nothing to happen to me, right?"

"I guess so."

"Sure he did. And if anything does, you'll be the one to get the blame, right?"

"I guess, yeah."

"That means he has something in mind for me. I'm not much looking forward to it, but if I were in his boots, I guess I'd feel the same way. But I need you to just help me straighten up, that's all."

Gage held up his left hand. It looked awful, covered as it was with drying blood, and he accentuated the shaking as if he had been struck with palsy. He hoped he looked sufficiently pathetic enough for the man to extend a hand, the rifle pointed at him. It would be an awkward pose, which is what Gage counted on.

Gage pulled a tight face and sucked in his breath through close-set teeth. "Oh, my hands are in bad shape."

"Yeah, well, you should have thought of that before you started setting fire to our feed barns, you heathen." Marstow rubbed a hand over his chin and scratched quickly at his modest beard. "Once you get on your feet, I am going to tie you up, just so you know."

Gage sighed. "Fine. Okay, if you have to, but please, for Pete's sake, help me stand."

He continued to hold up the trembling hand, holding his awkward pose, and the man let out a breath of disgust and nodded. "All right, then. But that's it, all you're getting from me."

He bent forward, the rifle held partially snugged under his right arm, his right hand near the trigger. He extended the left and grasped Gage's raised hand and pulled. Gage rose up to a standing position and kept on moving.

He brought his afflicted right arm around in a swinging arc and it whistled in, catching the Brethren man square on the left side of his head. Gage stifled back what pain he could as his already-torn and bloodied fist connected with the man's bony skull. It was a solid hit, and he'd willed himself to make it extra bold, considering his weakened state. It worked.

Gage's captor was plenty wiry and muscled, since he

was a subsistence farmer who worked from before dawn to well after dark at various tasks, most requiring strength and brute force.

Despite all this, he was not expecting the slamming blow, and a quick "Ah!" flew from his mouth as it happened. That staggered him to his right side and he collapsed, dazed, Gage could see, but not knocked cold.

Gage wasted no time in landing atop him, clawing at first for the rifle that had clattered to the hard earth in the fall, although still grasped, however loosely, in the man's right hand.

Gage's fingertips brushed the polished wood of the gun's forestock, scrabbled for it, even as his sore right hand drove again down against the side of the flattened man's head.

"Sorry," he grunted as his fist connected. "Truly," he gasped, sagging backward. He had no strength left. Even though the man was apparently unconscious, Gage knew it was but a matter of moments before the captor awoke or one of the other Brethren returned or came upon them fresh out of the frigid night.

All this had taken place in the glow of a single low-burning storm lantern set on a stump.

Of the old woman in the cottage, Gage saw and heard nothing. Perhaps she'd scuttled off into a corner for the night, he thought, then chastised himself as he dragged himself from the still man. There was no call for being petty about the old thing.

There was, however, plenty of call for him to actively

EVERYBODY HAS A GUN 317

try to stop these savages from continuing their war of attrition against the wagon train folks.

Gage wondered how the travelers had fared through this long day and into the evening. He'd set out with certain intentions in mind—to lob distraction into the path of the Brethren. At the very least, he hoped to slow them down in their attack, maybe disperse their numbers, separate them a bit so that somehow the travelers might be able to get a leg up on them. He had also wanted to rescue the stolen child, but that had quickly become Bewley's task.

He shoved to his feet, wondering how much more he would endure before he might curl up somewhere and rest, or just plain expire from exhaustion. At this point, Gage wasn't so certain he cared which happened.

He stood, chest heaving, and rested his left hand on his knee and regarded the man he'd lied to and then pummeled. He had to remind himself it was all for a just cause. But it still sat raw with him that he had to keep resorting to foul means to get what he felt he needed.

Shooting men and causing others to shoot them atop the clifflike ridge, then setting fire to the winter feed of innocent beasts, killing an admittedly vicious, dangerous dog that was doing its job—keeping intruders bent on destruction from doling out their worst—and now pounding a man's head until he lost consciousness.

"Jon Gage," he muttered low as he bent to retrieve the man's rifle, "this is not what you had in mind when you bought your new coat back in Higgins." He stood, trying to fight the urge to take the man's coat and hat—

he'll be found soon by his own kind—but hoping that bit of blackness was to disguise him. He devised the only plan he could think of—to walk back toward the pass.

That meant making for the road and walking eastward. He saw lantern light far to his right, westward toward the end of the valley, and although he spied three pricks of honeyed light here and there eastward, none were close to the road. Those were likely farm cabins.

Of the fires, he thought perhaps he saw the low glow of fire of the three, and that was at the spot of the first fire he had caused, but no dark shapes passed before the glowing, interrupting the meager view. He considered this heartening.

It was but a quick matter of time before Deacon and his followers—either several or all—were going to return to him and perhaps kill him. *But that,* he thought as he tugged on the man's coat and snatched up his broad, flat-brim, low-crown black hat, *is only if I linger here and wait for them.*

Deacon was plenty steamed, and Gage knew if the kid had not burst into their midst, Gage might well be dead by now. He slid his throbbing right hand into the coat pocket and felt bullets there. Good. That meant the rifle would be useful beyond what was already in it.

The hat fit his head snugly—a pinch more generous in sizing and it would be just right. Still, he tugged it low. He reckoned that the slight throbbing it caused around his pate would serve to keep him alert.

* * *

Holding the rifle in his big right hand, he snatched up the lantern's bail and, turning the wick even lower—just enough to barely help him see by—Gage set off eastward, back along the valley he'd earlier traveled, causing headache and havoc for its inhabitants. He was once more making for the maw of the beast, this time at the mouth where a good many of its teeth, in the form of the Brethren men, were gathered, no doubt seething with anger and knowing because they were obeying Deacon, that their homes and farms were being tormented with flame by their heathen enemy.

Gage stumbled here and there on half-frozen tussocks and fieldstones as he cut, in a long, slow angling, toward the valley's central lane. He wanted to make good time, and put as much distance as he could between him and Deacon and his followers back behind him, for it could be only a matter of moments before the cold-conked Marstow was found.

He had no doubt that they would see the lantern, and if Deacon had his way, they would shoot at it first and then apologize later, should he need to.

Gage reached the roadway and stepped as fast as his aching, torn body was able, aware that his every sound seemed to echo in the still night air about him. And then he heard more of the same sounds. He slowed and resisted the urge to raise the lantern, for that would reveal his visage, not one that any member of the Brethren would tolerate.

Yes, it was coming at him, and from ahead. He resumed his quick pace, and within a half minute, he distinctly heard boot steps on gravel, also traveling with no time wasted. He bent his head low as the person from the pass walked within view, and held the lantern even lower, down below his knee. He deduced it was a man, noting the boots and trouser legs.

"Ho there, hold up!" It was the newcomer, sounding as if he were in a hurry. "Friend or foe?"

Gage also held, shrugging deeper into the other man's coat and hat, and kept the lantern swinging from his left hand. "What is it?" said Gage, hoping to sound somehow like a member of this freakish band.

"Dill, that you?"

Gage grunted and hunched his shoulders, as if he were so cold, he didn't want to chat.

"I know it, my word, but it's turned cold tonight. Hey, whose places got it?"

Gage shrugged. "Going to the pass. Deacon sent me."

"Deacon!" said the strange Brethren man. "Where is he at?"

"He's coming," said Gage. "Straight back." He had altered his voice, made it sound higher, and kept his head bent so that the man saw little of him, save the right hand that held the long gun. His other hand, the scarred, bloodied left, was mostly hidden by the coat's cuff.

EVERYBODY HAS A GUN

"Okay," said the man. "Get back there quick, then. These heathens are killing our men left, right, and center! Can't believe it. I just can't believe it. You know that Heinz and his two boys are all dead, found up on the ridge! And Per Schneider, he was supposed to go spell them up there on lookout duty. But he's missing."

That would be the man who was shot and fell backward off the trail and landed impaled on the jagged pine trunk. They'd find him in daylight, no doubt.

Gage looked downward even more and shook his head, as if the news was too awful to hear.

"It's Deacon's doing," said the man. Then he leaned closer.

Gage checked his urge to back away.

"Heathens or no," said the man in a lowered tone, "it never should have come to this. Never!" He backed from Gage and said, "Okay, get going. See you."

Gage grunted and made tracks, lest the man prattle on. The fellow walked on and Gage heard the receding sounds of his boots crunching stiff earth on the roadway.

Maybe he should kill the light, but it was so dark and he was unfamiliar enough with the terrain. Still, he dithered on the notion as he walked. He came abreast of the little bridge, and as he was halfway across, he thought he heard something that he knew could not be possible. The sound of a baby crying, somewhere ahead.

A baby. Could it be?

Gage paused, and this time, he made to douse the

light, but set it close by the bridge side and walked as soundlessly as he could to the far side. He listened and soon heard cautious, slow steps beneath the whimpering of the baby's cry. And then he heard a woman's soft voice offering the child soothing sounds, but it was not working well. Still, the child was not offering a full-throated cry.

He heard voices then, low, whispered. *Are they saying something about milk?*

"Who's there?" he said, well away from his lantern.

"I . . . I was going to ask the same!"

It was a woman's voice. Gage did not respond.

He heard more footsteps; then the woman said, "I see your lantern. But where are you? I must get to the Brethren camp at the pass. Deacon sent me."

"Okay," he said, not certain what else to say.

There was a pause of a few moments and he thought he heard two whispering voices. "Who else?" he said, offering as few words as he could in his own voice.

"I . . . I have a prisoner. And a baby."

"A prisoner?" said Gage.

"Yes," she said. "One of the heathens. Deacon said to bring him to the pass. Kindly take your lamp and lead the way," she said, her voice sounding stronger with conviction.

Gage was confused. The only heathen prisoner he knew of might well be . . . "Bewley?"

There was a pause, a quick, barely audible flurry of whispers; then a voice familiar to Gage said, "Gage? That you?"

It was a timid bit of questioning, but Gage knew it was the scout. But he was a woman's prisoner? And a woman with a baby? How was that possible?

"Wait, are you a prisoner?"

Another pause of a moment, and Bewley said, "Are you?"

Gage hefted the rifle, just in case this was some odd trap. It certainly had the makings of one. "No. Here under my own steam."

"Oh, Gage. That's good. Me and Mrs. Schenk here, she's the boy's mother."

"But . . . you're not her prisoner?"

"No," said Bewley. "Now come over here into the light. We need to talk, get our stories to line up. Running into you changes everything. And I don't know if it's for good or ill yet."

During this exchange, Gage heard the woman doing her best to soothe the child. Finally he stepped toward the dim figures barely lit by the ground-set lantern. He lifted it and moved closer to them. He heard soft sucking sounds and saw the woman holding a blanket-wrapped bundle—had to be the baby—and a sugar-teat in her hand quelled the child's fussing for the moment.

"Evening, ma'am."

She offered a terse "Good evening."

"Gage!" said Bewley. "What on earth has happened to you?"

"A disagreement with a dog."

"*Disagreement?* If you gave better than you got, I pity the poor dog."

Gage said nothing.

"See you carried through with your plans," said the scout.

Gage knew it was a reference to the fires. "For good or ill," he said.

"For ill, I should think," snapped the woman, glancing at him. "You couldn't think of a more civilized way of causing a distraction, Mr. Gage, than by burning down the feed for our stock?"

"Maybe I should have shot innocent travelers and stolen their cattle and children."

She made no reply, but smarted visibly as if he'd struck her.

Good, thought Gage, *I'm weary as all get-out of this entire affair. It's a one-sided, greedy lot she's part of.* At the moment, he didn't know any other way of seeing them.

"And what's happening with the boy?" asked Gage.

"Well"—Bewley stroked his beard—"he run off."

"I know. I saw him."

"You saw him? Where?" said the woman.

"He came running up just as your precious Deacon was about to kill me, most likely. So I guess I have him to thank. Or you"—he nodded to Bewley—"for letting him go."

"Well, never mind that now. Where do you suppose he's at?"

Gage looked westward, back up the road, but saw no lanterns. "No idea, but I thought they'd be along by now. We have to get moving to the pass. Your plan will have to do. Now let's go." He turned and led the way.

Gage walked eastward along the road, toward the pass, carrying the lantern and hoping no one else would see them. In this, he was aided by a long rise in the land over which the roadway had been carved. They began walking upward, following that incline.

He recalled from earlier, seeing the valley from on high, that at the top of the rise, it would dip down slightly as they neared the pass. He hoped it would be enough to shelter them and their lantern's dim glow for a bit longer.

Gage paused. "When we get near the top, I'm going to douse the lantern," he said, holding the low-flamed light down by his knees, just in case. It was annoying to have to wrangle it and the rifle, particularly when his right arm burned like fire.

He wished that the moon he'd seen earlier had stayed with them, but then again, that would leave them to be seen, too, by others. At least with the lantern, they had a little control over others spotting them.

"Why?" said the woman, seeming annoyed that Gage would dare to speak up and take command.

"Those men ahead. No need to reveal ourselves just yet."

"But I told you," she said, "we have already discussed this and I am going to make as if Mr. Bewley is my prisoner."

"Do you really think, ma'am, that they're going to treat you well in all this?"

"You got any better ideas?" asked Bewley.

"Yeah," said Gage, nudging Bewley a few steps away from the woman and talking low to him. "I, for one, am going to keep on doing what I can to weaken them. Especially before this Deacon fellow arrives. He has a large handful of worked-up Brethren with him—"

"How many?" cut in the scout.

"I saw seven or eight, mostly men. But I stirred them up pretty well."

"Yeah, you did!"

"Look, I think our best bet is for me to create another distraction, while you and the woman take the baby to the wagon camp."

"But—"

"No," said Gage. "I'll think of something and you move fast. Stay off the roadway, on this right side, until my signal."

"What'll that be?"

"Oh, I'll shout something about babies."

"Babies?"

"Yeah," said Gage. "Now listen: Once you make it up there, hug tight to the west edge of the rock face. From there, you know the way, but it'll be up to you to get her and the baby there without getting shot by somebody from your train."

"If I do, it'll be that idiot, Chase," mumbled Bewley. "What are you going to do?"

Gage shrugged. "No idea, but it'll come to me."

Bewley explained things to the woman, who protested.

"Fine," said Gage. "Give the baby to Bewley and go home."

"No, no, I . . . I mustn't do that."

"Then what do you suggest? And make it quick, Deacon might be a dozen feet away and we wouldn't know it."

"Fine, fine," she said, "but I can't let anything happen to the baby, and Mr. Bewley will have to protect us from the . . ."

"Heathens?" said Gage.

"No, I . . ."

But they all knew she was about to say that very word.

"Look, Bewley," said Gage. "If this all goes off the trail and I don't make it back, tend to my horse, Rig, all right? He's partial to a good feed and he's more than earned it."

"Who ain't?" said Bewley. "Course I will, pard, but there'll be no need for that. Keep a tight rein on your thoughts and you'll make it through all right. It was Benjamin Franklin, after all, who said, 'Do not anticipate trouble, or worry about what may never happen. Keep in the sunlight.' Wise words from a wise man."

"Yes, a wise fellow, indeed," said Gage, though he was thinking that of Bewley himself. "Thank you for them. Now"—he handed the lantern to the old scout—"you may need it, but I don't."

"Ma'am." Gage touched his hat brim. "Good luck."

"And to you," she said, and it sounded to Gage to be more genuine in intention than said out of courtesy.

* * *

He checked the strange rifle as he walked, keeping his steps measured, hoping to avoid grinding rock or earth beneath them and giving himself away. He wished the man he'd taken the coat and hat from had been a tad wider in the shoulder and taller in the leg. But it was the garb of a Brethren he wore, and he reminded himself again that the clothing might prove useful in disguising himself.

By the sight of firelight ahead, perhaps two hundred feet or so, more so than by the leveling off of the land, Gage saw the dim shapes of men standing.

As he drew closer, he realized their line of offense had fractured, and the few Brethren men Gage saw looked frightened, tired, and confused. Every time a fresh pop from the firewood, or a snap of a twig under a boot, or the crunch of gravel under another boot sounded, several of them twitched, eyebrows rose, along with guns. Although seeing them so degraded was a situation he'd hoped for, it was not one he could have predicted when he and Bewley took to the ridgeline that morning.

They had left behind a camp full of haggard, weary, jittery travelers, but from the looks of things—and he hoped he was not incorrect or guessing in haste—the table had somehow begun to turn, and the Brethren were taking on that harried look that comes to the worn down.

Gage drew closer and knew what he was going to do. And it involved not taking pains to mask his footfalls any longer. He began to trudge, his boots stepping and scraping. It didn't take but a few strides before one of the men, then the others, turned.

"Who's there?"

Gage walked another couple of steps, gaining what he could while they were still uncertain. Then he stopped.

"Who's that?"

"One of your own," said Gage. He hoped his voice sounded sufficiently weary. He certainly felt that way.

"Who?"

He was about to say, "Rob!" when one of the men said, "That you, Joe?"

"Yeah," said Gage, hoping it wasn't a trap.

"Where you been?"

Gage walked a bit closer. "Fightin' fires."

"Is it bad?"

"Not good," said Gage. Then he decided it was time to press his luck and try his plan. "In for a penny," he whispered to himself; then toward the Brethren, he said, "Deacon wants everyone's help! Now!"

"What?" said one of the men. "But what about the pass?"

"Said not to bother. Heathens are all but done anyway."

"Don't know about that," said another of the men.

"Deacon says they need help to catch the men setting fires!"

"Didn't catch them yet."

"No." Gage let out a shaky breath. This was more talking than he thought he'd be doing. Any more and they might be wise to him.

"Well, if Deacon said so."

Against the poor fire's dim glow, Gage saw the outline of a man walking toward him, then stop. "Come on," the man said to his fellows behind him.

Gage heard at least two more men join him. How many more were there?

"What about you?" said the first man to the others.

"I'm sorry," said a voice that sounded like that of an older man. "But with the five men still missing from this morning's raid, I can't just leave this pass unwatched. That is not what we agreed on. Besides, Deacon insisted!"

"Suit yourself," said the first man.

Gage heard the steps of at least three men walking toward him.

"Where you at, Joe?"

"Be along shortly," said Gage, cutting wide of them, over to the right side of the road. He acted as if he had to make water. His intention was that he had to clear that last sentinel from the pass. He was also curious about the missing men from the morning's raid. Maybe the wagon train folks had scored a victory while he and Bewley were away.

"We'll wait for you," said the first man.

"No!" said Gage. "Deacon said for you to hurry!"

"Joe, you sound funny. You all right?"

"Was the smoke," said Gage, trying to sound as if his throat was ailing him.

"Oh, sure. Drink some water. There's a bucket up by the fire."

"Right."

Gage kept on toward the top of the pass. He heard

the others walk on by toward the valley, their steps hastening.

He watched the fire's glow and was surprised to see not just the one man who he presumed was the older one who'd spoken, but another as well, standing beside him. They were in low conversation. He walked on, stepping with no speed toward them.

One of them broke off chatting. "That you, Joe?"

Gage coughed again. "Yeah," he said. "Smoke got to me."

"Okay, get a drink of water. Then fill us in."

Gage approached, trudging a bit, giving himself a pinch of time to size up the situation. He hoped there were only the two of them, standing together on the far side of the fire, their backs to the field beyond, shrouded in the dark, cold night.

Little had changed about the camp. Beyond them, flanking the left side of the road, stood a supply wagon, wheels chocked. Alongside it, various crates were arrayed, and a barrel with three or four long guns poking out. He bet some of the crates contained ammunition.

Beyond that, in the darkness, he knew several horses would stand there. If there were five men missing, and at least six in the valley with Deacon, likely more, and three just walked by him, and two faced him, that made roughly seventeen or eighteen men.

He knew there had to be more Brethren men than that; he'd seen them that first day as they were rallying, listening to Deacon.

He saw the tall wooden water bucket with a dipper

hanging from it, over by the wagon. Keeping his low-pulled hat tilted toward them and the fire, and walking as if in pain, which was exactly how he felt, he moved along the near side of the fire.

"Joe, you look rough. You all right?"

Gage shook his head slowly. "Heathens made a mess down there," he said in a low voice, then forced a cough. "Houses, barns, a mess." He used the dipper and sipped the water, keeping turned from them.

He sized up the rest of the situation and decided they were the only two in camp. He could brace them with the gun, force them to go face down on the far side of the fire, away from the guns and bullets stockpiled.

That would give Bewley and the woman and the baby time to scoot on through and make for the wagon train camp. Was it a good plan to send him back in there? Gage hoped so. Bewley was their scout, after all.

"Where are the others?" he said, still affecting his husky, coughing voice.

"Five haven't reported back from the raid earlier," said the older man.

"I think it's six men unaccounted for. I fear the worst," said the second man.

"Yes, as do I. And we still have men out around the perimeter, trying to catch others of the heathens who might try to sneak out and sabotage us."

"Those heathens won't stand a chance, though. Plenty of men in the dark. And with the Maker to guide them, they will stop any of them dead."

One of the men walked over toward Gage. He had to

keep himself from shying away. He was pretending to be one of them, after all. And they all knew each other well.

"What happened to your arm, Joe?"

Gage gripped the forestock of the rifle in his left hand. The man stepped close and Gage bent lower over the dipper, not sipping any longer, but ready to swing.

"Hey, wait a minute," said the man, tensing as he leaned in and peered at Gage. The fellow worked his head side to side as a snake might, testing the air before him.

He leaned closer still. Gage risked a quick glance out from beneath the low-pulled hat brim toward the other man still by the fire. He held no long gun, but judging from the way his coat sat about his waist, Gage figured the man at the fire was wearing a holstered pistol.

Gage knew he'd have to act fast. And he had to do it . . . right away.

"Hey, you ain't—"

But that's all the time the man had for sharing his discovery with the world, because Gage used his crouching stance to force momentum into a hard upward swing with the rifle. He brought the shoulder stock whistling up in a quick, tight arc, straight into the right side of the nosy man's head, catching him from the chin on up to the temple, just before the ear.

The man's ear pinched beneath the hardwood and burst, sending a spray of hot blood spuming outward. The man squealed, then collapsed to his left side on the gritty earth. Gage was already in motion, keeping low and barreling toward the man at the fire, who had dropped low and was clawing at his sidearm.

Somebody should tell farmers to practice such maneuvers before they decide to tangle in a gunfight. Gage piled into the man and knocked him off his pins. Both men sprawled hard, and as Gage was already slowed by injury, he recovered slower than his opponent. The Brethren man growled and kicked at Gage.

His boots drove hard into Gage, one catching him unaware in the gut, forcing Gage's wind from him, and the other boot slammed into Gage's right arm, sending a wash of hot pain up his body. Gage felt his unhealed cuts gush anew with hot blood; and as he rolled, sucking in what breath he could, he wondered how much blood he had left in him.

Surely, he'd reach the end any second now and drop, spent and empty, like an old pine cone.

He felt himself losing what edge he had as a blur of flailing limbs walloped into him. This would be a poor end if he lost his fight with life right now. That notion alone vexed him enough to renew his attack on the thrashing Brethren man.

It was only then that Gage realized he'd lost his grip on the rifle. No worry, since it would not be of much use in an up close fight. His clawing left hand closed around whatever it could—the other man's black wool coat—and he jerked at it hard.

That one motion saved him from yet another fist raining down on his head. These blows were beginning to take their toll. The Brethren farmer grunted and growled and flailed, and Gage felt something jam into his right forearm and he guessed what it was.

He let go of his grip on the man's coat and snatched at the thing. Grim rage alone forced him to close his fingers around it and wrench it from the man's waist. The pistol felt all too familiar, and, as much as he did not dare to admit it to himself in that brute moment, it felt right somehow. It was as if a piece of him that had been missing had been found.

He ignored the sensation, but could not ignore the wash of bile and illness building within his gut. Even as he thumbed back the hammer, he fought the bubbling up of vomit from within himself.

It sprayed out and so shocked his foe that the man jerked back, confused and repulsed.

The distraction was enough to help Gage. In that sliver of hesitation, he acted, leaping at the man. He raised the revolver high and swiped it at a hard angle down at the man's head.

The butt of the gun smacked into the farmer's temple on the right side. Gage felt the man's beard and skin beneath his slamming left hand. He yanked the gunhand back for another immediate blow, but the one had been enough.

He sat back on his heels, his breath coming in ragged, quick jags; then he remembered the first man and jerked his head to his right, but that fellow was still sprawled on his back, unmoved.

It took him long minutes before he found something—a handy coil of hempen rope in the back of the work wagon—to bind their hands and feet. He used their own shirts, yanked up from the front, and stuffed into their mouths, to gag them, and more rope knotted at the back of their flopped heads, to hold the gags in place.

Once more he sagged, aware he had precious little time before Deacon and his fellow Brethren returned. He staggered over to the water bucket and dipped up the precious liquid, sluicing it over his face, on top of his hot head, and finally into his mouth.

He swigged a mouthful and spat it out, expelling the bitter taste of vomit before drinking. Then, when he had recovered his breath, he walked on shaky legs over to the low, glowing fire and nudged it to life with a few lengths of wood.

Then he cupped his hands about his mouth and shouted "Babies!" Not caring that nothing more clever had come to him. He doubted it mattered anyway, as Bewley was no fool. The old scout was likely already back at camp anyway.

Gage poured himself a cup of somewhat-hot coffee from a tin pot nested on rocks to the side of the fire. As he sipped and sighed, swearing to himself that a cup of coffee had never tasted so good to anyone ever, he took stock of the mess he'd made, and of the goods at the wagon. He made his way over there, and then stood on a crate and peered into each vessel, as much as the low light from the fire allowed.

CHAPTER 24

"That you, Gage?"

Gage knew the voice. He peered out around the crate with the rifles poking up, and looked eastward into the night. He let his eyes run along the edge of the vast field and the trees, skylined high above, against the purple-black sky. "Who's that?"

"Silks. I'm coming in. Alone."

"Come ahead."

Within moments, Gage saw the dim outline of the rangy woodsman. He carried a rifle and walked with a limp.

"How'd you know it was me?" said Gage.

"Got a sense, is all."

"Busy day?" said Gage, looking past Silks.

"Yep. Gave better than I got."

"You shot?" said Gage.

"Nope. Twisted the knee, is all. My fault."

"How many did you . . . deal with?" said Gage.

Silks chuckled. "You sound like one of those fool politicians. I laid low four. And a fifth might not make it. The rest, let's see, that'd be six more, I knocked them clean out and trussed them up. They'll live. Have themselves a hard time seeing straight for a while, but they'll live."

"And your boy?"

"Let's ask him. Son?"

From the shadows behind Silks, a younger version of the woodsman emerged. "Yeah, Pa?"

"How many men you come upon today?"

"Eight, all told. Three floated on downstream, the others will fare about the same as them you knocked in the head."

"Good man," said Silks. The woodsman looked at Gage. "That do?"

"You bet it will. I don't like to assume a thing before it's happened, but I'd say we're in good shape, going into what's sure to come."

"That'd be Deacon and the others." Silks said this as a matter of fact.

Gage nodded. "Headed this way, any second, I believe."

Then he explained the situation of Bewley, the woman, and the Henning baby.

Silks frowned a moment. "Son, you best trail them and see that they don't come to no harm. That Chase ain't trustworthy in a hot situation. And see if you can't get men to come on back here. We'll need help flanking the enemy. Make it quick."

"Yes, sir."

With that, the youth disappeared into the dark. Gage

barely heard his moccasin-clad feet as they set off for the wagon camp.

"Got to figure out our weapons," said Silks, limping over to peer into the crate with the long guns jutting out. "For a fella handy with a gun on his hip," he said, looking over at Gage. "You don't seem to favor one."

"You know what I am," said Gage.

The rangy woodsman scratched his chin whiskers. "I know what you were. Seems to me, you ain't that fella no more."

"I'd like to believe that. I'm not certain a man can ever outrun the demon dogs of his past."

Instead of saying what Gage thought he might, the placating words people used to help others feel better, Silks shrugged. "Maybe not. That's up to you to figure out. Me, I'm alive right here and right now. I don't have time to go brooding about the past. I got concerns about the enemy pounding at my own gates, seeking to lay low them I love and them I travel with and have come to know as friends."

Gage worked up a half smile. "That count for Chase, too?"

Silks looked sideways at the ex-gunfighter. "Still thinking on that one." He stretched his game leg out and flexed his foot. "So, what's the plan?"

Gage let out a long breath and looked toward the small rise that led up from the valley. "I can't think of any other way to do this—except to ambush them as they come up. Maybe let the bulk of them drift in and assemble, poke around, and we can flank them, cut them off, prevent them from retreating back into the valley."

"Good enough plan," said Silks. "Some might make for the field, eastward into the night. But we can't prevent what we don't know."

"As long as we don't shoot each other in the cross fire."

Silks nodded. "There is that, yeah."

"Hopefully, the first ones along might not know they've been bested."

"Won't take long for them to find out, though."

Gage nodded. "What do you think?"

"Sure be nice to cut the head off the snake. By that, I mean that wily Deacon fella. Might be the rest of the body will simmer down."

"That's what I'm hoping, too. It'd be easier if we had more men."

"Might be the boy will have luck in sending some back to lend a hand."

Gage nodded as he looked at the low-banked fire. *Seems like a fellow ought to be allowed a fire on a night such as this,* he thought, then stopped himself. He was beginning to whine, and it was a trait he did *not* like in the least in others, so he sure as heck wasn't going to tolerate it in himself.

Silks had followed his lead of rummaging in the available weapons and came up with six long guns and one revolver. It would have to be enough.

"You going to shoot to kill?" Gage asked.

"I struggled with that notion much of the day, which

ain't much like me. Usually, if I'm wronged, I give back what I got. But something about this situation makes me think I might be wrong somehow. Too late for some of them I done for earlier, but the others . . ." Silks let the thought hang between them in the cold night air. "You?"

"I would prefer to slow them up, any way I can, before I shoot to kill—a shoulder, a leg." Gage shrugged. "Painful, to be sure, but it's better than being dead."

"Sure. You shoot a man in the meat of the leg, he's going to take it hard, but he'll live. Now, the knee, that's a rough one with a bullet. Shatter that bone and he never will walk right, if at all. But I can kick a man from the side, take his pins out from under him, bust that knee sideways, and he'll heal up in time. Walk with a limp, but, as you say, beats being dead."

Gage nodded his agreement. "Mostly, I don't think the Brethren are bad folks. Just fools who let themselves get taken in by that foul Deacon."

"Sure, yeah," said Silks, inspecting a rifle. "Happens all the time. Why, back home, at least twice in a summer, roving preacher men would visit the holler. There was always a handful of the weak-in-the-head folks, we all have 'em in our families, who wail and moan and flop around, claim they've seen all manner of fancies that nobody else could. Me and Mother and the boy, we'd go just to watch the fools get themselves persuaded and such. Have us a picnic lunch and all. It was a nice time-out. Gives us something to chuckle about when it's cold out."

Gage smiled at the thought of such a strange family outing, and it made him envy the man his family. "What is it about preachers that turns normal folks into fools?"

Silks offered a rare chuckle. "We knew that, we'd be somewhere else, I bet. Say, I see you carry a belt blade, too," said the woodsman. "Looks to have some heft to it."

"It does, indeed," said Gage, lifting the sheath with his fingertips, then letting the blade flap back against his leg. "I'll show it to you when the night's over."

"Be morning by then," said Silks.

He knew that the man, under other circumstances, would like to talk knives. He also wasn't averse to a discussion around a campfire about the finer aspects of well-crafted tools. But at the moment, both men knew that would have to wait. For within a short time, there would be many other things to worry about. But at least each would have a solid blade at hand for close-in fighting. And Gage had no doubt it would soon come to that.

He did not feel ready for such an event. But who ever was?

He bit back a curse rising in his throat about feeling so worn down already, even before the fighting began—or make that *renewed*. It wasn't his fight, after all. *Hang on,* he told himself. *You're doing it again. And as a matter of fact, it is all your fight.*

"Looks like you're having a struggle on your own, even before these yahoos open the ball."

Gage looked to his left, and saw Silks looking back at him. The man handed him a rifle. "Here. I expect this will serve you better than that farming tool you've been lugging around."

"Thanks. Silks, how are you able to . . ." Gage shook his head. "Never mind. I don't know what I'm saying."

"I think you're wondering why I seem so chipper before the coming skirmish, no?"

Gage nodded. "Something like that."

"Well"—the man smoothed his beard—"it's like I said before. I have folks who are dear to me and who depend on me. That's about enough to keep me swinging. You? You got anybody, Gage?"

It was a topic he'd thought of before, certainly, but as soon as he let his mind nibble at the thought, it as quickly conjured the blond girl's face in his mind, her last moments, those blue eyes clouding in death, and he had to shake his head and force himself to think of something else.

"No, no, I reckon I don't."

"Well, if it's worth anything to you, I'd say you've earned a passel of friends since you wandered on down the mountainside and lent us a hand in this mess."

"Thanks, Silks. I appreciate it. I'm tuckered, fought with a dog, was attacked by an old woman, and a few other things. It's been a long ol' day already."

"I hear that." Silks nodded. "Why, I about laid myself down after the third—"

And then Silks raised a calloused hand in the air, as if about to swat a fly. He shifted his glance to Gage and offered a slow nod. Gage returned it, knowing what the man was on about, because in that moment, he heard it, too. The voices of men from beyond the rise in the pass.

Gage nodded to Silks, then to the south. Silks responded with a nod and, even with a sore leg, he retreated into the shadows without a sound.

Gage did the same to the north, at the rear end of the supply wagon that had been parked there since the Brethren began their campaign.

As agreed, each man took up his position to either side of the funnel the pass made. Each was aware that it would be a simple thing to accidentally shoot at the other man, but angling their shots at the pass would avoid any such accident.

Gage didn't hear much talking, or much in the way of voices from the approaching Brethren, but neither did it seem as if they were taking pains to keep quiet. He guessed they assumed it was a normal thought to have one of their own tell the men at the pass that Deacon wanted them back in the valley to fight the fires and find the culprit.

Soon the outer edge of a ring of lantern light, low but advancing, wagged into view, then shadows followed, wavering and long. "Hey!" a voice said. "You Brethren men hereabouts?"

Gage didn't recognize the voice, but that meant nothing. There were plenty of Brethren to go around.

That's when Gage saw the first men appear atop the small rise. Their shapes were but black outlines, and two of them held lanterns.

"Where is everyone? I thought you said there were two men still here."

"I did."

"Well, I called and they aren't answering."

Gage held his place, unmoving, and listened to them. He knew Silks was doing the same.

What they'd said would have filled Gage with caution, but this showed him that despite the foolish fight they were embroiled in, these men were not warriors, but farmers. Farmers led by their noses into something they would likely regret for the rest of their days.

Soon there were six, seven, and then an eighth man straggled on in. Still, Gage did not see that verminous Deacon. He waited as he listened.

So far, they hadn't ventured beyond the fire ring. The only thing one of them had done was to revive the fire. He'd knelt, dribbled on a handful of crushed sticks and twigs, and blown on the coals. Small flames soon licked upward, hungry for the air and the dry tinder.

It must have been the sight of it, for Gage soon found himself clamping his teeth together tight to stifle the chattering they wanted to get up to.

He didn't think it would take them long to begin rummaging about the camp. The cold, it seemed, was keeping them from nosing too far from the still-paltry fire. Soon that would change. And he was correct.

"I'll be back," said one stout fellow. He yawned as he made his way toward the back of the wagon and to the trees beyond. Gage watched him walk by, and soon he heard the man make water and sigh.

Just then, one of the two men Gage had clunked and tied up began to moan, a sound made odd because he had a wad of his own shirt stuffed in his mouth and held in place by a tight rope.

No wonder the fool is moaning, thought Gage. *It has to hurt.* But his concerns ended there, as the man who'd visited the trees stopped on his way back to the campfire. "Hello?" he said softly. "Hello?"

The bound man moaned again and the farmer, who had left his rifle at the campfire, walked closer to where Gage had bound and stashed the two unconscious men—on the far side of the wagon.

Gage gritted his teeth, regretting not dragging the two men away from camp. Too late now, though.

He watched the newcomer advance slowly. Someone from the fire said, "Roy—you okay over there?"

Another of the men giggled. Then Roy stepped even closer.

He was now less than a foot from Gage, and that's when Gage heard Silks's voice. "Easy men! You are surrounded! Hands high or we'll drill you in the heads!"

Gage froze, his leg muscles tensed to spring on the advancing Roy. Bold talk on Silks's part, he thought. Unless he knew something that Gage didn't, it was just Gage and Silks holding the fort here.

There was a moment in which everyone in camp was silent and immobile, save for the moaning, bound fellow a few feet behind Gage. He wanted to kick the man to shut him up.

That's when the men at the campfire made their choices.

They bolted in two directions. A pair of men lunged back toward the pass, and the remaining five made for the darkness that led to the field.

It was then that Gage realized the flaw in their plan—light. Or the lack of it. He wasn't able to see with any clarity the men to deliver bullets into their scrambling, nonvital parts.

But that didn't seem to stop Silks.

Gage heard two gunshots. Both, he thought, had come from the woodsman, and at least one had an unwilling host at the head of the small group of men making for the field—judging by the fact that one man screamed, his legs collapsing beneath him. He slumped to the ground, where he stood, and howled, clutching his ravaged limb.

The other four men, who had also been running eastward, kept moving, bolting deeper into the field.

The two men who'd decided on returning to the pass were just leaving the light when Gage leveled on them and caught one in the meat of his left calf. He was in the lead and toppled in a pile, clutching his leg and screaming, as had Silks's victims.

The other man—a tall, lanky fellow, and slow—actually tripped over his friend and landed hard on all fours. Then he scrabbled forward, as if imitating a dog for a child's amusement.

Gage *almost* let sentiment, and the foolishness of how the man looked, prevent him from doling out a wounding shot, but the lanky fellow surprised him. He spun in the dark, a pistol in his hand, and began firing toward the wagon.

Gage flinched and resettled his shot, tickling the rifle's trigger. His bullet caught the lanky shooter in the upper left arm, just below the shoulder. He let out a yip and threw his revolver in a high arc.

Before it landed in the dirt some yards away, the man clutched at his fresh wound and began rocking in place on his backside and sobbing.

Great, thought Gage. *Now we have four fresh Brethren men somewhere in the dark, just into the field, two wounded in the pass, and . . .*

That's when the one he'd overlooked, Roy, clunked a boot toe against a nail keg on his route away from the bound men behind the wagon.

During the shooting, he had made for the bound men and managed to free one. Then he'd pivoted and was in midlunge at Gage when his boot offered up the telltale sound.

Gage spun and, as much out of instinct as out of reflex, dropped low and to his right, and the effect of Roy's descent on him was lessened. His ample gut hit Gage's bent left knee a hair's speed faster than his grasping hands connected with Gage's shoulder and arm.

Gage was already in action, and shoved up to a near-standing position that flowed in a seamless arc, bringing the butt of his rifle down on the man's burly back.

He also jerked his left leg out from beneath the dropping, slop-gutted man, with no time to spare. Roy made a noise of defeat and pain as he smacked face-first to the dirt.

Behind him came the moaning man, who was moving toward Gage, but not swiftly or in a straight line. Even in the low light from the briefly blazing campfire—the fresh wood placed on it by the returned Brethren now catching well—Gage saw he was in little danger of being harmed by the man just yet. Still, he figured, why should he take chances?

He advanced on the lurching fool and delivered another hard blow with the side of the rifle stock, perturbed because the idiot had caused him to turn his attention from the still-coherent Roy, and the other wounded closer by the fire.

Too much happening, too soon, thought Gage, biting back annoyance at Silks and anyone else who, he thought, had kicked off this mess.

The man Gage had shot in the leg would not stay low and whimpering for long. And then there was the lanky, shoulder-shot fool, who Gage saw had disappeared. He thought he saw movement, however brief, in the dark by the rise in the pass leading to the valley.

Good riddance . . . for now, he thought, although he knew the man could cause them a pile of woes, should he tip off other Brethren men.

Gage had no solid plan, but he had wondered that if he and Silks had somehow managed to keep folks from inflicting too much damage to each other in the dark, they might be able to wait out the enemy until daylight and then rally the others from the wagon train.

He had tried not to give much thought to Bewley or the woman and baby. They should have made it to the wagon camp before the first bullets were swapped. At least he hadn't heard gunfire from that direction.

"Gage!"

It was Silks.

Gage spun on his right heel and slammed the flat of the rifle stock against Roy's waggling head. The man had been halfway up, holding his gut with one hand and trying to reach for his back with the other. "You need another hand to hold your aching head," Gage muttered as he watched the portly gent collapse once more. This time, Roy looked to be down for good. Or at least for a few precious moments.

"Yah!" Gage growled as he dropped low behind the scant cover of the water bucket.

"At least three, maybe four, made it into the field."

"Okay—can't worry about them. You hit?"

"Nope. You?"

"Nope."

As Gage looked into the dark beyond the fire, he saw that the man he'd shot in the leg had made decent time in nearly disappearing from view, hobbling bent over and whimpering and hopping on his one good leg and dragging the other like a hunk of log.

Gage let him go, but Silks didn't share that notion, because Gage heard a crack, saw a flash, and saw the retreating man's arms fly upward, as if about to drop low in prayer. He offered up a quick yelp of surprise, then collapsed face-first.

"Don't worry," Silks growled, as if he had been privy to the thoughts in Gage's mind. "I shot his other leg. He'll live—if he's tough."

"You're a hard man," said Gage.

"Yep," said Silks. "One who's sick of this mess—"

That was all the cozy discussion the two men got up to, because a voice from the pass interrupted them.

"What's all the yowling and shooting up there?"

Gage and Silks exchanged looks. It wasn't Bewley, nor did it sound like anyone else from the wagon train. And it was bellowed from just below the rise in the pass.

From the dark, close by Gage, Roy moaned and sobbed.

Apparently, whoever was approaching from the pass heard him, too. "Who's that?" said the voice.

Gage looked beyond the fire toward the dark of the pass, aware now that the speaker was not advancing. He also thought he heard other voices, murmuring and whispering. But breaking apart, as if the speakers were separating, spreading out . . .

Then he heard a light scuffing sound, and a sprinkle of gravel rained over him. "Gage!"

It was Silks, trying to get his attention. The woodsman spoke in a forced whisper.

"Yeah?"

"Ambush, both sides!"

"Yep." Of course—that would account for the fact that the voices Gage had heard sounded as if they were separating. Because they were. He dragged a crate to his left and waited. He didn't have to wait long to hear signs of them. They were Brethren, creeping along eastward, no doubt hoping to come up behind him and Silks.

Gage was no tracker, but he'd done his share of such over the years, and he knew that hunkering and reading signs were only part of the task. A goodly portion of it was dedicated to holding still, watching and listening; sniffing the air; and feeling, with fingers, on skin, on hair, however one felt, for shifts in the breeze; smells, carried along by the same, and sounds, too.

He employed all these tricks by remaining where he was and looking toward, but not seeing, the approaching, slinking men. He looked sideways toward the tree line and soon saw movement there. Then he looked to the side of whatever it was that had moved.

Another trick that Gage had learned about tracking—never look straight at a thing. If it is a beast, it will know it, will feel your eyes on it, and will feel threatened. It will either bolt or attack. Looking askance allows the tracker, as the watcher, to remain less threatening, and to pinpoint the quarry's location.

There were always exceptions to this general rule, but it worked much of the time. And it worked for Gage then, as he watched shadows within the edge of the forest to shift and shape and reshape. He had to believe that these were the Brethren, and he hoped they could not see him, although he had to assume they could.

Shooting at them was not yet a consideration, because he could not see them clearly enough. The matter was decided for him, once again, because Silks, he assumed, had grown weary of waiting and had opened the ball.

Gage heard a man to his right, over toward Silks, shriek. It was not the voice of the woodsman, so he kept on scouting his own shadowed side. From Silks's side, someone, not Silks, returned fire with one, two shots.

Silks remained quiet and Gage hoped for the best for the man. He refocused his attention on his own side, on the shifting shadows in the woods, and for the moment, he waited. He needed to know at what or whom he was shooting.

From the crunching, soft footfalls he heard, moving slowly and with measured steps, Gage reckoned there were three, perhaps four, men. What was their intention? Likely to circle him and come upon them from the east edge, from the field.

Gage felt he had waited them out long enough. He stepped low, to his left, and with the rifle held before him, he aimed at where he knew them to be; and ready to fire, he cut left, and soon was in the woods himself, pursuing them. Nobody was behind him—that he could decipher—no telltale sounds of slow movement, no scents of men drifted to his nostrils.

And then they were there, closing in on the few horses still tied where the Brethren kept them picketed. Gage waited them out, wondering if the men were going to defy his guesses and mount up or continue on, cutting to the right in an effort to close in on him and Silks.

He didn't have long to wait, for he saw them do just that, and move toward the field's edge. He saw three men now, skylined against the emerging morning light slicing in from the east, beyond and behind them.

He raised the rifle to his shoulder, felt a mild twinge of regret at what he was about to do to an unwitting man, and called to mind the fact that the wagon train folks had not asked to be made into targets and victims of these ruthless brutes. Then his fingertip squeezed the trigger.

The tip of the rifle's barrel spat a quick, explosive burst in the murky dawn light and a man screamed, stiffened, and slammed groundward, writhing and howling.

The Brethren fellow had earned it, but it didn't make it any more pleasant hearing the man suffer the leg wound. Gage's bullet drove into the meat of his thigh and he let the world know it hurt.

Gage tracked the other two men, who had also yelped. But they escaped his next shots, because they had rabbited it eastward, into the field. Fear, no doubt, renewed the fact in their minds that they were farmers, not killers, and they were being hunted.

He heard them retreating and decided to let them go without pursuit. He was about to turn back toward the campfire, to see if Silks was in need of help, when something stilled him.

It was not a sound, a scent—not much of anything, save for a feeling. And while it was slight at that, it was there. And if Gage had learned anything in his years on the trail, it was to trust that flutter of warning nested in him. Whether it lived in his mind, his gut, his heart, he had no idea, but it had served him well over time and he valued its presence in such dicey moments as these.

And this time, it was telling him not to act in haste, for there was another, a fourth man, one who had not advanced with the other three. One who had remained . . . but where?

Then Gage heard a horse whicker low. Of course, he thought. Someone was still hiding there, perhaps readying to make a run for it on horseback toward Higgins. Or just hiding.

Then, to his right, Gage heard growls and shouts and thuds, as of fists on flesh, then low curses and oaths muttered. They were words no so-called religious person would use, and the voice sounded a whole lot like Silks's. And the other sounds told Gage the man was engaged in close-in fighting.

Gage let whoever was lurking by the horses be for the moment, and, hunkering low, he cat-footed in a curve toward the field, then in toward Silks. He didn't have to travel far to see the back of a man, dressed in black, with arms wide and humped, hopping backward as if trying to avoid something, or someone, coming at him.

As Gage approached, he saw beyond the man that indeed someone was closing in. And that someone was snarling low and cutting off words of anger. And as morning light from behind Gage shafted in, he saw buckskins and a rangy arm wielding a big, wide-bladed knife.

It was Silks and he was riled, closing in on the man with speed and ferocity.

"Attack me?" said Silks, whipping his blade in a controlled, precise arc. But his combatant was a sizable fellow, too, and was not turning tail and running. He was sidestepping and looking as if he wanted to fight, for he, too, was armed.

As he advanced, now with more caution and cutting to his right, Gage saw that Silks's opponent held a rifle by the barrel in a big left hand and was raising it to swing as a club. Silks's game leg was hampering his intended advance, and Gage saw that this might well cause him injury any second.

So Gage bolted forward and slammed the butt of his rifle hard into the side of the big Brethren fellow's head, above the ear, in that spot that rarely failed to elicit results. Gage had thumped and clubbed plenty of men in that very spot, and the blow usually yielded satisfaction in the form of a groan and a dropped man, collapsing to the earth in a heap like a sack of wet sand.

And this time was no exception. The big Brethren brute offered up a gagging sound and then sort of turned in place, his boots tangling, and he dropped to the earth.

"Mighty thankful you showed, Gage. I was beginning to curse, and when that happens, it's a sure sign that I'm letting my temper ride on over the top of my reason."

Gage and Silks stood looking down at the unmoving man.

"Glad to help," said Gage. He looked up. "Others?"

"Two. I had to gut one, and shot the other. That one might live. They sneaked up on me, I'm shamed to say, and got right to work on me before I was set. But it all worked out."

Right about when they had trussed the man Gage had clubbed, and checked on the others—both had expired—Silks raised a long finger to his lips and nodded toward the lightening field.

Both men faded to opposite sides of the lane and waited for the approaching figure to show himself. It didn't take but a few moments; then Gage heard Silks say, "Son!" and he, too, emerged to greet the woodsman's boy.

"How'd you do, then?" said father to son.

Silks the younger said, "I kilt one. Had to, me or him. The others, five or so, will live, I expect."

"Good job, son."

Silks and his son exchanged nods.

"Anyone else from the camp out there?" said Gage.

The youth nodded, reminding Gage anew, with each movement and mannerism, of the boy's father. "Mr. Bewley and that Chase fella." He said it with the slightest sneer in his voice, but showed nothing on his face of his obvious disapproval of the man. "We all been busy. Lots of them Brethren about. Or there were."

"And the woman and baby?"

The kid nodded. "She's all right. She's with Ma, but she give the baby to Mrs. Henning first. There was some squallin' about that. I reckon Mrs. Henning was happy."

Gage had no more time for questions, because beyond

the kid, emerging from the low river-bottom fog hugging the field, he saw two shapes. He stepped to the side and whipped his rifle up to his shoulder. At the same time, Silks and his son bent low, spinning and raising their own rifles.

"Easy now!" growled one of the approaching men. "It's me, Bewley! Don't shoot! Or if you do, make sure you miss me and this one here behind me!" He let out a quick cackle.

"Hey!" shouted the second man. Gage recognized it as his mind picked out the other shape as belonging to the annoying Chase.

They emerged from the mist fully, and while both held their hands raised slightly, it soon became obvious to everyone they needn't.

"You made it," said Gage.

"Yep, about to say the same of you."

The scout looked about him in the purpling light at the various forms sprawled out or hunched up, those conscious were shaking and whimpering. All, he saw, had been trussed tight with rope.

"Anybody seen that Deacon beast?" Bewley questioned.

"I was about to ask you that," said Gage.

Silks looked over from eyeing the terrain behind Gage, and Gage did the same with his gaze, which had been roving the emerging shadows beyond Silks.

"Plenty of time to track him, now that we have daylight," said the lanky woodsman.

EVERYBODY HAS A GUN 359

"Are there others?" Bewley directed to Gage, but asking it of both of them.

"Not so far as we know. But I have no idea how many more there are waiting in the valley."

"I doubt we'll get a straight answer out of any of them," said Bewley, nodding toward the scatter of wounded and trussed about the campfire.

Then Gage's eyes widened and Bewley saw this.

"What is it?"

"I forgot—too tired, I guess," said Gage. "But I think there's still a man back in the trees, at the Brethren horses. Curse me for a fool!"

Bewley was about to offer a few placating words as they turned to make for the Brethren horses, when the younger Silks said, "Pa!"

Gage and Bewley and Silks and Chase all looked northward, to the tree line. There was movement there, back where the Brethren horses had been picketed. Just where Gage and Bewley were headed.

"Horse, son?" said Silks, squinting in the direction his son pointed.

"Don't think so. Man, I reckon. Mounting up."

"Come on," said Bewley to Chase. The tall man bent low and followed the scout, who led the way down the field. Gage knew the man was going to cut wide eastward and flank whoever it might be over there by the horses.

"You two go together," said Gage, aware that Silks was pained by his leg more than he was willing to let on.

The woodsmen nodded and made for the field, taking the center of the ambush.

Gage broke left, westward, and then in toward the trees. He figured if whoever it was happened to linger too long there, Gage might well be the first to come upon him, if it was a him. He didn't doubt the younger Silks's eyesight in the matter.

Gage made it halfway to the makeshift Brethren corral, close enough to see the shapes of three horses there, all standing alert, ears perked forward, and all gazing toward the field.

He stepped one stride closer, and that's when the last of the mist burst apart. He could now see the farthest of the three mounts hammered hard beneath a thick shape growling "Ha! Ha!" and whipping the beast's flanks hard and fast, the leather reins snapping loud and quick.

The distance was too great for Gage to see without doubt who it was, but he knew for certain it was a Brethren man, for the fellow wore black trousers and a black coat, and a black hat popped off and pinwheeled to the ground as the thrashed horse stampeded forward, whinnying a series of high-pitched, shrill sounds of shock and pain.

The horse and rider were soon beyond where Gage felt he could risk a shot, given that Silks and his son were out there in the general vicinity, and Bewley and Chase might well be, too.

Gage wasted no time and followed, keeping low and entering the slowly eddying mist, which as he advanced into the field, he saw was already fading with the dawn's slow-blooming light. He lost sight of the thundering horse and rider, but in a few seconds, he heard shouts, recognized Bewley's voice calling, "Stop!"—and then Chase repeated the directive.

A gunshot snapped, then another. Both reports were from a pistol, given the high, quick, cracking sound. Gage ran forward, rifle at the ready, moving as quickly as he could, given the preceding night's tortures.

He caught sight of the horse, then a man beside it, shouting at the horse to calm down. It was Silks. Where was the rider?

"Where'd he go?" Bewley growled as Gage ran up. Chase, Gage saw, was some distance to the southeast, on a rise in the field, and Silks's son was nowhere to be seen.

"Was it who I think it was?" Gage stated as he came up alongside, helping Silks gentle the beast.

"Deacon, yeah," said Bewley. "He tried to angle east, toward the Higgins road, but Chase managed to send him back this way, into the field. By the time we caught up to him, he was gone, out of the saddle!"

"He's around," growled Silks. "My boy will sniff him out."

"Any sign?" shouted Chase. Gage wished the man would keep quite and not stand out in the mist. He was liable to get shot.

"Aah!"

The cry, higher pitched than a man's, not as high as a woman's, came from the south, low down, and still in the mist.

Gage recalled there was a low spot in the middle of the field, where the land bellied.

They ran for it, Silks letting go of the horse's reins. "That was my boy!" he snarled, leading the way.

Game leg or no, the woodsman was not easy to keep up with.

All four men arrived at the same time, from different directions, arrayed along the slight swell overlooking the low spot. Below, in a swirl of parting mist, Silks's son lay on his back, at the bottom, unmoving.

The woodsman let out a bark of rage and leapt down the hill, colliding with his son's body and sprawling, then regaining his knees and clutching at the boy.

Beyond, making straight across the field, in the direction of the river, a burly form barreled. Gage raised his rifle, but the mist folded over the man again, enclosing him as if in a gauzy wrap. *A winding sheet, if I can make it happen,* Gage thought as he ran after him, not waiting to find out about the Silks boy.

As he ran, Gage heard other steps closing in behind him. He didn't turn to see who it might be, but assumed it was Bewley and Chase.

He came upon Deacon sooner than he expected. The plug of a man stood in the midst of a clear patch, his hands half raised, a rifle clutched in his right at the forestock. And beyond, Gage soon saw the reason that Deacon was brought up short.

A woman stood facing Deacon, not twenty feet away, with a rifle drawn on the man. Gage recognized her as Mrs. Hastings, the wife of the man who was shot in the back early in the attack on the first day. And Gage recalled thinking it had likely been Deacon who had killed the man as he fled, unarmed.

Gage also saw he was nearly in line with Deacon and the woman. He kept his rifle trained on the burly preacher, but sidestepped to his right, clearing himself from a bullet's path, should Mrs. Hastings's shot not find its mark.

He caught movement to his left and, glancing quickly, saw Bewley and, beyond, Chase.

"You shot my husband, you vile man!" shouted Mrs. Hastings.

"No!" shouted Deacon. "No! I swear it! I wanted none of this! These people, they wouldn't listen to reason! They are to blame!"

"Shut up!" she barked, cranking the hammer back all the way and snugging the stock to her shoulder and cheek.

"No, Mrs. Hastings! Don't do it!"

It was Bewley, advancing between the two, an arm extended toward the woman. "He ain't worth it—let others deal with him. You'll never live it down if you take a life like this, ma'am!"

His words seemed to rattle her a little, for Gage saw her arms tremble. Then she shook her head. "No! He killed my husband! The father of my children!"

"I did not do it!" shouted Deacon.

By then, Gage had covered the distance between himself and the Brethren leader and came up on his right side.

"Drop the gun, Deacon!"

The burly man glanced to his right at Gage. "You!"

"Yes, me. Now drop it!"

The man dithered.

"Now!"

Deacon let go his grasp of the rifle and it fell. Gage knew it belonged to the Silks youth, and he hoped the boy was alive.

Gage glanced to his right and saw that Bewley was now smack between Mrs. Hastings and Deacon, his own arms raised. He continued to talk to the woman, while slowly walking toward her. "He ain't worth it, ma'am. You know it and I know it. Those kiddies need a mama! They don't need to wake up screaming every night because they saw their mama kill a man!"

By then, she was crying, and as Gage looked, he saw for the first time that she was not alone. Behind and close to her left side, two small children stood, eyes wide, faces red, but it looked as if they were unable to breathe, let alone cry.

No wonder Bewley had risked his life to keep her from shooting Deacon.

She relaxed and lowered the rifle as Bewley's hand closed over the barrel and took the long gun from her. She turned from him and dropped to her knees, sobbing and pulling her children in close.

Gage moved in on Deacon, to within a step. To the thick man's left, Chase walked closer, rage pulling the tall man's face into a tooth-gritting mask of anger.

Deacon glanced at Gage, a sneer on his face, and said, "That stupid woman." He nearly smiled then, but Gage's left arm swung, hard and fast—in a move, he later realized, he had learned from seeing it come, hard and fast, into his own face, delivered by his father so many years before.

The back of Gage's big, bone-hard hand slammed into Deacon's face. Gage felt the man's nose collapse flat and smear as blood and gristle sprayed outward into the cold morning air.

The Brethren leader screamed and clutched at his face, falling to his knees in the brittle grass. He blubbered and howled and blood poured out between the thick fingers of both his hands as they groped his face.

Gage looked over the top of him and saw Chase staring down at the mess of a man, a sneer on his face, and a nod of approval working his head slightly. He looked at Gage and nodded again, then snatched at the man's coat and shoved him face down in the dirt and whipped out rope.

Gage left him to his task of binding the screaming man's wrists behind his back, so tight, he saw, that the man's skin puffed and purpled within moments. *That's good,* he thought as he picked up the dropped rifle and walked back to where he'd left Silks.

Relief washed over him as he saw the lanky woodsman and his son standing together, the father resting a hand on his son's shoulder, the son holding the side of his head with his left hand.

Gage walked up and handed the rifle to the youth and it was accepted with a sigh and a nod of thanks. Gage returned the nod, appreciating the simplicity of outward emotion that obviously masked a deep, strong affection, for Silks's eyes were moist and his face was wide in a rare full smile.

Chapter 25

"You could come with us," said Bewley, not looking at Mrs. Schenk, and so he did not see her weary smile.

"Mighty kind of you, Mr. Bewley. But I don't think the other members of your wagon train would take kindly to that notion. Besides," she said, holding up a hand to keep Bewley from giving voice to the protest he was about to offer, "I have a home here. It's a good little farm, in a pretty place, with a good many people. And a son who needs me."

"You think those folks are trustworthy?"

She shrugged. "I hope so. I knew most of them before Deacon came, and I will do my best to cut through the fool notions he laid atop them over the past few years. They're in there, I can tell."

"Then I wish you luck, ma'am." Bewley tugged off his battered felt topper and bowed low. She blushed and hugged him. "Goodbye, Mr. Bewley."

* * *

"What are you going to do with me?" Deacon growled and jerked his plug of a body trying to loosen the tight-wrapped bindings about his wrists behind his back. "I demand you let me go!"

"Oh," said Gage. "We will. Matter of fact, I think we might as well do that here and now." He turned to the man to his right. It was Silks. "What do you think?"

The rangy woodsman nodded. "Sure thing." Silks turned to Marstow, Quint, Fletcher, and a pile of other Brethren men, who were all joined, side by side, with women and youngsters.

Gage and Silks assumed they were their long-suffering wives and families. The gathered farmers of the Chosen Valley looked weary, bruised, and besooted, but there was a hard glint in their eyes and not a smile among them. Yet, none of them were directing their flinty gazes at the wagon train folks. They were looking straight at Deacon, instead.

The burly, self-appointed holy man's eyes widened and he took a step backward. "Hold on, I . . . I think you folks have the wrong idea." He looked over at Gage. "Yes. Yes, I have had a change of mind and I do believe you should take me along with you."

Gage scratched his chin, looked at Bewley, then Silks. "What do you think?"

The other two men shook their heads.

"No, I reckon not, Deacon. I think you'll be treated well by your folks here. After all, they are your Brethren, and this here is the Chosen Valley. Or at least the ones you chose, right? Seems to me, a man should stick by his people, and his decisions."

"But . . . but . . ." Deacon's face had bloomed bright red and he kept turning, looking at Gage and the others, then back to the Brethren, who were advancing on him.

Gage, Silks, and Bewley backed away and walked toward the waiting wagons. As Gage looked back, he saw the crowd of black-clothed farmers close around the plug of a man. At first, Deacon's shouts, then his pathetic, begging whimperings, sounded like music to his ears.

Twenty minutes later, the wagon train rolled through the far western pass leading out of the Chosen Valley. The land once more opened before them, revealing a vast, wide, rolling vista topped with blue sky, sparse white clouds, and fringed ahead and alongside with the rising foothills and flanks of the Chisley Range.

The wagons halted and men and women hopped down, checking and rechecking wagons, tending to stock, and taking care to look after anything else that might give them cause for concern. After this, Gage knew, they would not stop for some time; each member of the train—animals, no doubt, included—wished to put the distance of many miles behind them, away from the sour paradise that was the Chosen Valley.

Bewley rode back and halted beside Gage. "You should come along with us, Gage." He fluffed his beard and squinted over at him.

"Thanks," said Gage. "I'll ride along for a bit, keep an eye on the back trail out of this place. Just in case."

"And then?" said Bewley.

Gage looked to their right, toward the northeast and the peaks of the Chisley Range rising into the distance. The higher they grew, the whiter they became. "I don't think it's too late in the season to find a spot in a valley up there somewhere. Maybe alongside a cold, clear lake. I heard tell that with enough motivation, a man can build a cabin, trap, fish, and—"

"And smoke a pipe and read a little poetry in the evening." Bewley handed Gage a worn, thick book.

The former gunfighter tipped it sideways and read the spine: *Whittier's Complete Poems*. He looked at Bewley. "Thank you . . . friend."

"Safe journeys to you, Gage. You're a good man." Bewley offered him two fingers off his old hat's brim, nodded once, and rode his horse back up to the front of the train.

Gage watched him ride off, looked down at the book with a smile, and tucked it into a saddlebag. When he looked up again, the wagons were rolling westward. He heeled his old horse forward. "'A good man'? What do you think, Rig?"

The horse flicked an ear and walked on.

Turn the page for a plumb-entertaining preview!

**Johnstone Country.
Hold On Tight Because This Rodeo
Is Just Getting Started.**

Introducing a gun-blazing new series
from the masters of the classic Western.
Meet Jesse Derringer. Troubleshooter for
the Union Pacific Railroad.
Where there's trouble, there's Derringer.
And where there's Derringer, there's shooting . . .

On the Fourth of July, 1867, the Union Pacific
Railroad announced plans to expand their line
into the remote mountains of Dakota Territory.
They chose a site near Crow Creek Crossing to be
their headquarters and named it Cheyenne.
Almost immediately, new residents began to arrive:
dreamers and schemers, drifters and grifters,
good folks and bad.
The owners of Union Pacific knew
there'd be problems. Between settling land rights,
laying down tracks, and keeping the peace,
they'd need a troubleshooter.

His name is Derringer. Like the gun. Arriving by
cattle car with two of his beloved horses,
Jesse Derringer is not your typical railroad employee.
With the eyes of a scout, he looks for trouble before
it becomes a problem for the construction crews—
and sometimes starts trouble himself.
Usually, with a cool head and steady hand,
he handles hot-tempered troublemakers. But then,
there are problems like Felix Reardon.
A wealthy rancher with a sprawling cattle spread,
Reardon refuses to give up a piece of his land
for a new U.S. Army post.

Jesse Derringer is about to learn the true definition
of troubleshooting.

**National Bestselling Authors
William W. Johnstone
and J.A. Johnstone**

DERRINGER

First in a new Western series!

**On sale September 2025,
wherever Pinnacle Books are sold.**

CHAPTER 1

General Grenville M. Dodge sat beside a small fire on the bank of Lodgepole Creek and drank a cup of coffee. His column of 150 cavalry had totally routed a party of about forty Arapaho warriors, who had been raiding settlers between Crow Creek and Fort Laramie. They had been fortunate to attack the Arapaho camp while the warriors were still asleep in their blankets.

The forced march to catch the Indians was the suggestion made by the general's personal scout, Sergeant Jesse Derringer. It was Derringer who found the Indians' camp at the base of a line of mountains after they raided a small settlement north of Crow Creek. The few Indians who had escaped the attack disappeared into the steep mountains of the Black Hills, so Dodge decided to have breakfast before starting the march back to Fort Laramie.

"You send for me, General?" Jesse Derringer asked when he approached Dodge.

"Yes, I did, Sergeant," Dodge replied. "Did you get something to eat?"

"Yes, sir, I ate," Derringer said. "What can I do for you?"

Dodge smiled in response to Derringer's submissive attitude. The general would be willing to wager that he was the only person on the planet who commanded much respect from the burly sergeant. "Now that the horses have had a chance to rest, I'm going to go on a little scout up into those mountains to see if those Indians kept running. You wanna go with me?"

"I reckon I'd better," Derringer said, thinking that wasn't the smartest idea the general had ever had. "You want me to mount up a detail of fifteen?"

"No, I was thinking about just the two of us," Dodge said. "I feel pretty confident they're not thinking about planning to attack us. You said you were sure they headed for home, didn't you?"

"Yes, sir, but I didn't know you were plannin' to go ridin' up into the mountains by yourself." He paused for a few moments before asking a question. "This have anything to do with the railroad?"

"As a matter of fact, it would be interesting to see if there's anyplace that the railroad could go through on this line of mountains. It would sure cut off a lot of miles of track if it could, and they're too damn high to climb."

"I expect it would," Derringer said. He knew how interested the general was in the construction of the cross-country railroad and that he had already been involved in planning the path of that track. The general had told him it would shorten the route 150 miles if the tracks were brought this way from Council Bluffs, if they could go straight across this line of mountains. It was by coincidence that they followed the raiding party to the base of the very mountain range that was blocking Dodge's preferred path to the west for the Union Pacific Railroad. Since they were here by chance, it would seem a shame to leave without giving the general the opportunity to estimate the possibility of somehow getting past this mountain range.

"Jesse," Dodge said, "when we leave here, we're going straight back to Fort Laramie. I don't know when I might get a chance to get back to this place again."

"That is a fact, sir," Derringer responded. The general only addressed him by his first name when he was asking a favor, instead of giving a direct order. "I expect we oughta go up those mountains and take a little look around." He felt pretty sure they wouldn't find any of those Arapaho warriors waiting for them. "I'll get the horses."

They followed the path the fleeing Arapaho warriors had taken to ascend the mountain, since it was obviously the easiest way up. All the way to the top, Derringer kept a cautious eye on the trail left by the Indians. They had made no real effort to disguise their retreat, and once they reached the top of the ridge, they varied their direction, only to the extent of picking the easiest way down the other side. Only then was Derringer willing to dismiss them from his concern.

Dodge wanted to scout the ridge to the north first, so they made their way along it for almost a mile before they stopped when they found the mountains grew higher, the farther north they rode. "Too steep to climb and too far to tunnel through," the general conceded. When he looked at Derringer for a response to his comment, he found the sergeant staring at a large outcropping of rock ahead of them. Staring back at them, a lone Indian warrior stood motionless, as fully surprised as they were. When Derringer pulled the Henry rifle out of his saddle scabbard, the Indian turned and fled, disappearing in the rocks.

Derringer was immediately after him. "Stay here!" he told the general. "I'll try to see if he's alone!"

He gave his horse a kick and worked his way through the rocks, where he found a trail on the other side, leading down the mountainside. He caught a glimpse of the Indian just before he disappeared again when the trail bent around a clump of trees. When he got to that clump, he reined his horse to a sliding halt, because he saw the Indian he had been chasing pulling up before a camp beside a small stream.

A war party, he thought, for they were wearing paint. He did a quick count of those he could see and figured there were about twenty of them. The one he had been following didn't dismount, but was gesturing wildly and pointing back in the direction he had fled. "Damn," Derringer swore, and wheeled his horse around when he saw the warriors scrambling to get to their horses.

He started yelling to Dodge before he reached him. "War party! We've got to ride like hell!"

"Can we hold them off?" Dodge yelled back.

"Too many!" Derringer answered. "We've gotta ride like hell," he repeated.

The general still waited until Derringer caught up to him before falling in behind him, preferring to have the rugged scout lead the way. They rode south along the ridge as fast as they safely could, to the sound of war whoops from their pursuers. It began to look as if they might be trapped on top of this mountain ridge; so when they came to what looked like a narrow pass, Derringer didn't hesitate. He guided his horse down into the pass and followed it. To his surprise, it continued to gradually descend until it took them all the way to the prairie floor.

"You all right, sir?" Derringer asked when he reined back to let the general catch up.

"That was a helluva ride," Dodge said. "They didn't even see us drop down in that pass, so I expect they're wondering where we went." He laughed in relief. "I'll tell you the truth, I thought you'd lost your mind when you dropped down in that gully. And I thought I was crazy to follow you. How did you know that narrow ravine was a pass that would take us down to the prairie?"

"It just looked like a narrow pass that would just naturally lead down to the prairie," Derringer lied. In fact, he had given up hope of outrunning the war party and was looking for someplace where they might hold them off. But since it had turned out to be a safe way down to the bottom, he figured he might as well take credit for a smart move.

Dodge just shook his head, still amazed that they had

escaped. "I'll tell you one thing, though. If we can save our scalps, I believe we've found a pass through which the Union Pacific can go."

"Well, then, I reckon the scout was worth it," Derringer responded. "I expect we oughta get along back to the column now before those boys up there on that mountain figure out we ain't up there no more." He paused before suggesting another option. "Unless you wanna wait for that war party to find out we're down here on the plains, so we can lead 'em back to our camp. It ain't but about a mile from here and then they wouldn't waste all that war paint they're wearin'."

"I don't know what that war party was doing up on top of that mountain," Dodge remarked. "Where were they going? There's no settlement south of these mountains."

"That's a fact," Derringer said. "I suspect they mighta been thinkin' about settlements east, back along the South Platte and there's a few of them. Hard to tell what they're thinkin' now. They mighta run into those Arapaho we chased up atop that mountain. If they did, then they know there's a column of a hundred and fifty soldiers right behind them."

"I know we put a stop to that Arapaho raiding party, but we're two and a half days' march back to Fort Laramie," Dodge said. "I swear, damn it, I can't leave now when we know there's a war party of twenty or more savages probably on their way to attack some settlement east of here."

"I reckon I could go back up there and ask 'em what

they're plannin' to do, so we'd know what we oughta do," Derringer japed. "Since it ain't but about a mile back to camp, how 'bout we take you back to your command? Then I can come back here and keep an eye on this war party. There ain't no sense in makin' a hundred and fifty men worry about their commandin' officer when they could just have to worry about one sergeant."

The general couldn't help chuckling in response. "I'm sure Colonel Walsh is standing ready and willing to take command of the column in the event of my absence."

Derringer started to laugh, but stopped short. "He might get his chance," he said when he saw the warrior suddenly appear in the mouth of the narrow pass. "It's time to go!" He gave the general's horse a smack on the behind just as they heard the war cries coming from the base of the mountain. They were off at a gallop with what he assumed were twenty-two screaming Cheyenne warriors in hot pursuit.

"Head for the gap in that line of trees!" Derringer shouted to the general. "I'm gonna slow 'em down some!"

Dodge did as he was instructed and continued to gallop toward the gap in the trees that outlined the creek where his men were camped.

Derringer pulled his horse to a stop and wheeled around to face the war party chasing them. One particular brave was out in front of the rest and he was gaining on them. So Derringer again drew his Henry rifle from his saddle scabbard. He waited for the horse to be still while he cranked a cartridge into the cylinder, guessing the warrior was at a distance of about 120 yards and closing fast. Then he took dead aim and knocked the racing warrior off his horse. Thinking also to put the detachment of soldiers on alert, he fired twice more at the war party. It caused them to spread out and those with rifles answered fire.

"That oughta do it," he said, wheeling his horse again and racing after General Dodge. *Now it's up to you, Colonel Walsh,* he thought. The colonel was already up to the surprise. He stepped out of the trees and signaled the general to come to him. Seeing him, General Dodge headed straight for him, and Derringer was not far behind.

As he rode into the cover of the trees, Derringer passed through a long line of soldiers lying in ambush and waiting for the command to fire at the charging party of unsuspecting Cheyenne warriors. Derringer's first thought upon riding into the safety of the trees was: *That answers the question why they didn't run into the fleeing Arapaho on the mountain.* He and the general quickly dismounted and took cover, while Colonel Walsh commanded the men to hold their fire. When the war party was about thirty-five yards away, he gave the order to fire and the trees erupted in a long line of rifle fire, which decimated the hapless Indian war party. It was reduced to half a dozen in a few minutes' time, and half of them were wounded. They promptly retreated as best they could.

Walsh reported to General Dodge and asked if he

wanted to mount a patrol to go after the survivors. Dodge gave him a "Well done," but said no. He thought the war party had been sufficiently discouraged from any raids they had sought to perform on any settlement. "We'll start back to Fort Laramie after the noon meal."

With six other soldiers, Derringer walked out among the bodies left on the prairie. Their purpose was to make sure all the bodies were dead, so as not to prolong suffering. Those who survived the ambush would most likely come back to take care of the dead after the soldiers left. Derringer's purpose, however, was to identify the dead, and he found that he was right in thinking they were Cheyenne. He reported the fact to General Dodge and Colonel Walsh.

Walsh, known for his sense of humor, made a suggestion when planning future campaigns. "Instead of mounting patrols of fifteen or more men, why not just send you and Sergeant Derringer out as bait? And you can just lead them back to an ambush, like you did today." Overheard by some of the soldiers close by, it became a running joke among the regiment.

The ambush of the Cheyenne war party happened in September 1865. It turned out to be the last campaign of that nature for the general and the sergeant. During the following months, the general was called back to Washington to plan the building of the railroad, while the sergeant was assigned to a cavalry regiment. In May 1866, General Dodge resigned from the army, and later that same year was appointed chief engineer of the Union Pacific Railroad. When news of the general's appointment finally got around to Sergeant Jesse Derringer, he was not surprised at all and was happy for his old boss. He realized how much he missed the days when he was the general's personal scout, and how little he liked serving in a regular cavalry company. So he decided to resign from the army, fully convinced he had no desire to retire from it. He preferred to find out what else was out there to see before he became too old to see it.

It had been some time before the war since he had been back to the family farm near Omaha, so he decided to visit the old homeplace. His younger brother, Dan, and his wife, Shirley, took over the farm after his parents were gone. They had passed away while Jesse was serving in Dakota Territory.

Jesse's visit with his brother was a brief one, lasting only a couple of days. Although Dan and Shirley made a show of welcoming him home, Jesse was aware of a sense of concern from both of them that he was planning to claim his inheritance and move in with them and their two boys. He assured them that he had no desire to settle down on the farm, so he would be on his way again the next day. His statement relieved the tension immediately and they persuaded him to stay over an extra day. When he left, Dan asked where he was heading, and Jesse simply answered, "West."

CHAPTER 2

William C. Cartwright, the assistant construction supervisor, sat at his desk in the Council Bluffs office of the Union Pacific Railroad. He was studying a large map spread out across the desk when one of his clerks stuck his head in the door and announced that there was a gentleman who wanted to see him. Cartwright was not inclined to waste his time granting interviews to journalists, so he asked, "Newspaper reporter?"

"I don't know," the clerk responded. "He doesn't look like one. He was a rather direct gentleman, however, when he said it was important."

"Oh, he did, did he?" Cartwright replied. "Did he give his name?"

"Yes, sir. He said his name is Derringer."

"Derringer?" Cartwright responded. "The only Derringer I know about is no gentleman. Send him in here, Lewis. Hell, I sent word for him to come see me." He got up from the desk to receive him when Lewis withdrew his head from the door and opened it for Derringer to come in.

"Sergeant Derringer!" Cartwright announced, grinning from ear to ear. He stepped forward to extend his hand to the tall, serious-looking man.

"Sergeant?" Jesse Derringer responded with a genuine look of surprise. "It's been a while since anybody's called me Sergeant. I mustered out of the army when there wasn't nobody left to fight. How did you know I was in the army?"

"I know that you served as a scout for my boss at Union Pacific, General Grenville M. Dodge, and I know he's looking for you."

"I heard that General Dodge was workin' for the railroad," Derringer said. "I didn't know he was lookin' for me, though. How did you know I was in Council Bluffs?"

"I didn't," Cartwright responded, "but the general remembered you had a home in Omaha before the war and he thought you might be passing through here sometime in your travels. So I gave your name to the bartender at the Whistlestop Saloon. And I told him if Jesse Derringer ever stops in, tell him I want to see him and it's important."

"Yes, sir, it sure surprised me when he told me that," Jesse said. "Mickey Deal's his name, ain't it? The last I heard about General Dodge was that he won an election for congressman, but he's workin' for the Union Pacific Railroad now." He looked around and nodded, smiling. "I see they fixed him up in a nice office."

"Yes, but he doesn't spend much time in it," Cartwright was quick to reply. "My job is assistant superintendent of construction for the railroad across the country to connect with the Central Pacific Railroad to form a transcontinental railroad. The general is in the field with the surveyors, mapping out the right of way for the tracks, so I'm glad you got here when you did. General Dodge wants me to offer you a job with the Union Pacific."

"That's mighty thoughtful of the general, but I don't know anything about workin' on the railroad," Derringer responded as he pictured himself swinging a pickaxe or driving a spike, and it wasn't the kind of work that suited him.

"Mr. Derringer, the general says you're the best damn scout he's ever had the pleasure of working with," Cartwright informed him. "He said that maybe you're the only man he trusts to fill the job he's got in mind. The railroad has given him the task of planning the route of the railroad from Council Bluffs into Dakota Territory. Right now, General Dodge is at Crow Creek Crossing, where they're building a bridge across Crow Creek. After Crow Creek, they're faced with a rougher route to follow up across what the general's calling Sherman Hill. The general said that back in 1865 in the Black Hills campaign, your outfit had to escape from an Indian war party, and it was you who found a pass out of that mess. He said he thought at the time that it would serve as a pass skirting the Black Hills for the railroad, west of the Platte River."

"Yes, sir," Derringer remarked with a chuckle, "I remember that time."

"So, how about it? Are you ready to go back to work as the general's scout? You'll go on the Union Pacific payroll starting today if you are. I can authorize some advance expense money so you can get what supplies you need right away."

"Well, I could say I'd have to think about it, since I had other plans," Derringer said, "but that would be a lie. So I reckon I'm your man." He didn't say as much to Cartwright, but when he mentioned the money in advance, it was a done deal. His financial state was down to pocket change. When he rode into town the day before, the thought that he would ever see General Dodge again never entered his mind as a possibility. And with winter coming on, he was expecting to be riding the grub line, hoping to sign on as a cowhand with some rancher.

"Excellent!" Cartwright responded. "That's going to make the general very happy. He's told me some tales about your time in the army."

"Is that right?" Derringer responded. "Well, I hope you didn't believe all of them."

"When did you get into town?" Cartwright asked.

"Yesterday mornin'," Derringer answered.

"Did you take a room in the hotel?"

"No, sir, I spent last night in the jailhouse," Jesse told him.

"Oh? Did you drink a little too much of the demon whiskey?" Cartwright asked.

"No, sir, I only had a couple of drinks, but the fellow at the end of the bar had way too much to drink. And I reckon it affected his eyesight, because he said he didn't like the way I was lookin' at him. He invited me to settle it with our guns, and when I told him I druther not, he said he was gonna shoot me down anyway. When he drew his gun, I grabbed his arm and he shot himself in the leg. The bartender sent for the sheriff, and I reckon we musta caught him at a bad time, because he took me to jail, even though Mickey and I both tried to tell him I didn't shoot that fellow. I didn't put up too much fuss about it, though, since I'm a little short of money and I couldn't afford a hotel room. I figured I'd at least have a place to sleep and maybe a meal or two, and they put my horses in the stable, too. So I figure I came out ahead on that deal."

Cartwright shook his head, not sure if Derringer was serious or not. "If you're broke, what were you thinking about doing next?"

"I was thinkin' about maybe robbing the bank, but I hadn't made a final decision on that yet, so I'm glad you have a job for me."

"I'll get you a room in the hotel tonight," Cartwright said, thinking Derringer was joking, but not willing to bet on it. "So you'll have tomorrow to take care of your horses and any needs you might have in personal supplies or ammunition." He looked at the clock on the wall. "It's about dinnertime," he announced. "Let's go to the hotel to get something to eat. Then I'll get a room for you for tonight and tomorrow night. Then you can hitch a ride on a train that's leaving at ten o'clock Wednesday morning, heading for the end of the track."

"How far will that take me?" Derringer asked, since he was going to have to buy supplies for the trip. Cartwright said the general was at Crow Creek Crossing and that had to be about five hundred miles from Council Bluffs.

Cartwright took another look at his map. "Here's where they were when he wired me two days ago. Based on the rate they've been laying track, about three miles a day, that ought to put them close to Crow Creek."

"Well, I'll be . . ." Derringer started. "How many days will I be on the train?"

Cartwright shrugged. "Depending on how many hours they travel a day, I'd say about two and a half days."

Derringer shook his head and grinned. "I expect it would take me the better part of two weeks to ride my horse that far. I reckon I won't need as many supplies as I thought."

As Cartwright suggested, they walked down to the hotel dining room for some food. Jesse left his two horses tied at the hotel hitching rail. After dinner, they went to the front desk in the hotel to get Jesse a room. When that was taken care of, Cartwright took a roll of money out of his pocket and peeled off fifty dollars and gave it to him as an advance. "That oughta be enough to get you set to travel," he said. "Are your horses in good shape?"

"Yes, sir," Jesse replied. "I always take care of them,

so they'll take care of me. I'll take 'em back to the stable. I just picked 'em up before I came to your office."

"Tell John Walker to put the fee on my bill," Cartwright said. "He seems to take pretty good care of my horses. I've got to meet with some people this afternoon, so I'm going back to the office. I may not see you tonight, so check in with me sometime tomorrow. All right?"

Jesse said that he would, so Cartwright started back to his office with the air of a man who had accomplished an important item on his list of things to do. "Don't spend all that advance in the Whistlestop," he called back.

"Right," Jesse responded as he took his rifle and his saddlebags off the gray gelding. "I'll spread it around in the other saloons." Then he took his things up to his room before taking his horses back to the stable.

"Howdy," John Walker greeted him when he rode up to the stable again. "I didn't expect to see you back so soon."

"I got a job when I got outta jail," Jesse replied. "So I'm gonna need to leave my horses with you until Wednesday mornin'. But instead of the sheriff paying for 'em, this time you can charge William C. Cartwright's account, or the Union Pacific's, whichever."

"Is that so?" Walker responded. "You goin' to work for the railroad?"

"I reckon so." Jesse shrugged.

"Doin' what?"

"Whatever he says." Jesse shrugged again. "I worked for General Dodge for quite a while as a scout durin' the war and after that in the Indian wars. Looks like I'm gonna start out doin' that right away, scoutin' for the railroad this time."

"So you'll be leadin' the Union Pacific Railroad across the country to join up with the Central Pacific Railroad?" Walker asked.

"I wouldn't put it that way," Jesse said. "General Dodge is the one who says which way to go. My job is just to take a look to see if there's anything he might stub his toe on ahead of him."

"That still sounds important, so you better be careful you don't run into nobody else like Stony Packer before you leave town," Walker said.

"Who's Stony Packer?"

"He's the fellow you shot in the leg yesterday that landed you in jail," Walker said with a chuckle.

"I didn't shoot that fellow," Jesse immediately replied. "He shot himself. I tried to tell the sheriff that I was just tryin' to keep him from shootin' me. Hell, he pulled the trigger, the damn fool."

"Tell you the truth, Warner Black ain't really the sheriff. He's just takin' on the job until we get another one," Walker said. "He's the blacksmith and I expect the situation was a little bit unusual for him and he wasn't sure what to do."

"To be honest with you," Jesse confessed, "I didn't give him any argument that amounted to much, because I figured I could use a bed for the night. He was pretty reasonable about it this mornin', though. Even got me a breakfast before he let me go."

"I expect there's a lotta folks that woulda liked it better if you had turned Stony's gun up at his head, instead of down toward his leg," Walker said. "Him and those two saddle tramps he hangs out with think they own the town, now that Luke Collins left to take the marshal's job in Omaha. It wouldn't be a bad idea to stay clear of those two friends of his while you're at it."

"It'd help if somebody would hang signs around their necks with their names on them," Jesse said. "I really didn't pay much attention to who was with him yesterday."

"Travis Stacy and Rob Gentry," Walker announced. "Each one of 'em is worse than the other one."

"Well, now, right off, that don't sound too good," Jesse remarked. "I was hopin' to enjoy some of the town's hospitality before startin' out on a trip that's liable to take almost two and a half days on a train. And when we get there, there won't be a saloon to celebrate the journey."

Walker chuckled again. "Yeah, but you'll be part of history."

"That's right," Jesse replied, "the part they throw out of the chamber pot when they empty it. What time will you open up in the mornin'?" Jesse changed the subject.

"Usually around five-thirty or six," Walker answered. "So I reckon that's when I'll see you on Wednesday."

"I reckon," Jesse replied, "it's gonna be just like bein' back in the army again."

He left the gray gelding he called Clem, and the sorrel he called various names, with John Walker in the stable, while he spent some of the money Cartwright had given him to replenish his stock of ammunition. Cartwright didn't say anything about food during the train trip, so he figured he'd better buy something he could gnaw on during the journey. He found a message Cartwright had left for him when he came back to his room. It was an invitation for him to join his party for supper in the hotel that night.

Jesse was surprised to discover it was a bigger group of men than he had imagined. There were surveyors, which he had expected, but in addition, there were land agents and speculators, as well as military officers and personal friends of the general. He was left with little doubt that the Union Pacific intended to build a solid town at Crow Creek Crossing. Jesse enjoyed the supper and a couple of drinks afterward, but he felt like a square peg in a round hole in a social setting with officers, politicians, and executives of the Union Pacific Railroad. So he retired to his room at the hotel after a polite good night to Cartwright.

"Use tomorrow to get everything you think you'll need for a couple of days' ride to Crow Creek Crossing," Cartwright told him.

"Yes, sir," Jesse responded. "That gives me plenty of time to do the little bit I need to do." He took his leave then and Cartwright fully understood he was more comfortable elsewhere.

As he had told Cartwright the night before, he had very little to do to be ready. Much of his day was spent with his horses to make sure they were fit and ready to go on a long ride. As a consequence, he spent a great deal of time talking to John Walker at the stable and found the man to be one he would count as a friend. They agreed to meet after supper at the Whistlestop for a drink or two after John closed the stable and went home for his supper.

"You sure the little woman will think it's a good idea to let you out for a drink?" Jesse asked. "Better not let her know I was in jail, night before last."

"Ain't no problem," John replied. "I'm the one who does the thinkin' in my house. Course she tells me what to think."

"I reckon I'll just have to wait to see if you show up," Jesse japed. "And if you don't, I'll take a drink for all the poor men who took that rocky trail called matrimony."

Visit our website at
KensingtonBooks.com
to sign up for our newsletters, read more from your favorite authors, see books by series, view reading group guides, and more!

Become a Part of Our
Between the Chapters Book Club
Community and Join the Conversation

Betweenthechapters.net

Submit your book review for a chance to win exclusive Between the Chapters swag you can't get anywhere else!
https://www.kensingtonbooks.com/pages/review/